wine
OR lose

AMANDA CHAPERON

before you read

WINE OR LOSE IS a steamy small town romance full of explicit language and sexual content. To avoid—or locate—the open door chapters, please flip to the Dicktionary I've provided in the back. For the complete list of *Wine or Lose* content warnings, please visit my website at <u>www.achaperonauthor.com</u>.

For anyone who has ever been underestimated.
And for those of us who prefer a man on his knees.

IF ONE MORE GIRL touched my dick uninvited, I was going to start screaming.

Now I was all for a little hand and mouth—and, okay, definitely pussy—action where my cock was concerned, but haven't these women ever heard of consent? We were in a *club*, for fuck's sake, and not *that* kind, either.

My buddy Aaron must've noticed the look on my face when the latest one removed her hand from my groin, the one that said I was seconds away from bailing if I had to endure much more of this, because he quickly shoved another shot into my hand, clinked his glass against mine, and said, "To Cal!"

And, okay, I supposed I couldn't exactly leave my own celebration early, could I?

I tossed back the liquor, reveling in the way it burned all the way down, until it hit my stomach and the warmth spread. Mentally, I shook out my arms and legs, cracking my fingers and preparing to settle in for a long night.

Truthfully, I was excited to be here. Like I said, this was *my* celebration.

After finishing grad school two years ago, I'd moved out to Napa Valley and took an internship, that then turned into a glorified assistant's position, under one of the big winery's Chief Financial Officers. The pay was garbage—unless you counted endless free bottles of wine as a solid trade for sometimes wondering how I was going to pay my bills—but the experience more than made up for it. And when a friend sent me the job posting for a CFO position here in Michigan, I jumped at the chance to return to the Midwest. I'm originally from Wisconsin, but I moved to Michigan for college and fell in love with the area. This night out was a coming home party for me, and a celebration of my new position as Chief Financial Officer for one of the oldest and most successful wineries in all of Michigan.

I'd nearly shit myself multiple times during the interview. The CEO of the company was an intimidating bastard, and I had been terrified my answers to his questions hadn't been sufficient enough. No one was more surprised than me at the end of the interview when he stood, refastened the button on his suit jack, extended his hand to me, and said, "Welcome aboard."

As simple as that. *Welcome aboard.* At twenty-eight, I had officially secured my dream job.

That had been a week ago, and the surrealism still hadn't worn off.

Four days ago, I'd taped shut the last box in my apartment in Napa, loaded it into the moving truck, and caught an Uber to the airport with enough clothes and toiletries to last me until the rest of my things arrived. Two days ago, they had, and I'd been spending endless hours settling into my new home in a condo not far from this bar.

Fortunately, I still had a few friends in the area from my college days, and when I began to go stir crazy staring at the same blank white walls, I called them up, and we agreed to check out this new club, Lawless. It had recently opened and was apparently owned by Owen Lawless, former—now retired—Detroit starting quarterback.

*Un*fortunately, there were people everywhere, and I was chafing a bit from the constant unwanted physical contact. Women had repeatedly sloppily poured drinks down my jeans or thrown up on my shoes when they couldn't make it out of the crowd fast enough, not to mention the not-so-subtle cock groping.

Yeah, tonight was not going well.

After the latest vomit incident, I left the group to head to the bathroom and clean up. I was wearing my favorite pair of suede loafers, and I was already planning a small funeral service for them in the morning, when I woke up, studied them in the light of day, and inevitably deemed them a lost cause. Still, I was stuck with them until I got back to my apartment, so I wetted a paper towel and mopped them up as best as I could.

I washed my hands and dried them on my jeans—because I'd unwittingly used the last of the paper towel on my shoes—then exited the restroom, taking a moment in the hall outside to allow my eyes to readjust to the dimness. Still blinking, I started making my way back out to the main room when the door to the women's room opened and a girl stumbled out, plowing her head right into the center of my chest. Instinctively, I threw my hands out to steady her.

"Fuck," she breathed, rubbing her forehead. "Are you wearing armor or something?"

"Uhm...no?"

"Your chest is hard as a rock," she said, and reached out, placing her palm atop one of my pecs, unabashedly feeling her way around. "Fuck."

"Is something wrong?" I asked. "Are you okay?"

"Yeah, yeah, I'm fine," she said dismissively, though she still hadn't lifted her head. "I just...how often do you work out? Your pecs are ridiculous."

At last, she looked up at me, and based on how little she had to crane her neck to meet my eyes, I put her somewhere in the five seven to nine inch range. But I forgot all about the height difference the moment our gazes locked, because...holy shit.

Her eyes, fringed by thick lashes coated in mascara that I was willing to bet she didn't need and lined with kohl and glitter, were the most peculiar and stunning shade of hazel I'd ever seen. Hazel typically presented as a combination of brown-gold and green, but hers were all gold, shining brightly even under the near-complete absence of light in this dingy hallway. They were pools of honey I wanted to drown in.

Vaguely, I remembered she'd asked me a question, but as her slightly open mouthed stare turned to a full on grin as I studied her, illuminating her entire face with the same light shining from her eyes, I had no idea what it was—nor did I care.

"Cal," I said.

"Cal?"

"That's my name," I explained, aiming a thumb at my chest like a tool. "Cal. Short for Calvin. Calvin Ryder." I was rambling and couldn't make myself stop. Something about the way this girl had plowed into me had shaken something loose in my chest—and probably my brain. I wasn't exactly firing on all cylinders.

"Amara," she said through her smile. "Pleasure to meet you, Calvin Ryder."

The name dimly rang a bell in my brain, but I was too intoxicated, too entranced by that golden stare to figure out why.

"Would you like to join me for a drink?" I asked.

"Sure," she said. "Lead the way."

Boldly, I reached for her hand, and she threaded her fingers through mine.

When we pushed through the throng and found my buddies once again, I was unsurprised to find our small table completely surrounded by them and a group of women.

"Boys, this is—" My introduction was cut off as one of the girls lunged forward and hauled Amara into a hug, squealing her name and other statements of excitement, her voice so high-pitched I was certain she was tearing the sound barrier to shreds. Or my eardrums, at the very least.

When Amara pulled away, she looked up at me with a smile. "I see our friends have met."

"That they have," I replied. "That makes me feel less guilty about hogging your attention for the rest of the night."

"Who says I won't be the one hogging yours?"

I stepped closer and pulled her against my body. "How about we agree that you stay right here for the rest of the night?"

"Here?" she said, shuffling her feet a little. "In this exact spot of this bar?"

"Smart ass," I growled through a grin. "I meant *here* as in at my side, and you know it."

"And what if I find someone better?"

This girl.

"Trust me, Amara, you won't find *anyone* better."

"Is that so?"

"Definitely."

She pressed impossibly closer, entering the danger zone of a beautiful woman in my personal space that meant my dick could come out to play at any moment. But still, I let her, settling my hands low on her hips, feeling the lush curves of her body beneath her flimsy top and short shorts.

Something about her had me wanting to test my limits, to push my luck, so I slid my hands even lower, resting them on the curve of her ass and lightly flexing the tips of my fingers against her flesh.

"Cal!" she protested with a giggle and light shove of my chest, attempting to put some space between us. Unfortunately for her, I was basically a brick wall.

The muscles she'd been feeling up earlier were hard-earned, thank you very much.

"What?" I said innocently, batting my eyes.

"You're dangerous."

I shot her a wolfish smile, but I silently agreed. I *was* dangerous. Dangerously on the verge of making this girl my entire personality.

A moment later, she stepped away from me, and I mourned the loss of her heat immediately. I meant what I said about her staying right next to me all night; I didn't want to waste a second of time with her. The air around us shimmered with something new and exciting, and I wasn't in a hurry to let it go. But she only went as far as her friends, and after a brief confab, she laced her fingers through mine and tugged me toward the stairs that led upward.

At first glance, it appeared to be only a mezzanine level, essentially a place where people could stand at the railing and survey the crowds below. In actuality, it was a loft, a VIP section of sorts, open to anyone in the club.

When we reached the top, I was pleased to find the random assortment of oversized chairs and couches arranged in conversational groupings were mostly empty.

It was intimate without being secluded, a way for us to have quiet conversation without being away from prying eyes where we could get in trouble.

Because this girl? She had *trouble* written all over her. Not that I minded; it had been a long time since I'd had a little fun, always too focused on getting through my internship and landing a full time position to think too much about having sex—or the fact that I was *not* having it.

I learned a lot about Amara in a short amount of time: she was twenty-three and recently graduated from the University of Tennessee, where she earned her business degree. Originally from the area, she decided to move home for the summer before she set off on her next adventure in Europe. I gathered her family was well-off but not in a showy, pretentious way. More in the quiet, old money kind. Amara loved to travel, and was able to do it frequently thanks to her family's business, but she was also incredibly grounded in the sense that she seemed perfectly content to sit here with me, her legs slung across my lap in the armchair we shared, glass of white wine dangling from her long, pretty red-tipped fingers.

The other rested almost indecently high on my thigh, and her pinky was an inch from brushing my dick—my *painfully hard* dick.

"So what's your story?" Amara asked after we'd gone shot for shot and I'd lost count of how many we'd done.

Although, I supposed that explained why she was so comfortable draping herself across me, and why I had my free hand buried in her hair, rubbing circles across her scalp.

God, I didn't even know her last name, but I knew I wanted to fuck her more than I'd ever wanted anything in my life.

"I went to Grand Valley for college," I said, returning to myself, ignoring the ache in my cock enough to answer her question. "And then MSU for grad school. After college, I moved out to California for a job, and now I'm back for a job."

"What kind of job?" I opened my mouth to answer, but she held up her hand. "No, let me guess!"

Her golden eyes narrowed, sweeping over my face and body as though my physical appearance would yield the answers she sought. She even reached out to sweep her hands over my shoulders, arms, and chest, and dug her fingers deep in the mass of my red-brown hair. I laughed but didn't stop her; I loved when she touched me, and I loved even more that she felt so comfortable doing so. At last, her gaze returned to mine, and she said, "Finance."

My jaw dropped open. "How..."

She shrugged, taking a little sip of her wine. "It's a gift."

"You are...so unexpected."

Amara blinked at me, cocking her head to the side so her curtain of dark, heavy hair fell over her shoulder, fanning out along the length of my forearm. "How so?"

"I'm not sure yet," I answered honestly. "All I know is I hadn't intended to meet anyone tonight, much less anyone like you."

"Like me?"

I shifted my hand to tuck her hair behind her ear, then leaned forward until my lips brushed the shell. "Sexy. Sassy. Smart. Someone I could spend hours talking to." I dropped my voice lower. "Someone I want spread out beneath me as soon as possible."

A shiver passed through her, and I chuckled.

"We're drunk at a bar, Cal," she said, pulling away enough to look me dead in the eye, though still close enough that only a few inches separated my mouth from hers. "Will you still want to talk to me in the morning?"

"Why don't we find out?"

The words were out of my mouth before I could second guess them, and Amara's eyebrows shot up in surprise.

"Is that an invitation?" she asked.

"Do you want it to be?"

"Badly."

Abruptly, I stood and withdrew my wallet from my pocket, taking out a bill and throwing it across the table at Aaron, my eyes never leaving Amara's.

"For whatever I owe," I told Aaron.

"You don't owe me anything, dipshit," Aaron said, rising and stuffing the bill into the pocket on my button up, patting my chest with a wink and a glance at Amara. "Go spend it on your girl."

This time, only one of Amara's eyebrows rose. "So I'm your girl now?"

"For tonight, anyway," I said with a smirk before I grabbed her hand and towed her from the bar.

I only lived a few blocks away in downtown Traverse City, and soon we were pushing through the door of my condo. Before I could get my bearings, kick my shoes off, or even attempt to show Amara around—not that there was much to see since much of my belongings were still packed and I'd had zero time or energy to decorate—she had me backed against the wall, and her mouth was on mine.

I inhaled deeply as I kissed her back, my hands roaming her body, stamping every sensation of this moment on my memory so I could revisit them over and over when we were apart. If this was all I got from her, if this wound up being a fluke brought on by too much cherry whiskey, I didn't want to forget a thing.

Her perfume was some sexy, spicy blend, so at odds with the usual floral notes I'd come to expect from women's colognes. And my god, her body. Her full breasts flattened against me, her chest tapering into a trim waist before once again flaring out into curvy thighs and an ass I wanted to sink my teeth into. I hadn't even gotten a good look at it, but I already knew it was perfect.

And her hair was a fucking dream. Like I'd been wanting to do all night, I grabbed a handful and wrapped it around my fist, angling her head where I wanted her.

She ran her tongue along the seam of my mouth and I opened for her, brushing my tongue against hers and swallowing the moan she released. She tasted incredible, something bright and refreshing mixed with the spicier notes of the shots we'd done.

"What kind of wine were you drinking?" I asked, pulling away to nip a path across her cheek, along her jaw, and down the column of her throat.

"Chateau Delatou Pinot Grigio," she answered, tipping her head to the side to give me better access. "It's my family's."

All the blood drained from my head—no, my body—in an instant, and I stilled.

I pulled away and scrutinized her face. "Your family's?"

"Yeah," she said, leaning in to press a kiss to the hollow of my throat. "Like...we own that winery."

"Amara Delatou," I said suddenly, the inkling I'd had earlier when she introduced herself fully forming in my mind, and she raised her head to look at me.

"That's me," she said, dipping to lave her tongue against my throat.

Before her mouth could land on my skin, before she could further distract me with her...everything, I gripped her upper arms and held her away from me.

"The job I just got," I croaked. "I'm your new CFO."

Amara's eyes widened so much it would've been comical under other circumstances.

For a painfully long time, we simply stared at each other, considering next steps.

During my interview, I wasn't only terrified of Leon Delatou because his classic Greek features made him sharp and intimidating, like a statue you shouldn't get too close to, or because he was a shrewd businessman who had successfully been running

Chateau Delatou since he was in his mid-twenties. No, the thing that terrified me the most were his parting words.

"And Mr. Ryder?" he said as my hand landed on the door knob, readying to leave.

"Yes, sir?"

"I only have one rule: stay the fuck away from my daughters."

And here I was...getting ready to fuck one of his daughters.

"You have to go."

"What?" Amara asked, wrenching free from my grasp and stepping back in a move so smooth I wouldn't have been surprised to learn she'd perfected it in some sort of self-defense class. "What do you mean?"

"I can't do this," I said, pushing away from the wall and past her into the open living room, giving myself some space to breathe, to quell the panic rising like high tide in my chest.

"Do what?" she asked. "Kiss me? Fuck me? I'm not a virgin if that's what you're afraid of."

"I'm not worried about that," I said, not turning to her but not moving away when she settled a hand in the center of my back. "I'm worried about your dad."

"My dad is harmless. Plus I'm twenty-three. I make my own decisions."

Twenty-three. She'd said as much earlier, but it was only now sinking in. Five years and practically a lifetime of experience separated us. For all intents and purposes, she was still a child.

"To you, maybe," I said, finally spinning to look at her. "But as of today, he signs my paychecks. And you're so young."

"I'm not that young."

"Younger than me," I countered. "And no offense, but I'm not about to risk my career for some fucking"—I mentally grasped at straws, searching for something to say that would send her running. If she hated me, it would make things so much easier, because I wasn't sure I had the strength to push her away myself—"party princess one-night stand, no matter how hot you are."

"*Party princess?*" she spat, and I had a feeling it wasn't the first time she'd been referred to as such. "One night stand? Is that what this is now? Because earlier, I distinctly remember you telling me how unexpected I was, and how you wanted to spend hours talking to me." She snorted a derisive laugh and turned away from me, taking heavy, angry steps toward the door. "You know what, Cal? Fuck you. If you see me at the offices—no you didn't. Never speak to me again."

I let her go, though I still stepped up to the window and watched her stalk down the street back in the direction of the bar. I knew I should go after her, should placate her, find some way to smooth this whole thing over before it became a bigger deal than it needed to be.

Instead, I locked my door, crawled into bed, and prayed I'd still have a job on Monday morning.

I'D DONE AND SEEN a lot I didn't agree with in my nearly five years as the CFO at Delatou, Inc., but standing by while my boss handed over the company to his incredibly incompetent daughter was proving to be the most difficult to swallow.

Since the night I'd met Amara Delatou, I'd done my best to ignore the attraction between us. Thankfully, she made it easy. That first night, I'd called her a "party princess" as a joke, a way to show her how little she meant to me compared to my shiny new job. Since then, she'd managed to live up to the moniker in the most obnoxious of ways.

Amara Delatou was, simply put, a spoiled brat who had been content to coast on her good looks and family money for the last five years. And now she was being handed the reins to the oldest and most successful winery in the state of Michigan on a silver platter.

The official vote would take place the following morning, though considering Leon Delatou, Amara's father, held the majority share in the company, it was basically a done deal. The vote, at this point, was a simple formality. And the fact that the board was comprised entirely of Amara's immediate family meant, even if Leon hadn't agreed with the plan, his four other daughters and wife could combine to overrule him.

I had set up this meeting with him and his wife, Lena, in a last ditch effort to convince them to see reason. But even before I walked into the room, I knew it was a lost cause. What tipped me off was Leon asking to meet in his private office instead of the conference room. This wasn't level playing field; this was home field advantage...for him.

Then again, this entire place was his home field advantage.

Chateau Delatou, the winery nestled in Apple Blossom Bay on Michigan's Old Mission Peninsula, was founded in 1911 by Leon's grandfather. Since then, it had passed through three generations, always going to the eldest son. Unfortunately, Leon didn't have sons. No, Lena had given him five daughters. The eldest, Chloe, had been groomed from her preteen years to take over this company and continue the legacy. But a few months ago, with the help of her lawyer boyfriend—now husband—Chloe had found a way to break the bonds that shackled her to this company. She'd never wanted to run it, but Amara had. As the next oldest, she was up to bat when Chloe stepped down.

It was a fucking mess, and I needed to put an end to it before Leon and Lena ran their company into the ground.

I knocked on the door, a gruff "come in" greeting me. After a fortifying deep breath, I stepped into the office.

It was well appointed, decorated in chrome, glass, creams and navy blues, with a full wall of sturdy light oak shelves displaying award-winning wines, plaques, photos of the Delatou family throughout the generations, including a heartwarming number featuring Leon's daughters.

Or, they would be heartwarming if I wasn't here to convince this man to give one of them the axe.

To my right sat his desk with those shelves behind it, and to my left was a conversational grouping consisting of a couch, two chairs, and a bar cart stocked with an array of glasses and bottles, centered around a coffee table. Leon and Lena Delatou sat side by side on the couch, his arm tossed casually across the back, toying with a lock of his wife's shoulder-length brunette hair—the same shade as each of her five daughters but streaked with silver. She was a beautiful woman who had given birth to a basketball team's worth of beautiful women.

And beside her, her husband was as strikingly handsome as she was drop dead gorgeous. Their daughters had inherited an amalgam of their features, including an array of his green eyes and her strange golden ones, the dark hair, sharp but almost regal bone structure, her curves and his height. They were a beautiful family, and I stuck out around here like a sore thumb.

With my red hair—so dark it was very nearly brown—forest green eyes, and paler, freckled skin, my Scottish heritage was completely at odds with these olive-toned Greeks. Normally, I didn't mind it, but today the contrast was stark and intimidating.

I walked toward them, extending my hand for Leon and bending to press a chaste kiss to Lena's cheek before turning and dropping my ass onto one of the arm chairs across from them.

"Thank you for seeing me," I said, the words coming out rough around the dryness of my throat.

"We agreed to hear you out," Lena said. "That's all this is: a courtesy."

I nodded and swallowed hard before launching right into it.

"I don't think Amara is ready for this kind of responsibility," I stated plainly. If I'd learned anything about these two in my time here, it was that they didn't mince words, and they didn't appreciate beating around the bush. Cutting to the chase was my best bet.

"And what makes you think you're qualified to comment on what Amara is ready for?" Leon asked, those emerald eyes locked on mine, never wavering, never blinking. That unyielding focus was unsettling. I thought I'd grown used to it over the last five years, but there was nothing in the world that mattered more to Leon and Lena than their daughters—including this company—and I was pointing a loaded gun right at Amara's head.

"I've been here for nearly five years," I reminded him. "And in that time, I've had the unique opportunity of being on the fringes of your family while you operated this business and raised those girls."

"*Those girls*," Lena said, her tone edged in displeasure at my choice of words, "are adults. They are responsible for their own actions."

"Thank you for making my point," I said. "From the time she was twelve, Chloe was in these offices, working side by side with you guys to learn the ins and outs of this business, to prepare her for taking it over one day. She's proven to be nothing but dependable, steadfast, and stolid when it comes to business matters. The only time I have ever seen her get emotional about anything was when she finally told you she wasn't interested in running the company. And you saw that passion too, which is why you're allowing her to give up her legacy. Amara, however, was not afforded that same education, and she has spent the five years since I started here doing nothing more than partying, showing up here when she felt like it, and generally thumbing her nose at everything this company—and your family—stands for."

"There's far more to Amara than meets the eye," Leon said. "There are things about Amara and her role in this company that you've not been privy to."

"So enlighten me," I snapped.

"Watch your tone, young man," Lena said, eyes blazing. "I'll remind you that while your work for us has been exemplary, you are replaceable. Our daughters are not."

Inhaling deeply, I leaned forward, resting my elbows on my knees and shoving a hand through my hair. This was not going how I'd planned...and I'd known it wouldn't. Still, I firmly believed I would be doing them a disservice if I didn't make my reservations of Amara's appointment known.

Eventually, when the silence in the room became too oppressive, I lifted my head and looked Leon and Lena dead in the eyes in turn.

"I think you're making a mistake."

I'd managed to save myself from such a mistake, to extricate myself from an entanglement with Amara before things had gone too far. And that had only been where sex was concerned. This was a whole fucking company, one Leon's grandfather had founded after immigrating to the States from Veria, a city in central Macedonia, in the early 1900s. This was his legacy and, in my eyes, Leon was spitting on it.

"Then that is our cross to bear," Lena said. She rose from her seat, and I knew before she even spoke her next words that this meeting was over. "We'll see you in the morning."

I stood before Leon fully got to his feet, not wanting to be towered over by these two, not wanting to feel smaller than I already did. This time, there were no chaste kisses or handshakes as the Delatou parents herded me from the room.

I was halfway down the hall when Leon's quiet, steady voice floated to me.

"Calvin?"

I half turned, looking at him over my shoulder. "Yes, sir?"

"Remember that, as one of the top officers in this company, you're invited to tomorrow's vote as a courtesy. But as my wife said, you are replaceable, and if you cause any problems, I will see to it that your office is packed before you can even exit the conference room."

And with that threat hanging over my head, I simply nodded and continued on my way.

⁂

When I arrived at the conference room the next morning, cameras and reporters from local news stations and publications lined the walls. This was a momentous occasion, not only for this family but for the area at large. The passing of the mantle only happened once a lifetime for some people who lived here, and as the winery was the largest enterprise in Apple Blossom Bay—hell, the entirety of Old Mission—today's vote was, naturally, a newsworthy human interest story.

The Delatou family was already seated at the table—Leon at its head, Lena to his left, Chloe to his right, the other four daughters spread equally down both sides after them. The remaining seven chairs at the opposite end of the table remained empty. As I had every time I entered this room, I wondered why they'd purchased such a large table if no one outside the family was ever allowed to own stock in the company.

Trust me, I'd looked into it. I wasn't exactly a legal whiz, but I'd studied enough contracts in my day to recognize when no loophole to the bylaws existed, and the bylaws specifically stated—in ironclad legalese—that no one without Delatou blood was able to purchase stock unless by unanimous vote. In over a hundred years of this winery's operation, no such thing had ever happened.

At its core, this was a family business, and the Delatous took that seriously. As Lena had reminded me the evening before, I was nothing but an outsider, a fly on the wall, tasked with making sure this company didn't tank by keeping a close eye on their finances. They could bring in anyone off the street to do that. Lately, I'd been desperately searching for a way to make myself indispensable.

I took up a spot near the door, almost directly behind Amara's chair. As though she sensed me standing there, a slight turn of her head had her looking over her shoulder at me, that golden gaze fiery and practically boring holes in my skin. I offered her a crooked smile and a little finger wave, satisfied when she looked away from me with a huff.

Beyond the windows, snow blanketed the fields of vineyards, the vines themselves brittle and brown, a skeletal representation of their warm weather verdancy. It was New Year's Eve, and the winter wind whipped and shrilled against the stone exterior of the building we stood in.

New Year's Eve...a day for shaking off the old and ushering in the new.

A new era that would surely mean the end of this company as we knew it.

God, this was going to be a shit show.

Leon rose from his seat at the head of the table, and all chatter in the room died off, leaving fraught silence in its wake. The air hummed with something I couldn't quite put my finger on, but it was obvious this was a big moment for this family.

"We all know why we're here," he said without preamble, then dropped his hands to the table and pushed a stack of papers to his right, placing them in front of Chloe. "This is an agreement officially relinquishing your right to be named CEO of this company, as well as any heir you may produce. If this is what you desire, simply initial at the tabs and sign on page four."

I knew the man loved his daughters and was warm by nature, but within these walls, he was all business. Brusque, even, as he told his eldest daughter what she needed to do.

Leon was one of the most impressive and successful businessmen I'd ever had the pleasure of working with, which is why this whole mess was so surreal to me. He wasn't blind, and after nearly forty years, he knew what it took to keep this company solvent. So why was he turning a blind eye to all of the flaws his replacement presented? Daughter or not, he had to realize appointing Amara was a horrible idea. An idea that would more than likely sink this company in her first year.

As Chloe began inking her initials and name onto the agreement, officially signing away her legacy, I bit my tongue so hard to keep from protesting that the taste of metal coated my mouth. My chest tightened as I watched the best shot this company had give it all away.

"And now what we've all been waiting for. I, Leon Delatou, as president and CEO of Delatou, Incorporated, and owner and operator of the Chateau Delatou winery, do officially nominate Amara Danae Delatou as my successor, a transition that will happen immediately. All those in favor, please raise your right hand." Before he'd even finished speaking, Leon raised his own.

Six hands rose into the air in unison as the six Delatou women—yes, Amara even voted for herself—officially agreed to pass the mantle to the second oldest daughter.

My heart stopped dead in my chest. There was no coming back from this now, and I watched in mute horror as Leon slid the agreement to his wife, who signed and passed it down. The last in line, Chloe, signed with a flourish and a wink at her sister. I couldn't see Amara's expression from this vantage point, but I knew a smile adorned her face.

The reporters politely clapped when the company attorney stepped forward and notarized the documents. I wanted to throw up, and was seconds away from leaving the room to drag some fresh air into my lungs when Leon spoke again.

"Now that that's settled, it's time to restructure."

Restructure? Isn't that what they just did?

"As the new president and CEO," he said to Amara, "it's only fair that you hold majority share in the company."

I blinked in surprise. It made sense, but I also hadn't expected this to happen in front of the reporters. This was a conversation that should've been held behind closed doors. I had no idea who owned what currently, or what a Delatou, Inc. stock was even worth, only that Leon held the bulk of the company's thousand shares. Leon had something up his sleeve, and all thoughts of exiting the room were forgotten as my interest and confusion piqued.

"I've had the attorneys draft a proposed stock redistribution, and I think you'll all find it to your liking."

He passed a piece of paper to each of the Delatou women, and I resisted the urge to move to the table and read it over Amara's shoulder. I'd find out soon enough.

A gasp sounded from the end of the row on the far side, and my gaze latched onto the youngest sister, Brie.

"Daddy..." she said.

"You're giving us...everything?" Chloe asked, her voice shaking with shock.

Everything? What the fuck was going on?

Leon nodded, then said, "Well, not everything. Your mother and I are retaining thirty shares, split evenly between us. As you'll see, Amara, you'll be getting two hundred. Chloe, Delia, Ella, and Brie, you each get one-ninety."

My mind leapt into the mental calculations, and realization dawned.

"There are still ten shares up for grabs," I said, ignoring the fact that I was expressly prohibited from speaking during these proceedings.

Lena glared at me, but Leon nodded, the ghost of a smile playing on his lips. "Correct, Mr. Ryder. For the first time ever, Delatou, Inc. is selling shares to a non-Delatou party."

"I want them."

He'd planned this. I didn't know *how* I knew, only that I did. Leon had to have guessed that working under a CEO I didn't believe in wouldn't sit right with me, and that I would immediately be seeking other employment opportunities. He was offering this stock up to me on a silver platter, giving me a reason to stick around. Maybe he realized I was our best chance at survival, at keeping his daughter in line.

I had no idea what this stock was valued at, or how much of my nest egg I'd just spontaneously offered up, but it didn't matter. I'd been looking for a way in for five years, for a way to become more than just the man who managed this company's finances without reaping any of the benefits. I didn't know what the profit share looked like, or what hoops I'd have to jump through to make this happen. If it required my first born child, I'd do it.

But this, at last, was my in. My chance to make myself indispensable. As a stockholder, I'd be wholly involved in business decisions for the corporation moving forward, not just as the CFO, but as someone whose bottom line would be directly affected by everything we did from here on out.

Including personnel decisions.

Maybe, I could...

No. I wasn't going there right now. One thing at a time.

Leon surely clocked the desperation in my gaze as I silently implored him to give me this. He studied me for several long moments, unblinking, and I refused to be the one to break first. At last, he turned back to his family.

"All those in favor of selling the remaining ten shares of Delatou, Inc. stock to Calvin Ryder, raise your right hand."

Per the bylaws, this vote *had* to be unanimous in order for the motion to pass. I held my breath, desperately trying to choke the life out of the hope threatening to rise in my chest.

With a sigh, Lena lifted hers, and her daughters fell like dominoes after her.

All but one.

"Amara?" her father implored.

"No."

I should've known it wouldn't be that easy, and that the party princess would deny me. I brought the girl home one time and kicked her out before anything happened that we couldn't come back from, and suddenly, I was the worst man to ever walk the planet.

"Amara, *please*." My tone was borderline begging. "Please let me have this."

Amara stiffened with my words, her back going ramrod straight, and she angled her head slightly but stopped herself, as though she'd been about to look at me but thought better of it at the last second.

"Amara?" her father asked again.

With a sigh that had her entire torso rising and falling dramatically, and a sound from the back of her throat that couldn't be confused as anything other than disgust, Amara raised her hand.

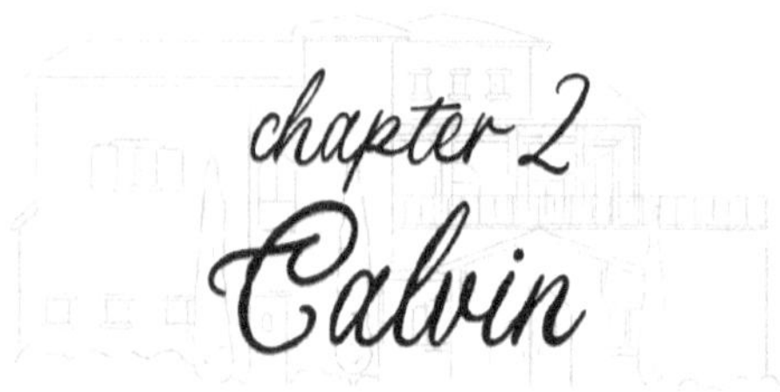

My attempt at getting Leon and Lena to see my side of things and not hand over the reins to Amara obviously hadn't gone as planned, so it was time to try a different tack.

I approached Chloe first.

Once the meeting ended, and the reporters conducted their interviews and left, the sisters began filtering from the room. I said a silent prayer of thanks that Chloe was the last one out, too busy tapping away on her phone to realize she'd been left alone with me until it was too late. Once everyone else had exited, I quietly closed the door behind me, and her gaze shot up to mine.

"Cal?" she asked, clearly confused. "What're you doing?"

"We need to talk."

"*We* don't need to do anything," she said coolly, rising to stand and folding her arms over her chest. "You lost. Get over it."

"See, that's where you're wrong. You know Amara better than anyone. You *know* she's not cut out for this. This was supposed to be you," I said, gesturing to the empty room around us but meaning a whole lot more than that. "And I understand wanting to give it up to pursue your dreams. I really do. But this can't be what you wanted for the company. This is just as much your legacy as it is your father's. You can't be okay with the way this is going down."

"What exactly is it that you think I don't want, Cal? Or are you forgetting I willingly voted for my sister today?"

"You don't want this company run into the ground. You may have signed away your right to serve as CEO, and that of any children you and Logan have, and your last name might be different now, but you're still a Delatou. Your parents refused to see reason, but with the restructuring—"

"You spoke to my parents about this?" she asked, incredulous.

"I talked to them yesterday evening. They, of course, are backing Amara one hundred percent."

Chloe studied me for a long time, her green-hazel gaze sweeping me from head to toe. I could tell by the slight curl of her lip that she didn't like what she saw.

That was fine. She didn't have to like me; she simply had to agree with me and vote on my side when the time came.

And the time *would* come. If I had anything to say about it, Amara wouldn't be CEO of this company for long. As far as I was concerned, she was nothing more than a figurehead, a placeholder until someone more suitable could be found.

"My dad ran this company for nearly forty years," Chloe said finally. "He took over at twenty-six when his father had a stroke that forced him into a wheelchair for the rest of his life. He and Mom had barely been married for six months at that point, but she stuck by him. They put in the work, turning this tiny little winery into a national—and international—brand. They instilled those same work ethics into each of their daughters. So tell me, Cal...what makes you think you know better than my parents about who is fit to run this company?"

I chose to answer her question with another. "Has Amara told you how we met?"

Chloe blinked in surprise. "I assumed it happened when she came back from Europe."

I shook my head. "We met five years ago at Lawless."

She blinked, surprised. "What happened?"

"We had...a moment. One that ended as soon as I realized who she was. I made her leave, telling her I wasn't about to risk my career for a one night stand with a party princess."

"What—" Chloe began, anger blazing in her eyes, but I cut her off before she could go to bat for her sister.

Amara didn't need defending. She needed to be brought down to earth, to be reminded of her place—which wasn't at the top of Delatou, Inc.

"Don't try to convince me otherwise, Chloe. I've seen the receipts and the credit card statements from her...*adventures* abroad. I've seen the bar tabs from her weekends in Paris and Monaco and Ibiza. I've seen how much she spent on simple meals in restaurants in Greece and Spain. I *know* who she is, and she isn't someone who should be in control of this company."

Chloe's gaze hardened, her expression unreadable, but I could only hope that meant she was seriously considering what I'd said. That having her sister's antics explained so plainly by someone who didn't love her—hell, who didn't even *like* her—would peel the blinders from her eyes.

I considered it a small victory when she said, "I'll think about it," and pushed past me to leave.

Bracing my hands on the edge of the conference table, I bowed my head and inhaled deeply.

I may have just opened a whole can of worms I'd sooner avoid, but at this point, now that the contracts were inked and notarized, now that Amara's first day at the helm was *tomorrow*—the first day of a new financial quarter, no less—there were few things I could do to remove Amara as CEO without proving gross negligence or having her step down of her own free will. Seeking out her sisters and imploring them to see reason was my last chance.

I'd started at the top, and now it was time to go in for the kill with the littlest Delatou.

Normally, Brie was easy to locate on Chateau Delatou grounds. The girl lived to bake, which is why her family affectionately referred to her as Baker Brie. She never strayed far from the kitchens—or Ezra, the restaurant's head chef. From the outside looking in, her little crush on him was honestly adorable, and I idly wondered if any of her sisters had picked up on it yet.

Ezra, for his part, seemed completely oblivious, which wasn't entirely surprising given what he'd been through. I'd been in the interview when Leon had hired him three years ago—right around the time Brie had wrapped up culinary school and moved home—and had gotten to know him decently well in the time since. Ezra Wendt had two focuses: food, and his son,

Hansen.

When I walked into the kitchens an hour later, I fully expected to find Brie glued to Ezra's side.

Only, she wasn't there.

"Hey, Cal," Ezra said when he caught sight of me, tossing a dish cloth over his shoulder and turning the heat down on whatever sauce was simmering on the burner in front of him. Damn, it smelled delicious, and my stomach grumbled in response.

"Hey, Ez. Where's Brie?"

"In town at the bakery," he said, waving a hand like, *where else would she be*? "I could've really used her help on lunch today. Nobody browns the grilled cheese quite like her."

"The girl does have a special way with carbs," I said with a chuckle.

Ezra's expression turned serious. "She's the most talented pastry chef I've ever met."

Which was saying something considering he himself was a Michelin starred chef who left a highly lucrative job in New York City to come work for this middle-of-nowhere winery.

Not that I wasn't grateful. His cooking was, unsurprisingly, some of the best I'd ever had. The grilled cheese, in particular, was my personal kryptonite, and I stared longingly at the steaming pot of what I now knew was his homemade tomato soup bubbling on the stove.

He caught my gaze and grinned. "Want some?"

"As much as I'd love to say yes and absolutely destroy some of that soup right now, I really need to talk to Brie. Save me some?"

"You got it, bud," he said, and I made my escape.

In addition to being the pastry and dessert chef at the winery's restaurant, Brie also owned a little bakery in the heart of town, right on Main Street. The awning over the front door was pale orange and cream-striped, reminding me of a creamsicle and glowing bright in the gray December afternoon, with a sign above that read "Brie's" in fanciful lettering.

Apple Blossom Bay was a town of about a thousand people that encompassed almost the entire population of the Old Mission Peninsula. The "city" limits were nestled along the shore of West Grand Traverse Bay, which looped between Old Mission and the Leelanau Peninsula, with Traverse City planted firmly in the middle.

Downtown was about as picturesque as it got, even during the cold, blustery winter. There was the main thoroughfare, a street that ran perpendicular to the city docks, so if you stood all the way at the top of the low, gently sloping hill, you could see straight out onto the water. It was like that Manhattan-henge thing everyone was obsessed with, only with the bay. Alongside the docks was an expansive bayshore park with a gazebo that had seen a lot of weddings, a playground, and amphitheater for outdoor movies and concerts. The park was also where the town held all major citywide celebrations, such as the annual cancer awareness fundraiser and the Fourth of July festivities.

I'd seen pictures of the town as it was when Andreas Delatou, Leon's grandfather, had settled his family here in 1908. Back then, there wasn't much beyond a few rudimentary houses and a church. Once Andreas bought basically the entire northern half of the peninsula for the winery, got it up and running, and started hiring people to work for him, the population in the area increased. Now, a number of businesses lined Main Street, including gift shops, an ATV rental place, Blossom's, the flower shop, Granny Smith's Tavern, Sydney's Diner—the building one of those lunch car styles that had been around since 1935—Bob's Grocery, a post office, bank branch, and Brie's. They each held a piece of historical charm while being firmly rooted in this century. The town as a whole was a seamless mix of modern and vintage, making it unlike any place else in the state—or, perhaps, the world.

When I parked my truck and got out, even fifteen feet from the white oak door of the bakery, the scents of sugar and freshly baked bread met my nostrils, exacerbating the emptiness of my stomach.

Hopefully Brie would take pity on me and serve me up one of her special cheese danishes.

The bell above the door tinkled softly as I pushed inside, the warmth of spices and fresh brewed coffee smacking me in the face. I took a deep, fortifying inhale as I approached the counter.

"Welcome to Brie's!" the young girl said brightly. "What can I get started for you?"

"I was hoping to speak with the boss, actually," I said with a sheepish grin. "Would she be available?"

The woman herself appeared from the back, wiping her hands on the front of her orange apron that was already heavily dusted with what looked like flour.

"Cal?" she asked skeptically.

"Hey, Brie. Got a sec to chat?"

"Uhh...sure," she said slowly. "Let me just—"

"Take your time," I said with a wave of my hand, then I hooked my thumb over my shoulder toward a table in the corner. Thanks to the weather, the place was deserted anyway. "I'll just be over here."

"Can I get you anything?" she asked. "Coffee?"

"I'm good on coffee," I said, "but I won't say no to a danish."

The corner of her mouth twitched. She may not understand why I was here, but she knew how much I loved those things. She turned to her employee and said, "Cheese."

The girl sat the pastry in front of me moments after I dropped onto the chair, and I practically inhaled it, wiping the crumbs from my lips and fingers as Brie took the seat across from me.

"So, what can I do for you?" she asked.

Straight to the point, then. I liked it.

"I think you can guess why I'm here."

"If it has anything to do with the text Chloe sent me an hour ago, then yes, I think I can."

Fuck, I thought. If Chloe was texting her sisters, warning them I was making the rounds, it was only a matter of time before word got back to Amara, and that was a problem I couldn't have. Amara knowing I was staging what was essentially a coup would only wind up with my ass on the street, unemployed.

"We haven't said anything to Amara, if that's what you're wondering," Brie said, correctly interpreting the fear that surely crossed my expression. "We agreed learning that her CFO was trying to undermine her leadership on day one would only hurt her in the long run."

My shoulders relaxed from my ears, and I slumped in my chair.

"I'm not the bad guy," I said quietly.

"I never said you were."

"But Amara is your sister."

Brie nodded, indulging my statement of the obvious. "She is."

"Then why aren't you nailing my balls to the wall right now?"

"First of all...ew. I have zero desire to be anywhere near your balls, Cal." I snorted, but she plowed ahead. "Second, I like to see the best in people. I grew up with the benefit of my sisters' mistakes and triumphs to inform my decisions and perceptions of the world, and I'm a firm believer in second chances. I genuinely think you're a good guy, this little—and, I have to say, sad—attempt at a coup notwithstanding. I think you're coming from a good place, and you're strictly looking at this from a business standpoint. I know my sister, and I could see how, on paper, she's not the ideal candidate for the job. But, *on paper*, my twenty-six year old father who assumed he'd have at least ten to fifteen more years before taking over wasn't exactly the best man for the job either. And I think that all turned out pretty well, don't you?"

I was momentarily taken aback for a few reasons.

First, I'd known Brie Delatou for nearly five years and that was the most I'd heard her speak in my presence in one go. As the youngest sibling, she—at least at first glance, and at least *to me*—appeared quieter and more reserved than her big sisters. But I should've known she'd have an opinion, and be loud and proud about it when it came time to defend someone she loved.

The second was the shocking realization that Brie...respected me. From the moment I'd found out Amara was being anointed as the new CEO of Delatou, Inc., I had been outspoken in my disagreement with the decision. At that stage, my only stake in the game had been, admittedly, quite large—my job.

But now that I had my own little slice of the pie to protect? Now that the success of the company would directly affect my bottom line? I had to make some tough decisions, and I had to make this family face some tough realities.

The problem with family owned companies like this was that everyone refused to look past those blood bonds and view people practically and in terms of whether they were an asset or liability to the company.

I knew which one Amara was, and I was taking it upon myself to prove the same to the rest of her family. They could love her and still recognize she wasn't meant to lead this company. She would still be their sister and daughter even when she was no longer CEO. The two were not mutually exclusive.

"Well, yes," I said slowly at last. "But Amara isn't your father."

"You're right," Brie agreed. "But that doesn't make her any less qualified."

"Actually, I think that's exactly what it makes her. Look," I said, leaning forward onto my elbows and staring Brie dead in the eyes. "I'm not asking you to make any decisions now. Think about it. Talk to your sisters. But just know that I *will* find a way to force Amara out, with or without you. Wouldn't you rather be on the winning side?"

"Not at the expense of my family."

"But it's like you said, Brie," I told her as I rose to stand, towering over her. "This isn't personal. It's just business. And the fate of that business is on the line here."

I didn't know if any of my words had hit their mark with either Brie or Chloe, but as I stepped back out into the cold, I certainly felt better for having tried.

Taking a deep, soothing breath and steeling my spine, I pushed into the conference room.

My parents were already seated at the table, dark heads bent together as they quietly murmured to each other. Even this simple act, having a soft conversation while they waited for me to arrive, had my insides twisting. It was so clear how much they loved each other, and...God, I wanted that. I had always wanted that, the partnership and the soul-deep bond they shared. My parents were the paragon of a happy, healthy marriage, the kind I strived to find for myself.

I shook my head, clearing those thoughts and shoving down the pang in my chest. Now was not the time to let my silly dreams and desires rule my mood.

Here, in these offices and in this conference room, I was the boss, and I needed to act like it.

"Hi, Mom," I said, crossing the room to drop a kiss on her cheek, then my father's. "Daddy."

"Hi, kiddo," Dad said. "You ready for your first big board meeting?"

No. "Of course," I said, tapping the stack of papers I held in my arms.

Truthfully, I was shaking like a leaf inside. This wasn't technically my *first* board meeting; we'd had a few smaller ones in the five months since I'd taken over management of the company from Dad. But this was the first major one, where instead of voting on issues that had already been in play for ages, I was bringing something new to the table. Lucky for me, about eighty-five percent of the board consisted of my family—my parents and my four sisters. *Un*lucky for me, the remaining member happened to be Calvin Ryder, better known as a giant asshole and the bane of my existence.

He also happened to be our Chief Financial Officer despite my best efforts to get him fired.

Suffice it to say...Calvin didn't take too kindly to my appointment as CEO, and he definitely didn't like the fact that I was now his boss. Over the last five months, he'd taken every possible chance to rebuff my efforts to usher in a new, more modern era of our business. Every little change I wanted to make was either picked over with a fine-tooth comb under the guise of making sure it was a "sound financial decision," or outright vetoed.

It amazed me that someone who only held ten shares of our company stock had managed to make my life and job such a living hell.

Then again, Calvin had been making my life a nightmare since the night I met him.

What an absolutely cruel twist of fate that the man I'd instantly had such strong chemistry with wound up being the same man my dad had just hired as our CFO. I've spent the last five years questioning...everything.

But again...now was not the time.

I specifically arrived early for this board meeting so I had the chance to run my new marketing ideas by my dad. There was no one on this earth I trusted more than him when it came to business, and I knew he'd shoot me straight. Before I went ahead and made a fool of myself—or, hopefully, not—he'd be the one to save me from myself.

Even though he was retired, his opinion mattered more to me than anyone else's. His grandfather had built our family fortune on the backs of Chateau Delatou, the winery that remained our flagship business. My grandfather had taken it over from him in the sixties, and my father in the late eighties.

I was officially the first woman to head this company, and I had to admit...sometimes I was definitely in a little over my head. But I had some truly genius ideas to usher us into the twenty-first century, and today's meeting was my opportunity to pitch them to the board and get approval to move forward.

Not only was I owner and operator of the winery, but I was also in charge of managing all our other business ventures, which included the restaurant on the grounds that had been my father's major brain child during his tenure, our short-term rental, The Villa, and my sister Brie's bakery in town. It may have her name on the building and I had no active hand in running it, but it was still considered a DI asset. Delatou, Inc. also owned nearly half of the land on Old Mission, from the town limits all the way up to the point that jutted out into Lake Michigan, where Mom and Dad's house was.

So, yeah…maybe I was a little overwhelmed, and maybe I needed reassurance from my parents that I was on the right track.

After I handed Mom and Dad one of the bound packets I'd created as a guide for my presentation today, I took my seat at the head of the table and reviewed my notes, resisting the urge to fidget while they studied my plans.

Unfortunately, my mind floated back to thoughts of Calvin, and all the ways in which he could ruin my day during this meeting. Hell, him simply walking into the room would be enough.

Unbidden, my cheeks heated at the memory of that night five years ago, when I met him at the bar, fell under his spell, and almost had sex with him. It had taken me some time to realize he'd done me a favor when he kicked me out of his place, but that didn't stop his final words from ringing in my head with irritating frequency, threatening to shatter my already fragile confidence.

I'm not about to risk my career for some fucking…party princess one-night stand, no matter how hot you are.

Shame coiled in my stomach. Thankfully, Daddy had never found out what went down that night. He chalked up the animosity between me and Calvin to some childish perceived slight that we'd allowed to fester all these years and had never bothered me about it.

I'd grown a lot in those five years, but it was clear that to Calvin, I'd always be the twenty-three year old recent college graduate who partied too much and wasn't worth risking his career for. God, that stung. I didn't have any delusions about where that night would've taken us. I had just gotten home for the summer and went out to celebrate finishing undergrad with my friends. I hadn't been looking for anything more than one night—maybe two or three or, who knows, an entire summer of them before I officially started working for the company and my job duties, not to mention grad school, took me to Europe.

From the moment I'd run face first into his impossibly hard chest, I'd been entranced by Calvin. He was funny and sexy. Within a few hours of quiet conversation in the VIP at Lawless, I'd become so mesmerized by him. How his focus had been solely on me the entire time. How he made me feel treasured—like a princess.

Now, that term of endearment had become anything but.

"These ideas are good, Mar," my father said, pulling me out of my reverie. "Really good."

"You say that like you're surprised."

He shared a look with my mom before returning his gaze—those green eyes, like emeralds flashing with something I couldn't name—to me. "I'll admit, kiddo, this wasn't exactly what we had planned. We spent years grooming Chloe to take over. We'd never anticipated it being you. But now that it is, now that I see how seriously you're taking this, how seriously you've *always* taken the success of this business, well...we're just so proud of you."

I gave him a watery smile and reached out to squeeze his hand. "Thanks, Daddy. The only thing I want to do is make you proud, so I'd say my tenure is already a success."

"With ideas like these," he said, tapping the booklet in front of him, "I think we can expect great things from you."

I moved to his side and he rose from his chair, wrapping me in a bear hug that did everything to calm my nerves.

And not a moment too soon, as the conference room door swung open to admit my sisters.

As the eldest, Chloe entered first, her dark hair—the same shade the five of us shared—recently cropped for her usual mid-back length to just above her shoulders. She was the only one of my sisters older than me, having entered the world the year before I did. Lately, she'd been so busy with deadlines while pursuing her novel writing career that I'd hardly seen her, and I relaxed further as she pulled me into a warm embrace.

"How's it been going?" she asked.

"Really well," I assured her with a smile, and I meant it. Getting acclimated had taken some time, but I knew what I was doing.

At least, I thought so.

"Good," she said. "I'm excited to see what you've come up with."

"Me too," my younger sister Delia said, flipping her long hair over her shoulder. Delia was the middle child, and Ella and Brie arrived quickly after her. With barely four and a half years separating the five of us, I knew Mom and Dad had been busy in the second half of the nineties, something I didn't want to think about too hard.

"Do I even need to be here?" Brie protested, focusing on the end of her signature braid instead of meeting my eyes. "Literally none of this concerns me."

I snorted, and the four of us rolled our eyes at our littlest sister. Brie was an incredibly talented pastry chef and in charge of preparing all desserts and snacks for the winery's tasting room on top of owning the bakery in town. She also worked closely with our chef, Ezra, and rarely left the kitchen if she could avoid it. She actually lived in the small flat above her bakery, saying she didn't need anything bigger and wanted to be close to her kitchen.

"Yes, you need to be here," Mom said as Brie sat on her left, Ella in the spot next to her. Chloe and Delia sat across from them, leaving the spot to my immediate right open for Calvin.

Brie *hmph*ed and sank down into her chair, pulling out her phone to distract herself with endless inspiration Pinterest scrolling until the meeting started.

"I, for one, am excited to be here," Delia piped up.

Next to me, Delia was the one Delatou sister most interested in the inner workings of our company, and in the months since I'd taken over, she'd approached me a few times about possibly heading her own project. As her sister, I loved the idea. This was a *family* business, and the more family involved, the better. But as the CEO, I needed to get my bearings and focus on modernizing our marketing strategies and rolling out our new product line before I could start allocating money for my little sister's whims and dreams. For now, I was grateful to have her as the company's social media manager, and her help implementing those new marketing strategies would be invaluable.

"Thank you, Lia," I said, shooting her a wink. "I have a lot of ideas that I'm excited to run by you guys."

"Lovely," Ella said, and I rolled my eyes.

My second youngest sister was the lone sibling who wanted absolutely nothing to do with our family business—even Chloe was an active participant in these meetings—content to work at Blossom's and live in the apartment above the shop, and it left all of us at a bit of a loss as to how to connect with her.

The fact that we couldn't stand her boyfriend also didn't help matters.

"And exactly how much will these ideas cost us?"

The joy in the room evaporated like a popped soap bubble the moment Calvin's words rang out. His voice was like a piece of gravel stuck in my shoe that I couldn't shake no matter how many times I dumped it out; it grated on every one of my nerve endings. I rolled my eyes and ignored him, turning my attention instead to getting my laptop connected to the digital screen for my presentation.

Still, I couldn't help tracking his movements out of the corner of my eye.

Calvin strolled to my father's side and shook his hand before taking the seat across the table from him, completely ignoring my mom and sisters. We all watched in stunned silence as he withdrew a notepad—the kind of yellow legal pad I had only ever seen Chloe's husband, who was an attorney, use—and set up his pens and water bottle next to them.

At last, he looked up at me expectantly, and I was struck momentarily breathless by just how green his eyes were when they caught the sunlight slanting in through the floor to ceiling windows, like fresh maple leaves glinting in the spring sun.

"I asked you a question, Amara," he said.

"What?" *Fuck.* It was too early in the meeting for him to be messing with my head this badly. He'd just walked in the door, for crying out loud.

My question made him smirk, and he repeated, "How much will these ideas cost us?"

"How about you let me pitch them before we discuss the budget?" I sniped back, and his grin only grew.

"Amara..." my father warned, his tone rumbling through the room, through my very bones, despite the lowness of it. His voice had *always* settled me, and did so now.

"Sorry, Daddy," I muttered, then turned to the sideboard behind me and picked up the stack of bound and laminated marketing proposals I had prepared for this meeting. I walked around the table, passing them out to my sisters, unceremoniously tossing Calvin's down in front of him so hard it would've slid to the floor had he not slapped his palm down on it at the last second. With a satisfied, victorious swish of my hips, I returned to my place at the head of the table and picked up the remote for the screen, clicking it on and simultaneously cuing up the first slide of my presentation.

Despite Calvin's gaze like a brand on the side of my face as I spoke, I easily settled into my speech. It was easy to be here, to present these things to my family, the people in the world who mattered most to me and would never outright shoot me down or belittle me or my ideas.

Unlike the one person in this room who thought I was a vapid party girl, *they* actually believed in me.

"If you turn to page one, you'll see I've outlined a three phase marketing approach to start increasing the winery's visibility overall as well as reaching some new target audiences that I think will be a big help in taking the CD brand to new heights."

Step by step, I walked them through my plans for marketing on TikTok, canned cocktails, and the Labor Day Weekend party I intended to throw, inviting sales reps from our wholesaler to stay at the Villa and experience all we have to offer.

When I finished, my sisters and parents chimed in with questions, and I answered them easily and honestly. I had come well prepared. Not even Calvin's stormy gaze could break my stride. Still he stared, leaning back in his seat with his thick arms crossed over that broad chest, brow furrowed. I tried my best to ignore it, to shut him out.

And I succeeded...until he spoke.

"You're just going to...give up an entire weekend at the Villa, one of our busiest of the year, for *free*?"

I ground my teeth together, fighting the urge to snap back at him. He didn't have a say in what we did with the Villa. While it may seem like a company asset because it was located on the vineyard and operated in tandem with the winery, it wasn't. The title was held jointly by me, my parents, and my sisters, making it, technically, a personal one.

I grew up in that Villa; we split time between it and our house in Traverse City. I spent long, hot summers there, running up and down the beach, playing in the cool waters of Lake Michigan with my sisters and other kids who were staying at the small, nearby cottages that dotted the lakeshore on small parcels of land my family had sold over the years. I had my first kiss in the basement, and lost my virginity in my bedroom upstairs.

When Brie graduated high school, the last of us to turn eighteen, Mom and Dad made the decision to sell the house in TC and move into the Villa full time. About five years ago, they'd begun construction on their dream home up on the northernmost point of the peninsula. According to Mom, they needed *more space,* which meant going from the sprawling vineyard home to an even larger three thousand square-foot house.

"We need more room for our babies…and their babies," my mom had said pointedly with a wink and a smile when we all ribbed them about the size of the new house.

Now, the Villa served as a seven bedroom Airbnb perfect for bachelorette parties, couples' trips, or girls' weekends.

All of us except Chloe still lived on the peninsula, which was funny considering she was the only one who had used the piece of winery land we were each deeded at eighteen to build her dream home.

The dream home I was now renting from her since she and her husband moved into Traverse City after their wedding last December to be closer to his law firm. At the moment, my own lot sat vacant. I'd spent too much time away from home in the last ten years to do anything with it. When I'd come back from Europe late last fall, right in the midst of Chloe finally breaking free from the family legacy, I had nowhere else to go, and I refused to move in with Mom and Dad again. Thankfully, she'd let me move in with her and Logan. I missed having them as my roommates—but mostly, I missed seeing my sister every day.

Still, I adored Chloe's house on the beach. Everyone was still close by, but far enough away that I had privacy. In the more temperate months, I could walk to work—the winery was less than a mile up the road—or ride my side-by-side if it was raining or I was feeling lazy. In the winter, I could drive or take my snowmobile. I didn't even mind showing up to work smelling like exhaust.

Not to mention the two hundred feet of sandy beachfront I had to myself.

In answer to Calvin's question, I finally said, "As a condition of inviting them here for an all-expenses paid weekend, I'm requiring mandatory training for each sales rep who has Chateau Delatou in their portfolio."

Calvin snorted. "How can you be sure anyone will actually pay attention?"

"Because I'm going to test them on it."

"Seriously?"

I nodded. "Seriously. Making sure our sales reps are completely knowledgeable about our product offerings is important to me. So, yes. I'm putting together a presentation including videos of everything from the harvesting process all the way up until we push product out the door. And at the end, they'll be tested on how closely they paid attention. If they get any less than eighty percent, they can't come for Labor Day."

"I think that's a truly inspired idea," my mother said

"Agreed," my father said. "Not only because in-depth product knowledge makes all the difference when it comes to sales, but also because I think having them come out here and showing them around the winery, meeting our family, getting to know the team...it's easy to promote a brand you whole-heartedly believe in and stand behind. This will give them the chance to put their faith in us."

I beamed, studiously ignoring the storm cloud gathering to my left.

As my sisters piped in, thoughts on my plans and ideas on how and where to improve floating around the room, I sank into my chair and opened a blank document, tapping away at the keys as they chattered, writing everything down for review later.

This meeting had gone better than I dared hope it would, and I felt like I was floating. Proving to my family that I was capable of not only running this company, but doing so successfully, was one of the most important things to me. I'd say today was a resounding success.

That was, until Calvin opened his mouth.

"There's just one problem here, princess," he said, leaning his elbows on the table and steepling his fingers under his chin.

His words were quiet, yet all conversation died.

I reared back like I'd been slapped, and Calvin's smirk said it all. He'd lobbed that nickname at me on purpose, aiming to cut, and he'd surely hit his mark. Instantly, I was transported back to that night, when things had started so promising and ended in a ball of flames.

The confidence I'd been feeling a moment before, that sensation of floating on a cloud, vanished in an instant, leaving me feeling like the rug had been pulled out from underneath me. I hated how easily he riled me, how a simple word speared right through my heart. Reasonably, I knew I shouldn't let one man hold so much power over me, but it was so much easier said than done when faced with him day in and day out.

I had to get out of here. Away from him and his giant ego sucking all the air from the room. I needed to compose myself, and I couldn't do that with him watching me, his eyes narrowed like he was a hunter zeroing in on his prey.

He had me right where he wanted me, and I fucking hated him for it.

I inhaled deeply through my nose and plastered a saccharine smile on my face.

"And what's that?"
"I control the money around here."

50

chapter 4
Calvin

I DIDN'T KNOW WHAT it said about me that I couldn't help but needle Amara at every opportunity. This time, I could've gone about it in a different way, because, to be fair, what I'd said wasn't a lie, nor was it strictly out of line. I *did* control the money around here.

"I hate you," Amara said under her breath, though everyone else in the room no doubt heard it.

"Doesn't make what I said any less true."

Amara ignored me, returning her attention to her family.

"So what do you guys think?" she asked, the apprehension in her voice so slight I would've missed it had I been paying less attention.

And God, what the fuck was wrong with me that I studied her intently enough to decipher the nuances of her tone?

"It's all genius," Chloe said. "I think this will all really help our profit margins and foot traffic to the winery."

"Which means I get to bake more treats!" Brie quipped excitedly, and I couldn't help but grin at her enthusiasm. I appreciated the youngest Delatou child's spirit. Save that fire in her eyes I'd witnessed when I approached her about voting Amara out—a deal I still hadn't been able to close thanks to these stubborn women around me, too damn loyal for their own good—she didn't cause problems, and was content to spend her days in the kitchens, out of my way.

Amara could take some notes from her baby sister.

"Whatever you need, Mar," Ella said without looking up from the booklet in front of her. "I'll help with whatever. Maybe we could make sure the rooms at the Villa with arrangements of fresh flowers for when new guests check in? I can talk to Fanny about that and we can work something out."

The words shocked me as much as her actually having a plan for how to chip in. Ella Delatou was not what I would consider a team player. Where the family business was concerned, she generally seemed withdrawn and apathetic, preferring to keep to herself instead of indulging in the incessant family bonding that seemed to happen around here.

I think a lot of it had to do with Alfie, her douche bag boyfriend. I didn't know much about Ella outside of the intricate floral designs inked like sleeves on her arms and the piercings that lined her left ear from lobe to tip, but I knew she could do better than *that* guy. Something I'm sure her sisters had told her on numerous occasions.

Honestly, she kind of scared me a little. Where her sisters were all bubbly and outgoing, fresh-faced and dressed in the latest fashions, Ella was...their opposite in every way. Her mid-length dark hair was streaked with pink, and she wore fishnet stockings under ripped jean shorts, a heavily distressed band tee, and a studded collar.

To a board meeting.

You see what I have to deal with here?

"Thanks El," Amara said to her sister with a soft smile. "I would love that actually. Get me a number and we'll go from there."

"Let me just nip that little idea in the bud right now," I said, narrowly holding back a chuckle at the pun I'd unintentionally made. "You're not getting money for flowers, or *anything*, until you tell me what all this"—I gestured to the booklet in front of me—"shit is going to cost."

Amara slowly turned toward me, and I resisted the urge to shrink under that gaze. I'd be damned if that glare didn't make me feel as big as an ant. And I'd be double damned if I wasn't still completely entranced by her golden eyes.

Amara tossed a number at me, and I snorted, the flicker of desire I'd experienced instantly doused.

"No. Absolutely fucking not."

"What do you mean, *no*?" she asked, leaning her hands on the table to get in my face. "This is *my* company."

"That may be true," I said, rising to my feet and mirroring her pose to look her square in the eye. "But I control the money, and I said no. I'm not giving you that much for these yet untested ideas."

Amara huffed out an irritated sigh. "They're not *untested*," she said, doing a poor job of mimicking me. "TikTok marketing is a tried and true strategy, and canned cocktails have continuously grown in their percentage of the market share over the last few years. These are sound ideas that will make us a lot of money and truly put CD on the map."

"The answer is still no."

For untold moments, the only sounds in the room were our heavy breaths. Unbidden, my gaze flicked to her mouth, and when she captured my stare once again, her eyes had darkened from their usual honeyed hue to a deep golden like the color of top-shelf whiskey. Her pulse tripped against her long, slender throat, clueing me in to the fact that she was...*turned on*. The realization made me feel better about my cock thickening in my pants.

Honestly, what was I? Some fucking teenager with uncontrollable urges? This was a board meeting, for fuck's sake. And I *hated* this woman, didn't I? Arguing shouldn't be foreplay. It should just be...arguing, yet another demonstration of how deeply our mutual disdain ran.

Her lips parted slightly, and my entire world narrowed to that tiny gap, to the minty breath fanning across my face. To how easy it would be to drag her toward me and capture that unfairly plush mouth with mine. Would she taste as minty as her breath? Would she feel the same as five years ago? Would she make those same, chest-deep moaning sounds that sent shivers racing across my skin? That had ideas of bending her over this table and sinking into her swirling in my mind?

I hated how badly I wanted to find out.

The room came into sharp focus again as someone cleared their throat, and Leon said, "Maybe you two could come to some sort of compromise."

Amara jerked back like she'd been shocked, and I blinked

rapidly, trying to remember where I was, what I was doing—my own damn name.

A hand clenched at her side, and I could practically see the little wheels spinning in her head as she considered whether or not she could get away with driving it into my face. When she flexed her fingers, she said, "What's it going to take to get you to agree to this?"

"I'm not sure," I said. "But I'll let you know when I find out."

"Calvin," she ground out. "We don't have time for this shit. Memorial Day is in three weeks, and I want to get the ball rolling on this as soon as possible. Traffic to the area is already picking up, and I've got the bottling department on standby, ready to start production on the cocktails. If we get our asses in gear, I can have this stuff rolled out to market by mid-June at the latest, just in time for Fourth of July sales. Time is of the essence here, and you're standing in my way."

"And I'm going to keep standing in your way," I told her. "I'm not giving you that kind of money up front."

Amara's cheeks pinked beneath her olive skin, a sure fire sign that she was ready to blow her top.

"Fuck you," she said, hastily scooping up her things and rushing toward the door. Before she flung it open, she turned back to me and said, "You're making a huge mistake."

And with that, she was gone.

In the wake of Amara's outburst, her family took that as their cues to leave as well.

"You didn't have to rile her up like that," Lena said as she passed me.

"We know you're not exactly on board with it, but she's still your boss. Treat her with some respect."

Leon's parting words were a demand I had no intention of complying with, but I simply nodded and gave him a cheeky little salute as he and Lena left.

"What the fuck is wrong with you?" Chloe asked the moment her parents were out of earshot. "She put a lot of work into this. And I know you two don't like each other, but this conference room and these offices are no place for personal feelings. You're stuck working together unless she decides to fire your ass. And need I remind you, Cal"—Chloe rose from her chair and moved so she was in front of me, one hand leaning on the table as she got within an inch of my face—"that stock you own does not save you from getting the axe."

"We could avoid all of this if you guys would put your feelings aside and agree to vote her out once and for all."

"You know that'll never happen," Ella said.

"It might."

"Not in a million years," Chloe promised, then swept from the room.

The three remaining Delatou sisters followed the eldest out, each shooting me glares and offering disappointed shakes of their heads.

Alone at last, I leaned my elbows on the table and dropped my head in my hands.

As much as I hated to admit it, Chloe was right. Amara and I *did* have to work together, and whether or not she hated me for an *almost* that happened five years ago, and whether or not I found her lazy and incompetent, didn't matter here. She was my boss, and I controlled the money. We were locked in a truly unfortunate and twisted symbiotic relationship, and we needed to find a way to coexist that wouldn't burn this place to the ground.

So I did what any sane person would do: I followed her to her office, intent on hashing this out, right here, right now.

Amara's assistant rose from her chair as I approached.

"I'll let her know you're here."

"No need," I said, moving past her desk without breaking my stride and pushing into Amara's office.

"You do realize that storming out of a board meeting is only fuel for me, right?" I said when I walked inside, dropping onto one of the cozy armchairs grouped on the left side of her office.

"Absolutely fucking not," she said, rising to her feet and stalking for the door. "Cindy!" she yelled, and her assistant appeared. "Why didn't you warn me Mr. Ryder was here?"

Mr. Ryder, huh? I hated the way my last name on her lips had my cock twitching.

"He didn't give me a chance," Cindy said sheepishly, and Amara whirled on me.

"You need to leave."

I shook my head. "No can do. We have things to discuss. Now sit down and let's talk."

"Don't tell me what to do in my own office."

"Stop acting like a child, princess, and *sit.*"

With a world-weary sigh, she shut the door and moved to the chair across from me. Instead of sitting, she folded her arms over her chest and tapped her pointy toed heel on the floor. My eyes trailed from those shoes—shiny, black, red-bottomed—and up her body. She wore a black suede skirt that molded to her thighs, leaving nothing of her curves to the imagination. Tucked into it was some sort of gauzy blouse, white and patterned with flowers, short, flowy sleeves brushing against her upper arms. A delicate golden chain hung around her neck, clinging to the edges of her collarbones and dipping against her cleavage. When I met her gaze at last, she was less than impressed with my perusal.

"Keep your eyes to yourself," she said.

"*Sit down*," I growled.

She opened her mouth as though to argue with me further, but finally dropped onto the chair. I studiously avoided lingering on the way her skirt rode higher, revealing even more of those delicious thighs.

I shifted uncomfortably in my seat, willing my dick to remain calm. I was too old to get worked up over someone's *thighs,* for fuck's sake.

Especially if I hated the woman attached to them.

Even if they were spectacular.

"Speak," she commanded, directing her attention to her manicure instead of at me.

"I can't give you all that money upfront and let you run wild with it without receiving some assurances. You had to know walking into that meeting that I'd never agree to it. This may be your family's company, princess, but it's my job to make sure you don't bankrupt us."

Ignoring my not-so-subtle dig, Amara said, "What kind of assurances?"

"The kind that involve knowing you won't go out and blow it all on some three day party in Ibiza."

She rolled her eyes. "That was one time, and I didn't use

company funds."

If there was one thing I'd learned over the last five years while working here, it was that with family owned companies such as Delatou, Inc., the line between business and personal often blurred, especially where money was concerned. I had seen the credit card bills from those benders, and I knew she was lying. Unfortunately, while Leon had been in charge, I'd been unable to put a stop to it. He assured me Amara was acting within the purview of her role with the company.

Plus, that man scared the shit out of me. Amara didn't scare me at all, and I wouldn't be intimidated into turning a blind eye any longer. Maybe that weekend in Ibiza hadn't been bankrolled by the company, but I could name ten other weekends just like it that had been.

"We'll be discussing your irregular and frivolous spending habits more in depth later," I assured her. "For now, I'm telling you...you're not getting approval for this. Not this plan as it stands, anyway."

I hated to admit my mind had been whirling since she'd named her sum earlier. I wasn't going to give her that kind of money carte blanche, but...I'd be more amenable to a discussion if she were willing to compromise on something on a smaller scale.

"What do you need from me, Calvin? I'm telling you my ideas are going to be huge for this company, and I'm ready to move on this now. You're making a really piss poor business decision if you don't give me what I'm asking for."

"Three months," I blurted.

Well, I had hoped to make her sweat for it a little bit more, but apparently my stupid ass mouth had other ideas.

I think that skirt she wore was short-circuiting my brain.

"What?"

"I'll give you three months. Or a little more. From now until Labor Day. Summer is our busiest time of year, and if these things are going to work, it's going to be now. What do you need for three months?"

She opened her mouth to respond but I added, "And statewide only. Three months and execution within the boundaries of Michigan."

Amara studied me, squinting, clearly apprehensive.

"I'm not fucking with you if that's what you're thinking," I assured her. "If we do a controlled, statewide roll out of the cocktails and start using your silly little TikTok strategies, and everything works out, I'll give you what you need to take it nationwide. But if it doesn't"—which I suspected would be the case—"then it's back to the drawing board, and we won't have wasted all that money for nothing."

Amara's gaze remained locked on my face, her eyes darting back and forth. I wasn't sure what she was searching for, but I held her stare, waiting for her to work through whatever was holding her back.

At last, she said, "You're really not fucking with me?"

Her voice was so soft, so quiet, that I almost felt bad for all the shit I'd given her over the years. I almost allowed myself to remember that she was only twenty-eight and had never been in charge of a multi-million dollar company before. I almost succeeded in convincing myself that, since she hadn't been prepared for this, I should cut her some slack.

But that mentality would only drive this company into the

ground. I couldn't let Amara's pretty face, inexperience, obvious desire for approval, or her attempts to make a big splash in her first year as CEO distract me from the fact that she didn't deserve her shiny new title. My mission was simple: prove to the rest of the world what I already knew—that Amara's appointment to head this company was a mistake.

"I'm really not fucking with you. What do you need for three months and a statewide execution?"

She rose from her chair and moved behind her desk, opening her laptop, her long fingernails clacking on the keys filling the silence in the room. After several minutes, she looked up and gave me a number—a far more reasonable budget that didn't have my blood pressure and anxiety rising to dangerous levels.

Still, I couldn't make it that easy on her, so I countered with something much smaller. She groaned but shot back a new number. Far less than what she'd initially asked, but a budget I could get on board with.

"Deal."

Amara quirked an eyebrow. "Just like that?"

"Just like that," I said, offering her a reassuring smile. "You have until the end of summer to prove to me that these are good ideas that will make the company money instead of costing it. And by make money, I mean I want to see a return on every single penny you put into this stuff. We'll re-evaluate at the end of Q3 and go from there."

She blinked briefly in surprise before her golden eyes narrowed on me, as if she couldn't quite believe I was willing to work with her on this. Honestly, I couldn't believe it myself. And fuck...I felt that stare *everywhere.* My chemical reaction to this woman was pissing me off. My cock and hormones really needed to get it together.

"You do realize I could call a meeting and vote your ass out of this company, right? Then I could do whatever the fuck I wanted, and you couldn't say a word about it."

"You could," I agreed. "But you won't."

"And what makes you so sure?"

"Because," I said, rising to my feet. Brazenly, I moved toward her, coming to a stop at her side and spinning her desk chair so she faced me. With one hand gripping the arm rest, I reached up with the other and tucked an errant lock of hair behind her ear. Those silky strands were the softest things I'd ever felt, but I needed to remain focused, not grab a handful, tug her head back, and capture her mouth with mine. Her sharp intake of breath when my fingertips skated across her cheekbone told me just how strongly she reacted to my physical presence in her personal space. I wished I could say she was the only one. "You thrive on the challenge. You *like* me standing in your way. You *like* that you being the boss doesn't intimidate me. You like that *I* own *you*."

I loved knocking this girl off her game, forcing her out of her comfort zone. One of these times, I knew she was going to do something she couldn't take back. I was biding my time, waiting for her to prove to me she was exactly who I thought she was.

And hell, if one of her moments of weakness resulted in her letting me sink into her body...well, that was just the cherry on top.

After all, what was more unprofessional than the boss fucking her CFO?

She sucked in a breath, slowly releasing it before she said, "You have no idea what I *like*."

I rose to my full height and turned away from her. When I reached the door, I paused and looked back, grinning at the blush in her cheeks, and the way her chest rose and fell.

"Maybe not, princess. But I look forward to finding out."

chapter 5
Amara

"I SHOULD REALLY FIRE you for that," I said to Cindy after Calvin had disappeared down the hall. "You're supposed to announce people, or stop them from coming in altogether."

"I didn't hear any screaming in there, so I'm assuming it went well?" she asked, ignoring my comment.

It went a little too well. I'd expected it to be a knockdown, drag out fight. Instead, he'd approached me with...a plan. A way to give me what I wanted without potentially hurting our bottom line as a company. While he royally pissed me off—simply looking at his face, that damn dimple and the way his deep red-brown hair waved over his head always made my blood pressure rise to dangerous levels—he was good at his job.

And okay, the words he'd uttered as he left *may* have had my toes curling inside my heels a bit. I chalked that up to them being sore and smushed.

"I got what I wanted...on a trial basis," I told her.

"Better than nothing," she assured me.

"That remains to be seen," I grumbled. Her eyebrows drew together, and before she could question me, I changed the subject. "What's on the agenda for the rest of the day?"

I flicked my wrist, checking my watch. It was shortly after three p.m., and I was already looking forward to getting home, uncorking a bottle of wine, and sinking into my bathtub with my Kindle. There was a new small town romance calling my name.

"You've got a meeting with Liam and those grower douche bags in twenty minutes."

"Cindy," I scolded.

"Sorry, boss," she said sheepishly. "After that, though, you're free until Monday."

I gave her a tight smile before moving to the free standing armoire near her desk. If I was walking the grounds, I wasn't going to be doing it in my Louboutins.

Once my beat up tennis shoes were laced, I clipped my hair back, slipped my arms into a Chateau Delatou branded zip-up hoodie, and saluted Cindy. "Wish me luck."

"You don't need luck," she reminded me. "You're Amara Delatou. You own these guys."

I certainly owned something, but it wasn't the men I'd been forced to surround myself with in this job. Five months in and I was still struggling to get anyone to take me seriously. Calvin Ryder was simply the tip of the iceberg, albeit a particularly sharp, pointy, and obnoxious one.

I stepped outside through the back door of the office, the one that opened right onto the vineyard. Despite the sun shining brightly, there was a bite to the early May air, and I was glad I'd thrown on my hoodie.

"Amara!" Liam Danvers said as I strode toward the four men gathered atop the hill, two side-by-sides waiting on standby to take us into the vineyard.

"Liam," I said warmly when I reached him, extending my hand in greeting. He wrapped it in his inked one, the lines of the rose on the back stark in the afternoon sun. "It's good to see you."

"You as well."

I turned my attention to the older man next to him. "Victor."

Vic's response was a grunt, which was honestly as good as a warm hug from the man. Vic had been working for my family for what seemed like a hundred years. According to Dad, he'd started here in the seventies when he was fresh out of high school, doing odd jobs both inside and outside. Eventually, Papou promoted him to head grower, and Vic became a permanent fixture at Chateau Delatou. Now in his seventies, his years spent outside in the elements were evident in his physical appearance. His grey-blond hair was long and scraggly, perpetually tied back with a thin strap of worn leather. The skin of his face was deeply tanned and creased, his forearms brown and dusted with white hair.

Despite his gruff manner, he was one of few people who treated me with the respect owed to my position. The only person he seemed to show any sort of positive emotion for was Liam, which was all I could've asked for as we underwent a sort of changing of the guard. The two were thick as thieves, and I'd often look out the windows of my office to see them surveying the vineyard, talking animatedly as they planned the future of the winery.

"You ready?" Liam asked.

Before I could offer a response, the door to the offices opened, and I shielded my eyes against the sun, squinting to make out the figure approaching us.

"Hey, Liam!" Calvin said brightly as he approached, then shot a quick glance in my direction. "Princess."

"Ryder," I ground out. "What are you doing here?"

"Coming along for the ride."

"But you weren't invited."

"Actually—" Liam opened his mouth, but Calvin cut him off.

"Actually, I ran into Liam earlier this week, and he was kind enough to invite me. It's been a while since I've been out on the grounds, so I figured now was a good time to reacquaint myself with what we've got going on."

"Great!" I said with forced cheer, then spun away from the men and slid onto the bench seat of the side-by-side. Desperately, I wished Vic was joining us, giving me another buffer against Calvin, but he rarely went deep into the vineyard anymore. He said it was because his old joints couldn't handle the ride. Secretly, I thought it was because he didn't want to step on Liam's toes.

Liam got behind the wheel, and I was about to tell him to leave Calvin behind when the man in question approached, blotting out the sun.

"Move over," he said, glaring down at me.

"No. Ride in the back."

"The back wouldn't fit a small child," he said. "I'm six-three. I'm not folding myself up back there."

I looked to Liam for help, but all my grower did was shrug and mouth, "I'm sorry."

I truly despised Calvin Ryder, and I happily plotted all the ways in which I could murder him and bury his body out here where no one would find him as I scooted over and let him drop down beside me.

It took every ounce of self-control I had not to react when the length of his thick and solid thigh pressed against mine.

How was it possible that I hated him so wholly, yet my body craved him in a bone-deep way?

The contradictions had me in a constant state of distress where he was concerned, and the heat of his body seeping into mine certainly didn't help matters.

And when Liam took a bump a little too fast and we rose in the air and dropped back down, instead of grabbing the oh shit handle like a normal human, Calvin's broad palm came down on my bare thigh. Did I imagine the small squeeze he gave my leg, or was this yet another one of his moves in the game we'd been playing?

Whatever it was had my heart beating so loud, I was sure he could hear it, and I willed my breathing to slow.

I'd been looking forward to this meeting for a few reasons. First and foremost, I loved being out on the vineyard, especially this time of year when the weather was still mild enough that I didn't sweat through my silk blouse. The vines were just beginning to sprout leaves and little baby fruits. Everything smelled crisp and inviting, and it calmed me in a way few other things ever had. With the fresh air blowing in my face and little to no conversation from Liam, I could simply...be.

Leave it to Calvin to ruin the whole thing. The two developers already hated me, and both considered my presence for these outings an unnecessary nuisance. The last thing I needed was

Calvin egging them on, encouraging their negative impressions of me.

Those guys were what Dad would call "good ole boys," meaning they were stuck in their ways. There wasn't anything I could do to make them like me, outside of miraculously becoming a man. Unfortunately, properly planting wine grapes required planning, and none of us had exactly been in existence when great-grandpa Delatou first seeded and harvested this land, nor did we have the time or energy to accomplish the schooling required to do so. During my dad's tenure, he'd hired a company to take care of that sort of thing. Liam was our grower who, along with Vic and a small team of men and women from the area, tended to the vineyard daily. The developers were here for the big picture stuff like optimizing our land to ensure maximum yield.

Even with these guys here to help, I didn't make any decisions without Liam's input. Liam had only been employed by Chateau Delatou for a handful of years, joining us after finishing some fancy bio-agricultural studies program out in Napa Valley. He'd introduced some truly amazing practices and changes into our harvest techniques that made the vineyard more environmentally sustainable.

He was also a genius mixologist, which reminded me...

"When we get back, I need you to come inside. We have to get something on the books to sit down and finalize the canned cocktails."

Liam's gaze darted to me, both eyebrows raised. "Cal gave you the go ahead?"

"He sure did," I said, shooting Calvin a wide smile. "So we

need to put our best foot forward with these recipes."

Liam simply nodded. "Whatever you want, boss."

I snorted. "This is your brain child too," I reminded him. "Don't sell your involvement short. I can't get these out to market without you."

Liam blushed, offering me a small smile, and I grinned in response.

Truthfully, I enjoyed Liam's company. He was around my age, warm and kind. Despite the brisk air, he had his shirtsleeves rolled to his elbows, displaying corded forearms decorated with an impressive assortment of random tattoos.

"So what's the plan for today?" Liam asked me.

"There's that empty plot down the hill from the newest Riesling vines? I'm curious if it would be a good idea to add some more on that slope. Riesling is our best seller, and I've got a hookup with a guy out in northern California who can get us ten acres each of them, Pinot Grigio, and Muscat for a steal. But I wanted you to come take a look at the soil, and see what the developers say about the growing potential in that spot."

"How much are these ten acres going to cost?" Calvin asked.

I ignored him as Liam launched questions of his own at me, which I did my best to answer truthfully—even with my limited knowledge.

Trust me, if I knew what I was doing one hundred percent of the time, I would not be in this side-by-side, smushed between Liam and the spawn of Satan.

There were a lot of things I was good at, but the agricultural side of this business was not one of them. I was grateful for Liam, who had treated me with respect and easily adapted to the change from my father to me. He was patient and kind, even when I asked stupid questions—which, embarrassingly, had happened quite frequently in my early days. He was knowledgeable enough for the both of us, and honestly, it wasn't my job to know everything. The mark of a good leader, in my opinion, was the ability to seek help when my own expertise failed. Running a business, I could do. Everything that happened outside the offices I left to Liam and Vic, their team, and the developers.

At last, Liam pulled to a stop at the crest of a hill, looking out over a field of grass and random brush. He turned to me. "Ready to kiss these guys' asses for the next half hour?"

"No," I groaned. "Don't they realize they should be the ones kissing my ass?"

"I don't think they care," he said as we exited the vehicle. I didn't even bother to see if Calvin moved, simply slid out on Liam's side. "They see your tits and figure there's nothing worthwhile in your brain."

I glanced down at my chest, at the ample gift I'd been given. "It is a pretty great rack."

Liam snorted, covering his laugh with a fist over his mouth, smoothly turning it into a cough as we approached the developers. "That it is."

I shot him a cheeky grin, which he briefly returned before turning his attention to the developers.

"Excuse you," Calvin said haughtily from behind me. "This is a work meeting. Act like it."

"Oh, fuck off, Ryder," I said, moving to follow Liam down the slope.

Liam's comment about my rack stuck in my mind, and I couldn't help myself from openly admiring the man. His thick forearms, dusted with dark hair, beautifully tatted, and deeply tanned from all the time spent outside. His broad shoulders and chest, tapering into a flat abdomen and trim waist, his thighs straining against his well-worn pants.

He and Calvin could not be more different. Liam, with his tattoos, beard, dark, shaggy hair trapped under a Chateau Delatou ball cap, Carhartt work pants in a deep green, dirt under his fingernails and tee sticky with sweat exuded *working man* energy.

Calvin, on the other hand, in his pressed chinos, long-sleeved, collared Ralph Lauren button-up shirt in a pale blue gingham pattern, deep red-brown hair perfectly styled, hands that I was sure he had regularly manicured, and clean-shaven face, looked every inch the white collar man he was.

Naturally, I was far more attracted to the pretty boy I shouldn't want, the bane of my existence and the one man I couldn't shake from my thoughts no matter how hard I tried. The one man I refused to let anywhere near me.

"So...you and Liam, huh?"

Goddamnit, why couldn't he leave me alone?

I snorted. "Absolutely not. He's my employee."

"Somehow, I don't think that would stop you."

With you, it probably wouldn't, I silently agreed before whirling on him and crossing my arms defensively over my chest.

"What's that supposed to mean?"

He leaned closer and dropped his voice so we wouldn't be overheard by the other members of our party. "You were fully prepared to fuck me that night five years ago, even after you found out I worked for your dad."

"That night was an egregious lapse in judgement on my part," I said. "Trust me, it'll never happen again. And you weren't *my* employee."

"Your name is on the door, isn't it?"

Funny how he only seemed to remember that when it suited his false narrative of me. "Fuck you."

"You won't," he said with a smirk, mirroring my posture. "You'll fuck everyone else, though."

I narrowed my gaze, my heart racing so fast I thought it might beat out of my chest at any moment. The steady, pounding rhythm was surely tattooing a bruise on my sternum. I wanted to rage, to pound my fists against his chest and beg him to let go of the version of me he had in his head. To finally let free all of my accolades and make him look as stupid as he's made me feel since the night I met him.

"You don't think very much of me, do you?" I asked with a resigned sigh, turning away from him so I didn't have to see the triumph I knew would flash across his face as my concession.

"I think of you plenty," he said, tone indecipherable, and my gaze shot to him. It wasn't victory I found in his eyes, but something else. Something unreadable. He cleared his throat and tacked on, "Just...nothing particularly flattering."

With a disgusted noise from the back of my throat, I stomped away from him, joining Liam and the developers in the middle of a conversation about estimated rainfall for the coming summer.

Physically, I was on that hillside.

Mentally, I was a thousand miles away.

It shouldn't sting so badly to hear so plainly how much he

disliked me, but still. This was a man I had to work with day in and day out. A man, it seemed, who not only thought I would fail, but expected it.

How could I feel confident in myself, to *want* to continue coming to work each day when the team around me didn't believe in me?

No. I mentally shook those thoughts off. I deserved to be here, had worked my ass off to prove I could do this. I knew I wasn't the Delatou woman they had planned on captaining the ship, but I was here now.

Calvin had thrown me off my game by coming to me willing to compromise, solution in hand, instead of with his usual animosity and condescension.

And again when he'd shown up for this excursion.

And yet again when he blatantly told me he disliked me.

Not to mention the way he'd gotten in my space at the end of our earlier meeting. Those green eyes of his were mesmerizing, entrancing enough to make me forget my own name.

And what the fuck was with his parting words?

I look forward to finding out.

Then there was the palm on my thigh, that subtle flexing of his fingers against my flesh. That foreign flash in his eyes when he said he thought of me plenty.

Who the fuck was this guy? Did he get off on messing with my head? Was it his goal to get me so twisted up that I gave up and ran away?

Well, I hated to break it to him, but I wasn't going anywhere.

"Amara?" Liam asked, his forehead lined with concern. "Are you okay?"

I blinked, clearly having missed an important question, if the expectant yet irritated looks on the developers' faces were any indication. Calvin, meanwhile, was particularly smug, as though he knew he'd weaseled his way into my brain and was the reason for my distraction.

Not today, Satan. This is my *show.*

I heaved a deep breath, squared my shoulders, and said, "I'm sorry. What were you saying?"

"We were just discussing the timeline for getting these new grapes in the ground," one of the developers said. Honestly, I hadn't even bothered to learn their names. They refused to respect me, so I gave them the same courtesy in return. "How soon do you think your contact in California can get them on a flatbed and driven out here?"

It was an innocent question, and one every man standing around me deserved the answer to. Unfortunately, it wasn't that simple.

"So," I said slowly, turning to Liam. "I was actually really hoping you could drive out there and inspect the plants and grapes before we make any further decisions."

"What do you mean...drive?"

"I mean, I want you to take one of *our* flatbeds out there, inspect the product, and drive it back if you deem the quality good enough for us."

"And if I don't deem it good enough?" Liam asked with a raised brow. From the outside, I'm sure it appeared as though he was pushing me, testing his limits with me just like every other man I'd dealt with in this business. Hell, one of the developers had an almost proud smirk on his face, like he was silently congratulating Liam on a job well done.

But I knew Liam better than that. The man was practical and logical, almost to a fault. I knew he was asking because he couldn't see the point in wasting his time when we could easily send someone else out.

"Then you'll get a nice, once in a lifetime, cross country road trip out of it," I said with what I hoped was a reassuring smile.

"I can't go right now," he said. "I have too much to do this summer."

I nodded, having known that was coming. "Fall, then. After Labor Day."

"That's harvest time."

"Shit," I breathed. "Winter. You can go after Christmas."

"So we're not getting the grapes in the ground this summer?" the other developer asked.

I shook my head. "No."

"Then why the fuck are we here?" he exploded.

"Watch it."

I looked up in shock. I'd expected Liam to come to my defense—not that I needed the help—so I was surprised when Calvin's voice echoed into the air between the five of us.

"She's fucking with us," the developer said with a sneer.

Calvin opened his mouth again, but I cut him off.

"I'm not *fucking* with you," I said, stepping closer to him, emphasizing the word as though doing anything involving its many connotations with this man made me sick—which wasn't far from the truth. He wasn't particularly tall. I'd guess either my height at five-nine, or just an inch over. It made things easier when I moved into his space and looked down my nose at him.

"I *do* want to develop this land. But there's only one man whose opinion I trust when it comes to our grapes, and that's him." I pointed at Liam. "If he's unavailable until after harvest, then we plant next spring. Your job, in case you forgot, is to determine whether or not this is a good spot for them *whenever* we plant them, or if we should consider another spot on the property. It isn't your job to decide *when*. Understand?"

The man's face was beet red with suppressed rage, but he wisely kept his mouth shut and merely nodded.

"Good." I spun back to Liam and clapped my hands. "Now that that's settled, do your thing, my friend."

Not needing any further encouragement, Liam sprang into action, gesturing for the developers to follow him, and I breathed a sigh of relief at a crisis averted.

chapter 6
Calvin

Honestly, deciding to crash the meeting with Liam, Amara, and the developers had been a genius move on my part...until it wasn't.

I didn't know what came over me when the one guy got belligerent and started swearing at her, but I'd been helpless to resist stepping in to defend her.

Since when did I *defend* Amara Delatou? What the fuck was happening to me?

But really, this was a *business* meeting, and all of these guys—myself included, as much as I tried to forget it—worked for Amara, not the other way around. They were way out of line in swearing at her and treating her like she didn't belong here.

And when she lit into him, proving she really didn't need my help after all? Fuck, I hated how hard it got me.

I needed to get laid, but unfortunately, the thought of being with anyone but Amara made my skin crawl. Seriously, something had drastically altered my brain chemistry. Maybe all the alcohol I'd consumed in my lifetime was finally catching up to me.

Liam returned to my side after traipsing up and down the slope for a half hour, Amara on his heels, taking pictures while the developers took notes, asked questions, and gave suggestions. I had to admit, Amara was holding her own out here. Being the only female with her male counterparts actively gunning for her couldn't be an easy position to be in, but she handled it with poise and professionalism—except where I was concerned.

The thrill that gave me, knowing I was the only one who could elicit that sort of reaction, was unmatched.

"So, about California," I began.

Liam crossed his arms over his chest and gave me a side-eyed glance. "What about it?"

"You don't think she's sending you on a wild goose chase, making you go all the way out there for potentially nothing?"

Liam shrugged. "No, why would I? She trusts my opinion, and I like being busy. It's not like I'd be doing anything else that time of year but staring longingly at the fields, waiting for the snow to melt."

I snorted, but the expression on his face said he was serious, and I quickly schooled my expression.

"Just seems like a lot of work is all."

"Amara is my boss," he said. "I do what she tells me. If she wants me to drive from here to California on the *possibility* of bringing back some new grapes...then I drive to California. It's pretty simple."

After giving me a long look, he walked away then, leaving me to mull his words over. I suppose his comment meant he thought

I should adopt his school of thought. But the idea of submitting to her, of throwing in the towel and fully accepting her role within this company just...didn't sit right with me. Plus, I was beginning to get addicted to our antagonistic repartee.

When we returned to the winery and Liam parked by the back door, I practically ran inside, unable to get away from Amara fast enough.

Thankfully, it was late on a Friday, so most of the staff—in fact, everyone but me and Amara—had cleared out of the offices. No one was around to see me power walk down the halls with a boner the size of Texas.

I'd never understand what it was about that girl that got me going so easily, and I was afraid of what it might mean for the last of my self-control. It had been easy to walk away five years ago. I didn't know her then. I only cared about saving my own ass, about making sure I didn't lose my dream job before I even started.

And even five months ago, I wasn't all that impressed with her. As I'd told her, I'd seen the credit card statements from her adventures across the globe. The bar tabs at London pubs, the orders from the hottest—and most expensive—restaurants in Paris and Rome, the endless string of penthouse suites in the most luxurious hotels in every major European city.

The day I met her, she'd been a fresh-faced twenty-three year old girl who knew every eye in the room was on her, no matter where she went. She knew with her face and her body, she could get anyone—man or woman—to fall at her feet, begging to do whatever they could to make her happy.

And what Amara Delatou wanted, she got.

Except me.

I'd be damned if I hadn't been one kiss, one swipe of her tongue, one breathy moan into my mouth away from ripping every shred of clothing off her body and fucking her into the next week that night. It was pure luck—and Herculean self-control—that had me kicking her out instead of sinking into her body.

Still, I could admit, in the five months since she'd taken over, I found myself unwillingly impressed by her. On occasion, she proved to be a shrewd and competent business woman.

But she still wasn't right for the job.

Her outburst during the board meeting today? Strike one.

Her complete and utter distraction with the growers out in the vineyards this afternoon, not to mention that grossly inappropriate conversation with Liam about her tits? Strike two.

Amara Delatou was walking a very fine line, and one more wrong move would have me snipping that tight rope and sending her to her doom.

Yeah, Amara losing her job would solve a lot of my problems.

When I slipped back into my office, I closed the door behind me and heaved a deep breath, willing the blood away from my groin and back into my head. If I was going to survive working with Amara, I needed to keep my wits about me.

Unfortunately, my cock had other ideas.

Traveling over the grounds with the entire left side of my body pressed against her, the warmth of her skin seeping into mine, the blend of her fucking sexy, spicy perfume sticking up my nose...I was in a bad way.

And guilt clawed at my insides over the things I'd said to her today. I hadn't missed the flash of hurt in her eyes when I didn't have any particularly flattering thoughts about her. It didn't help that she took my words at face value, refusing to look too closely at the admission I'd made moments before.

I think of you plenty.

Too much, in fact.

I imagined what the long, silky strands of her hair would feel like wrapped around my fist as I tugged her head back to suck on her neck.

I pictured her long legs wrapped around my waist as I pumped into her.

Fuck.

Before I could think better of it, I flipped the lock on my door and dropped heavily into my leather desk chair. Within seconds, I had my shirt unbuttoned, pants and boxers dropped around my ankles, and my dick in my hand.

The moment my fingers wrapped around my flesh, I groaned, biting down hard on my lower lip to keep myself quiet. All that did was make me think of Amara's mouth, those bee-stung lips that were painted a glossy pink today. I remembered how they tasted that night at the club, how she felt in my arms, the sounds she made. My hand moved faster, pumping up and down frantically, squeezing almost hard enough to hurt. But pain was good. Pain reminded me to stay the fuck away from her, even if it was her face that filled my mind as I pleasured myself.

My release snuck up on me, barreling down my spine as I thought of her outfit today, of the way that pencil skirt hugged her shapely thighs and showcased those long legs. I was glad I'd unbuttoned my shirt as I came in spurts all over my hand and stomach.

I sat there for a moment, staring at the mess I'd made. I knew I should be ashamed. Here I was, intent on pushing Amara out as CEO, yet I could barely keep my dick in my pants at the thought of her. But I *wasn't* ashamed. The orgasm had done its job—taken the edge off so I could do *my* job. And as long as I kept my dick out of her, there wouldn't be any problems.

The following Wednesday morning, I buzzed my assistant on the intercom. I figured I'd made Amara sweat long enough, and it was time to ante up.

"Yeah, boss?" Jeff said when he picked up.

"Draw up the promissory note to allocate the funds for our CEO's new marketing strategies and the canned cocktail roll out."

I could practically hear his eyebrow raise. "You're...giving her the money? What about—"

"Forget about all that," I said, cutting him off before he could say whatever he'd been about to. He didn't have the luxury of being ensconced in an office, and anyone wandering the halls could hear. "Get her the money. I offered her a trial run."

"Okay," Jeff said. "How long?"

"Labor Day. Well, technically the end of Q3, but we'll give her those extra few days. It's not like they'll matter."

My assistant let out a low whistle. "You're ruthless."

"Just doing my job."

He snorted but tried to cover it up with a cough. "I'll draw it up and bring it in for review. Give me twenty."

"Thanks, Jeff," I said.

The kid hung up without a response, and twenty minutes later, right on schedule, his knock sounded at the door. Jeff had a bad habit of pushing inside before I bid him to do so, and this time was no different. I ground my molars together to avoid shouting at him to go back out and try again. Too many people in these offices already thought I was a prick thanks to my tenuous relationship with Amara; I didn't need to add my own assistant to that list.

The man got paid to do my bidding, and I didn't want him to *accidentally* slip up and replace the sugar in my coffee with arsenic one day.

He placed the sheet in front of me, and I studied the note. It was standard language, a template prepared by our legal team wherein we amended the specifics on an as needed basis. The kind of thing we'd used thousands of times. Only, I'd never compelled the fucking CEO of the company to sign one. Leon would've beat my ass on top of my shoulders and reminded me his name was on the door. I wouldn't be shocked if Amara did the same, but if she wanted her money, she'd sign the paper.

"Bring this down to Cindy for signature and come back here when you're done," I told him, handing the paper back.

That little chore took all of five minutes, four and a half of which I was sure Jeff spent flirting with Cindy. Amara must've been out of her office, because when Jeff returned, he was empty-handed.

Before he could retreat to his desk, I gestured to the guest chair across from me.

"What's up, boss?" he asked when he sat.

"I want you to keep an eye on those funds. Set up a separate account, give her a new credit card, do whatever you have to do to keep track of every penny of that money. I want daily updates. If she uses it for anything other than company business, I want to know about it. I expect to know every move she makes for the next three months. Got it?"

"Yessir," Jeff said with a sarcastic little salute that had me wanting to lean over the desk and slap him.

"That's all," I said, waving a hand in his direction, the universal sign *for get the fuck out of my face.*

I realized I was acting like a dick, but being around Amara always put me on edge. It was a constant battle in my mind between wanting to fuck her and wanting to tell her to her face she wasn't cut out for the job she'd be given. I wanted to hold her and push her away. I wanted to see what she was capable of while also knowing this wasn't her destiny.

"Fuck," I breathed, running a hand through my hair, filling my nostrils when the scent of my pomade.

I was playing a dangerous game here, and if anyone found out about this little stunt and added it to the failed coup I'd attempted to stage in January, my measly ten shares in this company wouldn't save my ass. *Nothing* would save my ass, because Leon would bury it six feet under somewhere on the vineyard and use me to fertilize next year's grapes.

Several hours later, once I'd become sufficiently cross-eyed from the endless spreadsheets and charts and figures scrolling across my computer screen, I rose from my chair for lunch. Before heading out, I took a moment to bend side to side, sighing in relief as my back cracked and popped.

"Remind me to order a better desk chair," I said to Jeff when I exited my office. "Better yet...order me a better desk chair. That's what we pay you for, isn't it?"

"Your wish is my command, boss," Jeff said. I didn't miss the snark in his tone, but I chose to ignore it.

"I'm off to lunch."

"Heading to Sydney's?" Jeff asked.

I normally went to Sydney's, the diner in town, for lunch, mostly to avoid any chance of running into Amara. But today, I didn't feel like it. I was in the mood for some of Ezra's cooking.

"Nah, I'm just gonna go down to the restaurant."

Jeff nodded. "See you in an hour."

When Andreas Delatou first constructed the winery building in 1909, it consisted of the tasting room and the cellars below. Since then, each new generation has added on to the original. Leon's father, Christos, had built the offices and expanded the tasting room into a lobby, gift shop, and outdoor patio. Leon, of course, had been the mastermind behind the restaurant, which he opened in the early 2000s.

I was borderline hangry after starting my day off with all the boring parts of my job like those lame ass spreadsheets, and I practically stomped all the way down to the dining room. I knew getting some food in me would do wonders for my mood.

At least, I thought so until I stepped through the archway into the dining room and came face to face with the bane of my existence and her parents.

"Cal!" Leon shouted the moment he saw me, and my plan to duck out and head for Sydney's flew out the window.

I wove through tables until I reached theirs, offering Leon and Lena a tense smile and studiously ignoring Amara, though I could feel her glare like a brand on the side of my face. If looks could kill, I'd be dead several times over.

"Why don't you join us?" Lena said. She was a formidable woman—she'd have to be if Leon married her; I couldn't imagine him with someone meek—but now that the transition of power had gone smoothly and we'd had nearly half a year to distance ourselves from the harsh words we'd all spoken in that final meeting five months ago, she'd warmed to me considerably.

"Oh, I really couldn't impose," I said, waving a hand. "I was just going to belly up to the bar and beg Ezra to feed me his famous grilled cheese."

"You're such a child," Amara said under her breath, so quietly I knew her parents hadn't heard. No, that barb was meant only for me.

"Says the party princess," I quipped.

"What was that?" Leon asked.

"He said he was leaving," Amara told her parents sweetly, a fake smile glued to her face.

"On second thought"—I moved around to the empty chair, right next to Amara, and pulled it out—"I think I will join you, thanks."

"Our pleasure," Lena said. Then she reached into the center of the table and lifted the bottle of Pinot Grigio. *The perfect lunch wine,* I'd heard her call it on more than one occasion. "Would you like a glass?"

"No, thank you," I said politely. "I still have half a day of work to get back to."

"Oh, c'mon," Leon said, already signaling for the waitress to bring over another glass. "The boss won't care," Leon added with a wink at his daughter.

"Actually—" Amara held up a finger, clearly ready to protest, but her mother shushed her.

"Relax, Amara. A little wine with lunch never hurt anyone."

"I don't think you need to remind *her* of that," I said.

Amara turned her head toward me so sharply that her hair whipped against my shoulder with a *thwack.*

"What's that supposed to mean?" she asked.

"Amara..." her father warned.

"Did you not hear what he just said to me?" she asked her father incredulously.

"I did," Leon said. "And I'm telling you to let it go."

"Don't you think it's time—" Lena began.

"No." Amara's tone was firm.

Time for what? I wondered. It was clear from the looks on the faces of each Delatou that there'd be no further discussion on the matter. While her parents frowned at her, Amara lifted her wine glass and knocked its entire contents back.

"Easy, tiger," I said, low enough so only she could hear. "It'd be a bad look if everyone figured out who you really are."

Amara turned to me slowly, so slowly it was almost robotic. Those enchanting golden eyes, currently flared bright with rage, locked on mine for a beat, then two. The moment stretched, and the muscles in her jaw bunched and jumped as she ground her teeth together.

Then she rose to her feet abruptly, nearly knocking over her chair in the process, and hissed, "Fuck you, Calvin," at me before stomping away.

I was getting really used to hearing those three words from her.

chapter 7
Amara

My mom caught me before I reached the door to the cellars. Instead of trying to stop me, she wordlessly wrapped her hand around mine, punched in the code, and pulled the heavy wooden door open.

Growing up, my sisters and I hadn't technically been allowed down here. These stone-walled rooms were full of invaluable bottles of wine, and our parents—rightly so—didn't trust us not to damage something. And these bottles weren't invaluable in that they were expensive or exclusive; they were invaluable because a lot of them were the last of their kind, and the sentimentality made them irreplaceable.

The first bottle great-grandpa Andreas ever produced.

The first bottle Papou ever produced.

The first bottle Daddy ever produced.

New labels and vintages, the first bottle of red, of bubbly. The first *everything*, the turning points in the company, the history of Chateau Delatou spread out on the walls, a living, breathing timeline of my family legacy.

Even the simple act of descending the stairs, the temperature dropping as we went, my mom's hand wrapped firmly around mine, steadied me, grounded me, eased some of the weight off my chest.

I didn't want my first bottle down here. As far as I was concerned, bottled wine was old news. No, I wanted my first *can* immortalized along these perfectly maintained, temperature controlled shelves. I wanted to showcase the thing I'd done to leave my mark on this company, to take CD to new heights.

I wanted to be remembered not strictly as a winemaker, nor the CEO of this long-standing, family-owned company, but as the first woman to successfully run this company, and as a woman who didn't follow in lock step the path my forefathers had set for me. I wanted to break that mold, to usher us into the twenty-first century, and give my children a legacy they could be proud of—just as I was proud of my dad, and the men before him.

I only wanted to do things differently, and change was good. Necessary, even.

The problem with Calvin was that, to him, different equaled wrong. And maybe, if I didn't know what I was doing, he'd be right. But I'd spent the last five years preparing for this, first during my time in London, and then the years I spent doing market research and expanding our portfolio to all the hottest restaurants in all the major European cities

I was more than ready, willing, and able to lead this company, and Calvin was going to have to get used to it. He could oppose me at every turn, make it known to anyone who listened that he didn't think I could handle this job, but he was sorely mistaken if he thought I was going to give in that easily. If I gave up every time a man told me I couldn't, I'd never get out of bed. Corporate America was a boys' club, and I was here to fuck shit up.

My mother let loose a long-suffering sigh, pulling me from my swirling thoughts, and I braced myself.

"You shouldn't let him get to you like that."

I snorted. "You say that like it's the easiest thing in the world to ignore him when he takes potshots at my character. You know he tried to make me sign a promissory note?"

My mother stared at me for a beat, eyes wide, then said, "*Never* tell your father that. They'll never find Cal's body."

I chuckled, then sighed heavily. "Working with him fucking sucks, Mom."

"I don't understand why you don't just tell him that you're more than ready for this. We may have groomed Chloe to take over, but you've dedicated just as much time and energy to the success of this company as her. More, actually."

"Because that's not the point."

"Then what *is* the point?" Mom asked, throwing herself onto one of the armchairs in the corner.

Yeah, we had armchairs in our fifty-five degree cellars.

We didn't spend a lot of time down here, but sometimes it was nice to escape to this place where only Delatou family members could go and recenter before facing the world again.

Her question, though, gave me pause.

What *was* the point? I'd allowed Calvin to believe for the last five months—no, five *years*—that I was nothing better than some party girl who traipsed across the world on her family's money, using my charm and good looks to get me through the doors at the most exclusive clubs, restaurants, and parties in all those old European cities. And, okay, I had used my charm, good looks, and the Delatou money to get in the door. The money just happened to be out of my trust fund, not directly from the company coffers.

But those things weren't what kept me there.

And they weren't the things that had those clubs, restaurants, and parties serving CD products to their guests.

No, that had all been accomplished by my brains, not my boobs. But Calvin either didn't know about my MBA and experience, or liked to conveniently ignore that fact in order to fit me into his narrative.

The truth was, I knew from the moment Calvin had put his brand new job over getting into bed with me—which, okay, wound up being a blessing—that all he cared about was money. And I understood. Money was literally his job. But I could admit that I was still stung by his rejection that night. I didn't take kindly to being called a "one night stand." Who was he to say we couldn't have been more than that? In hindsight, I agreed it was the right call, but in the moment...twenty-three year old me had been crushed. And I'd spent every day of the last five years using that rejection as motivation. I allowed him to think I was a party princess capable of nothing more than using my tits to accomplish my goals.

It made it all the sweeter when I inevitably did everything he didn't think I could.

Not to mention the sense of satisfaction I got, the little thrill that zipped through me when I accomplished something and, for that brief moment in time, he looked at me as someone impressive. Someone he respected and believed in. Proving Calvin wrong was becoming an addiction for me, and I wasn't willing to risk not having him look at me like that ever again. It was all sorts of messed up, but what could I say? I'd been twisted into knots since the day I met the man. Sometimes, I wasn't even sure I *wanted* to untangle myself. I was ashamed to admit I craved Cal's attention, and antagonizing him seemed to be the only way I got it.

I wasn't sure how to explain that to my mom, though. She hadn't come up in an age where women weren't allowed to do bigger and better things than being homemakers. Women in her time had been frequently told by society that they had to make themselves small in order for a man to take an interest in them.

Not that my mother was a homemaker. She had been just as integral to the success of this company under my father's leadership as he had been. Mom had been responsible for the creation of our fruit wines and perfecting the ice wine recipe. Liam and I were naming our canned sangria after her, a small token of my affection and a nod to everything she'd done for the company. Exactly like me and my sisters, she was more than just a pretty face, and she got off on people underestimating her.

The apple really didn't fall far from the tree.

"I want him to take my title at face value," I said, answering her question at last. "I want him to look at me, recognize that I'm his boss, that I'm the one in charge, and accept that fact. I shouldn't have to explain to him or convince him that I'm a more than capable leader. He is our employee, and he should trust that. At the *very* least," I added, "he should take Daddy's decision as gospel. He worked for him for nearly five years, so he should know that Daddy wouldn't have voted in my favor if he didn't have the utmost faith in me. He could have easily brought in someone from outside the family, but he didn't. When Chloe stepped down, he chose *me.* And I'm fucking tired of Calvin bucking against that decision. Everything around here would be so much simpler if he'd just get over himself. We'd all be a lot happier if we worked *together* instead of him constantly working against me."

I sucked in a deep breath after that little diatribe, surprised to find my mother's mouth curved into a half-smile.

"You remind me so much of me at your age."

Those words had a full grin blooming on my face. "How so?" I asked.

I loved hearing about how my parents were at my and my sister's ages. To me, they were simply Mom and Dad. The wife of a CEO and the CEO. The woman who chose this life for herself and the man who was born into it.

It was hard to remind myself that they'd had lives before my sisters and I were born.

Hell, they'd had lives before each other.

"Did you know I worked here one summer when I was in college?"

I blinked, shocked. I hadn't known that. "Is that how you met Daddy?"

My mom nodded, a small, wistful smile overtaking her features. Even in her late-fifties, she was beautiful, laugh lines appearing around her eyes only now, her skin still glowing and clear. It gave me hope that I would age well.

"The year was 1986. I'd taken a job up here while I was on summer break from college because my dream had always been to become a sommelier."

Once again, my eyebrows rose. I always thought my mom loved wine because she was a part of this family, and being married to a Delatou meant you were forced into the life whether you wanted to be or not. I had no idea she'd *always* been a wine lover, and wanted to make a career out of it.

Although, I was proud to report she did eventually become a sommelier. She and Daddy working side by side were a fearsome duo.

"So here I was, this twenty-one year old girl, like a fish out of water. Detroit...it's not like it is up here, as you know. Life was so much slower here. Instead of feeling like I was being pulled in a thousand different directions, I could slow down, take my time, stop and smell the flowers."

"Or the grapevines," I chimed in.

She winked. "Or the grapevines. Anyway, your dad was twenty-five and the most beautiful boy I'd ever seen. You think he's a hottie now? Just imagine him thirty-eight years ago."

"Gross." My dad was attractive, yes, but did I think he was a hottie? No, of course not. He was my *dad*. Although, I'd seen thousands of photos of my parents as kids, teens, and young adults. I was familiar with what they looked like back then, and it wasn't shocking to me that these two gorgeous humans found their way to each other.

Nor that they'd produced the five of us.

"Anyway," she said with a flippant wave of her hand, "everything about him was magnetic. He drew every gaze when he walked into a room, mine included. I was working in the tasting room upstairs, hoping every day I'd get a glimpse of him."

"So what happened?"

"One day in late July, I finally weaseled my way into a meeting with the head sommelier here at the time. I was walking down the hall toward his office when Leon came barreling out of his father's. Plowed me right over. And the moment he landed on top of me and looked into my eyes...it was one of those meet-cute moments you see in movies, you know? I couldn't look away. The entire world faded away around us. If his father hadn't come out to see what the commotion was, I'm sure I would've kissed him right then."

"But you didn't."

"No," her mom said, smiling again. "I let him go in for the first kiss."

"And when was that?"

"The next night!" she said with a gleeful laugh and clap of her hands. "The next day, he tracked me down in the tasting room and asked me if I wanted to join him for a sunset picnic on the vineyard. How could I say no?"

How, indeed. We grew more grapes now than we had back in the eighties, but the rolling hills beyond this building still had to have been lush with vines back then. You could see the water on both sides of the peninsula from our perch up here, which would've made it a truly romantic spot for sunset.

"That was the first of many," my mom continued. "Before I met Leon, I always thought that whole 'when you know, you know' stuff was just bullshit. But...it's real, and it happened to us. We were saying 'I love you' before the end of our first month together, and we were married by Christmas."

I'd known their romance had been a whirlwind, but I'd never bothered to ask the particulars of it all. Still, photographs of their wedding day were displayed all over each of our homes, and while it might not seem like it, their winter vineyard wedding looked nothing short of magical.

Although, I had some idea of how perfect the day had been since Chloe and Logan had chosen to have their own wedding at the winery last Christmas. The snow-covered vines, the twinkle lights, those opaque little igloos set up outside for people to enjoy the season without suffering frostbite—it had all been a dream.

"How *did* you know?" I blurted. I couldn't imagine that, knowing without a doubt that you'd found the other half of your soul in another person, knowing implicitly that you were meant to share your life with them.

"I felt it right here," she said, placing a palm over her heart. "Everything felt right when I was with him. Easy. I couldn't think of anywhere else I'd rather be than in his arms. And the day we got married, and every time we brought another one of you girls into the world...I fell in love with him all over again. He's been there, holding my hand for every up and down. I couldn't do life without him."

Once again, that wistfulness settled over her face, and I smiled in response, my eyes going misty. It was a beautiful sentiment, and such a rarity to find your soulmate—especially that young. At twenty-eight, I was well past the age my parents had met and gotten married, and I didn't have high hopes for my love life going forward. Running a multi-million dollar company consumed nearly all of my time. Carving out an hour or two a week for dating seemed impossible and, honestly, wasteful.

Mom rose to her feet, but I remained seated, and she didn't question me. Though I was chilled, I wasn't ready to head back upstairs and face the firing squad—Calvin—just yet.

"I, for one, am thankful you and Daddy found each other," I said. "Although I could've done without the eight thousand siblings."

My mom threw her head back and barked out a laugh. "Your poor father. He wanted a son so bad."

"It certainly would've made things easier," I grumbled.

She stepped close and settled her hands on my shoulders, forcing me to look up into her eyes, their peculiar golden hazel so like my own. "No, honey," she said. "The company is in the most capable hands we could imagine. Your father and I are so proud of you, and we know you're going to do amazing things."

"I hope you're right."

She patted my cheek. "I know I am. But don't forget to take some time for yourself. You're still so young, and I know running the company is a big responsibility, but you have to take care of yourself too. Are you..."

Here we go.

"...seeing anyone?"

"Nope," I said, the "p" popping dramatically on my lips.

"That's something you should be making time for!" my mother insisted. "Your father and I aren't getting any younger, and we'd like grandchildren one day."

"Don't worry, I think Chloe will take care of that soon

enough."

My mother waved a dismissive hand. "Forget Chloe. She got her happily ever after. It's time you found yours."

She winked and took off, her feet scuffing against the stairs as she ascended. A moment later, the upper door creaked open, a blast of chatter and clinking glasses filtering down to me before it was abruptly cut off again. I remained rooted in place, my shivering shocked into stillness by the image my imagination conjured.

For some ungodly reason, Calvin's face came to mind. But...nothing about my relationship with Calvin was easy, and I couldn't help but think that meant I had to keep looking. That my person would find me eventually, and we'd walk off into the sunset together, hand in hand, happily ever after just like my sister and Logan.

Just like my parents.

Calvin

chapter 8

"WHAT THE HELL IS wrong with you?" Leon hissed when Amara and Lena disappeared from the table.

"I—I'm sorry," I said. "I overstepped."

"You did a hell of a lot more than overstep, boy. That's my *daughter*. Your *boss*."

"I understand, sir. Truly, I apologize."

"You could try giving her a chance, you know," he said, tossing his napkin onto the table in disgust. "She's not who you think she is."

"Everyone keeps saying that," I said, throwing up my hands, exasperated. "Yet no one will clue me in. When I look at Amara, I see a beautiful girl who wasn't taught financial responsibility. A girl whose family enabled her habits. A girl who used her face and body and charm and money to traipse across the globe doing whatever the fuck she wanted and not having a care in the world about exploiting her influence for any worthwhile endeavor save getting drunk every weekend."

Leon's brows pinched together, his mouth flattening into a line. Too late, I realized my mistake.

In insulting Amara, I'd also insulted him, the man who'd raised her.

Not to mention the fact that I'd called her beautiful and commented on her *body* in front of her father.

Fuck, I was an absolute moron where this girl was concerned.

"First and foremost, Amara has a trust fund that she gained access to at twenty-one. Every penny she used to 'traipse across the globe doing whatever the fuck she wanted,'" Leon said, putting air quotes around my phrase, "was her own. Did you know she has an MBA? Did you know she's been working for this winery since she was fourteen?"

I snorted, and he glared. But I mean...c'mon. Amara "Party Princess" Delatou, a diploma-carrying member of the MBA club? Doubtful. When would she have had time? Between getting drunk in Monaco and hooking up with the son of an earl in England?

Okay, that last one was purely a rumor, but honestly, I wouldn't put it past her.

"We may not have groomed her to take over like we did Chloe, but Amara knows this company inside and out," Leon continued. "Instead of jumping to conclusions, maybe you should ask her to tell you about her travels. Get to know her better. These past five years, you've done nothing but shun her at every opportunity. Amara is a beautiful girl, yes. And she did spend a significant amount of time in Europe over the last few years—the bulk of it in London, I might add. And did you ever stop to consider that maybe she was in those clubs and restaurants and hotels because I asked her to be?"

"No," I said quickly, because it was the truth. I have never once considered she'd been...what? *Working*? Doing market research? Absolutely not.

The night I'd met Amara, she hadn't struck me as overly intelligent. I'd looked at her and seen a drop dead gorgeous girl who I wanted to get naked and fuck into oblivion. She'd been fun to banter with, and the sexual attraction between us had been instant and staggering. That random slip of her family legacy had saved me from a colossal fuck-up.

It didn't matter that I still wanted her so bad I could barely breathe when she was around, that I could still feel the ghosts of her fingers pushing through my hair, her lips on mine, her tongue in my mouth.

Could I have been wrong? Could the reason she hates me so much be because I've refused to see who she is past that initial interaction? Have I misjudged her?

Could she be...capable of running the company despite all the evidence I've found to the contrary? Have I been making a mistake in antagonizing her all these years?

Fuck, my head was spinning. As if he could see what was going on in my brain, Leon offered me a sympathetic smile.

"Just...give her a chance, Cal. That's all I'm asking."

The request sounded simple enough, but how exactly was I supposed to undo five years' worth of bias to view this girl a certain way? How did the blinders come off?

At the very least, right now, I had to find her and apologize. My spirits perked up a little when Lena appeared at Leon's side...then fell again when I realized Amara wasn't with her.

"I'm...so sorry," I said to Lena, hanging my head. "I have no right to speak to her like that."

Lena waved a hand. "Amara is stronger than she looks, and"—she cut her husband with a glance before continuing—"there's a lot more about Amara and her role in this company that you don't know or understand. I know she's not who you would've chosen to take over, Cal, but...cut her some slack. We knew what we were doing when we voted."

It was one thing for Leon to tell me there was more to Amara than what I was seeing, but for Lena to come back after a presumably candid conversation with her daughter to tell me the same thing?

I supposed it was time I took their comments at face value.

Or, at the very least, *try* to. I still firmly believed there were more competent business men and women out there who would run this company better than Amara Delatou could.

"Understood," I said with a nod. "Still, I apologize for my behavior."

"It's fine," she said. "I'm assuming my husband already set you straight."

I grimaced. "He certainly did."

"Then everything is fine...as long as you apologize to her."

"Is she coming back?"

"Doubtful," Lena said, sliding onto the chair next to her husband. "She's down in the cellar, though."

She shot me a meaningful look, and I took that as my cue to leave and seek out Amara.

"Cal," Lena said as I moved to leave. "1-9-9-5." My forehead scrunched in confusion, and she added, "The code to the cellar door."

I'd never been down there before as it was a family only sanctuary. Lena must feel strongly about me patching things up with her daughter if she was handing the code over to an outsider.

With a nod, I bid Leon and Lena goodbye and stalked across the lobby, my mind whirring in a thousand directions. Quietly, I slipped through the cellar door and down the stairs. With each step closer, I felt like I was walking to my doom. This girl...she had the power to ruin me, in more ways than even she knew. But after that conversation with her father, and her mother's comments, I had to make some changes to my behavior. Because one day, her idle threats of voting me out wouldn't be idle any longer.

I found Amara where Lena said she'd be—curled up in one of the armchairs in the cellar. The contrast between the balmy late-spring air upstairs and the temperate, conditioned air down here rose goosebumps on my arms. For a moment, I leaned against the stone wall at the foot of the stairs, studying Amara before she acknowledged my presence and the serenity of her expression was wiped clean by her disdain of me.

I allowed myself to remember how it felt to have every curvy inch of that body pressed against mine. How her skin felt under my lips. The tiny sounds she made when I hit a particularly good spot, when my cock laid heavy between us...

"What the fuck do you want?" she asked suddenly, snapping me from my daydream.

Good thing too. The blood flow to my aforementioned cock was reaching dangerous levels.

"I came to apologize."

"Save it," she said. "I don't give a fuck what you have to say."

"Now, now, Amara," I chastised, unable to stop myself from needling her. "That's no way to speak to your partner."

"You're not my partner."

"I am if you want to get anything done around here."

"It's my name on the door!" she burst out.

"And you're going to have to get that temper in check if you want anyone to take you seriously. If you want to make a real difference around here."

"Real difference? I've been working here for fourteen years, Cal. That's half my life. I've already made a difference."

"Not in any meaningful way. That's why you're trotting out your new little marketing program, isn't it? And pushing so hard to get those RTDs to market? Because you want to leave your mark on this company."

I laughed when she said, "It's not little. And those RTDs are going to make us a fortune."

"That's what she said."

"Oh, fuck off."

"Gladly…as soon as you accept my apology."

"Well, that will never happen. You have no idea the shit I've gone through to make myself useful around here. You think I *liked* spending the better part of five years separated from my family by an ocean? No, I didn't."

I couldn't sympathize with the feeling, but I knew how close this family was, so I could imagine it hadn't been easy.

Then again, she hadn't really seemed to be hurting when she was getting drunk every weekend.

"I'm going to level with you: I don't give a fuck what your

parents think or say. I don't think you've got what it takes to run this company successfully. An MBA from some state school and a European club tour isn't job experience. It's just...you fucking around and wasting your time and money on stupid shit."

Amara blinked slowly at me, as though realizing something for the first time. "You really have no idea what I was doing over there, do you? You just looked at my credit card statements and receipts for reimbursement and assumed I was blowing money for no good reason other than to get drunk, screw my way through Europe, and live up to that 'party princess' nickname you're so fond of."

That rumor about her and an English earl slammed to the forefront of my mind, and my molars ground together at the thought of her screwing anyone but me.

And it was exactly those kinds of thoughts that would land me in a heap of shit if I didn't curb my urges immediately.

I couldn't go there. Not with her, not ever. No matter how badly I wanted to.

"Wasn't that exactly what you were doing the night we met?"

She ignored my comment and plowed ahead. "And for the record, my MBA isn't from *some state school*," she added. "It's from the London School of Business."

Wait...what? I could practically hear the record scratch in my head, the world coming to a standstill in the wake of that admission.

"You graduated from the London School of Business," I said dumbly, and she nodded. "With an MBA."

"With honors."

"Prove it."

"My diploma is literally displayed in my office, which you would've noticed had you bothered to pull your head out of your ass for five seconds."

For the first time in recent memory, I was speechless. This woman—had I seriously underestimated her that badly? I'd been so convinced she was walking around here like a fool while her family and her employees snickered behind her back, when in fact...*I'd* been the fool.

All the comments each of her family members had made about Amara not being who I thought she was—it all made sense now. In the blink of an eye, everything changed, and I had no idea what to do with this new information.

She sighed heavily, distracting me from my inner turmoil, and I could hear the exhaustion in it.

"I don't know why you have to fight me on everything," she said softly.

"Because I'm scared," I admitted quietly. If we were doing this, if I was going to be a better man and give Amara the benefit of the doubt, I had to come clean—about everything.

She cocked her head to the side. "Of what?"

"Of what'll happen if I don't." Amara quirked a brow and, heedless of the consequences, I added, "Of how badly I want you, and what that means for us."

"You're just saying that because my dad yelled at you," she said. "You don't mean that."

I snorted. "When have I ever lied to you?"

That gave her pause, those golden eyes widening, and she rose from her perch, arms wrapped tightly around herself to ward off the chill in the air and failing miserably. Even from ten feet away,

I could see the goosebumps on her skin.

"Me hating you is your fault," she said, stepping closer to me.

"I know," I said. "And I'm sorry for that. I—you make me fucking crazy. But the way I've been treating you is...inappropriate. I really didn't know—about London, about any of it. Fuck, Amara, I'm so sorry."

She choked on a laugh. "*I* make *you* crazy?"

"Absolutely insane," I confirmed.

"Yeah, well, welcome to the club."

"Either way," I said, waving a hand. I couldn't let myself consider if she'd thought about me the way I had her, if her mind had conjured images of me while her fingers, slick with her arousal, toyed with the pussy I'd been dying to devour for five years. "I'm sorry I've been a prick."

Her eyes narrowed, testing my words for verity. At last, in a breathy whisper, she said, "Apology accepted," she said breathily.

"Can I ask you something else?"

"Sure."

"Grad school should've only taken two years. Why didn't you come home right after? Why spend another three years in Europe?"

She shrugged. "My dad asked me to."

I waited for her to continue, and when she didn't, I raised a brow. "Care to elaborate?"

She shook her head, that heavy curtain of dark hair swishing around her shoulders and arms.

"If I do, you'll stop looking at me the way you do every time I surprise you. I'm not willing to give that up just yet."

Her admission surprised me. "How do I look at you?" I asked

quietly, gripped by a sudden desperation. It seemed as though everything hinged on the answer to this question.

Before she could respond, however, her chattering teeth filled the silence between us. Unable to stop myself, I removed my button up, stripping down to the thin white cotton tee beneath, and goosebumps rose on my arms. Even if this woman drove me out-of-my-mind insane, I was still a gentleman—or I liked to consider myself one—and I'd rather I freeze than she did.

"What are you doing?"

"You're frozen," I said as I draped my shirt around her shoulders, gripping it by the placket and tugging her toward me. I snaked my arms inside and around her waist, pulling her flush against me, warming her with my body heat.

"And you're gonna be the one to warm me up? Haven't we tried this before?"

"I was an asshole that night," I said quietly. "And every time after when I doubted your intelligence and ability to run this company."

She inhaled sharply, her chest rising and falling. With her tits brushing against my chest like that, I was having real difficulty remembering why I wasn't allowed to fuck her. I would give my left nut to see what they looked like bare and in my mouth, or bouncing as I fucked her.

What could I say? I wasn't superhuman, and this girl was proving to be my own personal brand of kryptonite.

She tipped her head back, offering me that mouth I'd been dying to taste again every day for the last five years. "I should go. I've got meetings this afternoon."

When she tried to pull away, I only held tighter. "Answer my question."

"What question?"

"How do I look at you when you surprise me?"

For a long moment, she stared at me, chewing on her bottom lip. I wanted to suck it into my mouth, to replace her teeth with mine, to make her moan my name.

"Like I'm someone you could be proud of," she said, so softly I barely heard her over the hum of the HVAC system controlling the temperature down here.

In that moment, that tiny seedling of excitement and promise that had rooted in my chest five years ago sparked once again, and I suddenly wanted nothing more than to claim Amara as mine.

"I *want* to be proud of you," I said. "I want so many things from you, and I'm sorry it's taken me so long to come around to the idea."

"I need you to trust me, Cal," she said. "That's all I'm asking for: some faith in me."

"I can do that," I said and crashed my mouth to hers.

Fucking hell, she was as sweet as I remembered. Her lips were soft and plush and so damn responsive. We molded together, every one of her soft curves aligning perfectly with my hard angles. Her palms swept across my chest, over my shoulders, nails scraping against my back through my shirt. Suddenly, I wanted nothing between us, to feel the sting of those wicked red points against my bare flesh.

With a tug on my bottom lip with her teeth, I opened for her. The first swipe of her tongue against mine had me groaning into her mouth and shifting impossibly closer. There was no hiding my cock and how hard it was for her when it pressed into her stomach.

"Cal..." she breathed, and a cheap little thrill zipped down my spine. Fuck, I shouldn't love the way she said my name so much.

Especially not since it was the first time since the night we'd met that she'd called me *Cal*, and not Calvin or Ryder.

Fuck, but I loved it. I'd love it even more if she was screaming it.

"Yeah, Princess?" I asked, the nickname coming out much softer than I'd ever spoken it before. Pulling my mouth from hers, I trailed kisses over her cheek, jaw, throat, pausing at her pulse and deeply inhaling the scent of her perfume. I could get high on that alone. The warm blend of it mixed with the clean scent of her body wash or shampoo or...*something* drove me wild.

"We can't. Not here."

"You worried we'll be caught?"

"Among other things."

"Fuck, just let me..."

Before she could say anything else, I lifted her off her feet. Despite her protests from a moment ago, her legs wrapped around my waist instinctively, and my hands snaked up her impossibly tight skirt, shoving it out of the way as best I could, resisting the urge to tear it open at that little slit in the back for better access. I palmed a handful of her backside, groaning at the perfection of it, at the sheer bliss of having her in my arms like this again.

"Cal." This time, my name was a gasp, and I'd forever be playing it on a loop while I palmed myself in the shower, thinking about her and this incredible ass of hers. How would it feel to slide my cock between those cheeks?

Our mouths once again collided in a sloppy, wet, messy kiss. I couldn't get close enough, and neither could she if the way she tugged on my hair and ground against me was any indication. A low moan escaped her.

It was so good, too much and not enough all at once.

"I've wanted this for so long," I said, my voice low and husky. God, it should scare me how much I meant that.

I shifted my hips a bit, searching out the warmth between Amara's legs, and she stiffened a little in my arms.

"Right there, huh?" I asked, pulling the collar of my shirt out away from her throat and shoulder to suck the skin of her neck into my mouth, scraping my teeth over the spot.

I expected Amara to respond in kind, to let me fuck her, touch her...*anything*.

Instead, she shoved me away and dropped her feet to the floor. When she was steady, she righted her skirt, shrugged out of my shirt, and whipped it at my face.

"What the fuck are you doing?" I asked as she stalked off.

"I can't do this with you," she responded when she reached the foot of the stairs. "It's too much at once. I—I need some time."

Before I could protest, Amara disappeared up the stairs.

I remained rooted to the spot, blinking slowly. Knowing I needed to get out of here but unable to move thanks to the whiplash Amara had just dealt.

At last, my body caught up with my mind. I adjusted my dick, stuffing the tip into the waistband of my pants, the pressure of which elicited a hiss from my lips that forced me to take several deep, calming breaths.

Fucking Amara Delatou.

chapter 9
Amara

Fucking Calvin Ryder.

I stomped up the stairs and pushed into the lobby, inhaling my first full breath since I'd stormed away from the table a half hour ago. The warmer air was a welcome balm to my frozen skin, and I rubbed my palms up and down my arms to further dispel the chill.

When I approached my parents, my mom must've seen how frazzled I looked, because she asked, "How'd that go?"

"Fine," I clipped, then gathered my purse. "Sorry. I hate to cut this shorter than I already have, but I have meetings I'm going to be late for if I don't get going."

I bent and kissed each of my parents' cheeks in turn, my dad murmuring that he loved me as I strode away.

My main objective was getting out of here before Calvin reappeared, and I power-walked through the lobby. I was nearly to the door that would take me back to the offices when someone shouted my name.

I whirled to find Brie striding toward me.

"Where are you off to in such a hurry?" she asked.

"I've got meetings I'm going to be late for," I said. Not a lie, but not the whole truth, either, and Brie could see through me like I was three hundred-year-old paper.

She narrowed her hazel eyes—more green than gold, a trait she shared with both Chloe and Ella. "What aren't you telling me?"

"Nothing," I said quickly. "I just...ugh. Fucking Ryder."

Brie nodded sympathetically. "That explains the look on your face."

"What look?"

"Like you want to murder someone."

Did I ever.

At that moment, the devil himself pushed through the cellar door, eyes locking on mine. The entire world narrowed to that point; I couldn't tear my gaze away from him. How was it possible that I wanted to stab him and tear his clothes off at the same time? How could he drive me so fucking insane in the worst way yet drive me absolutely wild in the best?

My reaction to Calvin Ryder was a study in contradictions, and I needed to figure my shit out because the back and forth was making my head hurt.

He walked away at last, and I sighed, giving my sister a look that I hoped conveyed I had no idea what I was doing.

My sister simply settled her hand on my shoulder, gave it a squeeze, and said, "Good luck."

I snorted. "Thanks. I'm gonna need it."

❧ ❦

The meeting with the design team that afternoon was a resounding success, especially considering I had Liam by my side to pick up the slack when my mind continued to travel back to the events that occurred in the cellar.

Thankfully, I didn't see Calvin for the rest of the day, and only caught glimpses of him the rest of the week.

By Friday, I was dragging, and I desperately needed a night out. The moment I sent four words out in the sister group chat, the responses started pouring in.

Me: let's go out tonight
Chloe: ugh I'm on deadline
Me: fuck deadline
Chloe: this book is due by Memorial Day!!!!!!!!

I chuckled. Chloe had recently sold her debut novel to a publisher and was deep in the editing trenches. We'd hardly seen her since, and I'd be happy when she sent this current draft off and could take some time off, out of her writing cave.

Delia: here or in TC?
Me: here. I don't feel like making the drive after the week I've had
Delia: hell yes. I haven't been to Granny's in ages.
Brie: I'm in!
Ella: whatever

I snorted. That was as good as excitement from my second youngest sister. Truthfully, I was worried about her, and getting her out of the tiny apartment and surrounding her with her obnoxious sisters—myself included—would be good for her.

Me: I'm just leaving work now, so meet at my place in an hour!

My phone continued to beep with incoming messages, but I ignored them as I traded my Louboutins for my Nikes and pushed out into the mid-May air, bypassing my side by side in favor of the well-trodden path between the winery and my house.

Truthfully, I desperately needed the fresh air to give myself the opportunity to sort through what a mess my life had become. Hopefully the mile walk would get my head right.

I mean, honestly. It had been two days, and I still couldn't get those kisses I'd shared with Calvin out of my mind. And who the fuck did I think I was, making out with my CFO? On company property no less?

Calvin Ryder was driving me insane, and I didn't have time for distractions, least of all from a man who would love nothing more than to see me fail.

Although, his constant antagonism really lit a fire under me.

I'd given him a small piece of the puzzle when it came to me and the things I'd done for the company, but that didn't mean anything would change. If I'd learned anything about Calvin in the time I'd known him, it was that the man was stubborn to a fault. I shouldn't have been the one to tell him about London and my MBA—he should've known. Exactly as he should already know that I'd spent the three years between graduation and coming home to take over expanding our brand. But he'd made up his mind about me a long time ago. While that little romantic piece of my heart that inexplicably belonged to him would love nothing more than to show him exactly who I was...at what cost? If he hadn't gotten on board yet, who was to say he ever would?

Plus, it wasn't my job to convince him. No, my job was to *do my job*. And that didn't include exchanging heated glances and harsh words, or unbearably hot makeout sessions in the cellar that made me so horny, I'd gotten home from work on Wednesday and immediately crawled into bed with my vibrator.

It hadn't done anything to take the edge off, and as I rounded the corner onto the silty path of my driveway, my fingers absently brushed my lips, remembering the feel of his mouth there.

Wondering how'd they'd feel further south.

How his big hands had spanned the width of my curvy hips and thighs, and how those long fingers would feel inside me.

How easily he lifted me despite my five-nine height. How perfectly we fit together, and how wet something as simple as kissing him made me.

I shouldn't let my mind wander there, but I couldn't help imagining what he'd be able to do with a bed and a few uninterrupted hours to toy with my body.

I desperately needed to get laid, or at the very least makeout with someone who *wasn't* Calvin Ryder.

Maybe tonight would be the night.

The moment I pushed through the door of my house, my

shoulders sank from my ears, the stress of the week instantly sloughed off as though I were running a loofah over rough skin. I dropped my bag to the floor, kicked off my tennis shoes, and walked straight down the hall to the back door. A set of worn wood stairs, bleached from years under the fully exposed sun, connected to the beach beyond. The second my toes hit the sand, a wide grin overtook my face and a sigh of relief left my lips. With zero regard for my white paper-bag waist shorts, I dropped my ass onto the sand, close enough to the lake that the water lapped against my feet and under my bottom as it rushed ashore.

Inhaling deeply, I closed my eyes and let the soft breeze gently lift my hair, let it wash over me, let it wash away the stress and drama of the week. There wasn't anything that mattered more than this right now.

I blinked open my eyes, staring out at the endless expanse of the lake, and smiled. God, I was lucky to live here.

I lost myself in the sounds of the waves and the birds, and that's where my sisters found me forty-five minutes later.

"What the fuck are you doing?" Delia shouted down to me.

"Resetting!"

"You're fucking weird," Ella grumbled as I stood and dusted the sand off my ass before trekking across the beach to greet them. My backside was soaked, but I didn't mind. I was going to have to change for Granny's anyway.

"Sometimes, I just need a minute," I told her, slinging an arm around her shoulders as we moved up the path back to the house, surprised when she didn't shrug me off. "In case you forgot, I'm the CEO of a multi-million dollar company, and my CFO hates me."

"That's not what it looked like the other day," Brie said with a knowing smirk, and I cut her a glare that would've killed if looks could do such a thing.

"What happened the other day?" Delia asked as she moved around my kitchen, withdrawing glasses and rim salt from the cupboards, the bottle of tequila from the freezer, and the margarita mix from the fridge.

We may be winery heiresses, but we loved our tequila.

"Brie..." I groaned.

"What?" my littlest sister said with an unperturbed shrug. "You were going to tell them anyway. That's what tonight is for."

I sighed heavily, hating how well my sisters knew me.

Then again, having four built-in best friends was the greatest blessing, even if they meddled when they shouldn't.

"Tonight is for shaking off a long couple of weeks and letting loose before the summer craziness."

On the water beyond, a speedboat zoomed by, lazily trailed by three pontoons, bass-heavy music breaking the stillness of the evening. "Hate to break it to you, sis," Delia said, gesturing to the boats, "but the craziness is already here."

She wasn't wrong. Over the last week, like a switch had been flipped, traffic on the peninsula had increased tenfold from what it was during the slow season. So far, the uptick in reservations in the tasting room, for tours, and at the restaurant had mainly been from college-aged kids, groups of four or five girls coming up to celebrate graduations or the end of another semester.

But soon, once schools started letting out, those moms that spent the last nine months micromanaging their children's entire lives to make sure they survived the year would be in dire need of some "me time" and would flock to the area. The Villa was booked solid from now until the end of October, save Labor Day weekend, which I blocked off for my sales rep party.

"That's beside the point," I said to Delia, waving a dismissive hand.

"You're right," Brie said. "The point is, she and Cal had a *moment*."

"We did not!" I protested.

"Please." My baby sister pursed her lips, unimpressed with my attempt at deflection. "You were all sorts of hot and bothered when I ran into you on Wednesday."

"I was not," I said weakly.

"Save it. Anyone with two eyes and a brain can see the way you two have been circling each other."

I scoffed. "Calvin Ryder is a jackass. I wouldn't touch him with a ten foot pole."

"Except that time you let him stick his tongue down your throat and nearly let him fuck you."

"Delia!" I shouted. "I told you that in confidence!"

Delia only shrugged. "There's no such thing in this family."

I groaned, knowing she was right. When Ella and Brie made noises of protest at being out of the loop, I quickly told them about that night five years ago.

"Wait wait wait," Ella said, throwing her hands up in the air, and I couldn't help but smile. This was the most animated I'd seen her in ages, and it felt like getting a small piece of the old Ella back. The one who favored florals over black and wore a lot less eyeliner. "You're telling me he was seconds away from fucking you, and when he found out who you were, he called you a party princess and said he wasn't risking his job for a one night stand? Who the fuck does he think he is?"

"That's what I've been telling you guys for years. The animosity between us isn't just some childish butting of the heads like Daddy has always thought—like I've always let you guys believe. He…"

"He hurt you." Brie said it so simply that I should've realized the truth of the matter a long time ago.

"Yeah," I said quietly.

Thoughts of that night had continued to plague me for years, even when I was in Europe having the time of my life, burying myself in school and work—and okay, having a casual fling or ten. For the longest time, I thought the reason it stuck with me so incessantly was because I was embarrassed, and because he worked for our company so there was truly no getting away from him. He had his hand in everything I did; I *knew* he'd be the one reviewing my spending habits and reconciling the books. I knew every time my dad called me to gently warn me about going overboard with the dinners and the club nights that it was at Calvin's urging.

It never stopped me because I knew Dad didn't really care—and because I was using my own money. Truthfully, I liked pissing Calvin off. I liked picturing his face scrunching up in annoyance and the anger that would course through his veins every time the credit card statements came across his desk. Giving Calvin the middle finger from nearly four thousand miles away had been a blast.

I didn't realize until Brie stated it so plainly that he *had* hurt me. Having a man who I had such an intense and immediate physical connection to—and let's be real, more than that, even after only a few hours together—make such snap judgements about me and my character had me reeling for weeks after that night.

It's why I'd jumped into bed with Owen so quickly in the aftermath. I'd been willing to do anything to make myself feel better, and the sexy, retired NFL quarterback more than satisfied that urge.

Not to mention, Owen had become such a great friend after we stopped hooking up that it ended up being the best thing that could've happened.

But still...when someone repeatedly threw derogatory remarks out about your character, constantly undermined your work ethic and values, and generally seemed to abhor everything about you as a person—it was hard to stop those thoughts from weaseling their way in and taking root in your mind.

It was hard to stop yourself from believing they were right about you.

"So what happened the other day?" Brie asked, pulling me from my thoughts.

"Ugh," I groaned, slapping a palm over my face. "I let him kiss me."

"Like a peck or..." Delia prompted.

"Definitely 'or,'" I said, giggling and sighing. "He crashed my lunch with Mom and Dad, and the proceeded to make comments that pissed me off so much I told him 'fuck you' and stormed away. Mom and I had a good chat in the cellar, but I hung out down there for a bit after she went back up. You know, to collect myself. And I guess Daddy chewed him a new one, because he came looking for me."

I told them about our conversation, how I finally spilled the beans on my MBA. That damn "some state school" comment had been the last straw for me.

"One minute, he was giving me his shirt because I was freezing, and the next he had my legs wrapped around his waist as he pressed me into the wall and stuck his tongue in my mouth."

"What happened after that?" Brie asked. "Because when I saw you, you definitely didn't look like a woman who just had her world rocked by a kiss."

"He's so frustrating!" I said, leaping to my feet and diving my fingers into my hair, pulling on the strands at my temples. The sting grounded me. "He told me how he's wanted me for so long, but like...how can I trust anything he says? So I told him I wanted nothing to do with him, and I ran."

Once again, my hand flew to my lips, the ghost of his kisses still lingering even days later.

"But you *do* still want him, don't you?" Ella asked.

"What? No!"

"Mar..." all three of my sisters said in unison, giving me matching looks that told me to get real and stop lying—to them and myself.

"Fine, I want him!" It was the first time I'd admitted it out loud, and honestly, it felt freeing to finally get it off my chest. "I'd happily get into bed with Calvin Ryder and let him put that wicked mouth to good use for once."

"So...why don't you?" Delia asked.

I shook my head. Of course, she wouldn't see the complications in this. Of my sisters, Delia was the most...sexual. Professional boundaries wouldn't mean shit to her when her personal pleasure was in question. She'd simply take what she wanted and give any fallout the middle finger.

I wasn't like her, though. Did I want Calvin? Absolutely. My traitorous body fucking *sang* in anticipation whenever he was near.

But *wanting* Calvin and *having* him were two different things, and they were completely at odds with each other. We were oil and water, two things that would never mix.

"I'm his boss."

"Weak," Ella said, calling me out on my bullshit.

"It's not, though. I *am* his boss. A sexual relationship with him would cross so many lines."

"Maybe technically," Delia said. "But I'd consider you more on a level playing field than anything else. You hold the majority share, so what. It's not like you unilaterally make decisions. You require his input on everything. Hell, you require *our* input on everything. That's what having a board means."

I mean, yeah, if you wanted to get *technical*. But this was about a lot more than technicalities. Despite having gone nearly five years without seeing each other, and only having two al-beit incredibly hot, thigh-clenching makeout sessions that have spurred on a thousand fantasies of Calvin naked in my bed, there was too much history there.

Calvin had apologized to me the other day, yes, and I appre-ciated that. Maybe he'd start taking me more seriously around the office. But what Delia was proposing—a purely physical re-lationship with him? I couldn't get on board with that. Stupidly, I wanted more. I wanted Calvin to want my body *and* my brains.

It's what I would ask of any man I gave myself to, not just him. I deserved that, didn't I?

"It's too complicated and messy," I said, waving off my sisters' protests. "We have to work together, and it's not a road I'm willing to walk."

"So what're you going to do?" Delia asked.

"I'm glad you asked, little sister. Tonight, I'm going out with my favorite girls and getting drunk. Later, we're gonna come home and demolish all the food in my freezer. I'm going to spend my weekend curled up in bed with a book. And next week..."

"Yes?" Ella prompted.

"Next week, I'm going to do my fucking job, and show Calvin Ryder who's boss."

My sister erupted into cheers, and I smiled.

This was exactly what I needed: my best girls around me, slowly replacing all thoughts of Calvin with their laughter and love.

"Report."

Jeff scrambled into the seat across from me, arms laden with a sheaf of papers that flew everywhere when he dropped onto the chair.

"Shit," he said quietly, then looked up at me apologetically.

"What's all that?"

"Receipts."

I dropped my elbows onto my desk and pinched the bridge of my nose. "I don't know how many times I have to tell you, Jeff. Scan those into the accounting program and shred the physicals."

"I just thought you'd—"

"You thought wrong," I said, lifting my head to level him with a glare. Then I waved my hand. "Set all that shit down and tell me what's going on."

"According to Cindy, Amara's been hard at work with Liam Danvers to get the canned cocktail recipes perfected, and they met with the design team last week to finalize the packaging."

"And?"

"And what?"

"What's it look like?"

"Oh, right!" Jeff said, grinning sheepishly at me, and I glared in response. He rifled through the stack of papers balanced haphazardly on his lap until he came to the one he sought and held it out to me.

I took a moment to study the sheet, lifting a brow as I met his eyes again. "This is what they're calling it?"

"Yep," Jeff said. "Catchy, isn't it?"

Catchy definitely wasn't the word I'd use, not with the tangled knot of jealousy that had materialized in my chest and was currently pressing on my sternum.

Delatou & Danvers, a new line of canned, wine-based cocktails from Chateau Delatou, brought to you by Amara Delatou and Liam Danvers.

God, seeing their names together like that made me fucking sick.

Amara was a beautiful woman; that wasn't news. What was news, to me at least, was how much the CD grower had taken notice. The comment he'd made about her rack last week when we'd gone out into the vineyard had been plunking around in my head since. It had taken Herculean self-control to not call him out beyond telling them to act more professional.

I was the only one who should be noticing that rack, and I damn well better be the only one who got to feel those tits pressed against his chest or filling his hands.

God, figure your shit out, Ryder. You don't own her.

But damnit, did I want to—and that thought scared the shit out of me.

"It's definitely something," I said to Jeff at last.

"They've got four recipes ready to go. Ms. Delatou gave Cindy some samples, and we tried them over the weekend. They're *amazing*," he gushed.

I wasn't surprised. Amara had spent more than enough time sampling alcohol all over the world; she'd accept nothing but perfection. And Danvers was a talented mixologist in his own right.

In fact, I was more surprised by the fact that my assistant and hers were spending time together outside of work. Seemed Jeff finally found the balls to shoot his shot. Good for him.

I sat back in my chair, balancing my elbows on the armrests and steepling my fingers in front of me. "Wonder where my samples are..."

"Oh, shit, sir. I'm sorry. I should've thought—"

I waved him off. "Don't worry," I said. "I'll approach Ms. Delatou about them myself."

Jeff frowned. "Are you sure?"

"Quite," I assured him with a smile. "What else has been happening? What's on her agenda for today?"

I flicked my wrist to check my watch, surprised to find it was nearing five p.m. I'd been so busy today that I'd worked right through lunch without noticing. The thought elicited a growl from my stomach.

"She had a meeting with a boutique hotel owner this morning. Not entirely sure what that's about. I'll head over and see Cindy when I leave here, see if she can clue me in. If not, I'll approach legal to see if any contract requests have come through today."

The words *boutique hotel owner* had the hair on the back of my neck rising. He couldn't possibly mean...

"What's their name?" I asked, though deep in my gut, I already knew the answer.

"Amie something," Jeff said. "Sorry, I can't remember the last name."

"Fulton?" I prompted.

Jeff nodded, snapping his fingers excitedly. "Yes, that's it!"

"Damn," I said, brushing a hand through my hair.

Amie Fulton had moved to the area about five years ago, right around the time I did, after purchasing an old, run-down Mc-Mansion on the northern outskirts of Traverse City, right at the base of Old Mission.

A year later, after a complete gut job and external overhaul, she opened her boutique hotel—The Harvest Inn. The name was a little too whimsical for my tastes, and I honestly expected her to fail within the first six months. I knew how much money she dumped into that property, and I couldn't see how she'd have any hope of earning back her investment and turning a profit.

Naturally, she'd proved me wrong.

Then again, that had always been her favorite thing to do.

I'd given Amie and our relationship roughly two years of my life, and in the end...I wanted more, and she hadn't. She was content with her hotel, and expanding her real estate empire to other properties across the area.

I had just turned thirty and was ready to settle down. Amie had been the ideal woman—intelligent, sexy, one hell of a business mind. We'd never run out of things to talk about, and the sex had been fantastic. I could easily picture living life with her at my side. I could imagine getting married, having a few kids, and setting roots deep into this northern Michigan soil.

Unfortunately, I'd been so blinded by what *I* wanted, and by the contentment I felt when I was with her, that I hadn't realized she'd grown more miserable by the day. The tighter I clung to her and our relationship, the further away she pulled.

I hadn't noticed until it was too late—when I was down on one knee.

Thankfully, my proposal had been a spur of the moment thing and not the elaborate public plan I'd initially concocted. I'd managed to spare myself *that* small bit of embarrassment.

We'd been on a day trip to Sleeping Bear Dunes, on a hike up above the sparkling expanse of Lake Michigan. It was a perfect early summer day. Not too hot, not too cold. The slight breeze blowing off the lake had ruffled our hair and dried the sweat on my brow. Amie had been hiking ahead of me, her long legs eating up the terrain. At one point, she glanced at me over her shoulder, her short, ice-blonde hair brushing the bare skin there and the nape of her neck. The smile she'd given me had been so damn pure—complete and utter happiness. Happiness over being in nature that I'd mistaken as happiness with me. My heart had swelled in my chest, and I couldn't think of a more perfect spot to ask her to spend our lives together.

I'd closed the distance between us and clasped her wrist, pulling her around to face me.

"What's wrong?" she asked.

"Nothing," I said. *"I just...there's something I've been wanting to do for a while, and I think it's time."*

I reached into my pocket and withdrew the small black velvet box I'd taken to carrying everywhere with me.

A grin split my face as I knelt onto the sandy ground, gripping one of Amie's delicate hands in my own.

"Amie Fulton," I began, keeping my gaze on our joined hands until I got the words out. "These last two years with you have been the best of my life. When I moved here, I wasn't looking for anyone or anything like this. Then you walked into my life, and everything changed. I want everything with you—a house on the water, a massive wedding, a few kids running around. More adventures. More love. More sex," I said with a smirk. "I want it all. Will you marry me?"

I glanced up at Amie then, expecting to see joyful shock.

Instead, I found a frown, the skin between her brown eyes puckered in confusion.

"Cal..." she started, and a lead weight settled on my chest. "That's not what this is."

I blinked slowly. Now I was the one who was confused.

Amie shifted uncomfortably on her feet. "Look...I care about you, but I thought we were just having fun."

"For two years?" I asked, incredulous. "You told me you loved me!"

Fuck, I sounded like a teenage girl having her heart broken for the first time.

"I thought you knew..." she said quietly.

I hadn't known. She'd completely blindsided me that day. With stiff, jerky movements, I'd risen to my feet and stalked away from her. I'd practically sprinted back to the parking lot, where a kind elderly couple had taken pity on me and driven me back to the city.

I hadn't spoken to Amie since.

Amara had no way of knowing my history with Amie, but I'd be lying if I said it didn't sting a bit. That was three years ago, and I hadn't been in a serious relationship since.

It was difficult to get back on the horse when my heart had been trampled.

And, unfortunately for me, lately my thoughts—and dick—had been drawn to the last woman on the planet I should want. Hot makeout sessions in the wine cellar were as far as we could take things, and even that had been grossly inappropriate.

Even if my cock still perked up at the memory of her body under my hands, of those tits flush against my chest and her long, curvy legs wrapped around my waist.

Fucking hell, Ryder. Get it together.

At thirty-three, the thought of settling down and starting a family was on my mind pretty much all the time, but Amara Delatou would not be the mother of my children.

"Boss?" A quiet voice broke into my reverie, and I blinked several times, clearing the cobwebs of my memory.

"Sorry, Jeff," I said, scrubbing a hand over my face. "You were saying?"

"I was just telling you she's also got a meeting with Brie and Ezra in about ten minutes to finalize the summer menus for the restaurant." He glanced pointedly at my stomach, which once again emitted an impressive grumble. "Maybe you should join them."

A slow grin unfurled on my face. Crashing another one of Amara's meetings *and* getting an entire meal from Ezra out of it, plus sweets from Brie?

"I like the way you think, Jeff," I said, rising to my feet.

He gave me a mock salute. "See you later."

Whistling a peppy little tune, I exited my office and made my way toward the restaurant.

I found Amara, Brie, and Ezra in the kitchen, an impressive array of sample dishes spread on the massive prep island. Amara had perched herself on a stool on one side, one of her long, silky legs crossed over the other, the smooth material of her flowy skirt having ridden dangerously high on her thighs. Her arms were bare, one elbow resting on the counter, her chin propped in it as she watched her sister and Ezra move around the industrial kitchen in a well-practiced dance.

But I only had eyes for her.

God, she was stunning. It was truly a shame we absolutely could never be together, because we could have a lot of fun together.

All those thoughts immediately dissipated like smoke on the wind when I cleared my throat and Amara turned those golden eyes on me, the joy in them instantly dimming to wariness.

"What are you doing here?"

"This is the tasting meeting for the summer menu, right?"

"Yes, but..."

"Great!" I said, cutting her off and pulling out the stool next to her. Sure, I could've put some distance between us—and the moment her intoxicating perfume hit my nose, I wished I had—but I'd never pass up an opportunity to make her squirm. I looked at Ezra and Brie, both of whom wore amused expressions, and said, "You don't mind, do you?"

"Not at all," Ezra said graciously. "There's plenty here for both of you."

The moment they turned their backs on us, and Amara hissed, "What the fuck are you doing here?"

"Eating dinner," I said, my point punctuated by a low grumble from my stomach.

"How did you even know this was happening today?"

"I have my ways," I said with a smirk.

"I'm firing Cindy," she groused.

"I would have to advise against that."

"Leave my assistant alone," she said. "Matter of fact, leave *me* alone."

"No can do, Princess."

Her eye twitched at my use of her nickname, and I bit back a full on grin. Before she could retort, Ezra turned and plated a dollop of mashed potatoes, topped it with three healthy-sized medallions of some sort of meat, drizzled it all with sauce, and sprinkled fried onions on top.

That was one thing I loved about Ezra's cooking—not only that he was an insanely talented chef and I'd eat whatever he put in front of me, but also because, despite having earned a Michelin star at his former restaurant in New York City, his food wasn't flashy. He used high-quality ingredients and put his own spin on classic comfort-food staples. In New York, I'm sure he'd experimented a bit more, but when a tragedy in his personal life had him re-evaluating his career and his role as a father, he'd decided to seek out a job somewhere quieter and slower-paced.

New York's loss was surely our gain.

"Alright, Ez" Amara said to Ezra, leaning forward to stick her nose dangerously close to a plate of some pasta dish in front of her. "What've we got?"

Our first dish turned out to be a cold pasta, which surprised me when I shoveled a bite into my mouth. The cavatappi were tossed in a cheese sauce that I couldn't even begin to guess the components of, and the noodles were topped with an array of colorful grape tomatoes that burst deliciously in my mouth, the sweet acidity the perfect balance for the heavier noodles and cheese.

Next to me, Amara groaned deeply, and my entire body froze.

I've heard that sound before—when I was sucking on her tongue and grinding her against my cock in the wine cellar last week.

No no no no, I silently pleaded with my body, but naturally, my dick didn't listen. I shifted uncomfortably on my stool, reaching down to adjust myself while Amara's eyes were still closed as she savored her food.

"Fuck, that's good," she said quietly.

"That's for the lunch menu," Ezra said proudly. "I wanted something carb heavy but still light enough that diners won't be too full to indulge in some of Brie's desserts."

Next to him, Brie's cheeks turned pink, and Ezra offered her a small—but proud—secretive sort of smile. I could practically see the stars in her eyes over the interaction.

While Ezra moved around to set another offering in front of us, I wondered why I couldn't find myself attracted to someone sweet and quiet, more like Brie instead of her sexy and infuriating older sister.

Because you'd be bored out of your mind.

Right. There was that.

I dug into the next course, the meat and potatoes dish Ezra had plated right after I walked in, pleasantly surprised to discover thinly sliced and circle-shaped pork chops. On the side, he'd plated a helping of Brussels sprouts, coated in oil and baked to the perfect finish, the edges of the leaves crispy and dark brown while the center was somehow both fresh and tender. The small diced and fried pieces of prosciutto added a nice saltiness to the dish.

Plate after plate passed in front of me, and I ate my fill of every single one. Ezra had truly outdone himself with this menu, the flavor profiles somehow simple yet complex, the ingredients fresh, the meals familiar but elevated to a luxuriousness people would expect from a high-end winery like ours.

And the whole time, Amara continued to make those sounds, driving me absolutely wild.

Ezra and Brie gave us a brief moment between the last meal course and the first dessert sample to collect ourselves. I leaned back on my stool, stretching my arms over my head and trying to figure out how I was going to fit anything else in my stomach.

But when Brie set a dish of some custard-like substance in front of me and wielded a miniature blowtorch with a wicked gleam in her eyes, I knew I'd eat every last bit of her creme brûlée. Next to those cheese danishes she made, the creme brûlée was my favorite of her desserts.

Once the sugar topping was heated and hardened, and Brie had sprayed her chai whipped cream on top, I dove in, sighing happily as the sweetness melted on my tongue.

Then, unable to stop myself, I turned to Amara and awaited her reaction. Surely sensing my gaze, Amara slowly dipped the tip of her spoon in the dish and brought it to her mouth, her tongue darting out for a taste before she closed her mouth around the utensil, tongue swirling around to collect every last morsel. Once again, that low moan left her throat, and my cock hardened completely.

The rest of the dessert course was the purest form of torture as I stuffed myself with Brie's decadent concoctions and listened to Amara unabashedly have a foodgasm next to me.

Without thinking, I reached out and closed my palm around her thigh, hoping the pressure of my fingers against her skin would shock her into silence.

Her eyes flew open, gaze darting back and forth between my hand and my eyes.

"What are you doing?" she murmured, shooting a semi-panicked glance at her sister and Ezra. Both of them had their backs to us, chatting in low voices as Brie stirred something on the stove. They weren't paying us a lick of attention, which emboldened me further.

"You're making me crazy," I said, slowly arcing my pinky across her skin, sliding my palm higher as I did.

"Get your hand off me."

"Why?" I whispered back. "Afraid I'll find out how wet you are for me?"

Amara's chest rose and fell, those ample breasts heaving in time with her breaths, and she swallowed hard.

I had her, and we both knew it.

I don't know what I expected from her, but she surprised me yet again when she threw my hand off her leg, rose from the stool and, with a rushed goodbye and weak excuses about why she needed to leave *right now* to Brie and Ezra, stormed from the kitchen.

"What the hell just happened?" Brie asked.

"I don't know," I said, tossing my napkin down and standing. "I'll find her."

Brie looked like she wanted to argue, but after a brief moment of hesitation, she simply nodded.

As close to permission as I'd ever get from anyone in her family.

Because right now, I was painfully turned on, and I was finally ready to do something about it.

chapter 11
Amara

How fucking dare *he?*

I fumed as I stalked back through the buildings toward my office. It was late—well after six—and everyone had cleared out for the day. Good for me, since it meant no one was around to witness my Godzilla-esque stomp down the halls.

I'd just thrown myself into my chair, shaking with rage, when my office door burst open and Calvin appeared.

"What the fuck do you want?"

Calvin didn't answer me. He simply closed the door behind him, staring me dead on as he flicked the lock. With a predatory gleam in his eyes, he stalked toward me.

"Don't you dare come any closer," I said, rising to meet him. "Who the fuck do you think you are, touching me like that? Saying those things to me?"

"Oh, don't act all innocent. Those noises you were making while you were eating? Can you honestly tell me you weren't doing that to get under my skin?"

I wanted to argue with him, but all I could manage was a satisfied smirk.

I *had* been toying with him, and a quick glance at his crotch confirmed it had done the trick. But maybe I'd taken it a little too far. The look in his eyes told me Calvin was done playing our little games, and the idea both thrilled and terrified me.

"That still doesn't give you the right to touch me whenever you please. I'm your *boss*, Ryder. You can't put your hands on me like that, or make comments about my...state of arousal."

He raised a brow, continuing to close the distance between us until he at last crowded my space, pushing the backs of my thighs into the edge of my desk. "State of arousal?" he asked quietly. "Tell me, Amara...how wet are you for me right now?"

Fucking dripping. "Dry as the Sahara," I lied.

He chuckled darkly. "You're so fucking hot when you're angry," he said, bending to press his face into the crook of my neck and shoulder, inhaling deeply. "God, your scent drives me wild."

I froze for a beat before my hands raised. I had every intention of shoving him away, but my body had other ideas, and I found myself curling my fingers into the front of his shirt instead.

I still wasn't sure if it was to pull him closer or push him away, but Calvin ultimately made the decision for me. In one quick move, he ran his hands up the backs of my thighs, goosebumps rising in their wake, and lifted me so I was perched on the edge of my desk. With his palms on the soft skin of my inner thighs, he pressed my legs wide and fit his hips between them. My heels slipped off my dangling feet.

"We can't keep doing this," I said quietly, smoothing my palms up his chest, belying my words by reaching for the top button of his shirt.

"We haven't even gotten started."

His thumbs drew lazy patterns on my skin, higher and higher, my breath hitching when he brushed them both against my pussy. He whispered a curse when he discovered I wasn't wearing panties.

"You know we shouldn't."

Honestly, I rarely wore them in the summer. They got sticky and uncomfortable, and even thongs left panty lines in my tight pencil skirts. It wasn't particularly warm today, and I wore a flowy skirt, so I didn't really have an excuse, but the way Calvin's eyes darkened when he brushed my smooth, bare skin made me glad I'd forgone them.

"I don't give a fuck anymore."

I shivered, grateful he was taking this choice out of my hands. I wanted him so badly I ached, and I was so damn tired of fighting it.

With the last button free, I pushed his shirt off his shoulders and reached for the hem of the tee beneath. He took it from me and whipped it off. I didn't need his clothes off for what was coming—not entirely—but I'd been fucking dying to run my hands and mouth over his bare skin for *years*. This may be my only opportunity. I leaned forward and pressed a kiss to the center of his chest, then flicked my tongue over both of his nipples, grinning when his breath stuttered.

Calvin plucked a string of the delicate bow holding one side of my tank over my shoulders, slowly pulling it free, then repeating the process on the other side. The top slid over my chest, catching on the tips of my breasts, and he tugged it to my waist. A moment later, my tits were in his hands, and I arched my back, pushing against him as he kneaded and squeezed and brushed his thumbs teasingly over my nipples.

I went for his belt, unhooking it, unzipping his pants, and pushing them and his boxers to his ankles.

God, he was perfect.

Arms, chest, and shoulders coiled with muscle, his pecs tapering into a smooth, flat stomach, accented by that delicious V indenting his hips. The ridges of his abdomen twitched under my fingertips as I ran a hand over them, following the trail of reddish brown hair that ran from his bellybutton, drawing my eye straight to his cock. I swiped my thumb over the tip, collecting the precum beaded there. Then, with my gaze locked on his, I stuck my finger in my mouth and sucked.

His eyes flared with heat when I moaned at the saltiness of him, the same sound I'd been making earlier as I sampled Brie and Ezra's dishes.

"Just this once," I said.

Over the last five months, and especially over the last few weeks, Calvin and I had gotten really good at toying with each other, at driving each other to the brink and then walking away. No line had been crossed yet, at least not majorly.

Because that makeout last week was nothing compared to what was about to happen, and by the look in his eyes, surely mirroring the one in my own, we were both done playing.

It was time to put up or shut up.

He offered me a knowing smirk. "Sure, Princess. Just this once."

"Condom," I breathed, anticipation prickling my skin. I shifted so I could pool my skirt around my hips and leaned back on my hands, spreading my legs wider. Then Calvin dug in his back pocket, flipped his wallet open, and tossed a condom onto my desk next to my left hip.

"For what it's worth," he said, "I get tested regularly, and my last physical came back with nothing to report."

"Me too," I replied. "Nothing to report."

Grinning, he moved closer and slid his cock through my wetness, slipping the tip around my clit in the most distracting way. I reached for the foil packet and ripped it open with my teeth. Withdrawing the rubber, I slowly rolled it down his length, and he hissed against my touch.

Then he leaned forward, gripped the back of my head, and slammed his mouth against mine at the same moment he drove into me in one powerful thrust.

I cried out against the intrusion.

It was...exactly as I'd always imagined. Too good, too perfect, too much and not enough. Everything I needed, and even now, when he hadn't even begun to move yet, I wasn't sure how I'd ever give it up after only one time. Maybe this was a mistake.

But the damage was done.

I had a feeling Calvin Ryder was about to become a drug I couldn't quit, an addiction I couldn't shake, injecting himself straight into my bloodstream and making sure I couldn't think straight, couldn't function, without having him just like this over and over.

He withdrew to the tip and drove back in, his hand slipping around to the front of my neck, cupping my throat, forcing me to look at him. "Anyone ever tell you that you have a perfect pussy?"

"Cal…" I whimpered, his eyes lighting with satisfaction.

I only called him that in situations like this, when he was pleasuring me instead of pissing me off. Here, in this bubble where it was just us, just *this*, his body against mine? It was the only time I'd felt safe doing so. Nicknames, even shortened versions of first names, could be a slippery slope. They could lead to a familiarity I was trying to avoid.

Then again, his cock was currently buried inside me, so I supposed that ship had already sailed.

"God, I need you," he breathed, and the admission twisted my insides further.

Yeah, I was a lost cause where this man was concerned. Somehow, the thought didn't bother me nearly as much as I'd expected.

"You have me."

"Look at us," he said, taking his hand away from my neck, using his thumb and forefinger to spread me open, both of us watching as he slipped in and out.

I was mesmerized by it all. By how perfectly I gripped him, by his cock wrapped in a condom coated in my arousal, by him pressing his thumb against my bundle of nerves in a way that made my legs shake.

"More."

"I can't—"

Cal stopped himself, that wicked gleam returning to his eyes a moment before he hauled me up and stepped backward, dropping himself onto my desk chair. The leather creaked under our weight, the sound drowned out by my low moan. The fit of him inside me at this angle had my eyes rolling back in my head. The way I stretched around him was fucking perfect in the way it toed the line between pleasure and pain.

I wanted him every day, just like this. Me above him, my nipples brushing his chest with each roll of my hips. His murmured curse words. The passion-filled confessions.

"How did we go so long?"

I didn't mean to say that, but God. Being with him had the floodgates open, had me defenseless against the onslaught of new and intoxicating emotions swirling within me. Suddenly, I wanted to give him everything.

"I don't know, but I'm regretting sending you away five years ago if it would've been like this."

I shook my head. "I've learned a few tricks since then."

His stare flamed when he met my eyes, and he settled his hand against my windpipe, squeezing just hard enough that my pussy pulsed and clenched tighter around him. Why was that so hot? I needed to breathe, but in these moments? I needed Cal more.

A growl tore free from his throat. "You're mine now. Do you understand? You don't bring your little fuck boys into this." I could only nod. "Good girl," he added, smacking my tit at the same time he pulled his hand away from my neck, and I gasped a moan.

Filthy words. Filthy boy. I was his in ways I didn't think either of us realized yet, and he was mine.

Our bodies quickly became slick with sweat as I raised and lowered myself on him. He held me tightly, not giving me much leverage. It was slow, lazy torture.

"Cal, please," I whined.

He wrapped my hair around his fist and tugged my head back, gripping my hip tightly with the other. He licked a path from the hollow at the base of my throat to the underside of my jaw. "You wanna come, Princess?"

My nickname was spoken with such reverence now; it made me impossibly wetter. How had something I hated so deeply so quickly become something I craved?

"Please."

His hold loosened, giving me free range of motion, and he said, "This is your show, then. Use me."

God, I loved it when a man let me take control. My orgasm coiled tighter.

I shifted onto my tiptoes and fit myself a little closer to him, bobbing up and down a few times until I found that spot where my swollen clit rubbed against the base of his cock with every shift of my hips.

And then I rode him like it was my goddamn job.

"That's it, Princess," he said, burying his face between my tits, a completely blissed out expression on his face as he cupped them against his cheeks. "You look so good bouncing on my cock."

"I'm close," I said, digging my fingernails into the skin of his shoulders. "I just..."

"What? Use your words, baby. I'll give you whatever you want."

"I can't," I said. I was so fucking close, but I needed..."More."

I didn't even know what I was saying. His words, his magical dick, his fingers digging into my tits hard enough that I'd surely have bruises—it was simultaneously everything and not enough.

Cal somehow knew what I needed before I did, and he spread

his knees, forcing my legs wider. With his big palm spanning across my lower belly, his middle finger dipped into my belly button as he thumbed my clit and bucked up into me.

Words eluded me; I could only throw my head back and moan. That was the spot, the one that had my vision going hazy, had my whole body clenching in anticipation.

"God, I just…" he breathed, eyes heavily lidded as he studied me. "You look so fucking good like this. Like a goddess, Mar. And I'm the man you're letting worship you? Unreal."

"Don't stop."

"Never," he promised.

We said more in those three words than I think we meant to. Cal didn't slow his punishing rhythm, and I hoped he never stopped worshiping me this way.

I was spread wide open for him, completely vulnerable as he rubbed my clit and fucked me hard and wild, but I'd never felt safer. The way he watched me, the way he looked at where we were joined, how my tits bounced freely, how fucking wet I was for him, the unashamed sounds I was making—perfection. I knew it'd be like this with him, but my imagination could never have prepared me for the real thing.

Magical dick, indeed.

My release built and built and built until I was sure I'd pass out before I ever came. It wasn't until Cal said "let go" that I went off like a bomb, only content to explode on his command.

My body was a traitorous bitch, taking her cues from the demands of a man, but I'd be damned if the edges of my vision didn't darken with the force of it. I collapsed against his chest, my face buried in his neck to muffle my cries, writhing through the shockwaves. He wrapped his arms tightly around me and continued to fuck me, and I clenched around him so hard that I triggered his own release. As he pulsed then spilled and spilled and spilled, he groaned curses and murmured my name against my skin.

When I was at last spent, no longer quivering in his arms, and our breathing had returned to semi-normal, I shifted so he could slip free, then lifted my head to look at him.

"Fucking hell, Mar," he said, a sated smile on his face as he brushed my hair off my damp forehead.

"That's the second time you've called me that."

"And you called me Cal."

"I guess all kinds of things changed in the last half hour."

The smile bloomed into a grin, and he cupped a hand around the back of my head to haul me in for a kiss. It was...soft, slow, and sweet—so at odds with our frantic joining.

I hated to admit how much I loved it. I wanted every version of Cal's kiss.

Surprisingly, the silence we fell into was...nice. Companionable, even. When we finally decided to move, he grabbed a tissue to clean me up before helping me retie the straps of my tank top, and I buttoned him back into his shirt as he finger-brushed the tangles from my hair.

At last, I gingerly unlocked and pulled open the door, checking the immediate area for any staff. Determining the coast was clear, I opened it fully and gestured for Cal to go out ahead of me.

We left the building in silence, and he walked me to my side by side, giving me an unreadable smile and a kiss on the forehead before heading in the direction of the staff parking lot, rounding the building and out of sight.

And I drove home, wondering what the fuck just happened, and what that meant for us going forward.

chapter 12
Calvin

It was official: I was fucking ruined.

My mind spun a thousand miles an hour as I sped down the peninsula, heading back to my apartment in the city.

"Skye!" I hollered as I stepped through the door, my shoulders instantly relaxing as the quick clacking of nails on the hardwood floor sounded down the hall, her collar jangling as she raced for me. She rounded the corner, and I knelt to her level, hugging her close when she threw her shaking golden body at me.

I stood, still holding her, all sixty pounds of her wriggling in my arms as she excitedly licked my face. Already, with my pup in my arms, I felt less like I was spinning out of control.

"What do you think, my girl?" I said as I walked into my room and dropped her onto my bed, no doubt returning her to where she'd been when I walked through the door. I'd never understand pet owners who didn't let their animals on furniture. Skye slept curled up next to me every night, and I wouldn't have it any other way. "Should we go for a walk?"

At the mention of her favorite four letter word, her glossy ears perked up, and I gave the white patch on her chin a little scratch before shedding my clothes in favor of some athletic shorts and a Detroit Warriors tee. Then I exited the room, Skye trotting dutifully after me. At the door, I clipped on her leash and set off through the city streets toward our favorite path along the bay.

I thought the walk would clear my head, and it minimally distracted my attention when I had to keep pulling Skye away from chasing the ducks squatting in the grass along the trail. A woman stopped me to tell me Skye was a beautiful dog, having her own Golden Retriever connected to a leash that hooked around her trim waist. Clearly, she was flirting with me, but I couldn't get excited about the conversation and left her frowning.

No, my mind was completely consumed by Amara, no matter how hard I tried to fight it.

The image of her writhing on top of me, her tits bouncing as I thrust up into her?

Fuck...I'd never forget that as long as I lived. The mental movie playing on repeat at the forefront of my brain was better than any porn I'd ever seen.

It was without a doubt the dumbest fucking thing I'd ever done...and I couldn't wait to have her again. *Just this once*, my ass.

When I'd pushed into her office and locked the door behind me, I'd had every intention of fucking her hard and fast, punishing us both for how badly I wanted her. And then I'd undressed her, and the first sight of her bare breasts, of her naked pussy beneath that flouncy little skirt, of the way she collected my precum on her thumb and sucked it off—I came undone.

Us being together like that was wrong on so many levels, but Amara Delatou was an addiction I'd happily indulge for the rest of my life.

And with *that* terrifying thought, I broke into a run, Skye keeping pace with me as we sprinted the last six blocks home. After I let us back inside, I filled her food dish and topped off her water, then went downstairs to lose myself in the gym for a few hours.

By the time I returned to my place and cleaned up, it was nearly ten p.m., and I was pulling a fresh t-shirt over my head when my phone buzzed with a text.

Owen: what're you doing right now

Me: just got out of the shower. I was about to drown myself in beer and an Outer Banks rewatch

Owen: come down to the club

Me: do I have to?

Owen: I mean, you don't have to do anything but it sounds like you could use it

Me: you're not wrong. but the club? can't we go some-where...quieter?

Owen: you asking me on a date, Ryder?

Me: shut the fuck up. I just had a long week and a...weird day. I'm not in the mood for that scene

Owen: fair enough. how about Overtime?

Me: deal

Owen: perfect. see you in ten

❧❧❧❧❧ ❧❧❧❧❧

Owen was impossible to miss when I stepped into Overtime.

For one thing, he was six-five so he towered over absolutely everyone.

For another, he had a head of wavy blond hair that, when he ran his hands through it—whether during interviews or on the sidelines after removing his helmet during a game, or now when he brushed it out of the way to focus on the beers he was pouring—he had the attention of every female within a twenty foot radius.

And lastly, he was a former pro athlete. He may have moved to Traverse City after retirement to lead a "quieter" life, but he was still easily recognizable everywhere he went.

Yeah, my buddy was *that* Owen. Owen Lawless, former Detroit quarterback and current bar and restaurant owner. I'd been to Lawless, his club here in Traverse City, enough times over the years that Owen and I ended up meeting and struck up a friendship. Now, I'd consider him my *best* friend. I didn't have siblings, so Owen was the closest thing I had.

"Perfect timing," Owen said as I slid onto a bar stool across from him, and he placed one of the beers in front of me. Then he grabbed the other and tilted his head to the back corner.

I chuckled, knowing he couldn't stand to be the center of attention.

We caught up over idle chit chat while I practically chugged my first drink, Owen saying nothing as he raised a hand to signal for another one.

I savored my second one, taking the time to study the sports bar. When Owen caught my attention, he jerked his head and rose to his feet.

"Let me show you around."

The storefront Owen had purchased downtown contained three levels, and I was impressed with the thought and the care my friend had taken in making this the kind of place all ages could feel comfortable coming to relax.

Downstairs was a game room of sorts, with pool tables, a shuffleboard, darts, and table games like cards and giant Jenga. Owen had affectionately named it The Locker Room. It had a separate entrance from the bar—though you could get there from the bar level—where kids could hang out without Owen getting in trouble for them being in an establishment that served alcohol.

The main floor was of course the bar. The bar itself was an impressive U-shaped monstrosity, the island in the center lined with shelves stocked with any liquor you could want, from the cheapest rail vodka to the most expensive bottle of Kentucky Bourbon. The floors were poured concrete, polished to a high shine I knew would wear down with traffic, and the walls were lined with tables and booths. Flat screen televisions were scattered around the place, offering an angle for every patron no matter where they sat. The back half was a large dance floor, and Owen routinely hosted DJs and open mic nights, and had plans to start offering line dancing classes.

The first time he'd told me that, I'd laughed in his face, but I could admit, the idea was growing on me. It would be something fresh and exciting for these Michiganders and tourists, and it was a nice little hat-tip to Owen's Idaho ranch roots.

The third and final level, the upstairs, was named The Nosebleeds, and was really just another bar masquerading as a rooftop entertainment space. Up there, it was quieter and more...romantic than the main floor. It was a good spot to meet a blind date for a drink, or have a glass of champagne and watch the sun go down with your beloved—not that I'd ever experience those things.

My ass was stuck obsessing over a woman I wasn't even sure *liked* me.

"So who is she?" Owen asked when we took a seat at the Nosebleeds' bar. The open air and the fire-bright horizon were calming, and I sucked in grateful breaths of fresh air.

Now that I'd thought about her, I couldn't help imagining Amara and I here, her back against my chest, my arm slung across her torso as we sipped our drinks and took in the sunset.

"Hmm?" I asked dumbly, taking a fortifying sip of my favorite IPA, mind a thousand miles away.

Owen, of course, wasn't buying my shit. "The girl that's got you spun out."

"I'm not spun out," I grumbled.

"Cal."

"Amara Delatou," I blurted, and I'd be damned if it didn't feel good to get that off my chest. I could picture Amara now, curled up on her couch with her sisters around her as she told them—in explicit detail, surely—what happened between us this evening. The thought of her telling her sisters about us unexpectedly thrilled me.

Owen blinked slowly. "As in...your boss."

"The very same."

"Damn, I forgot how small this town is," he said, slipping his hand through his mop of blond hair. My brows drew together in confusion, and Owen added, "I uhh...dated her for a time. 'Dated' actually isn't the right word. It was more like—"

My arm flung out, fist driving heavily into his shoulder before I could stop myself. Then I gaped in horror. I'd just *punched* Owen Lawless. The man may have been retired for the better part of a decade, but I knew he could still kick my ass. Not to mention, when he winced and rubbed his flesh, I realized I'd punched him in his throwing arm—which he'd told me before still pained him sometimes thanks to the rotator cuff tear and subsequent surgery that had effectively ended his career.

"Fuck, man," I said, scrubbing my hand over my face before picking up my pint and draining it again. "I'm so sorry."

"You've got it bad, my dude," he said with a grin and patronizing pat on my shoulder.

"So...you and Amara, huh?" I asked, grimacing at my tone. Now that I knew, images of them flashed through my mind unbidden, especially given the fact that I was newly but deeply acquainted with Amara's flesh myself. Owen was such a good guy, and I could easily picture the two of them living a happy life together. He was the kind of guy Amara *should* be with. Not me, the man who couldn't decide whether he liked or hated her, who simultaneously wanted to rip her clothes off and rip my own hair out when she drove me insane.

The man who had given up on love thanks to emotionally absent parents and Amie ripping my heart out and stomping it into that sandy Sleeping Bear Dunes hiking trail.

Something occurred to me then, and I was beginning to wonder...did I actually hate Amara? Have I actually hated her this whole time? Or did I simply hate that I shouldn't want or have her? Because even now, after only one fuck, I was feeling things for her that I knew now had been glaringly absent from my relationship with Amie. Things I shouldn't be feeling so soon after five years of "hating" her and everything she stood for.

"It wasn't serious."

"Serious enough that you're bringing it up now."

"You're my friend," Owen said with a shrug. "You deserve to know. I don't want it to come up later and be this whole thing. It ended a while ago."

"If it wasn't serious, then what was it?"

God, sometimes I wished I could just staple my mouth shut instead of asking stupid questions I *really* didn't need answered.

"Look, there's no other way to say it than to just say it. We didn't do the whole boyfriend-girlfriend, dates and sunset walks on the beach shit. I had just opened the restaurant and was busy as fuck that summer. She had just graduated college and was gearing up to head to London. She approached me about bringing Delatou wines into Birdie's. One thing led to another, and we just..."

"You just what?" I prompted, hating myself for prying, and hating the jealousy bubbling in my chest.

"We just fucked. For three months, the only time we really saw each other was when we wound up in bed together at the end of a long day. She was a good way for me to blow off some stress, and I got the feeling she was just using me to forget something."

Forget something? Could it be...

No. There's no way that one night affected her like that.

There's no way my rejection had driven her right into Owen's arms. I was reading too much into it.

"If it makes you feel better, I've seen her grow up a lot in the last five years. She's fucking impressive, and I'm excited to see what she does as head of the Delatou empire. We weren't right for each other, but maybe that's because she was holding out for someone better."

My next thought came to me unbidden.

Someone like me.

Thankfully, Owen saved me from diving too deep down that rabbit hole.

"So...what exactly happened?"

"You really want to know?"

He shrugged. "Of course. You're my friend. Just because I have...intimate knowledge of the girl shouldn't stop you from spilling your guts to me."

"Mention that again and I'm going to punch you a lot higher than your shoulder."

Owen held his hands in front of my face. "Please, not the face! It's my money maker."

I burst out laughing, the tension in my shoulders easing fractionally.

With a deep sigh, I launched into the story. Of that night five years ago, of dancing around each other for the last five months, of how much harder it had grown over the last few weeks to keep my eyes—and my hands—to myself.

How today, I just...snapped.

"She's so goddamn infuriating, but that body...fuck."

"I know," Owen said, a little too wistfully for my liking.

"Watch it."

"Right, sorry. Truthfully, we didn't really do much talking. We didn't really do much of anything but fuck."

"Then what good are you? The sex is definitely not the problem."

Well, the sex *was* a problem, not because it hadn't been mind-blowing and life-altering, but because we shouldn't have done it.

"Because she's your boss, so this is an extremely complicated situation you've found yourself in. Hey!" he said suddenly, perking up. "If you want to take that whole boss-employee thing out of the equation, you could come work for me!"

"In what capacity? A bar back?"

"No, dipshit," he said with a glare. "As my financial advisor. Now that I'm expanding my empire, I could really use someone like you to make sure I don't blow my entire fortune on money pits."

I snorted. "You're doing pretty good for yourself without my help."

"Maybe so, but wouldn't it be fun to work together?"

"Why would that be *fun*?"

"Because I'm your only friend and you love me," he said, shooting me a wide, cheesy smile.

I punched him, softly and in his good shoulder this time, but I grudgingly admitted he wasn't wrong; he *was* my only friend.

I ran a hand through my hair, a habit I surely picked up from the man across from me, my thoughts a swirling vortex in my head.

"What do you want?" Owen asked quietly. "Like in a perfect

world, if she weren't your boss and you didn't have this tenuous relationship?"

And that was the kicker, wasn't it? Because I wasn't sure I could voice what I wanted. Not to him, not to anyone. I wasn't sure I could even dare *hope* for what I wanted.

But man, in a perfect world? It wasn't hard to imagine a life with Amara at my side.

chapter 13
Amara

I WASN'T SURE WHAT to expect from Cal when I walked into the office on Monday morning. I'd spent all weekend considering the possibilities, analyzing every single angle, and picking apart our entire interaction from the moment he put his hand on me in the winery kitchen up until that kiss on the forehead as we left.

I wanted him badly. And I knew he wanted me. The question was whether or not indulging in that desire again was a good idea.

As I approached Cal's office, Jeff gave me a small wave from his desk outside.

"Good morning, Ms. Delatou."

I smiled back. "Good morning, Jeff."

I was nearly past when Cal's voice reached me.

"Ms. Delatou, a word please."

I came to an abrupt halt and spun on my heel, shooting Jeff a look. "Any ideas?"

Jeff merely shook his head, so I stepped into Cal's office, which may as well have been a lion's den for how safe I felt being in his space. This could go one of two ways, and I mentally braced myself for a rejection.

The second I crossed the threshold, he tugged me deeper into the room, slammed the door shut, and pressed my back against it.

A moment later, his mouth was on mine.

Okay, not a rejection then.

"Fuck," he groaned against my lips. "I've been dying to do that again all weekend."

Momentarily stunned, I could think of nothing to say in response, could do nothing but grab fistfuls of his shirt and pull his body closer, moaning into his mouth when he slipped his knee between my legs. A few moments in this man's presence, with his tongue in my mouth, and I was already drenched, dangerously close to making a mess of his slacks if he kept his thigh pressed against my clit like that.

"We can't," I said, pushing him away. I raised a hand to my heart, attempting to marshal my breathing while he frowned down at me.

"Why the hell not?"

"Because the office isn't even close to empty," I said. "And, in case you've forgotten, neither of us are very quiet."

Cal smirked, then dropped his head and nipped at my ear, his breath against my neck as he spoke his next words making me shiver. "The memory of your moans got me through a really long, hard weekend, Princess."

"Long and hard, huh?"

"So long," he breathed. "So hard."

To emphasize his point, he tilted his pelvis into me, his fully erect cock pressing against my stomach.

Once again, I shoved him off and moved further into the office, needing to get some breathing room. It was completely at odds with the reaction my body was having to him, but I needed to sort some things out—we did, together—before I could let him near again. All rational thought left me when Cal's body was within touching distance.

It amazed me how quickly we'd reached this point. Last week, we were fighting like cats and dogs. Even all the way up until Friday, when we'd been in that kitchen together, I wasn't sure I even particularly liked him.

Now? Well, I *loved* the way he made me feel. Sexy and powerful. Desirable. What was it he'd called me on Friday?

A goddess.

Yeah, that was me. Amara Danae Delatou, Greek Goddess.

And okay…I definitely liked him. A hell of a lot more than I was willing to admit to anyone, least of all myself.

"We need to talk about what happened."

"I don't want to."

"I don't care. We…that can't happen again."

Wait, what was I saying? I'd walked in here afraid of his rejection, and now I was the one doling it out? God, being near this man short-circuited my brain.

"But what if I want it to?"

Stunned, I could only stare at him. Surely I misheard him. Just because I'd been having the same thoughts myself didn't mean I expected him to want it too. Then again, he'd greeted me with a toe-curling kiss *and* told me he'd been wanting to do that all weekend, and that was saying nothing of how hard his cock was, so maybe I was reading too much into it. Could I take his words at face value?

For more orgasms? Hell yeah, I could.

"What are you saying?"

Cal shook his head, pushing a hand through his thick hair. "I don't know. I just know I want to do it again. I want to do *you* again."

"Cal," I said with a laugh. "Be serious."

This was safer territory, though. The physical connection between us, the magic our bodies made together. It didn't have to go any deeper than that, right?

Not so simple for me, considering that buried beneath all this animosity, I'd come to realize I harbored some sort of very real feelings for this man. If that weren't the case, I would've felt like shit about myself after Friday and probably ran screaming in the opposite direction. As it stood, while I knew having sex with Cal was a bad idea for a number of reasons, none of them had anything to do with my conscience.

Fuck, I didn't have the time or energy to analyze that right now. I didn't have the mental bandwidth to examine what kind of weird brand of Stockholm syndrome I'd developed.

"I am being serious. Preferably in a bed this time, where I can spread you out and take my time learning all the things you like and then doing them until you come over and over."

"Cal."

"Mar."

"Be serious," I repeated.

"I am! I don't know when or how or why, but...I want you, Amara. Badly, and only you."

"So you want to be, what? Fuck buddies? We're too old for that."

Cal shrugged. "I don't like that term, but sure, why not? We're *not* too old to enjoy each other's bodies, are we?"

"Why not? *Why not*? For starters, Ryder, I'm your *boss*."

And I think it could be really goddamn easy to fall in love with you.

I better keep that bit to myself.

"Fuck, it turns me on when you call me Ryder."

I only crossed my arms over my chest and glared at him, realizing my mistake too late, when his gaze had already dipped to my cleavage, his eyes going a little glassy as he stared.

Then again, my own had dropped to his dick as it swelled beneath his pants. I couldn't help imagining its weight against my tongue, of the wide tip pressing into me again, of how perfectly he stretched me...

"Eyes are up here, Princess."

I obeyed the attention grab, slowly dragging my golden gaze up the length of his torso, meeting those emerald greens of his.

With a wolfish grin, he crossed the room to me and spun us so he sat on the armrest of one of his cushy leather chairs and pulled me between his legs. Like this, we were eye to eye, and I couldn't resist driving my fingers into his hair, scratching my long nails against his scalp. He groaned softly, his eyes fluttering closed.

"You have the *best* hair," I said as I slowly sifted through the silky strands, mesmerized by the combination of reds and browns.

"Yours is better." Without opening his eyes, he skated a palm along my arm and over my shoulder until he could grab the length of my low ponytail.

Then he blinked his eyes open for a brief moment and leaned forward to seal his mouth over mine.

We hadn't spent nearly enough time kissing on Friday, and fuck I loved this man's lips. Soft and smooth, plush and firm. They worked against mine, opening as his tongue darted out, tracing the seam of my lips until I did the same.

And hell, that tongue. I wanted it so much lower. I wanted it on my nipples, between my thighs. I wanted the sharp sting of his teeth on my lower lip replicated on the curves of my breasts and against the throb of my clit.

"Just say yes, Mar," he whispered when we broke apart, both breathing hard. And when he slipped his hand beneath the skirt of my dress and brushed his fingers through my slit, I was help-less. I was putty in his hands, ice cream melting on a hot day. "We're consenting adults. Everything else is just...bureaucratic bullshit."

"That bureaucratic bullshit is my company," I reminded him.

"*Our* company."

"*Mine*," I said, pulling my mouth away to nip at his lip, his jaw, his neck and shoulder.

"Stop fighting with me."

"But I'm so damn good at it."

"Princess." My nickname was a heavy, exasperated sigh. "Please."

"Fine," I conceded in a whisper. "Yes."

He rewarded me by slipping a finger into me.

"So wet for me," he groaned. "Although, you should really start wearing panties."

"Too hot," I breathed, struggling to keep a grasp on the conversation as he added another finger and lazily pumped in and out of me.

"I think it's more than that," he said, his thumb brushing briefly against my clit in a way that had my knees buckling. He wrapped his free arm tightly around my waist, holding me upright. "I think you wanted to end up right here, with my hand up your skirt, making you come all over my fingers."

"I-I wasn't opposed to the idea," I said shakily as he picked up the pace. I dug my nails into his biceps, the muscles bunching beneath my touch as he worked me harder.

"I think we should start every day just like this," he said against my neck, where he leaned in to press an open-mouthed kiss to my pulse, lightly sucking the skin into his mouth and swirling his tongue.

"I think people are going to start asking questions if we—oh!"

My train of thought was completely derailed when Cal drove a third finger into me and curled them, rubbing against some hidden spot that caused my entire body to spasm. Already, my orgasm built, sending tingles skating up and down my spine, that pressure against my clit expanding the harder he pressed, the faster he pumped his hand, the more times he hit that secret spot he'd found far too quickly for my liking.

"People will start asking questions if we what, Mar?" he asked, his voice a low grumble. "If I fuck you so good that you forget to hate me?"

His words did the trick—because, damn, he *was* finger fucking me *so good*—and I exploded, my orgasm breaking free. I bit down on his shoulder to muffle my cries as goosebumps broke out along my arms and thighs, as my legs quaked against his touch, only his arm saving me from collapsing into a heap on the floor.

When I stilled, I lifted my head, unable to stop the sated smile that spread across my face. I absently smoothed the wrinkles from my teeth out of his shirt while he pulled his hand free, my body twitching at the loss of him.

He offered his mouth up to me, and I obliged with a soft, lingering kiss.

"So...fuck buddies," I said when I backed away.

"Fuck buddies," he agreed. "Though, we really should come up with something else to call it."

"I don't care what we call it as long as you keep doing that."

"Doing what?" he asked.

In answer, I lifted his hand between us, his fingers and palm slick with my arousal.

"Doing *this*," I said. "Using those skillful fingers and wicked tongue and magical cock for good instead of evil."

"You think my cock is magical?"

Mentally, I smacked myself. That should've remained an inside thought, and I should be embarrassed.

But embarrassment went out the window the moment he spread me open on my desk last week and speared me with that cock.

"You know it is," I said with an eye roll.

"And my tongue is wicked, huh?"

"Well, I can't say for sure quite yet..."

With a smirk, he brought his hand to his mouth, closing his lips around the three fingers that had been inside me and sucking them clean, moaning as my taste coated his tongue. "Fuck, Princess. You've already been in here too long, but mark my words...the next time I have you alone, I am going to *devour* that pussy. We'll see what you have to say about my wicked tongue then."

A shiver of anticipation zipped down my spine. If it wasn't barely nine a.m. on a Monday morning, if the offices and halls around us weren't full of people who fully expected us to hate each other until the end of time, I'd happily drop onto the couch and spread my legs wide for him. Give him the chance to make good on that promise right now.

I bent and slanted my mouth over his, twin groans leaving us when our tongues brushed, the taste of me becoming a sexy, shared secret between the two of us.

"I look forward to it," I said.

"So fuck buddies," he repeated, and I nodded.

"We...have fun until someone says stop. Then it's over. No questions."

"Deal," he said, extending his hand.

I grinned. "Oh, I think we can do better than a handshake."

Taking the bait, Cal stood and lifted me into his arms before meeting my mouth with his in a tangle of teeth and tongues that had a dull throb returning to my clit.

At last, he set me down and, with a swat to my ass, led me to the door. One more hard and fast kiss, and he was shoving me out.

It was a damn good thing I preferred plain lip balm to lipstick because he hadn't even given me time to collect myself.

My inner thighs were still sticky with my cum, for fuck's sake.

"I expect that report in my email by the end of the day, Ms. Delatou."

"Whatever," I said, tossing him a glare over my shoulder as I stomped off down the hall in the direction of my office.

"Good morning, boss!" Cindy said brightly as I approached, handing me a fresh cup of coffee from Brie's bakery, where she stopped every morning on her way up to the winery from town proper. My littlest sister's counter staff was notorious for being dialed into all the town gossip, and Cindy liked to get her fix while *getting her fix.*

"Morning!" I said, my chipper attitude coming easily.

I just had an orgasm. Of course I was in a great mood.

"You're running a little behind," Cindy said as she followed me into my office. "Everything okay?"

I waved a dismissive hand. "Yeah, everything is fine. Fucking Calvin stopped me on my way in to yell at me for not having gotten him the report on the canned cocktails yet."

"Oh, I gave that to Jeff last week," Cindy said with a frown.

"It's fine, Cin," I said. "I'll email it right now."

"Okay," she said quietly, turning her back on me to exit my office. "I can't imagine why Jeff wouldn't pass it along..."

A moment later, the door closed behind her, leaving me in blessed silence.

A dangerous place to be, given how I'd started my morning.

Fuck buddies? With *Calvin Ryder*? What the fuck was I thinking?

You're not, my conscience reminded me unhelpfully.

But she wasn't wrong. I wasn't thinking—unless you count allowing my pussy to make decisions. I just...now that I'd had him, I wanted him again and again. My clit still tingled slightly, the ghost of his fingers stretching me still haunted me. I couldn't help but hope that we found some alone time *very* soon.

In the meantime, I had a company to run.

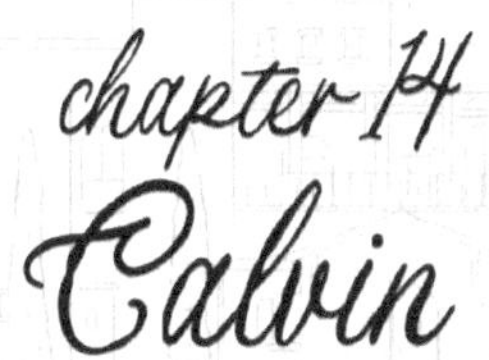

NORMALLY, I LOOKED FORWARD to bank holidays like Memorial Day. It meant an extra day out of the office and away from the temptation of Amara.

But now that I'd given in and bitten that forbidden fruit? I would spend twenty-four hours a day at the office, if only to get five seconds to kiss her behind a closed door, or twenty minutes to make her come on my fingers.

I hadn't had the chance to truly fuck her again yet, though, and I had probably the worst case of blue balls known to man.

But discussing our weekend plans wasn't part of the deal, and I was certain she was hitting the road with her family somewhere to celebrate the holiday.

Meanwhile, it was late Friday, and Skye and I were heading up to Torch Lake to spend the weekend at Owen's lake cottage. The weather was forecasted to be absolutely perfect straight through until Wednesday, which meant I'd be spending the next three days drunk in the sun, cruising around on Owen's pontoon or hanging out around the fire.

I'd come up here last year for the first time, and "cottage" was a woefully inadequate term to describe Owen's house. Perched atop a small hill on the northern side of the lake, the place was two stories, the side facing the water comprised entirely of windows. There were seven bedrooms, as many bathrooms, a fully stocked wet bar in the basement, a deck that spanned the entire length of the house off the upper level and a concrete patio with at least thirty handcrafted Adirondack style chairs gathered around a gorgeous stone fire pit. Stairs were cut into the hillside that led down to Owen's private beach and dock where he had his pontoon, speedboat, and jet skis tied up. There was also a small storage shed that held an impressive array of paddle boards, kayaks, and canoes.

If you could do it on the water, Owen had thought of it and provided the equipment necessary.

Perks of being a stupidly wealthy professional athlete turned successful multi-business owner.

The lake is a gorgeous place, with crystal clear waters that rivaled the Caribbean, and a sandbar on the south end that attracted a ton of tourist attention, particularly around the Fourth. This weekend wouldn't be as busy, but I knew when we headed out on the pontoon tomorrow, there'd be enough people down there to make it a party.

I wasn't wrong.

We set off around noon, Skye happily perched on the bench seat near the bow, her golden ears flopping in the wind. Looping around closer to the shore, Owen pointed out the vacation homes that belonged to a ton of prominent celebrities, including

Oprah, that tool Kid Rock, Eminem, and even Taylor Swift apparently.

When we reached the sandbar, we found an impressive crowd gathered in the shallow water skimming it. Girls in barely-there bikinis were shouting, dancing, and singing along to the music. Guys in board shorts and Speedos took beer bongs and roughhoused with each other. There were couples making out *everywhere*, which surprised me but didn't.

Something about hot summer days, alcohol, and being on the water simply turned inhibitions off. I'd experienced the phenomenon myself on more than one occasion. It was like here, in this little Torch Lake bubble, rules simply didn't apply.

I opened the back gate of the pontoon, and Skye took a running leap straight into the water, happily splashing around and attracting all kinds of attention. If I were inclined to be interested in anyone but Amara, my dog was the ultimate chick magnet, and soon a crowd of women gathered around our boat. When I wasn't buying what they were selling, they happily turned their attention to Owen. Though the bulk of them surprisingly had no idea who he was, it didn't stop them from being drawn to his all-American good looks and charm.

As I stood and surveyed the scene, Owen appeared at my side and pressed a cold beer into my hand.

"What happened to your fan club?" I asked.

He snorted. "Found something else to fawn over," he said, nodding to the group gathered in the water, squealing and gushing over a woman who apparently had just gotten engaged.

"This place is wild," I said with a small head shake.

"Paradise, man," he said, clinking his beer bottle against mine.

I chuckled and nudged him with my shoulder. "You're a long way from Idaho."

"Michigan is so different from Idaho in every way," he said, pausing to take a long swallow of his own beer. "Who knew places like this existed here? Before I got drafted, I thought it was all snow and trees. And it is both of those things at times, but...damn. We're lucky to live here."

I often felt that way myself.

Particularly when my eyes landed on thick, deep brown hair that trailed down a tanned and toned back, stopping just shy of a bright pink bikini-clad ass I'd know anywhere.

"Well, well..." I said, nodding my head in that direction. "Look who's here."

"The Delatou sisters," he said, shooting me a wide grin. "You hit that again yet?"

I shook my head. "Not yet, but that hasn't stopped us from doing...other things."

Owen barked out a laugh and held his fist up for a bump. "If the walls of that office could talk, am I right?"

"If those walls could talk, her father would've surely killed my ass and buried me on the vineyard where no one would ever find me."

"Fuck, he's scary, isn't he?"

"How do you know him?"

Oh, Ryder, get it together. Jealousy is not a good look on you.

"Easy, big guy. I carry their wine at all three of my places."

"Ahh, right," I said, grinning sheepishly at him.

"So what do you think?" He settled his gaze on Amara and her sisters once again. "You gonna make your move?"

"I don't know if that's such a good idea…"

"Brooooooooooo." Owen dragged the single syllable out annoyingly, and I was instantly reminded how many years he spent in locker rooms surrounded by dudes who threw that word around like confetti. "Look at where we are." He swept his arms around at the expanse of clear blue water and the crowds of people around us. "No one here but me and her sisters know who you are or give a fuck what your work relationship looks like, and I guarantee her sisters already know y'all fucked. So get your ass down there and go get your girl."

"She's not my girl," I grumbled weakly. But damn, did I want her to be.

One moment, I was standing safely on the deck of the pontoon, and the next I was being tossed over the side into the darker blue of the sandbar drop off—beer and all.

I came up sputtering and pissed.

"Fuck you, Lawless!" I shouted as I shoved my hair out of my face and wiped the water from my eyes.

"Appreciate the offer, Ryder," he said, grinning like a dick from six feet above me, "but you're not really my type."

"I hate you."

"Quit bitching. Your girl is headed this way." Then, like the gracious host he absolutely wasn't, Owen turned to greet the Delatou girls. I floated for a moment, watching as Chloe, her husband Logan, Ella, Brie, and Delia all climbed onto the deck of the pontoon, happily accepting Owen's invitation to take whatever they wanted from the cooler.

My eyes scanned the water around the boat, searching for the fifth sister.

"Looking for me?"

I spun toward the voice and found her standing ten feet away at the edge of the sandbar, arms crossed over her chest, her perfect tits squeezed together and pushed up, making my mouth water. Making me imagine what it would feel like to slide my cock between them.

Fuck, it was a good thing by bottom half was below the surface. I needed to get my shit together.

"Maybe."

"What're you doing here?" she asked as she waded deeper into the water, eventually pushing off the ledge and swimming over to me.

"Owen invited me," I said with a shrug. "Skye and I came up for the weekend."

"Skye?" I didn't miss the hint of jealousy in her tone, and I grinned knowingly at her.

"My dog, Princess."

"Oh," she said with a giggle. "So you and Owen are friends? I wasn't aware the devil made friends."

I rolled my eyes, ignoring her jab in favor of asking a question of my own.

"What are *you* doing here?"

"We own a house on the west side of the lake," she said, waving a hand in what I assumed was its general direction. "I'm surprised you didn't know that already."

"Must be a personal asset."

Amara laughed and nodded. "It was Dad's twenty-fifth anniversary present to Mom."

"What do you need a beach house for when you already live

on the beach?"

"Trust me, we asked them the same question. But honestly, it's nice to get off the vineyard and peninsula for a bit. And this is one of my favorite places in the world," she said as she tipped back to float on the surface of the water, her hair fanning out around her.

God, she was beautiful, like a siren luring me into the rocky shore of her body. And I, a mere mortal, was helpless to resist the call.

"Hey!" someone above us yelled, and my head shot up to find Delia leaning over the railing. "Get your asses up here. Logan wants to do jello shots, but Cal, I have to warn you. He's got a heavy hand with the vodka, so if they taste like paint thinner...just smile and say 'yum.'"

I glanced at Amara. "That bad?"

"He's the worst bartender I've ever met, and that's saying something given how many I've actually met."

Indeed.

I swam to the side of the pontoon and hefted myself on board, then turned to help Amara up, purposely stumbling a bit once she was on so I could pull her against me.

Just for a moment. I wouldn't indulge in PDA in front of her family, but I wanted her to know how even those few moments in the water with her and the sight of her in that bikini affected me.

"I want to untie this thing with my teeth," I said quietly, toying with the strings at her hips.

"Maybe later," she replied, then spun out of my arms and headed for her brother-in-law, who held out tiny plastic cups filled with bright green jello.

We all congregated in a circle as best as we could, and Logan raised his shot into the air. "To family and new friends. I still can't believe I'm standing on Owen Lawless's boat right now."

"Your brother-in-law is literally Brent Jean!" Chloe hissed, and the group devolved into laughter.

And wait...what? Logan was related to the Detroit Warriors' phenom? That's definitely a story I wanted to hear.

"To family and new friends!" Delia parroted, and we all squeezed the cold jello into our mouths.

I did my best not to gag as a small amount of liquid from the bottom trickled down my throat but damn. Delia hadn't been joking about the paint thinner. He must've used an entire bottle of bottom shelf on these things. There was no flavor other than the strong astringent of alcohol burning my tongue and its way down my throat.

"Fucking hell," Chloe growled. "I love you, baby, but that's the last time I let you make the drinks."

"What?" Logan said, looking genuinely confused. "I thought it was great!"

"Yeah, if you like drinking straight rubbing alcohol," Ella grumbled.

The comment from her was so rare that everyone aboard paused for a beat before bursting into laughter, her sisters tackling her to one of the benches and shouting, "You made a joke, El! You made a *joke*!"

The second youngest Delatou girl made an impressive show of attempting to shove them off and maintain her I-don't-give-a-fuck scowl, but she eventually lost the battle with her smile, giggling along with her sisters as they tickled and teased her.

This was a side of Amara I rarely saw. I was familiar with her European antics and the kind of woman she was at work, but around her family? This was new.

I didn't entirely hate it.

It was obvious in the way they interacted how much the sisters loved each other, and it reminded me how lucky I was that none of them had told Amara about my attempts to push her out of the company all those months ago. Their loyalty and desire to protect their sister was admirable, and a pang of jealousy lanced my chest. As an only child, I'd always found myself envious of sibling dynamics, found myself longing for that same connection to people who were forced to love me no matter what.

In fact, as I glanced at Logan, staring lovingly at his wife and sisters-in-law, I couldn't help picturing myself in his position.

What would it be like to join this family? To have siblings at last? To consider Chloe, Delia, Ella, and Brie *my* sisters? To spend family functions at Logan's side, shooting the shit with him and whoever Delia, Ella, and Brie ended up with, sharing a beer and watching the girls have moments just like this?

What would it be like to fall asleep with Amara in my arms and wake up the same? How would it feel to call her *mine* in every way? Right now, I had her body. But...maybe...I wanted the rest of her too.

The Delatous' cottage was only a few miles from Owen's, and

that evening, the girls and Logan came over for a fire. After a long day spent entirely in the sun, consuming far too many beers and Logan's heinous jello shots, I was struggling to keep my eyes open. But I didn't want to miss out on time with Amara—even if she chose to sit across the fire from me—so here I was, a lukewarm bottle of Michelob Ultra in my hand, legs coated in bug spray, listening to the girls tell a story about the time Brie nearly burned the winery down.

"I was twelve!" she shouted.

"You're lucky the buildings are constructed mainly of stone," Chloe said.

"You know, Cal," Amara said, pulling me into conversation for the first time since they'd arrived earlier, "you can still see scorch marks on the ceiling in the kitchen from where the flames reached before the fire department arrived."

With a chuckle, I said, "I'll have to check them out when we get home."

"All I wanted was to make soufflé," Brie said with a pout.

"Don't worry, sissy," Delia said, running her fingers soothingly down the length of Brie's hair, freed from its signature braid for once. "You've grown so much since then. You haven't set anything on fire in...at least two weeks."

"I told you that in confidence!" Brie exploded from her chair, tackling Delia to the ground, thankfully away from the fire, and the remaining Delatou sisters jumped up to pull them apart. Eventually, they all fell into a laughing heap on the ground, a tangle of long, tanned limbs glowing in the firelight and bright white teeth shining under the moon.

Once they were calmed down and dusted off and again settled

in their chairs, a mischievous glint appeared in Delia's eyes as she looked right at me, held my gaze, and said, "You should know by now that we don't keep secrets, little sister."

I didn't like that look in her eyes, the one that said she knew shit about me that could hurt me, and she wasn't afraid to use it. So help me, if she opened her mouth and ruined this thing between me and Amara before it ever really got started, we'd be having words.

And she wouldn't like what I'd have to say. It was one thing to fuck with her sisters, as I knew from my time around the family that Delia was prone to do, but to pull me into her bullshit was an entirely different story—and I wouldn't be so understanding.

"To be fair," Brie said. "With that incident two weeks ago, I was experimenting with a new creme brûlée recipe, and it was my own hair I accidentally set on fire with the torch, not an entire fucking building."

"Enough about that," Delia said, waving off her sister's comments. "Let's play a game."

The Delatou girls and Logan groaned, and Owen and I shared a skeptical look.

"What kind of game?" Owen asked.

"Truth or dare," Delia answered proudly.

"Absolutely not," Owen said firmly. "I'm too old for that shit."

Delia shrugged, unperturbed. "So just pick truth. We're not starting with you, anyway. We're starting with..." That wicked gleam was back in her eyes, exacerbated by the glow of the fire, giving her a demonic expression that I didn't think was too far off. She briefly glanced my way before swinging her gaze to..."Mar, truth or dare?"

"You little shit," Amara breathed.

"I'm sorry, sissy, that wasn't an answer. Truth or dare?"

Amara was silent for several long heartbeats, and the pieces worked their way into a fully-formed picture slowly in my head. Delia knew about us, obviously. I'd already guessed as much, but this was confirmation. Whichever option Amara chose, her question or dare would involve me. Delia was forcing our hand.

I'd always known Delia was a bit of a wildcard, but this was some next level bullshit.

"Dare," Amara said at last.

"I dare you to makeout with..."

I sat up straighter and dropped my half-empty beer into the cupholder. I wiped my clammy palms on the thighs of my shorts, preparing to do this, to indulge in a public display with Amara. Obviously I wasn't opposed to kissing her, but here and now? When she and I hadn't even had the chance to sort out what the fuck was happening between us? I didn't like being put on the spot, and this was like standing center stage, naked, while a crowd of people picked apart my every move. Just because I wanted the woman in a bone-deep way didn't mean I wanted to go broadcasting my personal life to the public quite yet.

"...Owen."

Owen? What about *me*?

"Lia..." Amara warned.

"What?" her sister asked innocently. "It's not exactly uncharted territory for you."

"Delia," Chloe scolded. "That's enough."

"She chose, Coco. Now she has to complete the challenge or

suffer the consequences. You know the rules."

Remember earlier how I said I could imagine joining this family?

I lied. At this moment, watching Delia toy with her sister, with me, *and* with Owen? I wanted out. I wanted Amara, but not like this.

"We're waiting," Delia said, tapping her watch when neither Owen nor Amara moved.

With a heavy sigh, Amara rose from her chair and circled the fire in the direction of me and Owen. He looked over at me, eyes pleading to do something, anything.

They could simply...not kiss, but what kind of consequences would Amara suffer for it?

I couldn't see a way out.

"I'm sorry," he mouthed a moment before Amara reached him.

Only...she walked right past him, threw herself onto my lap, and pressed her mouth to mine.

chapter 15

Amara

I WAS GOING TO kill Delia.

But with my lips against Cal's, with his tongue sweeping into my mouth and massaging my own, I was having difficulty remembering why.

Oh, right.

Because I was kissing him in front of my entire family and my *ex-fuck buddy* because my sister couldn't leave well enough alone.

Cheers erupted around us, and someone said, "About fucking time."

I'd bet good money it was Delia, but I didn't have the mental capacity to give a shit. Not when Calvin moved his hand to my neck, pressing his thumb against my jaw to angle my head where he wanted me. Not when he applied a bit of pressure to my windpipe, that massive palm spanning my entire throat, his long fingers delving into my hair.

I grinned against him when I felt him hardening against my backside, but I pulled away before we could get too hot and heavy, before I pulled him from his chair, hauled him inside, and had my way with him. That was fuel that certainly didn't need to be added to our already burning inferno. I was having difficulty catching my breath—a phenomenon I encountered frequently when he was near—and I wished time could just...stop for a minute.

"I'm so sorry," I whispered, resting my forehead against his, my breaths ragged.

"No," he said quietly in response, shaking his head slightly. "Never apologize for kissing me. Especially not since you saved Owen's life."

"Yeah?"

"*Yeah*," he growled. "I would've had to kill him if you touched him."

"Get a room!" someone shouted, and I groaned, remembering where we were.

My world had a habit of narrowing to Cal's entire presence when his arms were around me.

I slipped off his lap and reached out my hand for him.

"We should talk," I said quietly.

Cal only nodded, laced our fingers together, and pulled me away from the group.

The moment we were safely locked in a bedroom—his, if the spicy cologne and crisp body wash scents lingering in the air, combining to create a combination that was pure *Cal*, was any indication—Cal backed me against the door and fit his body to mine, fusing our lips together.

He had a habit of doing this, of pushing me into walls and doors, against desks, and every single time it thrilled me. The possessive way he towered over me until he blotted out every-thing around us had my body quivering in anticipation.

"Your sister is a pain in the ass," he said against my mouth, moving away to give attention to my jaw and neck. "But I'll admit, I'm not mad at this turn of events. It's nice not to have to hide us, even if it's just in front of your sisters."

Us. The word was perfection rolling off his tongue, spoken in that deep, rich voice of his. I wanted so badly for there to be an *us*, but I was quickly realizing that wasn't a good idea. As badly as I wanted to stay wrapped in his arms forever, I knew it wasn't where I was meant to be.

"That's actually why I wanted us to talk," I said as he dropped his mouth to my neck, laving my skin with his tongue.

"I don't care. Whatever you're about to say—I don't care."

"Cal..." I said weakly, making no real move to stop him. "I mean it."

With an exasperated sigh, he backed off and retreated across the room until he dropped down at the foot of his bed, patting the spot next to him.

Reluctantly, I crossed and sat, keeping a solid two feet of dis-tance between us.

"So...you kissed me." I nodded. "In front of all of your sisters."

"I did."

"Why?"

"Well, it was either that or kiss Owen, and like you said...I saved his life by not going near him."

"He knows about this," Cal said, gesturing between us. "I told him after that first night in your office."

My eyebrows shot up in surprise. Cal was...telling his friends about us? That meant something, right? That maybe I meant more to him than just a quick fuck and some good orgasms?

No, I scolded myself. *That doesn't change anything.*

"And how'd he take it?"

"Owen is fine," Cal said with a chuckle. "He told me the thing between you ended that summer, and now you're just friends."

It was the truth, and I was glad neither Owen nor Cal were making a big deal out of it.

"I'm sorry about Delia."

"Don't be," Cal said, reaching out to take my hand, slowly and soothingly brushing his thumb over the back. "Everyone out there already knew about us, right? This doesn't have to be some big secret anymore."

"I beg to differ," I said, rising to stand.

Cal's brows pinched together. "What do you mean?"

"I mean...we don't work with any of those people, Cal. Well, except Brie, but she hardly leaves the kitchen, so that doesn't count. And I need my employees to respect me. That won't happen if they find out I'm fucking you."

"And how do you think this looks for me?" He stood and bent over me, crowding my space until we were nose to nose. Until I had no choice but to stare straight into his eyes. "What are people going to say when they find out *I'm* fucking *you*?"

"What do you mean by that?"

"I mean...it's not a secret I wasn't on board with you taking over. How seriously will people take me when they find out I've changed my mind?"

Hope rose in my chest, and I did my best to beat it back. "Have you changed your mind?" I asked quietly.

He straightened and scrubbed a hand down his face. "I think I'm coming around to the idea."

Well, that was something, but...it wasn't enough. If we were going to do this, I needed him to believe in me. Full stop. No caveats, no ifs, ands, or buts. If he wasn't there yet, what the fuck were we doing? And maybe that wasn't fair of me, but the agreement was we could end this at any time, and right now was that time.

"This was a mistake," I said, turning away from him and walking to the door.

"What? No." He brushed a hand through his hair, the movement so similar to Owen's own stressed, nervous tic that I nearly laughed. They were really close, weren't they? And I had no idea, because I didn't know Cal. Not who he was at his core. That wasn't what this was, and I needed to get out before I gave him much more of myself—before I let go of pieces of me I couldn't get back.

I smiled at him softly, sadly, over my shoulder before pulling the door open. "It was...amazing while it lasted," I said, practically choking on the word. *Amazing* didn't even begin to cover how it felt to welcome him into my body. "But it's already too complicated. We were supposed to be having fun, remember? It's not fun anymore. So I'm ending it. No questions asked, right?"

Cal opened his mouth as if to argue, but wisely bit his tongue and gave me a rigid nod. Before I could linger too long and talk myself out of walking away, I shut the door behind me with a soft click.

Then, without a word to my sisters, Logan, or Owen, I walked home alone, with only the stars to witness my tears.

"I'm sorry, what did you just say?" my dad asked.

"I said...the Tigers just called. One of their game hosts tried Delatou & Danvers over Memorial Day weekend and was just raving about it to everyone I guess. One of the higher-ups in their food and beverage department heard about it and requested samples. He just called to offer us an exclusive contract as the official canned cocktail of the team!"

I still couldn't quite believe it. Even saying the words out loud, and the contract sitting in my email inbox, didn't feel real. We'd been on the market for a whole twenty days, and we were already signing exclusive deals with one of the oldest franchises in professional baseball.

I leaned back in my chair and pinched myself.

Yep, definitely awake.

"Mar..." my dad trailed off. "I don't know what to say."

"How about...congratulations?"

"Of course! Congratulations, sweets. I'm so damn proud of you, and Liam. I knew you could do it."

"Thanks, Daddy," I said, smiling wide. There was truly nothing better in the world to me than hearing my father tell me he was proud of me.

And damn, it felt nice to accomplish something big—my first major deal as CEO.

Before I even had a moment to consider what Cal would think of this, the man himself knocked on my open office door.

I held up my finger and said to my dad, "Sorry, Daddy. I've got a meeting to head into, but I'll talk to you soon."

"Of course, kiddo. I love you, and your mother and I are so damn proud."

"I love you too."

When I hung up, Cal said, "Got a sec?"

Word traveled way too fast around here, and I was going to need to have a frank conversation with Cindy about keeping her mouth shut sooner rather than later.

"I guess," I said with a sigh, nearly protesting when he shut the door behind him.

But I couldn't let him see how he affected me. It wasn't his fault the bolt clicking closed was like a gunshot, triggering the memories of our time together here.

Then again, maybe that *was* his fault.

It had been two weeks since I'd cut ties at Owen's cabin, and being in this office day in and day out was a trust test to my resolve. Every time I sat in this chair—which was all day long—I vividly remembered riding him atop it.

How he walked me outside and kissed my forehead after.

I gave in to an involuntary shiver, and the corner of his mouth twitched knowingly.

I needed a new fucking chair—actually, an entirely new office would be best.

"I heard about the Tigers' partnership," he said, stuffing his hands deep into the pocket of his slacks and leaning against the armrest of my couch. "Congrats. That's...a big deal."

"It is, thank you."

He stared at me, as though willing me to elaborate, but honestly, I had nothing else to say. Cal's praise would always come under duress, with conditions attached, and I wasn't willing to make an emotional investment in him when he couldn't make a professional one in me.

"Mar…" he began, but I held up my hand.

"You said what you came here to say, Cal. Now I've got work to do, if you don't mind."

"I do mind, actually. Because that's not all I came in here to say."

I quirked a brow, settling back in my chair and crossing my arms over my chest. "Alright then, let's hear it."

"I miss you," he said quietly, and I scoffed.

"You see me every day."

"That's not what I mean, and you know it."

"Here's the thing, Cal. I have too many eyes on me right now. Every single move I make is under a microscope, and no one is watching more closely than you. I can't afford to get entangled in something, have it get messy, and our already tenuous work relationship suffer further when shit inevitably hits the fan. I can't think of any good reason why we should hop back into bed together."

"How about because the sex is amazing? And we both know you're not getting that good anywhere else."

"I could always go back to Owen," I taunted.

The muscles in his jaw ticked as he ground his molars together. "You wouldn't."

He was right, but I didn't like the confidence in his tone. "You don't know that."

"I do know that," he said, rising from the couch and stalking around my desk, spinning my chair and leaning into my face until we were eye to eye.

With him in my space like this, the déjà vu was intense, bringing me right back to our meeting when he agreed to give me a shoestring budget and three months to roll out my new plans.

I could only assume that's exactly why he did it. Somehow, he'd figured out he still held all the cards here. This man lived for tipping me off balance, and knew he had perfected the ability to do so. One glancing touch from him and I'd be a goner, so I purposely shrunk myself as small as I could in my chair, careful to avoid brushing against his body in any way.

"You feel it too, don't you?" he whispered, his breath fanning across my cheeks. "There's this fucking...*tether* around my chest"—he tapped a spot right over his heart—"pulling me to you constantly. I couldn't get free, even if I wanted to."

"And do you?"

"Do I what?"

"Do you want to get free? Don't you think our lives would be so much easier without that tether?"

Because he was right: I felt it too, and it scared the ever loving shit out of me.

"Nothing about our lives was easy before we gave into temptation, Mar. The fire between us simply fueled that hatred."

"And now?"

"Now, the fire fuels something a lot more fun. And, maybe, something more lasting."

"What are you saying right now?" I asked, voice small, fear and excitement mixing together in my tone.

Almost in slow motion, I watched him reach for me, watched

raptly as he dragged his pointer finger along the full length of my right collarbone, trailing it over the silky fabric of my top at my shoulder.

"I want you, Mar. Only you."

"In what way?"

"All of them."

I sucked in a breath, barely able to believe what I was hearing. It was too much—too much to hope for, too much for him to ask from me, too much to ignore.

"Just say yes."

The first time he made that demand, it had been so fucking easy to give in. I'd been helpless to deny him anything.

This time, I had more steel in my spine. Except, just as I opened my mouth to protest, to say *no*, Cal dropped his lips to mine.

As it turned out, I was *still* fucking helpless to deny him any-thing.

The kiss was earth-shattering in its simplicity, in the soft way he massaged my lips with his, applying gentle pressure, coaxing a happy sigh from me.

That tiny, breathy sound was answer enough for Cal, because he pulled away, dropped his forehead against mine, and said, "Come over this weekend."

It was such a bad idea for an unbelievably long list of reasons, but my mouth formed the words and spoke them into existence before I could stop myself.

"How about you come to my place instead?"

If I was going to give my heart away, I was damn well going to do it on my own turf.

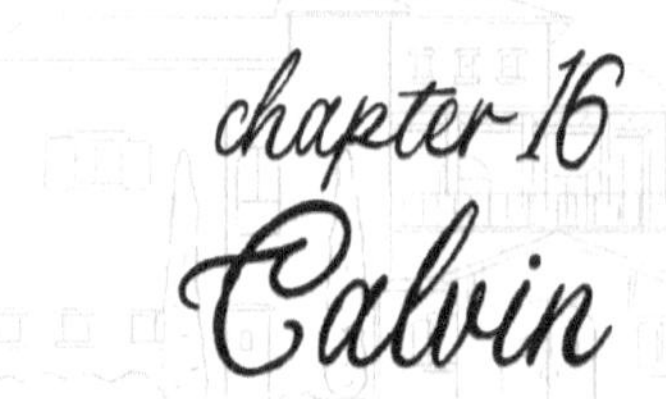

chapter 16
Calvin

I WAS A THIRTY-THREE-YEAR-OLD man. There was absolutely no reason why my hands should be shaking with nerves over the thought of going to spend the night with a woman. Not to mention, Amara was a woman I'd already had in the most compromising of positions, a woman I desperately wanted to take everything from.

But despite all that, Amara wasn't just *any* woman.

Things between us were changing fast, and I could admit now that, while my initial impression of the girl she'd been at twenty-three may have been spot on, Amara had grown a lot in the five years since, and the twenty-eight-year-old standing before me was more impressive than I ever could've imagined.

When it came to her, I didn't mind being wrong.

Especially not when she pulled the door open to her house the following weekend, clad in a lilac colored bikini with a sheer white cover-up tied around her waist and slung low on her hips. I was half hard from one drag of my eyes across all that exposed skin, and I couldn't wait to follow the same path with my lips and hands.

Skye bounded into the house ahead of me, her entire backside wiggling with the force of her tail wags, her excitement over exploring a new place mirroring my excitement over seeing the woman in front of me.

"Hell of a way to greet a guy," I said, backing her inside and wrapping my arms around her, holding her close so I could kiss her.

"This old thing?" she said when she shoved away. "I just had it lying around."

"I'll bet," I said, dropping my bags—one of which held Skye's food, enough for the entire weekend—and her dog bed onto the light wood floors in the entryway.

Skye continued to sniff around, and while I knew this used to be Chloe's house, that Amara's sister had built it specifically for herself with the idea of having a family of her own here one day, I'd never been inside. Following my pup's lead, I took a moment to study the space.

The floors were wide, light oak planks, the walls painted a cream so bright it was nearly white. The kitchen had beadboard cabinets with matte black hardware, white marble counters with deep grey veining, and a floor-to-ceiling wine rack fully stocked with exotic bottles from all over the world—an impressive testament to Amara's travels.

"You can wander if you want," she said from behind me, and I turned to find her smirking at me. "Or...you can come down to the beach with me. Your choice."

She sashayed past, her curvy hips swinging side to side hypnotically.

Yeah, there was no way I wasn't following that ass down to the sand.

I'd arrived late enough that the sun was near setting, but it was one of those rare days where it didn't cool off as the sky darkened, which meant Amara wasn't inclined to cover up to stay warm. For that, I counted my blessings.

Besides, if she caught a chill, I'd happily warm her with my body.

Skye raced down ahead of us, making a beeline for the water, and I grinned sheepishly at Amara.

"I'll hose her down before she goes back inside," I promised.

Amara waved a hand. "Don't even worry about it. That house has seen enough sand to fill this entire beach."

About fifteen feet off the foot of the stairs, she'd spread a blanket on the sand. An old fashioned wicker picnic basket sat off to the side, its contents spread around it. An array of cheeses, fruits, and chocolate, plus a hunk of crusty bread, crackers, thinly sliced meats, and, of course, four bottles of wine.

I raised a brow at the selection of bottles.

"What? I wasn't sure what kind you'd want."

"If it's all CD, it doesn't matter."

"You know it is," she scoffed. "You think I'd drink anything but the best?"

No, I really didn't.

I pulled my shirt off, feeling overdressed compared to her, and reclined on the blanket next to her while she poured herself a healthy serving of red wine. Before she took a sip, she moved to fill my glass, but I pressed a finger to her lips.

I crooked a finger. "Don't swallow that, and c'mere."

She obeyed and came to me, her lips pressed tightly closed around the mouthful of wine as she met my mouth.

"Open up."

We did in unison, the aromatic red liquid swirling from her mouth to mine. I let it run down my chin and linger on my tongue, allowing the layers to settle. I swallowed before kissing her again, sliding my tongue between her lips, tasting the wine on both of us. Leaning away slightly, I licked a small, errant drop from her jaw, and she kissed along mine, laving her tongue across my stubble, mopping me up.

"Pinot Noir," I said when we broke apart.

"My favorite," she said, grinning. "Although I've never had it quite like that."

"It'll never taste the same again, will it?"

With a happy sigh and a head shake, she poured another glass and handed it to me.

"Red wine grapes are so hard to grow well around here, though. Did you know it took my parents nearly ten years to perfect this recipe? And even now, we don't always get enough from the harvest every season to make a significant amount. That's part of the business though: making adjustments when the weather or the crop doesn't quite cooperate."

Despite the fact that we were literally in business together, I'd rarely actually listened to Amara when she spoke about work. Now I had no choice but to, completely mesmerized by her voice and her words. The way her eyes lit up, her hands waving in front of her. It was clear she loved her job, was passionate about wine and the work we were doing. How had I never seen it before?

"You are...impressive," I said at last, reaching out to tuck a lock of hair that had blown across her face back behind her ear.

She gave me a modest shrug and said, "That's what we've been telling you," though I didn't miss the blush that crept into her cheeks with my compliment.

"What was it like growing up around here?"

"Wonderful," she said wistfully. "I mean, during the school year, we lived down in TC, but in the summers we'd come up here and spend three months at the Villa. Both Mama and Daddy worked so much back then, but they let us roam free and trusted us to stay out of trouble."

"And did you?"

She gave me a mischievous smile. "Most of the time."

I could easily picture her and her sisters running rampant across the peninsula, letting tourist boys fall hopelessly in love with them before ripping their hearts out at the end of summer. I could imagine the five of them racing up and down these beaches, building sand castles and trolling the shore for Petoskey Stones.

Once again, that pang I'd experienced back at Torch Lake echoed through my chest.

I was an only child to a man and a woman who were in their late-thirties by the time I came along. They'd given up on having kids—or maybe they'd never wanted them; that wasn't a question I was keen to learn the answer to. They were content with a life spent loving only each other, so when I came along, they didn't really know what to do with me. Before me, they'd been nomadic, roaming across the country to where they wanted, when they felt like it. Mostly, I kept to myself. I was a studious kid, always getting good grades in school, and I graduated at the top of my class. I considered my best friends the characters I read about in my favorite fantasy novels like *Eragon* and *Lord of the Rings*. I didn't do drugs or break curfew—mostly because I didn't have one. I didn't even drink or really party at all until I left for college.

My parents are wonderful people who I love dearly. I never wanted for anything growing up, and I knew they loved me in their own ways. But when I stacked my own childhood up against Amara's? I'm sure it wasn't all sunshine and rainbows for her, either, but I'd seen her with her sisters and parents enough to know that I'd missed out on that kind of unbreakable, unshakable family bond.

But I lucked out when I got to college. Though we lived on opposite ends of the country, I still spoke regularly with my roommate, who I'd met freshman year and lived with until graduation, and was actually in his wedding. I made great friends out in Napa who I chatted with a few times a week, and since I'd met Owen, he'd become the closest I'd ever get to having a brother.

Maybe that's why I'd been so willfully ignorant of the red flags in my relationship with Amie. She'd been content to travel and party and work. There hadn't been a day when we'd had a frank conversation about the future, or what we wanted out of life. In hindsight, that relationship hadn't been much more than a couple of fuck buddies who decided to slap a more serious label on it in an attempt to hide its flaws.

I'd be damned if that hadn't been the most bitter pill to swallow at the time, though. I considered myself a fairly intelligent guy, but where Amie was concerned, I'd been too goddamn blinded by everything I wanted, and all the things I wanted *her* to want too.

That proposal was sheer stupidity, and as long as I lived, I'd never forget the pitying look on her face as she turned me down.

And sure, maybe Amara and I were doing the same thing, but I could say one thing for certain: I was already more entranced by this woman in a month than I'd ever been by Amie. Amie had been…easy. Amara was anything but, which was the whole point. I remember thinking the night we met that I'd be bored with someone who wasn't such a ballbuster. We'd certainly had our ups and downs since then, but I couldn't regret any of it—not since it led us right here.

"Where did you just go?" Amara asked quietly.

I'd been so lost in my head that I hadn't noticed the sun was kissing the horizon now where it had been floating above it the last time I'd looked. Soon, it'd slip below the water.

"Just…thinking about my parents."

"What're they like?"

"Distant," I said, and I didn't only mean geographically. "I'm sorry, Princess. I just…really don't want to talk about them right now. I don't want to ruin this."

Amara crawled over to me and fit herself between my thighs so her back was to my chest. Instinctively, I wrapped my arms around her. "Then let's enjoy this sunset together."

"Whatever you want, Mar."

She tilted her head back to look at me and said, "This is all I want."

I pressed a kiss to the top of her head, the scent of her shampoo steadying me. "Me too."

Upon seeing us cuddled up, Skye trotted over and dropped onto the sand at my hip, resting her head on my thigh. Amara brushed a hand over her head, and Skye's eyes drooped closed as Amara's touch lulled her to sleep.

Amara tipped her head back and gave me a wide grin at how quickly Skye warmed to her—I didn't have a heart to tell her that, as a Golden, Skye pretty much liked everyone. I pressed a kiss to the tip of her nose, holding her more firmly as we watched the sun sink below the horizon, painting the sky in pinks and oranges. Overhead, the stars were beginning to blink to life, and I couldn't think of anything more perfect than this.

"Is this a date?" I asked quietly. "Are we having our first date right now?"

Cautiously, she asked, "Do you want it to be a date?"

"Badly," I breathed.

"Me too."

"Are you one of those girls that withholds sex on the first date?"

"Cal!" she giggled, swatting at me. "I think we're a little past that, don't you?"

"Just a little."

Now that the sun had fully disappeared, Amara rubbed her palms over her arms. "Should I build a fire?"

"Or I could warm you up." I brought my mouth to the shell of her ear and whispered, "Remember what I told you about the next time I had you alone?"

I felt the shiver pass through her body and chuckled. "I believe there was mention of *devouring* my pussy."

"How about you let me make good on my promise?"

"Please," she whispered, then attempted to move away from me. My arms became a vise around her, holding her in place. She glanced at me again. "You don't want to go up to the house?"

"Only to lock Skye in," I said, shifting myself out from behind her and lifting my pup into my arms.

When I returned, I dropped between her legs and hovered over her, her hair a dark corona around her head on the white blanket beneath us. "You know, I saw some of Brie's desserts in that picnic basket," I said, placing soft kisses on her cheeks, her eyelids, and the corners of her mouth. "But I can think of something I'd rather eat instead."

"Cal!" she protested, albeit weakly, as I reached down and pulled the tie at one of her hips free, then she gasped as I released the other tie and brushed her bikini bottoms away, my fingers lingering against her sensitive skin.

"Mar," I groaned as I took a few exploratory swipes through her slit. "I've barely touched you. Are you always this wet for me?"

"Maybe."

I folded myself over her so we were eye to eye. "That's not an answer."

With a huff, she tried to turn her face away, but I caught her jaw and forced her to look at me. "Fine. Yes, I'm always this wet for you. Sometimes, just looking at you has me drenched."

I grinned. "That's my girl."

I shifted down and fit myself between her thighs until I was eye level with her pussy, then hooked her legs over my shoulders.

In anticipation, Amara dove her fingers into my hair and closed her eyes.

We couldn't have that.

"Eyes on me, baby. I want you to watch how much I enjoy this."

Those peculiar golden eyes snapped open, glowing even in the faint light of the dying day, and stayed locked on mine as I darted my tongue out for one long, slow lick from entrance to clit.

A moan escaped her as her nails dug into my scalp, and I chuckled darkly.

This woman was putty in my hands with my face buried in her pussy, but I didn't think she realized I could simply drown here and die a happy man. She was so fucking responsive to every teasing lick and glancing flick against her swollen clit, and the sounds she made had my cock painfully hard where it was sandwiched between the blanket and my stomach.

Amara unabashedly rode my face, using her heels on my upper back to leverage herself up and down against my tongue, and I fucking loved it. She was unlike anyone I'd ever been with. She knew exactly what she wanted, and she didn't need a man to give it to her—though I was all too happy to oblige.

"You're stealing my fun," I murmured against her flesh.

"I'm sorry," she said, a bit breathlessly. "Your mouth...so good...can't...help myself."

I splayed my palm against her pubic bone, both to hold her in place and to open her wider, trailing my tongue in a circle around her clit. "Just let me have this, Mar."

"I don't know if you know this about me, but I'm not exactly great at giving up—oh!" Her words were cut off by a yelp when I shoved two fingers into her slick entrance without warning. Goddamn, she was tight. I hadn't forgotten how good it felt to sink into her, and I couldn't wait to once again feel her clamped around my cock.

She didn't speak again as I fucked her with my hand, my tongue fluttering against her clit in time with the pumps of my fingers. I knew she was getting close when she began pulsing around me. With a curl of my fingers against her inner wall, I sealed my mouth around her clit and sucked hard.

She came with a scream, her thighs caging my head in as she cried out and quaked with the endless aftershocks as I maintained the suction and continued pumping my fingers. When her thighs fell open at last, I pulled away, placing a kiss against her belly as I rose to face her.

"How'd I do?" I asked, bending to kiss her.

"That tongue is definitely wicked."

I grinned. "You can ride my face whenever you want."

"Happily," she said, then shoved me hard so I flopped over, landing on my back in the sand.

"My turn," she said, working her hands into the waistband of my swim trunks. When I arched my back, she swept them the rest of the way off and threw them somewhere behind her.

All other thoughts eddied out of my head when she closed her fingers around my length.

She worked me slowly at first, lightly trailing her fingers up and down, toying with me in a way that had me bucking into her hand, desperate for more pressure and friction. Then she settled on her knees between my legs, bent, and swirled her tongue around the head.

"Fucking hell, woman."

"I'm just getting started."

Her lips closed around me and she pulled me in...and in...and in until I branded the back of her throat, almost my entire length disappearing into her mouth, then pulled off with a *pop*, following the path her mouth had just taken with her hand.

"No gag reflex?" I asked, incredulous. "Any other hidden talents I should know about?"

"Stick with me, Ryder," she said as she stroked me, giving me the pressure I craved, toeing the line between pleasure and pain—just how I liked it. "I'll show you everything."

This woman. She continued to surprise me.

With an easy flex of my abs, I was curling upward, gripping her beneath her arms, and hauling her over me.

"I wasn't done playing," she said with a pout, even as she rose onto her knees and reached between us, fitting my cock at her entrance.

"Yes you were," I said, then thrust up into her.

We'd spent too goddamn long on this beach, toying with each other. I was painfully hard, and if I was going to come, it was going to be in her pussy.

With a throaty moan, she collapsed against my chest, and I settled my hands on her ass, holding her in place as I bucked up into her over and over and over.

"Fuck," I breathed. "Goddamnit, Mar. You feel so fucking good."

"You get so deep like this," she said, sitting up and throwing her head back when I branded some new spot inside. "It's almost too much."

"You can take it."

"You're damn right."

She began to move above me, rolling her body, her tits bouncing with each of her movements, still covered by her bikini top. I quickly removed it, and I dug my fingers into her hips, hoping she'd wake up in the morning with bruises.

I liked the thought of branding her, of giving her something no one else could.

"Those European tools you messed with didn't fuck you this good, did they, Princess?"

I don't know what compelled me to say it, only that, even with her riding me like it was her fucking job, even with the pure pleasured sounds coming out of her mouth—and the fact that I'd already made her come once—there was some deep seated insecurity that needed her to confirm it. I needed her to tell me it hadn't been like this for her with anyone else, because I'd certainly never felt this before.

She stilled for a moment, leaning over me to brush a kiss to my mouth, then cupping my cheeks in her hands, meeting my gaze and holding it as she slid almost all the way off me then back down, painfully slow. "No one has ever fucked me this good, Cal. *No one.*"

With a satisfied growl, I lifted my hips and flipped us so she was on her back, sand flying everywhere as I fucked her against the beach like only I could.

Heavily lidded eyes met mine, mouth open around a soundless moan, neck arched. She was *everything*, and I was a fucking goner. As I fit my hand around her neck, pressing slightly, I pumped harder into her, and she widened her legs, gripping her knees back, practically folding herself in half to give me the angle I needed to get her there. Then she reached between us, and with three quick swipes of her fingers against her clit, her inner walls clamped down around my cock, and she fell apart.

Two pumps later, I joined her, slowing only enough to continue wringing every last bit of pleasure from her as she arched and quivered in the sand. While she chanted my name over and over into the cool, dark night, I spilled seemingly endlessly inside her.

When I was certain she couldn't take anymore, when I was entirely spent, I stilled and pulled free, then dropped myself onto the sand at her side and gathered her in my arms.

"I'm going to be washing sand out of places where sand doesn't belong for at least a week," she said, but I could hear the smile in her voice.

I pressed a kiss to her hair. "I could help you with that."

She trailed her fingers over my chest and abs, fingers closing around my impossibly still hard dick.

"How?" she asked.

"Have you seen yourself? You're always drenched around me, and I'm always fucking hard around you. It's our curse."

"Nah," she said quietly, pressing a kiss to my pec. "It's a blessing."

A blessing? Yeah, this woman in my arms absolutely was.

chapter 17
Calvin

I LOOKED UP AT the hesitant knock on my office door to find Amara standing at the threshold.

"Can I come in?"

"Always," I said quietly, and she smiled as she stepped in and closed the door.

I was out of my chair and on her in an instant, pressing my mouth to hers and inhaling deeply, trying to brand the scent and feel of her on my memory.

Though, now that I'd had her, I doubted I'd ever forget a single second of our time together.

"What's up?" I asked when I pulled away.

"The Tigers invited us down for a game this weekend. They're giving us a box, and I was wondering if you wanted to come. It'll be an overnight thing since it's a late game, so I'm going to book rooms at the Ren Cen."

"I *always* want to come," I said with a wicked grin.

With a smack to my chest, she said, "Cal."

"I'll join you on one condition."

"What's that?"

"You stay with me. Spend the night with me. We'll get a room far away from whatever floor of the hotel your family is staying on. We can order room service, and I can make you scream my name all night."

It wouldn't be the first time we'd done an overnight, but I didn't want her getting any ideas about staying with one of her sisters when she could be in my arms instead.

"Deal."

❧ ❦

That weekend, I dropped Skye off with Owen and hit the road. Despite agreeing to stay the night with me, Amara chose to travel down to Detroit with her sisters, saying she hadn't had a chance to catch up with them in a while and she missed them.

By "catch up," I knew she meant she wanted to fill them in on our little beach date last weekend—and the marathon night of sex that followed.

Was it weird for me to know the family that signed my paychecks knew the dirty details of my sex life with my *boss*? Hell yeah, it was. But it was also...flattering. To know that I fucked Amara so good she couldn't wait to tell her sisters about it was a powerful feeling. And it's not like sleeping with her was a hardship. She was the sexiest woman I'd ever laid eyes on, and the more I learned about her, the better I got to know her, the harder I fell.

Yeah, I said it.

I was falling for Amara Delatou. Fucking sue me.

I guess it took stripping her down to her bare skin, and seeing her at her most vulnerable physically, to start stripping away my preconceived notions about her character. But the more time I spent with her, the harder it was to ignore that Amara was an amazing woman—intelligent, loyal, hardworking, a natural born leader. All the things I would expect from the CEO of a family-owned company.

Her father had taught her well, and she was putting her education to good use.

Since it was a night game, the plan was to rendezvous at the hotel, check in, then head over to the ballpark together.

Naturally, the first face I saw when I walked into the lobby was Amara's.

The second was Leon's, which instantly doused any heat I was feeling toward his daughter and disabused me of the notion that I might give her a kiss hello.

"Cal!" Leon said, walking up to shake my hand. "How've you been, my boy? I haven't seen you in ages."

Oh, I'm great, Leon. Busy having the best sex of my life and falling in love with your daughter! How about you?

"I'm good, sir. Just been busy keeping the ship floating."

"Excellent," he said. "And I haven't heard any rumblings of drama between you and Amara lately. I'm happy things have finally turned a corner with you two."

You have no fucking idea.

At the mention of her name, Amara appeared at her father's side, and I could barely keep my eyes in my head. She wore a Tigers' branded baby tee and artfully distressed jean shorts, the waistband low enough to leave a strip of her tanned, toned stomach exposed, the hem cut high enough that her legs seemed to go on for miles, bare and smooth, and her feet were stuffed into a pair of bright white Nike dunks high-tops. Her deep brown hair was in a pony, pulled through the back of a navy ball cap with the Old English D on the front in orange.

She was breathtaking, effortlessly sexy, and it took every single ounce of willpower I possessed not to pull her to me and shove my tongue in her mouth.

"Ryder," she said coolly, then held out a keycard to me.

"Princess," I said in response, hoping her father didn't catch the way my fingers grazed hers a little longer and gentler than was proprietary for two people who presumably couldn't stand each other.

"Well, I guess not everything has changed," Leon said with a sigh.

When he turned away, Amara offered me a secret smile, and I returned it, hoping my eyes conveyed all the things I couldn't wait to do to her later.

Leon clapped his hands. "Well, let's get our stuff upstairs and meet back down here in, say"—he flicked his wrist to check his watch—"fifteen minutes?"

His daughters and wife murmured their agreement, and we made a mass exodus from the lobby toward the elevators. We all piled inside—Leon and Lena, Chloe and Logan, Delia, Brie, Ella, Ezra, Liam, me, and Amara. It truly was a family affair today, and I wondered, with all these people here, who was running the winery.

But all thoughts of Apple Blossom Bay fled my mind when

I found myself pressed into the back corner of the elevator car with Amara squeezed in front of me.

"What floor are you on?" I asked, so quietly only she could hear.

"Same as you."

"Good girl."

Without looking at me, she reached behind her and grasped my hand, giving it a quick squeeze before letting go.

I mourned the contact instantly, knowing it was the last time I'd get to touch her until I dragged her into my room later, stripped her down, and spread her out on my bed.

So I was pleasantly surprised when everyone but her and I got off on the same floor, leaving us completely alone. We didn't speak until it stopped again and we were pushing into my room. Amara made herself at home, dragging her suitcase over to the bed and setting it on top, then unzipping it to remove her cosmetics case.

"What are you doing?"

"I'm going to touch up my makeup."

"No, I mean...why are you acting like this is your room?"

"Because it is," she said, offering me a shy smile.

"You...what?"

"I made the reservations, Cal. I checked us in. I specifically requested we be put on a different floor than my family, and I purposely only booked *us* a single room. Together."

"Why?"

It was such a stupid question, but she'd caught me off guard, and my brain was sputtering to catch up.

She shrugged. "You asked me to stay with you."

I gaped at her, and then hauled her against me and kissed her.

Before I could deepen it, before I could snake my hand south and reward her forward thinking, she broke free and shoved away from me.

"We can't," she said. "We have to be back downstairs shortly."

"I want you so bad."

"I know, baby," she said, reaching out to wrap her arms around my waist. "And you can have me as many times as you want...later."

⁂

The Tigers had gone all out for us, practically rolling out the red carpet to welcome the Delatou family and their guests into the box at the park. The suite itself was fully stocked with Delatou wines and the new canned cocktails, as well as large platters of hot dogs, burgers, fruits, veggies, and other snack foods for us to munch on while we watched the game. Our party milled about, enjoying themselves, momentarily forgetting who we were and why we were here.

But I'd never forget. This entire day wouldn't have been possible without my girl, and as I watched her mingle with her family, pride surged in my chest.

I'd done my best to avoid Amara for the bulk of the day, but I decided to approach her in the middle of the eighth inning so we could plan our escape. I was hoping she'd be amenable to sneaking out early. It was already nearing ten p.m., the Tigers had a five run lead, and my skin buzzed in anticipation. I wanted her under me, my mouth between her legs until she came. And then I wanted to do it again with my cock. Then my fingers for good measure.

Extricating myself from my current conversation with Logan and Liam, I headed toward her, pausing a few feet away to simply study her for a moment. She stood on the opposite side of the small island counter from me, a can of Delatou & Danvers' Lena's Best Sangria in one hand, a Tigers' cup in the other. Amara turned on the charm as Delia filmed a video for the winery's social media accounts.

As soon as Delia finished, a petite blonde woman approached, wrapping Amara in a big hug, the two of them chatting and squealing like old friends, wide smiles plastered on their faces.

I wondered who she was, especially given she was decked out in an orange silk dress and high, navy blue heels, a microphone dangling at her side. On the opposite side of the counter stood a man, camera balanced on his shoulder, eye pressed against the viewfinder, lens trained on the women.

I wandered over for a closer look just as the blonde began her interview.

"Hey, Tigers fans! I'm Daniella up here in the section 122 suite with Amara Delatou, CEO of Delatou, Inc., and the owner of Chateau Delatou. This week, the Tigers inked a seven figure deal with Amara and her winery to make Delatou & Danvers, their new wine-based, ready to drink cocktail, the official canned cocktail of the team...a deal I had a large part in facilitating, if I do say so myself."

Amara laughed, and said, "Honestly, I can't thank you enough. These first five months since I've taken over for my dad have been trying to say the least, but now that I've got my first big win under my belt, I'm excited to see what the future holds."

"How does that feel, to be the first female to run the company that's been in your family for over 110 years?"

"Incredible…and daunting. My parents raised all five of us girls to work hard, and even from a young age, I was always interested in contributing what I could to the family business. It's why I got my MBA and spent the last five years in Europe. But I'm not the oldest, and I grew up expecting Chloe to take over. So when she officially stepped down, I couldn't help thinking, this is it. This is my chance. This is what I was meant to do. But, of course, there are people out there who view me as under qualified and would happily have someone else steering the ship. So it's been a bit of a balancing act, trying to do my job while having eyes on me constantly. I'm really thankful the Tigers approached me with this deal. Hopefully now, my naysayers will be a little quieter."

Her eyes met mine across the room as she spoke those last words, and irritation surged within me. No one could know she was talking about me—but *I* knew, and that was enough to urge my feet into motion until I was crossing the suite and stepping up to her side, the camera swinging to greet my smiling face.

I thought we'd moved past this, but apparently not.

"And who is this?" Daniella asked when I pushed into the frame.

"Calvin Ryder," I said, extending my hand, which she accepted. "CFO of Delatou, Inc."

"Ahh, the money man," Daniella said approvingly. "How's it been having this one for your boss?"

"Oh, I think we both know who runs the show up there," I said with a wink. Daniella laughed indulgently, but Amara surreptitiously drove her elbow into my side. "And she's not just my boss. She's also my girlfriend."

I swear to God, time stopped as soon as the word was out of my mouth. Honestly, I didn't even know what possessed me to blurt out that complete and utter lie, but now that it was in the air between us, shimmering, morphing, expanding, I found I didn't want to take it back.

"Co-workers *and* dating?" Daniella said, brow arching. "Do you spend any time apart?"

"Not much," I said, throwing my arm around Amara's shoulders and tugging her close. I didn't miss the rigidity of her body against mine, and I knew there'd be hell to pay later. "But I like it that way."

"Well, you certainly make a gorgeous couple."

I risked a glance down at Amara and found a tense smile—more like a grimace—on her face. "Thanks," she said.

Daniella asked me a few more questions about the deal with the Tigers, and I was effusive in my praise of Amara and my excitement over what this meant for the company going forward.

At last, when the next batter's walk-up music blasted out across the park, Daniella wrapped it up, thanked us, and disappeared.

"Mar, I—"

"Not now," she said through her teeth.

I simply nodded, though she was already walking away from me.

Sitting through the bottom of the eighth and top of the ninth innings was pure torture. Amara refused to look at me, be within five feet of me, and she certainly wasn't speaking to me. When the Tigers' closer struck out the last batter, earning a victory for the home team, the Delatou family wandered out into the bleacher seats and prepared for the post-game fireworks show.

Amara, meanwhile, finally looked at me for the first time in twenty minutes, jerked her chin, and moved toward the door.

I followed behind like a small child who knew he was about to be scolded.

I offered to order an Uber, but Amara ignored me, intent on stomping down the sidewalks. I could practically see the steam coming out of her ears, and I wouldn't be surprised to find the concrete paths crumbling beneath her steps.

She was royally pissed off.

The thing I couldn't quite figure out was...why? Given the progression of our relationship to this point, slapping the boyfriend-girlfriend label on it was a natural next step. Sure, the way I'd gone about it was a little fucked up, but I couldn't regret it. I wanted her to be mine in every sense of the word.

Maybe I'd misread everything, and maybe she didn't want the same things.

The thought had ice racing through my veins.

Once the door to our room clicked shut behind us, she exploded.

"How fucking *dare* you?" she shouted as she pulled her hat from her head and whipped it across the room.

I held up my hands placatingly, though I knew nothing would calm her right now. It had been a long time since I'd seen her this angry, and the woman was as stubborn as a bull. She wouldn't let go of the anger until she was good and ready. She'd keep charging me like I held that damn red flag in front of her.

"What did I do, Mar?"

"You can't be serious." I shrugged, and her eyes widened. "You are. You really have no fucking idea what you've done."

"Then explain it to me. Let me fix it."

"There's no going back from this, Cal!"

"Going back from what? From calling you my girlfriend? I certainly hope not!"

"You announced that shit on a *professional baseball broadcast*! What the fuck is wrong with you?!"

"*That's* what this attitude is about? Not that I said it, but because I did it so publicly?"

She crossed her arms over her chest and glared at me, the rage shining in her eyes so intense I was genuinely surprised the skin of my face wasn't melting off with the force of it.

"You took something about me and made it about you. You made it look like I can't accomplish anything without a man by my side. You've completely undermined everything I've been striving to do since I took over!"

I blinked slowly. Honestly, I'd never considered that. I had just been so irritated by her comments that were *clearly* directed at me, I jumped in, opened my mouth, and apparently stuck my foot in it.

Clearly, I was still having difficulty reconciling the Amara I thought I knew with the one standing before me.

I had to fix this, and fast, or I could kiss any chance of ever touching her again goodbye.

"I'm sorry, Mar," I said, slowly approaching her. "I wasn't thinking."

"You're right, you weren't," she said, taking a step back for each of my advancing ones, attempting to maintain our distance. She would've succeeded had she not bumped into the edge of the entertainment center. I closed the space between us in one large step and cupped her face in my hands.

"You're not entirely innocent here, either," I said, dropping my hands, gripping her hips tightly as I hauled her against me.

"Oh, really? And how exactly is that?"

"Those comments you were making about your *naysayers*," I said. "You were clearly talking about me."

With a huff, she pulled free from my arms and stalked across the room, the bed creaking slightly as she sat down on it. "Yes, well at least I didn't make you look like an incompetent twit who couldn't do her job without her *boyfriend* holding her hand. I have a goddamn MBA, Cal! I don't fucking need you. I've been successfully running this company for months, no thanks to you and your lack of faith in me."

Pushing my hand through my hair, I took a deep breath and turned to face her. "I thought we were past that."

"Well, I thought so too, until that stunt you pulled tonight."

"How can I make it up to you?" I asked. "I don't know what I was thinking, and I'm so sorry. Please, Mar. Please just...tell me what to do. I'll do anything."

I wasn't above getting on my knees and begging. We were still figuring things out, that much was true. But I couldn't let her go. Not yet. Maybe not ever. I wanted to work through this with her like a couple. And I knew she wanted to be with me. Under normal circumstances, I think she would've even been thrilled by me calling her my girlfriend in public. But these weren't normal circumstances, and I meant what I said. I'd do anything to vanquish that pain in her eyes—to keep her from walking away from me right now.

"Anything?" she asked.

There was a gleam in her eyes that surely meant trouble, but still, I swallowed hard and nodded. "Anything."

"Get on your knees, Cal."

As Cal lowered to his knees, I rose to my feet and quickly stripped down, kicking my shorts and thong to one side of the room, whipping my tee in another direction, tossing my bra carelessly onto the bed behind me.

Then I sat back down and spread my legs open, resting my heels wide and leaning back on my palms.

I was completely bare for him, more vulnerable than ever with him fully clothed and me completely naked. But the way he was looking at me? Like he'd never seen anything more stunning or perfect in his entire life? I'd never felt more powerful. His gaze heated as he took me in, eyes tracing across my flesh, goosebumps rising in its wake. As he studied me, I watched his cock harden until it tented the front of his khaki shorts.

My mouth watered, remembering how smooth the skin there was, the sexy sounds he made when I took him all the way in and swallowed around him, how his hips bucked when I lightly scraped my nails down his length.

But I could play later.

"Now what?" he asked, voice a low rumble.

"Now crawl."

Once again, Cal did as I asked, slowly moving on his hands and knees toward me until he was eye level with my pussy. He sat back on his heels, hands resting on his thick thighs.

Supplicant. Ready to atone. So goddamn sexy I barely stopped myself from pulling him onto this bed and putting us both out of our misery.

But I was getting mine before he got his. Consider it repayment for the emotional distress he caused me today. Did I want to be Cal's girlfriend? Yeah, I did, but the way he'd gone about the whole thing royally pissed me off.

"And now?" His breath fanned against my drenched slit, and I shivered.

"Now make me come."

"I don't think this is the punishment you think it is," Cal said, lifting a hand and dipping his fingers into my arousal, tracing a lazy path around my clit with his pointer.

"The punishment, Ryder, is the reminder that I hold all the cards here. If I tell you to stop, you stop. If I decide to leave and go stay with one of my sisters instead of letting you fuck me into this mattress all night, you let me go."

I reached down and gripped his chin hard in my hand, forcing his gaze up to mine. "And if you ever pull something like you did today again, I will fucking end you and your career. Do you understand?"

"Yes, Princess," he whispered.

"Good," I said, once again reclining and gesturing to my glistening sex. "Now get to work."

I wanted to watch, but holding myself up didn't last long as he buried his face in my pussy and set every single nerve ending in my body alight with the wicked, purposeful sweeps of his tongue. I flopped back on the bed and squeezed my eyes shut. The image of him crawling to me was forever branded on my memory, and I was halfway there already, picturing how easily he obeyed me, how he let me take charge.

And it wasn't just today, either. He'd been content to let me seek my pleasure however I needed to every single time we'd been together. Rarely, if ever, had I encountered a man so comfortable in bed that he hadn't needed to showboat for the sake of proving his sexual prowess. Cal was quietly confident as a lover, and thanks to watching me use him in whatever way I needed to get there, he quickly learned exactly what I liked and wanted, and he delivered on it every time.

I gripped the backs of my thighs and opened myself wider, both to give him better access and to keep myself from reaching for him. I wasn't ready to touch him, not yet. He let out a hum of pleasure against my clit, then backed off just a bit.

I missed him instantly, and made a noise of protest.

"Patience, baby."

Without warning, he spread my cheeks apart and licked a path from my rear entrance to my clit, letting out a low, long moan.

"Fuck," I breathed. "Do that again."

So he did, then blew on the wet trail, and my toes curled.

"Cal..." I whimpered.

"I know, Princess," he said, though I wasn't even sure what I was asking for.

As always, he knew what I needed before I did, because he unceremoniously shoved three fingers inside, not bothering to work me up to it first, and suctioned his mouth around my clit. The intrusion was fucking delicious. I loved how he played a little rough with me, knowing I could take it—knowing I *wanted* it. A few quick flutters of his tongue, a nip of his teeth, and three pumps of his fingers had me coming, digging my nails into his shoulders and screaming his name.

So fast I barely had time to blink, Cal abandoned me to free himself of his clothes, crawled over and hauled us deeper into the bed, then buried himself inside me in one quick pulse of his hips.

"Fucking hell, Mar," he said as he began to move, nothing gentle about the way he slammed into me. The room quickly filled with the sounds of our labored breaths, of our skin slapping together, of my moans and his groans.

"Harder," I said. "I need more."

"Whatever you want, baby," he growled as he picked up the pace, the slam of his hips against the backs of my thighs nearly painful.

But I'd never ask him to stop. I needed him unhinged and wild, to remind him that I was the only one who could give him this. I was the only one that could meet him thrust for punishing thrust.

"More, Cal."

"Flip over," he said, pulling free so I could turn onto my stomach.

Roughly, he lifted my hips up, angling me where he wanted, and slammed home again.

I dropped my head and moaned into the comforter. This was the first time he'd taken me this way, and only a few pumps of his hips had me quaking around him already.

Cal squeezed my ass cheeks, then pulled a hand away, only to swing down with a stinging slap.

"Oh, God. Again."

"I think about this ass all the time," he said, punctuating his words with a slap to the other cheek. "I fucking love your ass."

"You might love fucking it too."

I glanced over my shoulder in time to see Cal's eyes widen. "You'd let me?"

"Maybe one day," I said.

"Mar," he groaned, long and low. "You're ruining me."

The feeling is mutual.

I was fucking drenched around him, my arousal slipping down my thighs, and Cal continued the relentless, rhythmic pulse of his hips, branding his cock on that spot deep inside me with every thrust.

I was close, that pressure against my clit building to a near un-bearable level, my breaths becoming shallower, and Cal must've sensed it too. He reached out and wrapped my ponytail around his fist, tugging my torso back and holding me there as he reached around and settled his hand between my thighs. He pressed three fingers against my clit and circled in time with his cock moving in and out of me—fast and hard.

"You are fucking perfect," he said, then let go of my hair and gripped the front of my neck, angling my head toward the mirror on the wall to our left. "Look at you. Look how well you take me."

I shifted my eyes until I met my own gaze in the glass, but they didn't stay there. Cal and I? The picture we painted within that gilt frame? Fuck, it was the hottest thing I'd ever seen in my life.

Cal was a solid wall behind me, back arched slightly forward, hips tilted to keep that perfect angle as he pounded into me. In front of him, I was the epitome of a woman deep in the throes of passion: spine a graceful curve, the length of my ponytail dangling between our bodies, legs spread wide with Cal's fingers working against the apex of my thighs, his other hand at my neck keeping me right where he wanted me.

The slow build of my release gained steam until I was bucking back against him, begging for more, harder, murmuring other unintelligible words as he did exactly what I needed.

That pressure reached its peak and crashed, the edges of my vision going black as my climax pulled me under. I dropped my head back against Cal's shoulder and cried out. His hand against the underside of my jaw was the only thing keeping me upright as I drowned and drowned and drowned under the waves of my orgasm. My anger ebbed away with each tremor that passed through my body until there was only Cal and my feelings for him that bloomed bigger and rooted deeper into my heart with each passing day.

He followed close behind, burying his teeth in my shoulder to muffle his own cries, his hand at my clit stilling as he spilled long and hot inside me.

Hand still at my throat, Cal tilted my face to press a kiss against my mouth. Both of us were sticky with sweat, perspiration beaded on Cal's brow and at my temples. And I'd never been more sated, my entire body limp with pleasure.

At last, Cal let go of me, and I dropped face first onto the bed, every muscle like jello.

With a laugh, Cal dropped his hands to my shoulders, gently massaging my neck and traps, then sweeping down my spine.

Quietly, he said, "I really don't like fighting with you, but if the makeup is always that good? Fuck."

"Has it ever been like that with anyone else for you?" I asked before I could stop myself.

Instead of answering right away, he rolled me onto my back so he could hover over me. Greedily, I ran my hands over the taut muscles of his arms, needing to touch him, to remind myself that he was here with me.

Cal bent and pressed a sweet kiss to my mouth. "Being with you is unlike anything I've ever experienced before, Mar. I—fuck. This is the *best* I've ever had, in every way. And I don't just mean the sex."

I grinned. "Me too."

This entire time, I'd been seriously afraid it had just been me, that it had been so long since I'd had good sex—definitely since well before I left Europe, and even then, none of those guys could hold a candle to Cal—that I was attaching more importance to this thing with him than it deserved. But to hear that he felt it too? It was like looking at our relationship through fresh eyes.

I felt safer in Cal's arms than I'd ever felt anywhere else in my life.

But that comfort was dangerous for so many reasons, the main one being that, at the end of the day, we were still CEO and CFO, boss and employee. It's why I'd tried to push him away before—because I couldn't stand the thought of my entire life blowing up in my face if things between us went south. My parents would be so disappointed, and while my sisters were supportive of whatever—and whomever—I did, they probably wouldn't be singing the same tune if the company was forced to replace one of us to avoid further scandal in the wake of what would ultimately be boiled down to an illicit affair.

And him telling that reporter earlier that he's my boyfriend? That's the kind of publicity I *didn't* need, the kind of shit that could fuck me, and not in the good way.

God, I didn't even want to think about what would happen when my dad found out.

But for now, I let Cal rise from the bed and head into the bathroom for a towel, then clean me up before tossing it across the room, climbing in next to me, and nestling us both under the covers, my back to his chest, his hand splayed across my stomach.

While my mind continued to spin out, attempting to marshal my thoughts and make sense of everything I was feeling, Cal was quiet enough for long enough that I thought he'd fallen asleep.

Until he spoke.

"Question for you," he said.

"Shoot."

"What's your endgame for the winery? Like...what's the biggest thing you want to accomplish in your tenure as CEO?"

"To become a household name."

The answer flew from my lips. It was something I'd been considering for a long time, the deep, secret wish never far from the forefront of my brain.

"Like...Barefoot?" Cal asked skeptically.

"No, not like Barefoot, you goon," I said with a laugh, pinching his arm for the stupid response. "More like...Josh. You know, like how Joseph Carr founded Josh as a tribute to his dad? Those family-first beginnings are the kinds of stories people can identify with. And what's more 'family first' than a winery headed by four generations of Delatous? That's a big motivating factor for getting our sales reps up there this fall. I want them to meet us all—me, Mom and Dad, my sisters, Liam and Ezra, maybe even you"—I poked him in the stomach, and he caught my hand, quickly pressing a kiss to the back before locking our fingers together and settling them at my waist—"and understand that the whole 'family owned and operated' line on our website and bottles isn't just some schtick."

I shrugged when I finished, not sure anything I said made any sense to Cal. For all intents and purposes, he was an outsider at Chateau Delatou and within the company. He hadn't grown up playing hide and seek in the vineyard, or celebrating holidays at the Villa or the winery. Hell, he hadn't even grown up in the area. It was different for him. Despite his tenure with the company, he was still an outsider, a newbie. And while I knew he wanted the company to succeed, our situations were not the same.

There was just something special about being a Delatou and working for the company. Our products didn't exactly convey that, but I was certain I could convince anyone of it if I only managed to get them into a room with me.

Cal buried his face in my neck and said against my skin, "I think those sales reps will take one look at you and buy anything you're selling before you even say a word."

I rolled my eyes. Leave it to him to take a vulnerable moment for me and turn it sexual.

"Half of those sales reps are women."

"My point still stands," he said. "You should wear one of those flouncy little sundresses with the ties at the shoulders and flowy skirt that hits high above your knees. These legs, Mar,"—he ran his broad palm up and down my thigh—"could make anyone do anything."

"Anything?" I asked, shifting in his arms to face him and reaching between us to palm his hardening cock.

"Anything," he confirmed.

"In that case," I said, shoving him onto his back and climbing atop him, his hands continuing their slow exploration of my legs, "I have a few ideas."

chapter 19
Calvin

IN THE WEEK SINCE the Tigers game, Amara had done her best to avoid me, both at work and after. When we'd left Detroit, I thought everything was great, but apparently not. Every text I sent either went unanswered or received a one or two word response. Every time I stopped into her office, she barely looked at me and *always* made sure the door stayed open.

Something was up with her, and today, I was making it my mission to find out what.

It helped that it was the Fourth of July and her parents were hosting a party at their house. If I had it my way, Amara and I would clear the air between us and end the night wrapped in each other's arms.

Parking my car at her house and walking the mile to her parents' may have been a bit presumptuous, but I wanted to ensure she couldn't run away from me if it came down to that.

When I arrived at the Delatous', Skye hooked on the leash dangling from my hand, regret over walking sat heavily on my shoulders like the sweat sliding down my back and face. I skirted the house and joined the group of people in the backyard, going unnoticed for the moment. Before I sought out Amara, I beelined for the food table and used a stack of napkins to mop the worst of the perspiration from my skin, then headed to the bar for a glass of water. Once I slammed it—and two more refills that had my internal temp slowly dropping—I switched to beer. I'd trained Skye well, and she remained glued to my side, only interacting with other partygoers if they gave her attention first.

"Calvin!" a voice called out my name from behind me, and I turned to find Lena Delatou practically gliding across the concrete patio to join me in the shade. She settled her hands on my shoulders and pressed a kiss to my right cheek, then left, offering me a smile as she scratched Skye behind her ears. "It's wonderful to see you. I feel like it's been forever since we've had the chance to chat."

Yeah, since that lunch where I insulted your daughter in front of you. And now I'm fucking her! Funny how things change!

"I've been busy with work," I said instead, shrugging my shoulders in a *what-can-you-do* kind of way.

"That's what I hear," she said. "Though I'm glad you could join us at the Tigers' game last weekend. Although, I heard a rumor that's a bit concerning..."

"You wouldn't happen to be talking about that little stunt he pulled last weekend, would you?" Leon asked as he approached us, sliding his arm around his wife's waist.

"I was just about to bring it up," Lena said.

"Bring what up?" I asked, though I knew where this line of questioning was headed.

"The rumors swirling around town that you're now dating my daughter," Leon said, storm clouds gathering in his green eyes, turning them from emerald to pine in a moment. "What do you have to say for yourself, Ryder?"

A zap of cold raced down my spine.

When Amara called me by my last name? It made me harder than a rock, made me want to fuck her for hours just to hear her chant it again and again as I buried my cock in her.

But when Leon said it?

I wanted to run as far as I could in the opposite direction, or drop to my knees and apologize profusely as long as it meant he wouldn't punch my face in.

"We're not dating," I said at last, surprised by the evenness of my tone.

Technically, it wasn't a lie. We *weren't* dating—in so many words. But over my dead body would either of us be with anyone else.

This severe possessiveness that had taken root in my chest where Amara was concerned was a new development, pretty much showing up around the time I'd first said the word "boyfriend." I'd never experienced it before, which was yet another reason why I should've seen the signs that my relationship with Amie wasn't destined to go the distance.

Leon blinked slowly as my words settled, and I could practically see the gears in his mind turning as he abruptly changed tack. "Well, good!" he boomed. "I may not be your boss anymore, but that warning I issued the day I offered you your job still stands."

Stay the fuck away from my daughters.

Yeah...hate to break it to ya, Leon, but that ship has already sailed.

"Speaking of Amara, though," I said as nonchalantly as I could. "Have you seen her? I need to...apologize for last weekend."

"She was on the lawn playing corn hole with the girls last I saw," Lena said, already turning away from me, presumably to top off her sangria.

With a nod to Leon, ignoring the way his eyes narrowed on me, I turned away from them. The patio and "lawn" beyond, which was really an endless expanse of green space that wouldn't be out of place at some royal residence, were packed with people, including a lot of CD employees and their families. I pushed through the throng, craning my neck over the crowd to search for Amara's dark head.

"Do you see her, girl?" I asked Skye quietly, and she perked up, nostrils flaring like she was trying to scent Amara in the crowd.

I was just about to break through the mass of people onto the grass when a hand grabbed my elbow and pulled me around.

"Cal!" Logan shouted, apparently already deep in his cups, as he hooked his hand into mine and pulled me in for a sloppy bro hug. "Good to see you, man."

"You too," I said, offering him a tight smile.

"What've you been up to?" Logan asked. "I haven't seen you since Memorial Day!"

"You saw me last weekend," I reminded him. When his dark blond brows drew together in confusion, I added, "At the Tigers game?"

"Oh, right!" he said with an over-loud laugh surely brought on by too much of whatever was in his cup, slapping a heavy—and sweaty—palm down on my shoulder.

Not that I could talk. My clothes were still sticky from my walk.

Finally noticing Skye, he knelt to her eye level and said, "And who is this beautiful creature?"

"This is Skye," I said, chuckling as she licked Logan's face.

"I have a Golden too," he said. "Well, Chloe and I do, but I got him before we got together."

"Really? How old."

"Three."

"No shit," I said. "So is she."

"Really?" Logan straightened. "When's her birthday?"

"May 18."

"Holy shit," he breathed. "So is Benji's!"

My brows rose, and after comparing notes, we discovered Skye and Benji were brother and sister. It amazed me how small the world was, and I agreed easily when Logan said we should set up a playdate for them.

A playdate for the pups, and a double date for their parents was exactly my idea of a good time.

"Hey, have you seen the sisters?" I asked, remembering my true mission.

Logan waved a hand toward the water. "They gave up on corn hole when Owen and I beat them and decided to go for a swim."

I raised a brow. "Owen is here?"

"Yeah, man!" Logan said. "He's like one of the fam now. Isn't that so wild? I'm friends with *Owen Lawless*, and my brother-in-law is *Brent Jean*."

He shook his head as if he couldn't quite believe his luck, his slightly shaggy hair swishing around his head, reminding me strongly of the Golden Retriever at my feet.

I had bigger fish to fry, but that actually was a story I'd been dying to hear.

"Yeah, tell me about that," I said, steering him to a couple metal chairs lined with overstuffed cushions pushed up to a large table with an umbrella stuck through the middle, providing us some much needed shade. "How exactly did that happen?"

Logan waved a hand dismissively. "My sister met him while she was in her third year of law school. They dated, fell in love, the whole thing. Now they're married with a one year old and another on the way. Hey!" he said, perking up. "We should go to a Warriors' game this season!"

I grinned widely. "I'd love that."

As long as Amara hadn't killed me first, and as long as she was by my side.

❧ ❦

Almost the entire day had passed, the bulk of the partygoers dispersing unless they were directly related to the Delatous—and me and Owen—and I still hadn't managed to get Amara alone. The effort she'd put into avoiding me would've been impressive if I weren't so damn pissed off about it.

But now, we were heading down to the beach for the fireworks, and there was no way she'd miss those. Ambushing her there was my best—and last—bet.

The Delatou home sat on a cliff overlooking the northernmost point of the Old Mission. Apple Blossom Bay was about ten miles south of us, and until the nineties, the Delatou family had been in charge of the Independence Day Fireworks since they'd moved onto the peninsula and founded the winery in 1911. Now, there were two separate shows—one in town, and one out here.

I bided my time as the sun dipped toward the horizon, nursing a beer and shooting the shit with Owen as the volunteers raced up and down the long, L-shaped dock jutting from Leon and Lena's beach, prepping the fireworks for the show that would take place once it was dark enough.

And when that moment came, when the first warning *boom* echoed over the water, letting us know we had about ten minutes until the show, I made my move, bidding Owen goodbye with a wink. He gave me a head nod in response, Skye dozing at his feet.

I headed to the sand, eyes zeroing in on the littlest Delatou.

"Brie!" I said, jogging up to greet her, helping her spread her blanket out on the sand.

"Hey, Cal," she said slowly.

"Have you seen Amara?" I asked, cutting right to the chase.

"Oh," she said, twirling a lock of her hair around her finger, eyes darting everywhere but toward me. "I think she went up to the house."

"Brie..."

At last, she met my eyes, her expression pleading. "Don't do this to me."

"Where is she?"

"I can't tell you."

"Why not?"

"Because she made us all swear to run interference between you two today. Although, I can't say I blame her after that shit you pulled last weekend…"

"We moved past that," I said quickly. At least, I thought we had. "Please, Brie. I really need to talk to her."

"Why?"

I blinked, surprised. Brie had always been the quietest of the Delatou sisters, which I presumed to be a personality trait developed by being the last born into a family of outspoken women. I'd approached Brie because I thought she'd be the easiest to crack. So the way she was looking at me now? Pure malice shining in her eyes, arms crossed over her chest, feet planted firmly into the sand? Expression telling me I better give her a damn good reason for breaking her sister's trust?

This was an entirely new side of Brie, and I had to admit, I was impressed.

Even that day I'd cornered her at her bakery, she hadn't been this animus.

"That shit I pulled last weekend?" I began, using her own words. "I was mad. She'd taken shots at me during that interview, and…I felt my control slipping. I did the one thing I could think of to get it back. I *know* I fucked up, but *you* have to know I would never do anything to intentionally hurt her. At least, not like that…not again."

Lips pursed, Brie continued to stare me down, as though carefully weighing my words.

It wasn't until I'd spoken them aloud that I realized the truth in them.

This entire time with Amara, our whole work relationship had been a classic power struggle.

And guess what?

I was fucking tired of fighting.

I just wanted *her*.

At last, Brie said, "She's down the beach a ways. Just keep walking that way"—she pointed toward the west—"and you'll find her."

I did as Brie directed, following the curve of the point until I caught sight of Amara at last. She sat on a blanket alone, closer to the beach grasses than the water. The nearest group of her family was a few hundred feet away and around the corner, completely out of sight, though we could still see the dock from here.

I hated that she was hiding from me, the knowledge that she thought she couldn't just talk to me about whatever was eating at her.

Well, not any longer.

"Why have you been avoiding me all day?" I asked as I dropped down onto the blanket beside her.

Amara scoffed. "I haven't been."

"Mar, you won't even look at me right now. What the fuck is going on?"

"I'm mad at you, okay!" she burst out, careful to keep her voice low so as to not attract any attention.

"For what?"

"The whole boyfriend thing!" she hissed.

"I thought we got over that after the game," I said, willing my body not to react, forcing my mind away from thoughts of how she looked in that mirror, my cock in her pussy, my hand at her neck and fingers on her clit.

Christ, Ryder, I thought as my dick twitched. *Get it together.*

"Yeah, well...then I had to come back to work on Monday and deal with my entire staff and family giving me the goddamn third degree about how long we've been together and if it was serious and what that meant for the company. Not to mention the assholes on TikTok tearing me to shreds in the comments on our latest marketing video for the RTDs and"—she inhaled deeply—"it's all your fault!"

Goddamn, she was sexy when she was angry. I wanted to kiss that scowl off her face.

"I'm sorry," I said, though the sincerity of my words was undercut by the snort I let free.

She swatted at me. "This isn't funny, Cal! You're causing a lot of problems for me. Problems, I'll remind you, I wouldn't have to deal with if I was a man."

"I can't do anything about that," I said, taking a risk and reaching for her. Surprisingly, she came to me willingly, letting me tuck her against my side, my arm slung across her shoulders, fingers toying with the end of one of her braids. "I quite like you as a woman. In fact, it's my favorite thing about you."

"Don't be cute right now."

"You're spiraling," I said calmly. "Why?"

"I just told you!"

"There's more to it than that, Mar. C'mon, Princess. Tell me what's really going on."

I reached out with my other hand, brushing my fingers lightly up and down the length of her smooth thigh. Goosebumps that I knew had nothing to do with the slight breeze blowing in off the lake broke out on her skin.

"Don't you think this whole thing between us is just...too messy? Don't you think we're moving too fast?"

"No," I said firmly, "This thing between us? It's the best thing in my life right now. And so what if we're moving a little quicker than normal couples would. I don't know about you, but after five years of denying myself, I'm trying to make up for lost time with you." I gripped her chin in my hand and angled her head toward me, staring straight into her eyes. "I'm falling for you, Amara. I have been for a while. I acted like a jackass because I didn't know you like I do now, and I'm sorry for that. I'm sorry I ever doubted you."

Her gaze shot to mine, golden eyes, barely glowing in the light of the dying day, darting across my face, searching for any insincerity.

I knew she wouldn't find it.

"You mean that?"

I nodded. "The stuff about me being your boyfriend last weekend? I can admit now that was a power play. But I failed to consider just how bad it would make you look, and how deeply it would undermine your successes. And they are *your* successes, Mar. I may have signed off on the money, but you took what I gave you—"

"A fucking joke of a budget," she cut in.

"—and ran with it, turning it into a product offering that I know is going to make waves when we take it national."

"You mean it?" she asked again, her voice so small, so...unsure.

"Of course I do," I said, then scooped her up and onto my lap so she straddled me. "You are impressive. More so than I ever imagined. In the bedroom, in the boardroom. Everywhere. So yeah, maybe the boyfriend shit was a joke—at first. But the more I think about it, the more I truly would love nothing more than to be just that."

"Are you asking me to be your girlfriend officially?" she asked, a slow grin blooming on her face.

"Yes," I said, catching her lips in a quick kiss. "Do we have a deal?"

She tapped her forefinger to her chin, as though deeply considering it. In response, I rose and flipped her until she was on her back, laughing as I hovered over her.

"You've got a deal, Ryder," she said, then added, "For what it's worth, I'm falling for you too."

I grinned at the same moment the first of the fireworks exploded overhead, the multicolored sparkles reflected in her eyes.

"Tell me, Princess," I said, bending closer until our lips were a breath apart. "Anyone ever kiss the shit out of you below a fireworks show?"

"Just this super hot male model in Ibiza," she said with a shrug.

"What'd I tell you about bringing your fuck boys into our bed?"

"Technically, we're not in bed."

"Amara..." I warned.

With a giggle and a sigh, she lifted her hands to bracket my hips, pulling me closer. "No, Cal. No one I care about has ever kissed the shit out of me below a fireworks show."

"You're damn right," I said, then finally slanted my mouth over hers.

chapter 20
Amara

CAL AND I BARELY watched the fireworks, too intent on exchanging long, teasing, all-consuming kisses to pay much attention to our surroundings. By the time we stumbled back down the beach, bid my sisters good night—to knowing smirks and murmured comments from each of them, particularly Delia—we raced back to my house.

"Do you have to go home?" I asked as we tumbled inside, his mouth on my neck, his hands...everywhere.

"Why? You trying to get rid of me, Princess?"

"Never," I breathed as he sucked that sensitive patch of skin over my pulse into his mouth and released it with a *pop*. "Just wondering about Skye."

"Owen's got her," he said as he led me backward toward the stairs.

"So you're all mine?"

We crossed the threshold into my bedroom, and Cal pushed me down on the bed, towering over me, a wicked smile on his face.

"Always," he said, his hands going to the button of his khaki shorts. "Where should we start?"

I reached out and pulled him toward me with my hands on his hips, replacing his fingers on his fly with mine. With me seated and him standing, I was right at eye level with his groin.

"I want your cock," I said as I shoved his shorts and boxers to his ankles, his length springing free, mere inches from my watering mouth. He kicked out of them, then whipped his shirt off.

"You've got it," he said, hands going to my hair. "Do your worst."

I leaned away, my gaze roaming over his beautifully sculpted body, his golden skin glowing in the moonlight filtering through the curtains on my bedroom windows. Despite the fact that Cal spent his days at a desk, the man was built for hard work. Every muscle was perfectly honed, from the slopes of his shoulders and biceps to his strong, sinewy forearms. His pecs were ridiculous—no man needed a chest that big—and I reached out, tracing each dip and swell of his abdominals with a finger, smiling when they jumped under my touch. His thighs were thick, tapering to delicious calves.

Yes, *delicious.* Not a weakness I thought I had, but everything about Cal's body was kryptonite for me. I can't believe I'd ever called him a pretty boy. I'd happily run my hands and mouth over every curve and crevice, learn his body until I knew it better than I knew my own.

And I wanted to start with his dick. I'd already had it, but rushed, sloppy, on the beach when Cal refused to let me toy and explore until I knew exactly what got him there.

I took him in my hand, squeezing gently at the base then worked up toward the tip.

Brushing my thumb over the moisture beaded at the tip, I asked, "How do you like it?"

"A little rough," he admitted, his voice hoarse. "Use your teeth."

Fuck. The thought had me clenching my thighs together, desperate for friction. But my own needs could wait. This moment was about Cal, about making him feel good, about returning the favor—giving him a little taste of all the pleasure he'd awarded me the past few months.

I raised my eyes to his as I angled him so I could lick a long path on the underside of his shaft, and he groaned, the hand in my hair tightening.

"Hasn't anyone ever told you it's not nice to play with your food?"

I chuckled but squeezed him tighter at the root as I sealed my mouth over his tip.

"Fuck, Mar," he said, his hips jolting forward on reflex. I pulled off and swirled my tongue around his head, pressing the tip into that slit at the top, letting his salty flavor burst on my tongue before diving back in. "That's it, Princess. Eat that dick like the good girl you are."

I moaned around him. For the buttoned up business man persona he presented to the world, the man had a surprisingly filthy mouth. I could listen to him whisper dirty things in my ear all night and get off on that alone, never needing him to touch me.

But god, when he touched me, like now with the simple act of him tracing his finger around my lips as I took him deep, his head branding the back of my throat? I squeezed my thighs tighter together, desperately trying to relieve the ache.

As I picked up the pace, bobbing my head faster, circling my wrist as my fingers chased my mouth's path, he moaned.

His fingers dug into my scalp, and he held me in place as he pulled out. I made a noise of protest, but he tilted my head back, bending to look at me. "I need to taste you."

"Fine," I said, scrambling back on the bed. "But I get bottom."

Cal frowned. "No. I want you to sit that perfect ass on my face."

"And I want you to fuck my face."

"I can do that from the bottom."

"You're wasting time, Cal," I said, tempting him onto the bed over me by snaking my hand between my thighs and spreading my pussy open, showing him how fucking wet I was for him.

Cal climbed up next to me with a sigh, dropping a kiss to my mouth before shifting so his dick dangled in my face. I reached up as he settled his head between my thighs, his shifting until they rested along the sides of my head, and pressed a finger into his perineum.

He bucked. "Do that again."

"Get to work," I said in response, but did as he asked, this time gripping his hips to bring him closer and tracing my tongue along that smooth skin behind his balls. He rewarded me by plunging two fingers inside me and sealing his mouth over my clit.

Hell, I wasn't going to last long, but judging by the way he did as I'd asked earlier and fucked my face, his hips moving back and forth of their own accord, neither was he.

We entered some sort of unspoken competition, both of us trying our damnedest to make the other go first. Before long, there was nothing but sensation, of Cal's sleek, impossibly hard cock sliding between my lips, of his mouth slipping through my pussy, flicking at my clit as his fingers pumped in and out of me, curling against that spot that had my legs shaking well before I was ready.

I let go first, the clenching of my inner wall around his fingers, meant to hold back my building orgasm, only spurred it on and set me off. I moaned around Cal's cock as I writhed and shook beneath him, as he maintained exquisite suction on my clit until I came down at last.

Without a word, Cal rolled off me and palmed his cock, jutting obscenely from his body. I'd never understand how it fit inside me, but every time he pressed into me, that delicious burn only heightened my desire, only got me there that much quicker.

"Come sit."

He didn't have to tell me twice, and I quickly scrambled up and settled myself over his lap, replacing his hand with my own and lining up his tip at my entrance.

We let out twin sighs of relief as I sank onto him.

"Good girl," he said, though the words were bit off by a low groan as I swiveled my hips atop him, working him deeper.

Sex with Cal in any position was a guarantee for me—something I could grudgingly admit had never been the case with anyone else—but being on top like this was easily my favorite. I raised my hands to my head and buried them in my hair as I shifted my hips back and forth, raising off and dropping down in quick, smooth movements. Cal manscaped around his dick, which I'd always appreciated. Only, he left a little happy trail that extended from his root to right below his belly button just for me. He knew how much I loved the rough friction against my smooth clit when I rode him like this. Arching my back so my tits popped out and bounced, Cal reached up, filling his hands with them, and pinched my nipples between his fingers, the sensation jolting straight between my thighs.

It didn't take either of us long to get there as I rolled my hips against him, riding him into oblivion. When my walls clamped around him, when I fell onto his chest as I broke apart, Cal followed me off that cliff, and he spilled inside me, biting down lightly on my earlobe as he moaned low and long.

When we'd stilled, when the sweat on our bodies cooled and our breathing returned to normal, Cal pulled himself up to sitting, arms wrapped tightly around me so he could shift himself out. I could feel our combined releases dripping down my thighs, and Cal reached between us, swiping a finger through and stuffing it back inside me. I twitched.

"You like my cum running down your thighs?"

I nodded.

"Dirty girl."

"Only for you."

"Damn straight."

Then he rose, me still in his arms, and carried me to the bathroom, placing me on the counter. Wordlessly, he retrieved a cloth from the linen closet, wet it, and mopped me up with gentle swipes, knowing I was still sensitive.

"You are an enigma," I said when he tossed the rag and kissed my cheek, and Cal stilled, the skin between his eyes puckering in confusion. "You say the filthiest things to me, use my body as your own personal plaything, fill me with your cum...and clean me up after with such reverence. As though my body is your temple."

He bent to press his forehead against mine. "You deserved to be worshiped, Mar. I'm just doing my duty."

The words had my heart clenching, had a crazy, unthinkable phrase pushing against my teeth, begging to be set free.

But I wouldn't—couldn't—entertain it. Not yet.

I sucked in a breath and said, "Thank you."

His answering smile was so sweet, I could do nothing but mirror it.

Then he lifted me off the counter and set me on my feet.

"I don't know about you," he said, "but I'm starving—for food."

"I like the way you think, Ryder."

We moved back into my room, Cal pulling on his boxers as I shrugged on one of the tees he'd left here before and a pair of fresh panties.

Twenty minutes later, we were back in bed with bags of chips and bowls of macaroni and cheese. Cal reclined against the frame, the steaming bowl dwarfed in his big hands. I sat pressed against his side, my legs slung across his lap as I dug into my own meal.

"You grew up in Wisconsin, right?" I asked.

Cal nodded. "Near Green Bay."

"How'd you end up in Michigan then? I mean, I know you

went to GVSU, but...why?"

"Scholarship," he said. "I applied to probably fifty colleges across the country, and was accepted to most of them, but Grand Valley offered me the most money."

After that, the words poured from him, and I quietly ate while his own food grew cold as he talked. He told me about his parents, hippies who were nearly forty when he was born. Explained how they'd never planned on having children, and suddenly being responsible for one wasn't their idea of a good time, this man and woman who had since been traipsing across the country, smoking weed, picking up odd jobs in exchange for necessities, and living in an old school Volkswagen van.

According to Cal, they'd decided to settle near Green Bay before he was born because a man they'd met in their travels had offered his dad, Clint, a job at his mechanic shop. Unable to turn down steady work with the knowledge they'd soon have another life to support, one who needed stability and community, Clint happily accepted.

"It was an adjustment for them," he said. "Putting down roots after so many years going wherever the wind and their whims took them."

"In what way?"

Cal dropped his head, going quiet as he presumably lost himself to the memories of his upbringing.

"I don't think they knew what to do with me," he said quietly. "I was...a bit of a loner."

Difficult to imagine, considering how easily he managed to snag my attention the night we met—and never let it go.

A dam had broken now, and Cal spilled all his secrets at my

feet. How his parents had been present in passing. They'd ask about his homework when he started school, try to get him to talk about books he was reading, ask about friends and after school activities. They'd made sure he got where he needed to go when he needed to be there, and bought him a little beater of a truck—an ancient Chevy S10 with nearly two hundred thousand miles—when he turned sixteen, effectively checking out of his life.

"I came and went when I wanted, didn't have a curfew, and generally did what I pleased. They just...didn't seem to care. I could've been into drugs and alcohol, having all the sex in the world, and I doubt they would've noticed. By the time I reached my senior year, my mom had opened her studio, and Dad had retired from the shop and begun woodworking."

"And were you?" I asked, peering up into his face. "Were you doing drugs, drinking, and fucking your way through your pretty little classmates?"

I chose to ignore the hint of jealousy that laced my tone.

Cal did as well, simply placing a warm palm on my thigh and giving it a squeeze. Reminding me he was here with me and he wasn't going anywhere.

"No," he said with a chuckle, answering my question at last. "I've never done drugs, didn't get drunk for the first time until my first week of college, and lost my virginity shortly after."

I blinked, surprised.

"You're even more of an enigma than I thought," I said quietly. "But I'm not going to lie...I don't think that boy would've been able to handle me."

"You would've scared the shit out of eighteen-year-old Cal," he agreed.

"And how does thirty-three-year-old Cal feel?"

"I feel…" He trailed off, and I braced myself. "I feel like you could ruin me—and I'd happily let you."

"Same," I said, swallowing hard. "You're an amazing man. I hope you know that. Despite your upbringing, you're…pretty perfect."

"I just wish it hadn't taken me moving nearly four hundred miles away to find the family I should've already had, you know? The kids at school growing up didn't want anything to do with me. I was 'weird'"—he put air quotes around the word—"because I preferred books to people and wore thrifted clothes, or my dad's hand-me-downs when I got tall enough. I had glasses and was gangly. I didn't go through puberty until I was a sophomore in college."

A late bloomer, then. Not that I was complaining, because this version of Cal? Not only his body—which, admittedly, was a fucking dream and responsible for delivering me pleasure unlike anything I'd known before him—but his mind. His care and kindness. His loyalty. Every beautifully flawed and a little broken piece made him into the man before me. And for that, I would always be grateful.

"I spent my twenties searching for the relationships I never had growing up," he said. "The close friendships, the romantic relationships, the family. At least I found one of those."

"Two," I corrected, and he cocked his head. "We're in a romantic relationship, aren't we?"

"Yes," he breathed. "Yes we are."

The look in his eyes had grown distant, lost somewhere in the past, and I would do anything to bring him back to me. I took his barely-touched bowl from his hand and set it next to mine on the nightstand behind me, tucking the bags of chips in beside them.

Then I shifted over him, straddling his lap, and gripped his face in my hands. I didn't say anything, simply dropped my mouth to his, trying to imbue the kiss with everything I felt for him, trying to remind him that even on his darkest days, when his eyes took on that faraway look, he had me. His lips moved softly against mine, this kiss far more tender than any we'd ever shared before.

"Let's get some sleep," I said when I pulled away.

Cal simply nodded, then rose from the bed to brush his teeth, me padding along behind him. When that was done, I peeled back the covers and slid in. Cal got in behind me, pulling my body flush against his, burying his face in my hair. I could feel him relax behind me, as though I were an anchor keeping him from drifting away, a life raft in the middle of the vast sea.

And I'd happily be that for him, gladly do whatever it took to rid him of that hauntedness in his eyes.

I was straddling the line between awake and asleep when Cal's whispered words in the dark pulled me back like a vice around my heart.

"I've never been in love, I don't think."

"Neither have I," I whispered back.

"I don't think anyone has ever loved me either," he added. "Not even the two people who are supposed to."

My heart dropped. The pain in his words, the way his arms tightened imperceptibly around me—it was the most gut-wrenching thing I'd ever experienced.

"Your parents do love you," I said, spinning in his arms so I faced him, so I could snake my arms around him and rub soothing circles across the broad expanse of his back. His parents may have been hands off in his upbringing, but for both of us, I had to believe they cared about him in that way parents intrinsically loved the things born of their own flesh. They may not have understood him, but I had to believe deep down, they cared for him and loved him in their own way.

It would be impossible not to.

He pulled me closer, tucking my head under his chin.

His next words were so quiet, barely above a soft exhale into the room. "I'm really not sure they do."

There was nothing I could say in response to that, nothing I could say that would undo thirty-three years of this stubborn man believing this about himself—about his parents. So instead, I banded my arms around him, pressing my face into his chest and inhaling deeply. His heartbeat was a steady thrum between us, intertwining and beating in time with mine, and I let them wash over me.

Not long after, his breath slowed and evened out as he drifted off at last, though his arms maintained their grip around me. I pressed a kiss to his chest and burrowed deeper into him, wishing I could welcome him into my mind to see how much I cared about him, wishing I could absorb all of his emotional pain into my body so he would no longer have to live with it.

I'd been lucky to grow up the way I had. With four sisters and parents who loved each other and us, and weren't afraid to show us every day. Even when we screwed up, even when we angered or disappointed them, I never doubted that.

Cal needed that sort of presence in his life, someone who loved him through all the ups and downs.

Eventually, I fell asleep myself, making a silent promise to myself and Cal as I did.

Don't worry, I thought. *I'll love you enough for everyone who never did.*

THE NEXT MONTH CAME and went in a flash of work and Cal, and before I knew it, I was staring down the barrel of August. I had roughly a month to plan and properly execute my Labor Day Weekend event, and I was starting to realize I needed some help.

A quick phone call earned me a meeting with the hottest party planner in the area, but she could only squeeze me in this afternoon. In fact, I'd met with her earlier in the summer, but then life—and Cal—had distracted me from following up with her until now.

"Cindy, clear my schedule this afternoon," I said to my assistant as I breezed out of my office. "I have a meeting in town with a party planner and I'm not sure when I'll be back."

"You got it, boss!"

Fifteen minutes later, I was pulling up to my house, desperate to get inside and strip out of the slacks I'd chosen to wear this morning. It had been a lot cooler when I'd left for the office, but the clouds that had shaded the sun had dispersed by midmorning, and the temperature rose rapidly. I was sweating my ass off.

I rushed inside, dropping my purse and keys unceremoniously on the floor in the foyer, then took the stairs two at a time to the second floor. I sighed in relief when I hooked my thumbs into the waistband of my pants and peeled them off, the cool, air conditioned air a soothing balm to my heated flesh. I closed my eyes against a slight wave of dizziness, surely brought on by the heat and the fact that I hadn't eaten yet today. Once I was steady again, I padded to my closet and sifted through the hanging clothes until my fingers curled into the fabric of my favorite skirt—knee length, silky, slightly looser than form-fitting, and a shade of gold that mirrored my eyes. Paired with a short-sleeved white button-up with a little tie at the hem, right over my navel, I looked perfect for a midday business meeting.

A quick check of my watch told me I had ten minutes to make it into town to meet Amie at Granny's, where she suggested we get together for a late lunch and some drinks. I recommended the winery, but she said she was "in the mood for one of Granny's greasy burgers."

Truthfully, I hadn't even known the woman knew what Granny's was. She owned a boutique hotel at the base of the peninsula and this party planning business on the side. She was highly sought after and only took on select clients, so I was grateful my last name had at least gotten me a foot in the door.

Contrary to popular belief, it wasn't a card I liked to play, but I wasn't above using it when necessary.

And making this Labor Day weekend a success? That was my highest priority.

On my way out the door, my phone buzzed with a message from Cal, but I ignored it. He could wait until later; if I didn't leave now, I'd be late.

Honestly, the last month with Cal had been...surprising. After the confrontation on the beach on the Fourth, it was like a switch had been flipped between us. Where every glance, every touch before had been laced with simmering hatred and the desire to unsettle the other, now those glances and touches only fueled the fire between us. We could hardly keep our hands off each other, and we'd nearly been caught fucking at the office enough times that I'd had to implement a moratorium on having sex at work.

I'm not going to lie, keeping my hands to myself was a true test of my self-control. When he walked in wearing those chinos that clung perfectly to the sculpted globes of his ass, and he rolled the cuffs of his button up shirt to his elbows, exposing those forearms that, if you looked closely, bore scratches from my nails digging into his skin? I wanted to tear his clothes from his body and ride him right there.

But that was the opposite of professional, and I had an image to uphold.

Leaving my side-by-side where I'd parked it, I climbed into my little two-seater Jeep, the doors currently off and the top nowhere to be seen, hoping Amie wouldn't think me a slob for showing up with wind-blown hair. The vehicle wasn't practical in the winter, and I had an SUV I drove in the months we got snow, but I couldn't resist purchasing this as a fun toy for the warmer months. To me, there was nothing better than riding around with the windows down and the music up loud. My sisters and I had done that endlessly growing up, content to cruise the backroads of the peninsula, exploring the uncharted corners of winery lands, making plans for the future. What we'd do with our own property one day, what our houses would look like, how many rooms we'd need for imaginary children.

With the doors missing and no top, that nostalgia was amplified, a joyous bubble in my chest, expanding so large I thought I could burst with the force of it.

So yeah. I didn't give a fuck about my hair as long as I could experience a few moments of that childhood emotion again.

I'd just turned left out of my driveway onto the two-track that would take me to the highway that ran through town, but my progress was halted by a shiny silver truck approaching from the opposite direction. I steered off to the side and stopped as Cal pulled up next to me.

"Hey, beautiful," he said with a grin. "Where are you headed?"

"Hey, handsome," I responded. "I'm off to Granny's. Lunch meeting."

"Can I come?"

"Always," I said with a smirk.

Cal laughed and said, "Not what I meant."

"I know," I said happily. "But if you want to, go for it. Although I'm warning you, I'm meeting with the party planner for the Labor Day party. It's probably going to be boring as hell for you."

"Not possible as long as you're there," he said.

I lost the fight against the blush rising to my cheeks, then said, "Go park in the drive. I'll swing around and get you."

A minute later, I was back on the two-track, this time with Cal at my side, his hand resting indecently high on my thigh, Morgan Wallen blasting from the speakers.

"I haven't been to Granny's in ages," Cal said. "I can't wait to gorge myself on one of Tanya's buffalo burgers."

My stomach lurched at the thought. "Gross," I said, making a face that had him laughing. "I want a brunch burger and the biggest plate of sweet potato fries I can get my hands on."

"For you, I'm willing to bet that's a pretty big plate."

I shot him a glare, but he wasn't entirely wrong.

The Delatou roots ran deep in this town, considering the winery had been founded a scant thirteen years after the town itself, and remained the sole enterprise in the area until the mid-fifties, when my great-grandpa finally relaxed his iron fist enough to start selling some of the land that bordered the town. What had formerly been a church, five and dime store, and minuscule post office branch with a few blocks of small, craftsman-style homes quickly grew into an actual town practically overnight. By the end of the fifties, there was a diner, bar, and bank branch, as well as a small schoolhouse and double the number of homes.

The town continued to expand from there until it eventually reached the edges of the land great-grandpa had been willing to part with. Both Papou and Dad had since sold more, but on a peninsula that was only three miles across at its widest point, there was only so far the town could grow.

All that to say, in the early days of their marriage, Papou had gifted my grandma the stretch of land that now served as Main Street and a blank check, telling her to "go out and make yourself useful."

Granny had built the restaurant from the ground up and

named it after her maiden name, just to piss Papou off.

And thus, Granny Smith's was born.

Though my family no longer owned the business—Dad had sold it in the nineties, after Granny passed, in order to focus his time and attention elsewhere—we were still considered something of VIP guests around the place.

I supposed it didn't hurt that our family photos still lined the walls. Another long-standing Apple Blossom Bay family had purchased the restaurant from Dad and kept it exactly as is, telling us it didn't make sense to fix something that wasn't broken.

Although, the clientele had certainly changed over the years, as had the menu. During the day, it was great for greasy burgers and oversized plates of pasta. At night, they served appetizer platters and tap beer.

I pulled up in front and got out, Cal meeting me at the hood and grabbing my hand to pull me toward the door. The streets were teeming with people, adults and children alike, dashing around, cones melting in hands, bags full of souvenir trinkets weighing down arms. This was truly my favorite time of the year, when the town was once again full of life instead of the winter months when it seemed more like a desolate, post-apocalyptic, snow-covered wasteland than one of the hottest summer destinations in the entire country.

"So who exactly are we meeting?" Cal asked as he let go of my hand to pull the door open for me.

I blinked rapidly as my eyes adjusted to the dim interior, searching to see if she'd arrived yet. She caught my attention with a wave, and I pulled Cal toward her.

"Cal, this is—"

"Amie," he said, jaw tense, the muscles there jumping as he ground his teeth together. The joy from his face a moment ago had simply...vanished, replaced by something I couldn't quite put a name to. It looked as though he'd seen a ghost.

"Yeah, Amie," I said slowly, narrowing my eyes and glancing between them. "You guys know each other?"

"You could say that," Cal said.

"Calvin!" Amie said, approaching him, settling her short-nailed fingers—painted a pink so pale it was practically white—on his shoulders and leaning in to kiss one of his cheeks, then the other. "It's good to see you. It's been too long."

Cal offered her a tight smile, but Amie was already turning away. "Not long enough," he muttered under his breath.

"What the fuck?" I hissed.

"I'll tell you later."

I halted his path to the table with a hand on his arm. "Are you good? You don't have to be here."

"Actually, I think I'll run over to Brie's," he said. "Or the diner. I just...I'm sorry, Princess. I just can't."

He gave me a tense smile, dropped a quick kiss on my lips, and was gone.

I blinked after him, unsure what the hell had just happened.

"So, you and Calvin Ryder?" Amie asked from behind me. "Isn't he like...your employee?"

"Technically," I said, sliding into the seat across from her. "But...have you seen him? I couldn't stay away. And he's a really great guy."

"Trust me," Amie said with a knowing smile. "I know the

feeling. And I'm sure he's definitely not the same man he was three years ago."

"Wait...what?" I asked dumbly.

"He didn't tell you?" Amie said, that smile of hers going practically feline. "Calvin and I dated for, what was it?" She tapped her finger to her chin, thinking. Then, "About two years. He even proposed. But things just didn't work out."

Cal had *proposed*? No fucking wonder he couldn't get out of here fast enough. Clearly, I was oblivious to the specifics of their relationship, but if things had fallen apart after he'd proposed, I knew Cal well enough to know he'd see that as a personal failure, no matter who was at fault. He'd be embarrassed, and he would've wanted to stay away from Amie.

And I'd unwittingly dragged him back into her orbit.

No, I corrected myself. I'd unwittingly dragged *us* into her orbit.

And now, like a putz, I had to sit through a meeting with the woman, pretending I wasn't a swirling well of anxiety and questions, pretending I didn't know this woman was as intimately familiar with my boyfriend as I was.

This town was too small.

My stomach churned, my head light with anxiety and annoyance and...jealousy. Yeah, I was jealous of this woman, with her pointy features that somehow managed to be delicate and fierce, ice blue eyes, ice blonde hair, long, lithe body. And she was clearly successful, something I knew Cal admired deeply in a partner. How the hell had he ended up with me when he'd once been with her?

A waitress approached our table, saving us for the moment

from having to make awkward small talk while we ordered food and drinks. I got my brunch burger and sweet potato fries, requesting a buffalo burger for Cal to go, even though the thought made me want to vomit. I also ordered a margarita, hoping the alcohol would soothe the panic rising in my chest. Amie ordered a marg as well, and the green olive burger with onion rings on the side.

"I've been looking forward to this all day," she said sometime later when our food had arrived, then closed her mouth around a massive bite.

I'd never been an olive girl to begin with, but the scent of the green olives cooked into her hamburger stuffed itself up my nose, churning my already unsettled stomach. Between bites, I explained to Amie what I wanted for the party, where we were having it, the number of guests, and other pertinent information. Not that I was sold on working with her. If she made my man uncomfortable, I'd be a shitty partner to even consider hiring her.

While we ate, I rifled through my mental Rolodex, searching for another name, another company—anyone who could help me that wasn't Amie.

And then it hit me—I had four sisters who loved nothing more than party planning, *and* they were free. I wanted this party to be a success, and I knew my sisters would do whatever it took to make that a reality for me.

So, politely, I allowed Amie to take notes and run through ideas while I nodded at the proper moments and sipped my water, leaving my marg untouched after one sip had me gagging.

"I'm sorry," I said at last, holding up a hand to halt Amie

as she began discussing her fee and payment. "I really am not feeling well, so I need to find Cal and get going." Blessedly, the waitress arrived with Cal's to-go order, and I dropped some cash into her hand to cover the entire meal—mine and Amie's. "But unfortunately, this isn't going to work out after all. I appreciate you coming down here, and I'm sorry to have wasted your time."

A half-eaten onion ring fell from her gaping mouth as I turned away, and I couldn't help the small satisfied chuckle that escaped me.

Once outside, I inhaled deeply, willing the fresh air to quell the nausea in my stomach. Then I called Cal, who appeared at my side in moments.

"Can you drive?" I asked, passing him the keys. "I'm not feeling well."

"Sure thing," he said, pressing a kiss to my forehead then leading me to the Jeep.

The bumpy ride home was hell on my stomach, and I was barely out of the car before I was losing what little I'd managed to eat at the edge of my gravel drive. When I straightened, Cal swept me off my feet and carried me inside. I didn't have the energy to protest, especially not when we barely made it to my room before I was dashing into the bathroom to puke again. Cal followed me in, but the second he settled a hand on my back, I screamed at him to go away.

I didn't want him to see me like this.

Untold minutes—hours, days—later, I finally returned to my room, fully expecting to find Cal had left. Instead, he was propped up against my headboard, long legs stretched in front of him, watching reruns of one of the earlier seasons of *Southern*

Charm on the TV.

I crawled in next to him and buried my face in my hands.

"How are you feeling?" he asked quietly. A moment later, his hand settled on my head, his fingers brushing soothingly through my hair.

"Better," I said. "Hopefully it's just a bug from something I ate yesterday and not like the flu. I don't have time for the flu."

"Well, lucky for you," he said, rolling onto his side and scooping an arm under me to haul me against him, "it's Friday, so you don't have to leave this bed until Monday if you don't want."

"I had plans with my sisters this weekend," I grumbled.

"Don't care. You're staying here until we're sure it was just a little bug."

"Yes, sir," I said, grinning against his chest when he pinched my side.

"Brat," he said, squeezing me tight for a moment before letting go completely, his touch and weight next to me vanishing a moment later.

I lifted my head. "Where are you going?"

"To get Skye," he said simply.

"But...why?"

"You're sick, Mar. You don't seriously think I'm going to leave you here alone all weekend, do you?"

My heart swelled. For how tense and tenuous the early stages of our relationship was, it amazed me how easy it was to be with him now. How he was willing to spend time with me, take care of me because I wasn't feeling well, without me even having to ask. How he was going back to the city—a thirty minute drive one way—simply to get his dog so he didn't again have to leave my side until I was feeling better.

I don't know what I did to deserve him, but I was damn thankful for it.

Bending over me, he pressed a light, sweet kiss to my forehead. "I'll be back soon."

To his retreating form, I said, "We'll talk about Amie when you are."

Cal stiffened in the doorway, turning his head only enough for me to see his slight, terse nod before he disappeared.

chapter 22
Amara

C ALWASBACKIN a little over an hour, and he entered my house—Skye racing in ahead of him and slip-sliding across my hardwood floors—with his arms laden with shopping bags.

"What's all this?" I asked as I shuffled down the stairs toward him. Skye leapt at me, and I barely managed to stay upright.

"Skye!" Cal scolded. "Down!"

The pup obeyed, sitting her fluffy white-blonde butt on the floor, shaggy golden tail sweeping happily behind her as she stared expectantly at me.

In the months since Cal and I had gotten together the first time, Skye and I had perfected this little song and dance. With a scratch under her chin, I moved past her and opened the pantry, withdrawing one of the artisan dog treats Cal insisted on buying for her because the mass produced ones "are full of bad shit."

Approaching her again, her little head tilted at an unnatural angle as she tracked my movements, I knelt in front of her and said, "Paw."

She lifted her right leg, setting her paw in my hand.

I gave it a shake, then, "Other one"

Skye obeyed, and I rewarded her with the treat, which she devoured in one crunch of her teeth and one big swallow.

Then she trotted off to curl up in the dog bed I'd bought her a few weeks ago, and Cal heaved his load of groceries into the kitchen.

"I bought some stuff to make soup for dinner," he said, answering my question from minutes ago at last. "It's not Ezra's cooking, but..."

"It'll be perfect," I said earnestly, my heart squeezing as I considered his thoughtfulness.

I was struck then by how wrong I'd been about this man. But then again, maybe I hadn't been that wrong at all.

The night we met, I'd been drawn to him in a way I couldn't quite put words to. Even now, over five years later, I didn't think I could accurately explain it. It was just...there—some invisible string tying us together, pulling us in, connecting us in a way I'd never experienced with anyone else before. He'd once told me it felt like he had a tether around his chest, dragging him toward me, and it was an apt description. Truthfully, I'd never anticipated that I'd find this, find the same kind of happiness and bone deep contentment as my parents or Chloe and Logan.

Figured Calvin Ryder would be the one to prove me wrong.

Cal moved around my kitchen as though he'd been preparing meals in there for years instead of only a few months. The way he commanded the space was so sexy, and I could easily picture endless nights and mornings just like this one, where he cooked for me while I sat at the island with a glass of wine and we talked about our days, or when I cooked for him and he sipped a beer and studied me in that quiet way of his.

I let the comfortable silence between us stretch as he chopped vegetables and prepared the soup base, unwilling to pop the bubble quite yet.

But, eventually, I could no longer hold my tongue.

"So...Amie," I said slowly.

Cal, whose back was to me, stiffened at her name, and I winced. My intention was never to hurt him or dredge up painful memories, but if we were together now, if we were making a serious go at this whole relationship thing, I deserved to know.

Didn't I?

With a sigh, he lowered the heat on the stove to a simmer and turned toward me.

"What about her?"

Half expecting him to launch into some story about how she wasn't important and it was in the past, his question surprised me. Like he was giving me free reign to pry as deep as I wanted, to ask whatever questions came to my mind.

So I spit out the first one I could think of.

"What happened with the engagement?"

"There never was an engagement," he said. "I asked, she said no. That was the end of it."

The space between us went quiet. I was...shocked. That Amie had this man on a knee, offering to spend his life with her, and had turned him down was unimaginable.

"I'm sorry," I said quietly.

I was equally surprised when he opened his mouth and the entire story poured out. How they'd met not long after he'd moved to the area, shortly after Amie had bought the hotel. It used to have a tiny little cafe in the lobby that she'd since converted into a luxury gift shop for guests, and apparently they'd caught each other's eyes the first time Cal had gone there for lunch.

"It was...easy with her," he said, offering me an apologetic smile that I understood.

Nothing between *us* had ever been easy, but I honestly wouldn't have it any other way.

"Then why did she say no?"

"That just wasn't something she wanted," he said with a little shrug, though the brief flash of pain across his eyes belied the gesture. "She wasn't interested in the whole wedding ordeal, the kids, the house on the water. She was happy the way things were between us, and I couldn't—" He paused, swallowing hard. "I want all those things, Mar. A family of my own. To build a life with someone."

I knew that about him thanks to endless nights of pillow talk in which he'd filled me in on his upbringing. The older parents who weren't sure what to do with him, this precocious, curious, too-smart-for-his-own-damn-good little boy who had a heart too big for his chest. The kids at school who didn't really understand him. How he'd never really felt like he belonged until he moved away to college and started meeting new people outside of the same ones he'd known in his small town his entire life.

And as the second eldest in a family of five girls, I assured him that was something I wanted too—the house with a white picket fence, two or three kids, falling asleep next to my husband every night and waking up with him in the mornings. Forever.

That was the dream, and for all the flaws I'd perceived in Cal in those early days, it was surprising to find a man whose values and desires for the future were so in line with my own.

"I'm sorry," I said again. "But..."

"Here we go."

I reclined slightly on my stool and shot him a glare. "What's that supposed to mean?"

"You've been far too understanding up to this point," he said. "You met my ex today, Mar. The woman I wanted to *marry*. I know you well enough to know that can't be sitting well with you. Maybe that's why you puked your guts up when we got home."

"That's *not* why I got sick," I said defensively, though I couldn't entirely rule out the possibility. I hadn't truly started to feel nauseous until that bomb had dropped and exploded in my lap.

"Suuuuuuuure," Cal said, drawing out the single syllable with a wink. "Now let's hear this 'but.'"

"I wish you would've told me before," I said. "I was fucking blindsided in there."

"To be fair, it's not like I knew who we were going to meet until I walked into Granny's and saw her face, until you said her name. I don't know about all the skeletons in your closet, after all."

"You damn sure do!" I protested. "In case you've forgotten, you've taken every opportunity to throw my...European promiscuity in my face."

In truth, I hadn't been as loose as I'd let him believe, but any time he'd taken that particular dig at me, it had been easier to agree, to let him continue to think the worst of me. I'd truly believed there'd be no changing his mind.

Another instance in which I was glad to be wrong, but now that we were here, having this conversation, I supposed I *could* set him straight.

"It's not like you've ever kept that part of your life a secret, Princess."

Over the years, that nickname had been uttered in so many connotations—exasperation, anger, disgust, and more recently reverence, fondness, desire.

Now, we were back to sarcasm, where he tossed the term out to hurt me.

"It wasn't like I made you think," I said.

Cal raised a brow. "What's that supposed to mean?"

"I mean...yeah, I had fun in Europe. But I wasn't out fucking a different guy every night."

"Oh yeah? What about that son of an English earl?"

I grimaced. "Okay, that rumor was true. But that's one guy out of *five*, Cal. I had five partners while I was over there. In five years. I was too damn busy working to give much attention to relationships. You'd think by now you'd know that about me."

Something like shock and surprise flitted across his face, but he didn't back down—didn't apologize. "And you'd think by now that you'd know better than to be jealous of a woman I haven't seen or spoken to in nearly three years!"

"Well, how the fuck was I supposed to know that?" I said, standing from my stool so quickly it toppled over onto its side. The crash sent Skye skittering from the room, her nails clicking on the floors as she disappeared deeper into the house.

"You're supposed to trust me, Mar. That's how this works. Just like I trusted you when I found out about Owen, and we weren't even together then."

"Owen was a fuck buddy and nothing more," I said through gritted teeth. "The two are not the same."

"As far as I'm concerned, they are," he said, stalking toward me. Before I could protest, he'd hooked his hands behind my thighs and lifted me up onto the counter, sliding his hips between my legs. "What I'm saying here, Princess"—the nickname was softened now, sweet, more a term of endearment than the thinly veiled insult from a minute ago—"is that there's no reason to be jealous."

I pursed my lips, unimpressed. "Tell that to your fixation with the fact that I used to fuck your buddy Owen. The buddy I only started fucking because you rejected me!"

I clapped a hand over my mouth. Oh God, what had I done? I'd managed to keep that little secret to myself all these years, and now here it was. Out in the open, my heart bleeding on the floor.

An inhumane noise tore free from his throat as he brought his hand to my neck, thumb under my chin forcing my gaze to collide with his.

This man, the sheer possessiveness in his eyes?

Fuck, I wanted him to consume me.

"You don't fuck anyone else but me from now on."

It wasn't a question.

"Forever?"

"If that's what you want."

"Of course it is. I don't want to be with anyone else. Is that what you want?"

The admission had my heart lodged in my throat, and I swear I stopped breathing as Cal stared at me, not answering. I was laying myself bare here, exposing my soft underbelly, giving him the ability to cut me deeper than he could ever imagine. It was a big risk, one step shy of saying that four letter word, but it could mean a big reward. But Cal was worth that, and he deserved to know how deeply I cared about him. I wanted him and everything that came with it.

"I've always only wanted you, Princess."

With a rough kiss to my mouth that ended too soon but promised all the filthy things he'd do to me later, Cal let go of me and returned to the stove.

"I love you," I blurted at his back. He stilled, turning to me slowly.

"Say that again."

He stalked toward me, hands coming up to cup my face and brush away the wetness I hadn't even felt. "I love you," I said with a laugh.

"I love you." Bending, he peppered my face with kisses. "And I'm sorry I hurt you," he added quietly, staring deep into my eyes. "Then, and any time since."

"I forgive you. Just...don't do it again, okay?"

"Never," he promised.

A half hour later, he set two bowls of steaming soup on the counter in front of me, the other at his own seat, and dropped down next to me. The domesticity of it all made me downright giddy.

I groaned loudly around my first bite. It wasn't anything fancy—a simple chicken dumpling soup with a medley of vegetables to fill it out—but he'd seasoned it to perfection, the dumplings light and fluffy, the vegetables tender and bursting with freshness on my tongue.

"You keep making sounds like that," Cal said softly from my left, "and I'll find something else to shove in your mouth."

I turned to him, smirking, and lifted another spoonful slowly to my lips.

And moaned when it hit my tastebuds.

"That's it," he said, rising from his seat and lifting me off mine, easily throwing me over his shoulder like I was a sack of flour instead of a fully grown, five-foot-nine woman.

"Cal!" I said with a laugh as I pounded against his back. "Put me down!"

"Not a chance, Princess. You wanna play games? I'll give you games."

We reached my room then, and he dropped me unceremoniously on the center of my bed, reaching for the ratty sweats I'd put on after my bout of sickness earlier. Tugging them and my panties from my body, he tossed them across the room and reached for the hem of my tee. I arched my back enough that he could lift it up and over my head.

Now fully naked before him, I laid still as Cal dragged his eyes—then his hands—over my flesh.

"You are breathtaking," he said, peeling away and rising to stand at the foot of the bed again.

"And you are taking too long," I said, slipping my hand between my legs, spreading my pussy open, and circling my clit with the pads of my fingers.

Cal was on me in a flash, one big hand capturing both of my

wrists and forcing them over my head, but the moment he let go, I slid one between my thighs again.

"Amara…" he warned, and hell, it had been too damn long since he'd called me by my full name. I wanted him groaning it into my flesh, shouting it into the void as he climaxed.

"What?" I asked innocently, my fingers making slow passes over that bundle of nerves.

Surprisingly, Cal didn't respond. Instead, he turned away from me and stalked into my bathroom. A moment later, he returned with something in his hands—the tie from one of my fluffy winter robes.

He approached the side of the bed and stared down at me.

"Do you trust me?"

"Yes."

"Arms up."

I did as he asked, raising my hands over my head, which he gathered together, looping the sash around my wrists then slipping the ends through and wrapping them around one of the posts of my metal bed frame. My arms were tugged higher as he tied a knot.

"Too tight?" he asked.

I yanked experimentally, but they held comfortably. "No."

Cal's grin was wicked as he moved around to settle between my thighs. "Good," he said, face inches away from my pussy. "Now here's what I'm going to do. I'm going to tease you—with my tongue, my fingers, and maybe even my cock—until you're fucking begging for me to let you come. And even then…I might not let you."

"You're a fucking sadist," I said, even as desire curled in my core.

"Only for you, Princess," he said as he lightly trailed his finger around my clit. "Only for you."

And then he made good on his promise.

It was pure fucking torture, being entirely at his mercy, not being able to do anything but shift my hips, attempt to trap him with my thighs, and plead with exasperated and desperately turned on sounds. I wasn't coming until Cal decided I'd suffered enough, and while I was openly panting for him, my release brewing, the pressure between my thighs damn near unbearable under his ministrations...I was also more turned on than I'd ever been in my entire life.

I was a panting, exhausted, sweaty mess of desire by the time Cal took pity on me at last.

When he'd apparently grown tired of torturing me with his fingers and tongue, he pulled away, stripped, and settled between my thighs once again, his cock rock hard and weeping as he lazily pumped it with his hand.

Slipping the tip through my sex, coating himself in my arousal, he said, "Do you want to come now, my love?"

"Yes," I hissed, curling my legs around his waist and attempting to pull him toward me. Unfortunately, the man was an immovable wall of muscle, and he didn't budge so much as a centimeter.

"Tell me how bad you want it."

"Fuck, Cal," I said, wriggling. "I've wanted you since I first laid eyes on you. That night you turned me away? I was so embarrassed, but that didn't stop me from going home and taking my vibrator to myself with your face in my mind, imagining if your lips would feel the same between my thighs as they did against my mouth. And when I moved back from Europe and was forced to work with you every day? I pictured you fucking me in every room of our offices."

Cal's grin turned feline. "And you've made every fantasy a reality now, haven't you, baby?"

"You're damn right."

"I've had you just like this in my mind more times than I can count," he said, still idly toying with me, rubbing his cock against all the places I desperately needed something, anything, *more*.

"Cal..." I whined, working my hands, trying to free them from their binding. I only succeeded in tightening it.

"Shh," he said, then at last gave me what I needed, sliding into me so slowly. I clamped around him, and he groaned. "Fuck, you take me so good."

He began to move then, shifting his hips back and forth, pumping steadily in and out. I wouldn't last long, but after the torture we'd both just endured, I wanted him unhinged, wild and fucking me recklessly. I might love the man, and he might love me back, but I didn't want him tame and romantic right now—or maybe ever.

"Harder," I said.

"Where's that vibrator?" he asked, ignoring my request.

"Top drawer," I said, nodding to the nightstand to my left.

Still inside me, pressing as deep as he could go, hitting that spot that had me moaning, my legs twitching, Cal reached over and withdrew the bright pink toy from the drawer.

"Not as big as me," he said.

"And yet it still got the job done."

He resumed his lazy rocking into me and said, "Do you still use this?"

"We're talking too much for my liking," I said, exasperated.

"Answer the question." He pressed the power button until a low, insistent buzzing filled the room.

"I haven't needed to in a while."

"Not since I started fucking you so good that this puny little toy doesn't do it for you anymore?"

I laughed, the sound choked off my gasp when he pressed the toy to my clit.

"Something like that."

He shifted the vibrator a bit lower, angling it so the tip pressed against the topside of his cock as he thrust in and out of me, the length of it resting against my clit.

"Fuuuuuck," he groaned. "That's—"

"Amazing," I said. I could feel the vibration not just against my clit, but inside of me, buzzing along his length and against my walls. Begging, I said, "Harder, Cal."

This time, my request was granted, and Cal unleashed himself. Soon the room filled with the obscene sounds of his hips slapping against mine, of my moans as my orgasm built and built until—

"Cal!" I cried out as I shattered, my release sending me reeling as Cal followed me down, never once letting up in his punishing thrusts, never once taking the toy away from my clit.

My orgasm went on and on and on, tearing me apart, scattering my remains across the bed. And when I'd come down, when I stitched myself back together, just when I was sure this was the time it'd let go, another wave crashed, and I was once again lost.

At last Cal slowed, and the endless shaking in my legs stilled.

As soon as he stopped, Cal reached up and untied me, and my hands were instantly on him, burying in his hair as I brought his mouth to mine. I nipped and licked, dragging my tongue against his and my teeth against his lip, his jaw, his neck.

Then we collapsed side by side into a breathless tangle of skin and limbs.

"Fuck, Mar," he said. "That was..."

"Next time," I said, voice a nearly breathless whisper. "I'm tying you up."

He simply pressed a kiss to my forehead. "It's a date, Princess."

chapter 23
Amara

WHEN MY SISTERS FOUND me, I was curled into a ball on the floor of my bathroom. My tears had long since dried, the tile beneath my cheek cooling the heat in my face from the seemingly endless crying.

Okay, let me back up a bit.

After my meeting with Amie, my and Cal's miniature reckoning in regards to our pasts, and saying "I love you," things between us had been perfect. He'd been incredibly attentive, and we'd started to feel like a real couple.

Unfortunately, though I hadn't thrown up again in the two weeks since, my stomach was still unsettled, and a ball of anxiety had taken up residence in my chest, pushing on my lungs and making it difficult to breathe.

It wasn't as simple as anxiety, though I wished more than anything that was the case. But I had an inkling after that first time I'd gotten sick, and I hated how true that intuition had proved to be.

For the first week, I'd ignored the signs, unwilling to admit to myself that it was even a possibility. But pulling the wool over my eyes wouldn't make the potential problem go away, and at last, my nerves were frayed enough that I had to take steps to rule out the prospect. So this morning, I'd run the errand I'd been avoiding.

Those were the longest three minutes of my life, but I knew I'd feel better once it was over, once I put the scare to bed once and for all.

I'd never expected the test to come back positive.

"Mar!" Delia shouted as she knelt at my side. "What's going on? Are you okay? Are you hurt?"

"I—no."

Physically, yeah I was fine. But mentally? Emotionally? Everything was a fucking mess, and I had no one to blame but myself.

Well, and Cal.

The tears sprang forth once more, and a broken sob escaped my chest, echoing through the room. The next thing I knew, I was being lifted off the floor. Delia gripped me under the arms while Ella took my feet, shuffling into my room and dropping me on the bed. It was completely undignified, the way they lifted me off the floor like I was a heavy sack of grain instead of their sister in clear distress, but I couldn't summon the energy to care. Once nestled on the white down comforter on my bed, I shrunk into myself, and my sisters curled their bodies around mine. They didn't push. They didn't even speak. They just held me.

Fuck, I wished Chloe was here too. She'd know exactly what to say right now to make me feel better, to convince me that my life wasn't falling apart thanks to a couple pink lines. And Brie would bake for me, firmly believing carbs could fix anything.

But still, if only Delia and Ella were able to answer my SOS text, that was enough. I was safe in their arms, their embraces holding me together when that stupid pee stick threatened to shatter me into a million little irrevocably broken pieces.

"Mar," Brie—who I clearly hadn't realized arrived—said quietly some untold moments, hours, days, who the fuck knew, later. "What's going on?"

I considered staying quiet, keeping the secret to myself. The longer I held the words in, the less real it was. The moment I released them into the universe, I'd have to face the fact that this was happening. That there was a tiny life growing in my womb.

At last, I croaked, "I'm pregnant."

One of them gasped, but all three hugged me tighter.

God, I'd been so stupid. I was twenty-eight, for fuck's sake. I *knew* birth control was fallible. But...the odds had been so slim. How often do you hear of babies being conceived while their mother was on the pill? Rarely.

We should've used condoms after that first time. We'd never even talked about it. Like a fucking teenager, I'd been so consumed by everything Calvin Ryder was that I'd waved a flippant figurative hand at the protests my mind screamed at me.

I should've listened.

We never should've slept together at all.

Now I was a damn statistic, my baby an *oops*, the product of a relationship that never should've happened in the first place.

I had to breathe. I was spiraling too fast, thinking things that made no sense. I loved Cal, and he loved me. That would be enough to get us through this.

Right?

Delia spoke next. "What are you going to do?"

"Keep it," I said quickly.

The circumstances were all sorts of fucked up, but this baby was a gift.

I shifted so I could settle a palm across my abdomen.

"What the hell is going on?"

The voice from the doorway startled the four of us, and I whipped my head in its direction, meeting the emerald gaze of my big sister.

"Chloe!" I cried, shakily rising to my feet and throwing myself into her arms. "What are you doing here?"

"I got your SOS text," she said, as though it was the most obvious thing in the world. "You needed me. I came."

"How did you get here so fast?"

She and Logan had been in Detroit for the weekend, visiting his family and meeting his sister Berkley's new baby—their new nephew—Bentley.

Looked like Chloe was about to be an auntie again.

"Mar, you sent that text four hours ago," Delia told me.

"*Four*?" Fuck, I was in worse shape than I thought.

Chloe held me at arm's length, eyes darting across my face. "It doesn't matter," she said. "I'm here now, and someone better tell me what the fuck is happening."

"I'm pregnant," I blurted, eyes welling with tears again.

Whatever happened with me and Cal didn't matter in the end, because I knew I'd be okay, and so would my baby. Because these women around me? My sisters, my best friends? They were all we needed.

Fuck, this kid was barely into its existence and it was already the luckiest alive.

Chloe's eyes lit, mouth pulling into a bright, wide smile.

"Me too," she whispered.

My sisters and I erupted, and I wrapped my arms tighter around Chloe, tears streaming freely down my face, a mix of happy and sad, the two emotions warring for purchase.

"Shut the fuck up!" Delia squealed, rising from the bed to tackle me and Chloe to the ground. "We're gonna be aunties! We're all gonna be aunties!"

"Delia!" I shouted, my shoulder digging uncomfortably into the hardwood floors. "You just tackled two pregnant women!"

"Shit," she said sheepishly as she rose, and Ella and Brie helped me and Chloe to our feet. "Sorry. I'm just so excited!"

We moved out of my bedroom and downstairs to the living room, piling together on the massive sectional, looking out over the expanse of West Grand Traverse Bay beyond my windows. I felt calmer than I had before my sisters arrived, comforted by their presence and the knowledge that I wouldn't be doing this pregnancy thing alone.

"When did you find out?" I asked Chloe.

"About a month ago," she said, and Ella reached out to slap her. "Sorry! I just...we decided to wait until I was out of my first trimester to tell anyone."

"How far along are you, then?"

"Thirteen weeks," Chloe said, and I squeezed her hand.

If I had to guess, I'd say I was probably eight weeks along. Based on my missed period, the date of which had come and gone about three weeks ago, I'd bet good money I'd gotten pregnant in that Detroit hotel room, while he fucked me as we watched ourselves in that mirror.

I shivered as I let the memory wash over me—and then I let it go. Memories of our nights together only made my body ache for him, and I had some shit to figure out first.

Growing up, Chloe and I had always talked endlessly about our desires for a family one day. We both wanted at least three kids, and we wanted them to be as close as we were to each other and Delia, Ella, and Brie. We dreamed about our husbands, about having a love like Mom and Dad did. And we always discussed putting our roots down right here on this peninsula; we wanted our families close, to have our kids grow up together, to have Mom and Dad be fully involved in the lives of their grandchildren.

Chloe, at the very least, had gotten the husband and the love of a lifetime. She was doing this the right way, with a partner who would be there for her through every up and down of her pregnancy and the responsibility of raising a human.

It wasn't fair of me to make assumptions about Cal, not when I hadn't even told him he was going to be a father. I knew he wanted a family too, but to have one like this? Before he could plan and prepare himself for being a dad? How would he handle that?

"How are you going to tell Cal?" Ella asked, pulling me back into the conversation.

"I have no fucking idea," I said, dropping my head into my hands. "I haven't even talked to him in a few days."

Cal deserved to know he was going to be a father; I wasn't questioning that, or debating whether or not I *should* tell him.

The problem was I knew everything would change once I did, and to be quite frank, with everything about to change for me in the most epic of ways, I was holding onto any sense of normalcy for dear life at the moment.

I hadn't talked to him since Tuesday, when he'd taken me to the winery restaurant for lunch. By then, I'd already begun to question whether or not I was pregnant, and I was barely present for the conversation we had over our meal. I knew he sensed something was off, but he didn't press, and I brushed it off when he asked if I was okay, saying I was distracted over all the stuff I had to get done to prepare for the Labor Day weekend events happening in two weeks.

I'd been pulling away to protect us both, but whether I liked it or not, Cal and I were about to be connected for life. I'd be a liar if I said I wasn't terrified to drop this bomb on him, practically shaking with fear and anxiousness at the simple thought of his reaction.

"Mar..." Chloe said slowly, and I turned toward her. "There's something about Cal you should know."

My sisters shared a look, something entirely unreadable to me, and Delia said, "Coco...are you sure?"

"I thought we agreed we wouldn't," Ella chimed in.

"For the record, I never agreed to that," Brie added, petulantly folding her arms over her chest and turning her nose up at whatever my sisters were talking about.

My eyes ping-ponged between the four of them, anxiety rising with my confusion.

"Stop talking about me like I'm not here and tell me what the fuck is going on!" I burst out.

A myriad of emotions crossed each of their faces—apprehension, fear, discomfort, dismay.

At last, Chloe opened her mouth.

And the whole sordid story spilled free. About how, the exact same day Dad had signed over the company to me, Cal had gone behind my back and approached Chloe and Brie, begging them to see reason, imploring them to vote me out of my CEO position when he eventually called for my removal. How he'd approached my parents *before* my official appointment, pleading with them to take a step back and seek an outside candidate.

From the beginning, Cal hadn't believed in me. That wasn't news. And maybe he'd come around to the idea, and maybe he believed in me now. But this? This cut deeper than I would've liked.

I loved him, and I thought he loved me too.

It fucking wrecked me to think he could've been pretending all along.

As the details unfolded from Chloe's mouth, the pain in my chest morphed and shifted until it became something else entirely—rage.

So...yeah. I'd tell him he was going to be a father, that I was having our baby. But I'd be damned if he ever had *me* again.

And I'd be extra damned if he had anything to do with running *my* company.

This was the end of the fucking road for me and Calvin Ryder, both personally and professionally.

"Why didn't you tell me Cal was essentially staging a coup before I'd even officially taken over the company?" I asked my dad when I'd unceremoniously pushed into their house the following morning.

I'd given myself a day between breaking the news to my sisters and telling my parents.

For their parts, the girls hadn't left my side since they showed up at my house the day before, content to binge cheesy eighties romcoms and gorge ourselves on popcorn and chocolate. Delia, Ella, and Brie had dipped into my red wine selection, taunting Chloe and I by swirling the glasses under our noses.

Surprisingly, the scent of my favorite Italian Rioja made my stomach clench dangerously, and Chloe had never liked red anyway.

This morning, I showered and pulled myself together, my sisters hovering as though they feared I'd try to drown myself or something. Before I left, I made Chloe promise to give me a half hour head start. I knew she was chomping at the bit to make her own pregnancy announcement, and I figured if she told them after me, they'd be less likely to crucify me for getting pregnant out of wedlock by a man who was, for all intents and purposes, an employee.

A man they thought I hated, and who hated me in return.

God, I was not looking forward to my dad's reaction.

Blessedly, I wasn't sad and woebegone anymore.

Now, I was pissed off, the fury and rage at Cal fueling my every move.

Before I nailed his balls to the wall, however, I needed to have a frank conversation with my parents.

"Hello to you too, sweets," my dad said, raising a brow. He was seated at the breakfast nook in their expansive kitchen, half-moon glasses perched on the tip of his nose, the Sunday paper propped up in front of him as he read what I knew was the business news.

You could take the CEO out of the company and all that.

"Don't 'sweets' me," I said, throwing myself into a chair across from him, leaning my elbows on the table and staring him down. "Tell me what Cal said to you before I took over."

My dad sighed and folded the paper, laying it on the table and removing his glasses to set them on top. He was in no hurry, and his lack of urgency only stoked the fire in my blood.

With a sigh and a pinch to the bridge of his nose, as though he wished he could be anywhere but here, he said, "It's nothing you haven't heard before, Mar. He wasn't on board with you taking over."

"Why didn't you tell me then?" I implored them both as my mom strode to the table and sat beside Dad.

"Because it wouldn't have changed anything," Dad said. "You were taking over whether he liked it or not. It wasn't up to him—and it still isn't."

"Did you know he went to Chloe and Brie when he couldn't sway you guys to his side?"

My parents blinked in surprise; clearly, that tidbit was news to them.

I quickly filled them in on what my sisters had told me, my

father's face darkening with each of my words. When I finished, he rose, practically vibrating with rage.

"I'll fucking kill him," he said through clenched teeth. "He had no right."

"I agree," I said, maintaining my calm. It wouldn't do any of us any good to introduce a second Delatou temper into this conversation—not when I had yet to drop the biggest bomb of all, and mine was already consuming me. "But there's more I have to tell you."

My mother reached up and laced her fingers through my dad's, tugging him back into his seat. Then she studied me, and I swear she knew exactly what I was about to say. Call it mother's intuition or whatever, but something like understanding flashed across her eyes. Understanding and...acceptance.

She would be okay with this, but it was never her I was worried about.

My father was the best kind of girl dad. It was fairly obvious his life would've been easier had he been granted even a single son, but he'd never made us feel less than, never made us feel like burdens or like he wasn't the most proud man on the planet to be our father. He raised us to be hardworking, to be girly when we wanted to be, but also taught us how to change a tire on a car, change our oil, use power tools. He was a white collar man who had been raised with a blue collar mentality. My father had never been afraid to get his hands dirty, and he instilled the same work ethic in his daughters.

But on the flip side of that ultra-supportive coin was a man who was also, at times, overprotective. Leon Delatou didn't take kindly to slights against his children, and he'd go to bat for any one of us at the drop of a hat.

And I mean that literally, but we didn't have time to dive into the great prom debacle of 2014. Plus, that was Brie's story to tell, not mine.

"What is it, sweets?" he asked slowly. "What's going on?"

There was no going back from this. Once the words were out, my relationship with my father would change, and I was terrified I was about to break his trust and pride in me irrevocably.

At last, I squared my shoulders, my gaze darting between the two of them, and said, "I'm pregnant."

Surprise flared in my father's eyes while a smile bloomed on my mother's face at the same moment. A heartbeat later, she was out of her seat and moving around the table, pulling me to my feet to wrap me into a warm, reassuring hug.

"That's wonderful news, my girl," she said when she pulled away, cupping my face in her hands. "But I'm assuming there's more."

My father remained a statue across from us, and I looked him dead in the eye as I said, "It's Cal's."

The tether on his temper snapped, and Dad burst from his seat.

"What the fuck were you thinking?" he shouted, stamping around the kitchen, pulling on his hair and muttering what I knew were Greek expletives.

Damn, if he was speaking Greek, he was *really* mad. But I'd anticipated this. I'd been fully prepared for him to look at me with hurt and disappointment in his eyes.

"Do you have any idea how this will affect the company?"

"Trust me, Dad," I said with a sigh, once again dropping onto a chair. "I know exactly what this means for us."

"No one will ever take you seriously again."

"That remains to be seen."

"You're having a *child*, Amara. Your whole life is about to change. You're not going to be able to give nearly as much time and attention to the company as you do now."

"You had *five*," I reminded him. "And you did just fine."

"I had *help*," he snapped. "A partner who could pick up the slack when I faltered, and vice versa."

"And I have help too," I said, my voice breaking. "I have you guys. I have my sisters. What more could I need?"

All at once, the fight and anger left him, his shoulders slumping as he approached me and lifted me to my feet—off them—and into his embrace.

"Of course, sweets," he murmured into my hair. "You always have us. I'm sorry for my reaction." He let me go and held me at arm's length. "I'm just worried about you. This is a lot at once."

I swallowed hard, fighting the tears that threatened to fall. "I know, Daddy. But I have a plan."

He must've recognized the twinkle in my eye, because a smirk spread across his face as he released me and sank onto a chair once again. I mirrored him, my mother returning to his side.

"Let's hear it then."

SOMETHING WAS SERIOUSLY WRONG.

I'd lived my life by the principle that I always trusted my gut, and right now, my gut was screaming at me to get back in my truck and disappear somewhere far, far away.

Instead, despite the intricate knots my stomach had twisted itself into, I pushed into the conference room for the emergency board meeting Amara had called for this afternoon.

It was Monday, and I hadn't seen her since last Friday—hadn't even spoken to her. Considering we usually exchanged flirty texts back and forth when we were apart—hell, we rarely spent a weekend anywhere but each other's arms—her radio silence was a cause for concern.

Coupled with this meeting that she had *Leon* call to inform me of?

Like I said, something was seriously wrong.

When I entered the room, the entire Delatou family was already gathered at the table. My usual spot immediately to Amara's left had been occupied by Leon, Lena seated across from him, Chloe and Delia next to her, Ella and Brie on Leon's side. Uncomfortable with the abrupt departure from our usual seating arrangement, I dropped down next to Brie.

No sooner had my ass met the chair than Amara started the meeting.

"Thank you all for meeting on such short notice," she began. "There are only a few items on the agenda today, so I'll try to make this as brief and painless as possible."

How had it taken me so long to realize how easily she commanded a room? How perfectly she held the attention of every person here as she stood at the head of the table, hands sometimes resting in front of her as she leaned over and spoke, other times standing straight, shoulders square as she gestured to the flatscreen on the wall behind her.

"First order of business: the Labor Day event. Now, initially, I know I mentioned inviting all the sales reps in the state to join us for the weekend, but unfortunately, once I started doing my research, I realized that wasn't feasible."

She continued to speak on the sheer number of sales reps Michigan's largest wholesaler—*our* wholesaler—employed, and how it wasn't an option to give them all free room and board for a weekend. I didn't miss the way her eyes narrowed on me when she referred to it as an "unwise financial decision."

So she did listen to me on occasion.

Apparently, she'd decided to extend the invitation to each of the territory managers instead, which totaled around thirty people instead of over one hundred.

"Twenty of them are able to make it," she said proudly, "which is great considering that's that exact sleeping capacity in the Villa." Her family chuckled, and she continued. "It's unfortunate we couldn't get them all here, but I understand people have families and other plans that they weren't prepared to change or cancel. Twenty is still great, and I'm excited to welcome them all to Apple Blossom Bay and the property in a few weeks."

I still thought it was insane to open the Villa to these people for free, to expend precious resources on education and a party for them when it probably wouldn't make a lick of difference. But I couldn't deny Amara's excitement was contagious, and I found myself smiling at her as she relayed the plans she had for the weekend, including tours through the grounds with Liam, dinner at Owen's restaurant, Birdie's, and the Labor Day party itself, which would be held here at the winery and catered by Ezra and Brie.

"For drinks, we'll be offering the canned cocktails exclusively. Sales of all four offerings continue to trend upward, and as we move into the slower months, I want reps pushing them out to market whenever possible. I'm hoping for at least eighty percent account retention by the end of the year."

"Lofty," I said before I could stop myself, the word holding a slight edge.

"Doable," Amara quipped in return, then used talk of account retention to launch into Q4 projections.

Another departure from the norm—in standard board meetings, as the Chief *Financial* Officer of this company, it was my job to relay sales projections to the group. As far as I could remember, I hadn't even emailed the reports to her yet, which meant she circumvented me and went straight to Jeff. Being who he was, and Amara being who she was, I knew Jeff wouldn't balk at giving her what she'd asked for, wouldn't even question the otherwise abnormal request.

What the fuck was going on?

I hadn't realized I'd spoken the words out loud until Amara turned to me, a wolfish grin on her face.

"You know, Mr. Ryder, I'm really glad you asked."

Mr. Ryder?

"I didn't mean—"

"Oh, don't start backpedaling now," she said. "After all, you were the third item on my agenda today."

Fear raced down my spine, anxious sweat instantly breaking out on my brow, the surge of adrenaline prickling my under arms and raising my heart rate.

I couldn't explain how I knew, but the look on Amara's face right now? The utter, almost unnatural calm on the faces of each of her family members?

This was a witch hunt, and I was the one about to burn.

"I was?" I asked, fighting and failing to keep my voice steady.

"It's recently come to my attention that you attempted to stage a coup."

"That was months ago."

Amara raised and lowered a single shoulder in an unaffected shrug. Only the tightness around her eyes and the sheer molten fire blazing in her golden irises alerted me to the level of her anger.

The depth of my betrayal.

"And then," she continued, "we entered into an albeit inappropriate physical and emotional relationship."

My heart stuttered. If she was dropping *that* bomb without

care for her safety, everyone in this family was already well aware of who Amara and I were to each other.

I supposed that explained the murderous gleam in Leon's eyes.

"I don't think your family needs to be here for this, Princess. If you're mad at me, let's go somewhere and talk."

"I'm past 'talking,'" she said. "And don't call me that."

"What do you want from me right now? Do you want me to tell you how I approached Chloe and Brie on New Year's Eve and tried to take you out before you could run this place into the ground? Yeah, I did that. But like I said, *that was months ago.* I don't feel that way anymore, and you know it."

"What else?" she asked, ignoring my last statement.

"What do you mean, *what else*?"

"How about the fact that you gave me a fucking joke of a budget to roll out the canned cocktails? Or the fact that you tried to make me sign a promissory note to secure funds from *my own company*."

"You did *what*?" Leon asked, his cheeks flaming red as his temper flared further.

Fucking hell. If I got out of here with my head still attached to my body, I'd consider that a win.

"But you never signed it," I protested weakly to Amara.

"The simple fact of the matter, Calvin," she spat out my name, and I winced. It had been ages since she'd called me by my full first name, and I fucking hated it, hated how clipped and disgusted the two syllables sounded falling from the lips that had brought me so much joy and pleasure over the last few months, "is that you think you're the one in charge here. And I let it slide because I was still getting my bearings, and you and I had enough shit to fight about without adding that to the mix."

"I *am* in charge of the money," I reminded her.

"You're in charge of tracking our finances, of offering solutions to our weaknesses and exploiting our strengths. Tell me, Calvin: when my father ran this company, did he ever have to ask—no, *beg*—you to give him money to run a new campaign or begin R&D on a new product? Did he ever have to deal with the bullshit you've put me through?"

"Let me answer that for you," Leon said, smiling at his daughter. "No, sweets. I never had to deal with any of the bullshit you've had to. And you"—he turned to me, raising a finger to point accusingly at me—"have grossly overstepped."

I looked around the room at the Delatou family, knowing I was fighting a losing battle, but still unable to stop searching for a foothold as I stared down a thousand foot drop to the bottom of a canyon. At last, my gaze settled on Brie.

"Remember what you told me that day?" I asked, and surprise by being addressed flashed in her eyes. "You told me you knew I meant well."

"I also told you that your opinion of her didn't make Amara any less qualified."

"And *I* told you," Chloe piped up, "that you didn't know better than my parents about who was fit to run this company."

Up to that point, I'd been trying to save face. My relationship with Amara was terribly damaged, and I didn't know if there'd ever be any coming back from this. I knew how deeply I cut her. I'd listened to her ideas, her dreams and plans, fears and hopes over the last few months. I knew how hard she worked, and how much this company—and leading it successfully—meant to her.

I knew that, and I should've come clean about the attempted coup ages ago. If I had, we probably wouldn't be sitting here right now. God, I was so fucking stupid. I'd give anything to take it back.

I stood then, palms slapping down onto the table, reading to make my final stand. I wasn't going down without a fight. Next to me, Brie flinched.

"Tell me, Cal," Lena said, speaking for the first time, taking the wind right out of my sails. "Have you ever bothered to study our international distributions beyond reconciling the shipping invoices each month?"

I scrunched up my face in confusion. "What does that have to do with anything?"

"We've been telling you all along that Amara knows what she's doing. About her MBA and every other thing she's done for this company. But have you ever bothered to look into any of it, or have you just been content to coast on your opinion of her?"

"My opinion of her—"

Amara waved a hand, cutting me off. "It's not important, Mom. What is important is that I'm calling for a vote."

Ice ran through my veins. She wouldn't, would she?

"Mar—"

"All those in favor of removing Calvin Ryder as Chief Financial Officer of Delatou, Inc.—"

"Please don't do this."

"—effectively immediately—"

"You're making a mistake."

"—raise your right hand."

Six hands rose into the air instantaneously, the hammer on the final nail in my coffin.

"This is bullshit."

"You had to know your actions would catch up with you eventually," Amara said with no amount of sympathy in her voice.

No, my girl was ice cold.

Even in those early days, when I'd openly scorned and disdained her, there had always been some heat in her gaze, in her tone. Now, there was nothing, not a single trace of the woman I'd fallen for showing within the harsh lines of her face.

"Mar?" Brie asked quietly.

"Can Calvin and I have the room?" she said suddenly.

"Are you sure?" Chloe asked, sitting forward and leveling Amara with a concerned gaze.

"Yeah," Amara said, her shoulders sagging a bit. "It'll be better this way."

Though the members of her family shared unreadable glances, they all rose from their chairs and moved toward the door, Leon passing by Amara and pressing a kiss to her temple.

"We're right outside, sweets." Amara only nodded.

As he followed his wife and daughters out, Leon paused at my side, his glare heated.

"I had one rule, Ryder. What was it?"

"Stay away from your daughters," I mumbled.

"You're lucky she fired you before I had the chance to do worse."

What could possibly be worse than this? I'd lost my job. I'd lost my girl. My paltry ten shares in the company wouldn't do shit for me now beyond making me a nuisance to this family. In fact, I should leave here right now and have legal draw up a contract to sell my stock back to Leon and Lena.

A chill racked my body. It didn't bear thinking about, especially not when I once again faced Amara. Her jaw was clenched, hands white knuckled where they gripped the edge of the table.

But it was more than rage—there was pain in her gaze too.

Amara leaned forward on the table, leveling me with a dark glare, and my entire world narrowed to her pupils, to the swirls of honey around her irises, the eyes I'd been fully prepared to stare into and find love shining back at me every day for the rest of my life.

And then she pulled the trigger.

"I'm pregnant."

All the air was instantly sucked from the room, the force of the admission jolting me back into my chair with a dull *thud*.

"What the fuck are you talking about?" I hissed.

"I'm pregnant," she said again. "Eight weeks according to the ultrasound I had this morning. And you're the father."

"I can't—you're on—" I couldn't grasp a single thought and speak it with any sort of coherence. This day...it had been too much. I needed to sit Amara down, somewhere far more private than this board room, where I was sure her family waited outside, eavesdropping on our conversation. We needed to have a frank conversation, discuss next steps, *fix* this fucking shitstorm we'd found ourselves in the middle of.

"Birth control is fallible," she said simply.

I knew she was right, that nothing was one hundred percent save abstinence. It's not like we'd used condoms after that first time, and while I knew Amara was on the pill, I'd never stopped to consider the effectiveness of it.

As a man, I'd never considered that my job.

I should've been smarter.

Because now, this woman who clearly felt strongly for me—and not in a good way at the moment—was pregnant with my child.

As though all of my thoughts were being openly broadcast on my face like a sports ticker across the bottom of a television screen, Amara gave me a sad smile, the lone bit of sympathy she'd shown me since I walked into this room. She'd already come to terms with this, and knowing her, already had a plan in place for the future. Meanwhile, I was lost at sea, grappling for purchase as the waves crashed and crashed over my head.

While I drowned, Amara began gathering her things and took a step toward the door.

"No!" I shouted suddenly, shooting from my chair and halting her progress across the room.

Amara turned to me slowly, her family rallying at her back. "No, what?"

"You pull the pin on a grenade and launch it at my face and you expect me to just, what? Take that lying down? Absolutely fucking not. Sit down and talk to me like a grown up."

"You have treated me like some vapid figurehead with one foot out the door since the moment the company got signed over to me, Calvin. You have gone behind my back to my sisters *and* my parents, trying to stage some fucking coup, and you're lecturing *me* about acting like a grown up? Fuck you. We'll talk when you've had a chance to get your head on straight."

And with that, Amara stormed from the room, leaving me

standing in the middle of the wreckage of my life.

chapter 25
Calvin

ONCE AMARA LEFT, I moved to the conference table and leaned my hands against it, blankly staring out the windows at the vineyard beyond, the words of the last hour looping endlessly in my mind.

When I'd walked into the offices this morning, I'd known something was wrong, but I'd never anticipated *this*. I'd never expected my whole life to be upended and ripped to shreds in the span of sixty minutes.

Without my job, I was listless, floating in space. But there were other jobs. I could easily move away, move back out west to California, Oregon, or Washington. My winery experience would get me in the door at a number of places out that way. And if I wanted to leave wine altogether and enter an entirely new industry? Well, I could kiss a letter of recommendation from either of my former Delatou, Inc. bosses goodbye, but I had five and a half years of experience to draw from, and I was confident that would speak for itself.

But without Amara? I was untethered, on a hairpin trigger, the slightest pressure away from snapping completely.

I was just replaying the part when Lena spoke up that my attention snagged on her words.

Have you ever bothered to study our international distribution?

At the time, it hadn't made any sense. There was absolutely no context to the question. But now, cycling it back, and knowing Lena the way I did, I realized—she'd said it for a reason. Most likely because she knew I hadn't studied the international distribution as closely as I'd studied the statewide and national numbers since Amara had taken over. The international distribution numbers were solid, and had been for the last few years. Sure, I'd noticed a steady increase in sales in the last three or four, but I'd never given it a second thought. I figured it was a product of international consumers trying our wines and requesting them at new bars and restaurants.

But now, I wondered...

With a renewed sense of purpose, I rose from my chair and stalked down the hall to my office. Surprisingly, Jeff was MIA, so I pushed into the room, closing and locking the door behind me. I settled myself behind my desk and a few keystrokes had the international distribution reports from the last five years pulled up on my screen alongside the program I used to keep record of all receipts and credit card statements.

Amara's receipts and company credit card.

It didn't take me long to recognize the pattern, the realization drawing an uncharacteristic gasp from me.

Time and time again, every member of the Delatou fami-ly—hell, even Amara herself—had told me Amara wasn't who I thought she was, had implored me to let go of my preconceived notions about her and see her for who she truly was. And here I'd been, moving along with the wool pulled over my eyes like a fucking putz.

Every single weekend, every "bender" I'd accused Amara of going on in all those old European cities? Each one directly corresponded to a large shipment of Chateau Delatou product being shipped out to various bars and restaurants in that area within a week of her visit.

The entire time I'd called her "party princess" and gave her shit for fucking around for five years, she'd been...working. Expanding the company's reach, growing our distribution to include the hottest spots in the hottest cities across the European continent. Even after I'd found out about her MBA, hell even after I'd fallen in love with her, I'd still never considered she was capable of *this*.

I wasn't big on social media. For a numbers guy, I'd never given a fuck about increasing my following, of broadcasting my entire life on the internet for strangers, of monetizing it. I loved my job—and I was good at it. I loved living in Traverse City, my dog, my friends.

Amara.

I hadn't needed the approval of strangers to know my worth, hadn't needed endless likes and follows to make me happy.

But I did have an Instagram account that I used only to keep tabs on the lives and growing families of my college friends—and, ironically, my parents. My mom used hers to grow her business, and my father used his as a way to display his woodworking projects, which, even I could admit, had grown more complex and impressive with each passing day. And I also had a TikTok that I created at the beginning of summer to keep an eye on the new marketing strategies Amara wanted to roll out, though I couldn't tell you the last time I checked it.

Up to that point, I'd studiously avoided Amara's profiles. She was the kind of woman so comfortable in her own skin, who knew she was beautiful, and didn't mind showing off her assets for her followers. Before we'd gotten together, I hadn't needed the temptation, hadn't needed to be clued in on what her lush body looked like beneath her sexy work clothes.

And after we had gotten together, the real thing was much better than getting my rocks off looking at a picture of her.

But now, I navigated to her Instagram profile, scrolling endlessly through her pictures until I came to the posts from five years ago when she'd first moved to London.

And right there, in full technicolor, was a photo of her posing outside her new university, participating in that classic "first day of school" picture in front of the London School of Business.

Why had I never looked before? It was all right there, carefully edited photos in beautifully curated snapshots, detailing her travels, her studies, her work for her family's company.

What is that old saying about the pride coming before the fall? Yeah, I'd fallen alright. In love with Amara and flat on my fucking face when I lost her.

Wondering what else I'd remained so willfully—stupidly—ignorant of, I moved to TikTok, where I located her profile—and another gasp left me.

Endless videos of us. Of our hands linked, Skye's leash wrapped around mine as the pup trotted in front of us on one of our sunset beach walks. Of the curve of my shoulder, in bed next to her while she filled her followers in on her plans for the day. My back to the camera as I stood at the kitchen counter, chopping something, with a suggestive caption about getting you a man who could do both—whatever that meant.

I clicked on the one pinned to the top of her profile, and my heart clenched painfully in my chest. It started as a montage of the two of us, quick snippets of video and photos flashing by, set to some Taylor Swift song. At the end was a longer clip of us dancing on the beach at sunset, me swinging her in my arms, her head thrown back in laughter.

She was always laughing.

We had been happy, hadn't we?

She'd love me so much—it was plain as day on her face.

My God, I was such an idiot. What the fuck had I done?

Without a job—for now—I suddenly had a lot of time on my hands. Instead of holing up in my apartment and wallowing in self-pity until I concocted a plan to get my job and my girl back—although I'd settle for just the girl—I decided to hit the open road.

I packed up a couple weeks' worth of clothes and food for Skye, loaded my camping supplies and the dog into the truck, and set off for Wisconsin.

For all their years of wandering, and the nearly twenty-five years they spent in Green Bay, my parents had at last settled in Door County about ten years ago. They liked being near the water but away from the big city, and had lucked out when a younger couple was selling their starter home. Upgrading it was a new adventure for them, and they'd loved every second.

There wasn't an easy way to get to Sturgeon Bay, short of taking a boat straight across Lake Michigan—which was an option but not one I was interested in—so I chose to make an adventure out of it, traveling through the Upper Peninsula and stopping at all the nature hot spots on the way.

I worked my way along M-28, skirting up to Tahquamenon Falls, then on to Grand Marais and the log slide. There, I met a woman who owned a fine wine and goods shop that stocked CD products, which made my chest puff up with pride. I gave her my card, telling her to call if she was ever in TC.

Yeah, I was studiously ignoring the fact that I no longer had a job, sue me.

Then I went through Munising, taking a day to kayak along Pictured Rocks National Lakeshore and another to hike the Chapel Loop, spending the nights on a sandy Lake Superior beach. The disconnect from reality, from my entire life, was exactly the reset I needed before facing my parents.

After all, I'd been so wrong about Amara, so the chances were high I'd been wrong about them too. I owed it to myself to find out.

Five days later, I pulled up to their cottage front door.

"Calvin!" my mother said, throwing her arms around me when she found me standing on their porch, Skye jumping excitedly against the leash dangling from my hand. "What a pleasant surprise!"

"Sorry to show up uninvited," I said with a wince. "I should've called, but I had some free time, and I wanted to see you guys."

"Psh," my mother said, waving a hand. "This is your home too, honey. Come on in. I'll get the guest bed outfitted while your dad brings your stuff inside."

"Oh, that's not necessary—" I started to protest, but she was already shouting down the hall.

"Clint! Calvin's here! Go out and get his things, would ya?"

"Yes ma'am." My dad's grumble entered the hall a moment before he did. He approached me, squinting jokingly as though he didn't recognize me. Then he pulled me into a hug. "Good to see you, son."

"You too, Pops."

Mom had the bed made up by the time my father returned with my bag, which I was fully capable of getting myself. But I visited so infrequently that I figured I could let them spoil me a bit. Never mind that I'd essentially come here with my tail between my legs; they didn't need to know that.

That was, until dinner that evening, when my mother leveled me with that probing gaze of hers—her eyes the same shade of green as mine—and asked, "So why are you here, Calvin? Not that we don't love having you home, but something is clearly wrong."

I snorted. Leave it to her to sniff that out within a few hours in my presence.

Colette Ryder had a knack for that sort of thing. She was a well-sought after yoga instructor and meditation specialist, and she'd always been adept at reading moods and energies—particularly that of her only child.

"How do you know something's wrong?" I asked, and she shot me an unimpressed look.

"Your energy is dark. Troubled."

Heaving a sigh, I decided my best course of action was to simply rip the bandage free. "I uhh...lost my job. But...I lost my girl too, and that's even worse."

My mother gasped and my father gaped. "I'm sorry, honey," Mom said, settling her warm palm over my hand. "What happened?"

As much as I didn't want to, I couldn't hold myself back from spilling the entire sordid story at their feet.

Which took me all the way back to five years ago, to Amara the night I'd met her flashing through my mind. God, she'd been almost ethereal in the low lights of Lawless, her thick, deep brown curls falling around her shoulders and down her back. The memories of her body beneath my hands that night instantly melted into images of her speared on my cock in her desk chair. My head between her thighs on the beach, her mouth around my length in her bedroom. Every time and all the ways I'd had her.

But the quiet moments were there too. The innumerable nights spent on the beach at her house, watching the sun go down, or rising early in the morning—sometimes after not having slept at all—to watch it once again rise over the bay. The way she easily folded into my arms, her slow, deep breaths fanning across my chest, thigh flung over mine as she slept next to me. Cooking meals together, endless bottles of wine and picnics in secluded spots along the water. The day trip we'd taken to Sleeping Bear Dunes—Amara's idea to wipe away the bad memories the place held, replacing them with new ones, ones of *us*, happy and falling in love.

Riding to work together in the morning when I'd stay over,

going into town for coffee and danishes at Brie's, getting drinks at Granny's, watching movies on her couch or mine when it was raining.

Running the Delatou empire side by side.

I wanted all of that forever, and I'd fucked it up.

"Maybe I'm just not meant to be loved that way. Maybe I'm not meant to be loved at all," I said after spilling my guts on the worn-wood table between my parents and me. Tears sprang to my eyes as I met each of their stares and asked the question that had plagued me for thirty-three years. "Why didn't you guys ever love me?"

A pained sound escaped my father, and my mom's hand tightened on mine.

"It wasn't that we didn't love you, Cal. We did—*do*—love you, so much. But our lifestyle before you came along wasn't exactly conducive to raising a child. You were never the problem. We simply struggled with what to do with you, this kid who, despite the way we'd each grown up, despite the parenting—or lack thereof—we'd each received, was so damn smart, with his head on straighter than either of us could ever hope for. We may not have ever planned on you, Calvin, but you are the biggest blessing we've ever received. You forced *us* to grow up. We love you so much, but you're so different from us, and we didn't want to fuck you up with our admittedly jilted world views. We wanted you to make your own assumptions and perceptions of the way things worked. We wanted you to read those fantasy novels that took you to distant lands. We wanted you to get the education we'd both scorned. We wanted the world for you, and still do. It was just difficult for us to show that properly."

It all made sense now, why I'd never managed to connect with them. It wasn't that they hadn't cared about me—it was that they'd cared about me so much they hadn't wanted to mess me up the same way they'd each been messed up.

The realization was staggering, completely shifting my worldview on its axis.

"I'm afraid I'm making your same mistakes," I said quietly.

"Whatever you think you've done," my dad said, "I can assure you...you're doing just fine. Against all odds, you turned out to be a great man, Cal."

I gave Dad a watery smile and said, "I got her pregnant."

"Amara?" my mom gasped. I could only nod in response.

"And I'm afraid I'm going to fuck it all up. She—I hurt her. Badly. And she fired me, effectively cutting all ties between us. I don't know what to do from here."

"Do you love her?" my mom asked softly.

"More than anything," I whispered without hesitation.

And that emotion—I'd only felt a fraction of it before. Before I'd opened my eyes to the full picture of Amara, allowed myself to see how truly talented she was, how much business she'd single handedly brought to the company over the years, how intelligent and sexy and funny and truly *perfect* she was, I *thought* I'd loved her.

But it was nothing compared to the way my heart belonged entirely to her now. How every single one of my thoughts was full of her—her laugh, the smell of her shampoo when I dug my hands in her hair, and the scent of her perfume at the base of her throat where I loved to press my face, the way her hand felt in mine. How, the moment she'd told me she was pregnant, the life we could have together flashed so clearly in my mind, only to be shattered by the fact that she thought she'd have to do it all alone.

Amara was a good woman, and I knew if I pressed, if I asked, she'd give me time with my child.

But I didn't want *time*. I wanted *her* and the baby and the family I'd dreamed of having for as long as I could remember. I wanted to introduce her to the man and woman sitting here with me, proud to call them my parents, proud to call Amara my everything, proud that they would soon have a grandchild. I wanted Amara's entire crazy family to become mine.

I wanted a life with her—the entire thing, from now until we took our last breaths.

I just had to find a way to make that dream a reality.

chapter 26
Amara

THE EMERGENCY BOARD MEETING had been exactly the shit show I'd anticipated. After having my showdown with Cal, I expected to feel better. I expected the anxious weight that had settled on my chest over keeping my pregnancy secret from him to be lifted now that he knew.

Unfortunately, I wasn't so lucky.

The meeting had been a week and a half ago, and I was still struggling to come to terms with all I'd lost.

I loved the man, so sue me. I may not like him right now, but that didn't magically turn off my feelings. It would take a while to stop caring about him, especially since the baby growing in my womb was half him.

Every time I settled a hand on my abdomen—which remained flat for the moment—I was reminded that Cal and I weren't over. At the very least, we'd have to come to some sort of co-parenting agreement, and I dreaded the day I'd have to see him again.

Not because I didn't want to see him, but because I was afraid when I did, I'd throw myself at his feet and beg him to forgive me for acting crazy.

But there wasn't anything I could do about it now. What was done, was done, and I had a company to run. I could think of nothing I wanted more than to bury myself in work, and when Owen texted asking if he could come in for a meeting, I jumped at the opportunity, equal parts curious about what he wanted and desperate to pick his brain about how Cal was doing.

Owen arrived twenty minutes later, and I welcomed him into my office with a hug and kiss on the cheek.

"It's good to see you, kid," he said as he dropped onto my cushy leather couch.

I groaned as I padded across the room. "I hate when you call me that."

"I know you do," he said with a wide grin. "Why do you think I do it?"

"You're not that old, you know."

"Please," he said with a snort. "I'm pushing forty."

"Thirty-seven is *not* forty," I said. "And let's be real, you look damn good for your age."

"You hitting on me?"

I grinned as I approached the drink cart. "Just stating fact."

It was so easy to fall back into this banter with him. The reason we'd managed to stay friends after our physical relationship ended was because we genuinely enjoyed each other's company—even if, that summer, we hadn't enjoyed it much *beyond* the sex. But once the sex had fizzled, once I'd moved away and he'd continued to expand his empire here, we'd kept in touch. He'd text me occasionally, checking in and picking my brain about his random business ventures. I'd send him pictures of soccer matches I'd attend, teasing him about it being "real football."

Being friends with Owen was easy because, when we took sex out of the equation, we learned we actually had a lot in common and made far more sense as friends than we ever did as lovers.

"You want a drink?" I asked.

"Bourbon," he said. "Whatever you've got."

I poured him two fingers of Four Roses and filled a glass of water for myself.

He raised a brow. "You're not drinking?"

"I can't," I said as I handed him his tumbler and took a seat across from him.

"Are you okay?"

"Fine." I settled a hand on my belly. "Great, actually."

"Ho-ly shit. You're not..."

"Just over two months," I confirmed.

He bit down on his lips, as though considering his next words. At last, he uttered only one. "Cal?"

I could only nod, that weight in my chest growing a bit heavier with the mention of his name. "I'm assuming you've talked to him."

"Yeah," Owen said, "but he didn't tell me about this." Kicking one of his worn cowboy boots up until his thick thigh had the denim of his pants stretching tightly across his muscles. He was a perfect male specimen, the paragon of physical fitness, his athlete's body still beautifully honed despite being thirty-seven and retired for the better part of a decade.

He was going to make someone very happy one day.

"How is he?"

Owen's gaze softened. "Off in the wilderness somewhere," he said. "He was heading to visit his parents, but he went through the U.P., taking a few days to unplug."

"That's good," I said. "He needs that."

"After you fired him and ripped his heart out? Yeah, I'd say so."

"So he told you he got fired, but not that he got me pregnant?"

"We didn't exactly talk. He sent me a text saying he got fired, that y'all were done, and he was going off the grid for a few days so I wouldn't be able to reach him if I needed to. And that he wanted to talk about the job I'd offered him a few months ago when he got back to town."

I blinked, surprised. Cal had never mentioned anything about a potential job opportunity with Owen. "What job?"

"I want him to manage my finances," Owen said, dropping his foot back to the floor and leaning forward, resting his elbows on his knees. The way he wrung his hands together had the muscles of his forearms flexing, making the tattoo of his last name along his left ulna wave like a flag. That ink had mesmerized me once, had lured me into the whole Owen Lawless package.

"He'd be perfect for that."

"I know. That's why I want him."

"Well, he's suddenly unemployed, so I think it'll be pretty easy to convince him."

Owen sat back, the leather of the couch creaking with the movement, and folded his arms over his broad chest as he studied me. His cornflower blue eyes may as well have been lasers for how deeply they cut, and I resisted the urge to squirm.

"There's no chance of him getting his job back?"

As much as I wanted to say yes, that possibility *did* exist, I kept my mouth shut. Even if Cal and I managed to patch things up enough to form some sort of amicable relationship, with the baby on the way, I simply didn't think it was a good idea for us to be working together anymore.

With a sigh, I simply shook my head, and Owen gave me a small nod in response.

"I'm not going to ask what happened because quite frankly, it's not my business. I did, however, actually come here to discuss my business."

Business I could do, so I took a sip of my water and said, "Lay it on me."

"I want to buy a piece of Delatou land."

I raised a brow, confused, and Owen launched into his plan. A carefully thought out and fully realized new business venture—and he wanted Delatou, Inc.'s help to make it a reality.

Owen wanted to open a distillery, the first—and only—of its kind on Old Mission. He had plans for five spirits—vodka, rum, whiskey, gin, and bourbon—with batches of each in the works to perfect the recipes. He had plenty of capital to get the business off the ground, including buying the land outright, but what he needed was a place to build.

That's where I came in.

"I'd also love to offer you a partnership opportunity," he said at the end of his explanation. "What you're doing here is impressive, and I'd love to work with you on this. Hell, maybe one day we can even branch out into spirit-based cocktails."

I liked the sound of that, of expanding our portfolio to include a new product offering. But unfortunately, owing to the fact that I was pregnant, I wasn't prepared to take on anymore responsibilities at the moment. I told him so, hating the way his face fell. Despite his golden boy exterior and the fact that—career being cut short thanks to an injury notwithstanding—he was one of the most successful and talented quarterbacks to ever play in the NFL, he was also a shrewd businessman. I wanted to help him—wanted him connected to Delatou, Inc. in some way beyond deeding him the land and sending him on his way.

Then an idea struck me.

"Delia," I said.

"Your sister?" Owen asked. "What about her?"

"She's been begging me for a project for ages," I said. "I think this would be perfect for her. She's a marketing whiz and has been looking for a way to become more involved in the family business. Right now, she manages our social media, but I can tell she's getting restless. This isn't quite what she had in mind, I'm sure, but I think you two would work well together."

"No."

"No?" I raised a brow.

"She's too…young. And don't think I forgot the shit she pulled at my cabin over Memorial Day."

"She's only a year younger than me," I said. "And that's all water under the bridge."

Although…was it? Looking back, that night was the beginning of the end for me and Cal. In fact, I had *tried* to end it with him then, and he'd come crawling back anyway, pulling me in with his…everything. Making it impossible to resist him.

And now look at me. Pregnant, single, and without a Chief Financial Officer for my company.

What a mess.

"I'm not doing it," Owen said firmly. "I'll find someone else."

"Just meet with her," I said. "Please."

"No."

"I'll sell you the land if you do."

"Are you...bribing me?"

I totally was. "No," I said. "I'm making you an offer. Meet with Delia, and I'll sell you the land. I'm assuming you've got your eye on a particular parcel."

He shifted to withdraw a piece of paper from his back pocket, tossing it onto the table between us. I picked it up and unfolded it, studying a copy of a plat map of the northern end of the peninsula and a parcel outlined in red. I chewed on my lip; I could admit, it was the perfect spot. High on the hills above the water that would afford guests with stunning lake views, but flat enough for the distillery and a parking lot, and not too far off the main road that wove like a vein through the middle of the peninsula. Land I had zero plans to develop for the winery in the future.

"How much?" he asked.

"I'll have to ask my dad and get back to you."

"See that you do," he said and he rose to his feet.

"Get that meeting on the books with Delia and I will," I shot back.

"You drive a hard bargain, Delatou."

"I'm more than just a pretty face."

"Don't I know it," he murmured as he dropped a kiss on my cheek. When he straightened, he added, "For what it's worth, kid, I'd give Cal a chance to explain. When he talked to me about you, he was completely spun out, and that was months ago."

I perked up, surprised. "He talked to you about me?"

Owen gave me a sad smile. "Just talk to him, Mar."

Then he was gone, and I was once again left alone with my thoughts.

I should've gone back to my desk and dug through the mountain of paperwork I had waiting for me, and put the final touches I had to put on the Labor Day weekend festivities, which began in three days. Instead I kicked my heels off, tucked my feet under me, and draped the throw blanket on the back of the couch over my lap, letting my mind wander.

It was a dangerous thing, to give my thoughts free rein like this, but I knew I wasn't getting anything done no matter what I did. The day dreaming—or whatever the nightmare equivalent was—would happen regardless, so I dropped my head back and closed my eyes.

Immediately, Cal's face stamped itself on the back of my eyelids. Three months ago, I'd stormed in here after that summer menu tasting with Brie and Ezra, steam practically pouring out of my ears over the nerve of Cal. How he'd put his hand—*his hand!*—on my thigh under the table and had the gall to ask how wet I was.

I hated how much I'd liked it, though I'd never had any intention of acting on my desires. Desires that hadn't gone away in five years, no matter how many miles and men I put between me and that night.

And then he'd followed me in here, wordlessly locking that door behind him and prowling into my space, saying all the right things, convincing me it was "just one time," that we'd get it out of our systems and everything would be fine.

What a bunch of bullshit.

He'd been lying to me the entire time, and it had started right here in this very office, on that very desk to my left, when he'd spoken such soft, passionate words to me and fucked me until I could hardly stand afterward.

Anyone ever tell you that you have a perfect pussy?

God, I need you.

I'm regretting sending you away five years ago if it would've been like this then.

You're mine now. Do you understand?

You look so good bouncing on my cock.

I'll give you whatever you want.

And my personal favorite, and my greatest undoing...

You look so fucking good like this. Like a goddess, Mar. And I'm the man you're letting worship you? Unreal.

And in the days and weeks after, when those filthy words hadn't stopped coming but had been supplemented by compliments and tenderness? How could I do anything but fall for him? He was a wet dream and my dream man all rolled into one, and right from the jump, I'd been powerless against him. Naturally, I'd gone and given my heart to him anyway, and look where that had landed me.

Barefoot and pregnant.

"Fuck," I breathed. "What the hell am I going to do?"

A knock came at my office door, and Brie peeked her head in, carrying a plate of something that I knew would be a delicious short-term solution to all my problems.

"You busy?" she asked.

"Nope," I told her, patting the seat next to me. "Just sitting here thinking about the utter fucking mess I've made of my life."

Brie frowned as she dropped onto the couch, sliding the plate of whatever decadent pastry she'd recently concocted onto the table in front of us. The dish was covered with tinfoil, but a buttery and sweet aroma wafted from beneath it. When I went to peek, she slapped my hand away.

"Talk first."

"Are you bribing me into sharing my feelings with dessert?"

"Yes," she said quickly, and I laughed. At least, unlike me with Owen earlier, she had the decency to be honest.

"I don't even know where to begin."

"How are you feeling physically?" she asked, her eyes dipping to my stomach.

"Really good," I said. "Still a little nauseous around midday, but nothing some Gatorade and a granola bar can't fix."

"You better not be eating store-bought granola bars, sissy! Those things are so bad for you."

I gave her a sheepish smile. "I'm sorry?"

Brie slapped her hand over her face. "From now on, I'll make sure your office, car, and house are fully stocked with homemade ones."

"You're the best," I said, reaching out to squeeze her hand.

"And how are you doing with everything else?"

I didn't want to tell her, mostly because I knew even one word from my mouth about Cal and last week's drama would open the floodgates that would be damn near impossible to close again.

Still, maybe an emotional purging is exactly what I needed.

So I laid it all out there. My fears, my worries, my stresses. How

I loved him but I didn't like him right now and wasn't sure if I should trust him. How the thought of raising this child alone terrified me, not only for my sake, when I knew the days and nights would be long, but the years would pass in a blink, but for the sake of my child, who would have to split its time between two homes, two families, two parents who couldn't find a way to love each other enough to make it work.

"Do you even want to make it work?" Brie asked quietly.

"No. Maybe. I don't fucking know, B," I said, dropping my head into my hands.

And that's when the first tear fell.

Like a crack in a dam, once that first drop was free, I exploded into noisy, messy crying, the kind that had me wailing like I was in physical pain. That had my baby sister curling her arms around me and pulling me onto her lap like I was a small child that needed comforting.

I mean...obviously, I needed comforting.

"I don't want to do this alone," I said, the words broken by sobs. "And I hate him for doing this to me, for doing this to *us*."

And I didn't mean only me and him. I meant me, him, *and* our child. Whether we liked it or not, we were bringing another life into this world. We could've had it all. The family, the happy home, the unwavering love and support. I'd been prepared to give him everything.

"How can I love someone who refuses to see the best in me?"

Brie sighed. "Unfortunately, us Delatou girls have a habit of falling for men like that," she said with a sad, knowing smile.

I didn't have to ask who she meant, but I hated that she understood this pain. I hated that she knew what it was like to give her heart away to a man who'd probably never look at her the same way as she did him. It gutted me, for both of us.

But Brie could escape her prison eventually—hopefully.

Unfortunately for me, I was locked in this cell for the rest of my life now, and no one was coming to save me.

Wallowing wouldn't do me any good.

So I crawled off Brie's lap and sat up, squaring my shoulders and wiping the tear tracks from my face. I certainly looked like hell, and I'd have to touch up my makeup before I could set foot outside this office and face the world again, but at the moment, I had bigger fish to fry.

Namely...

"So...what's under the tinfoil?"

Brie laughed, a high, melodic sound—still girlish despite the fact that she was in her mid-twenties—that had always been my favorite of my sisters'.

"Just this new recipe I've been experimenting with. Tanya Geralt found this old cookbook of Granny's when she was cleaning out the attic space at the restaurant a few years ago, and she thought I might like it. I've slowly been working my way through it."

"You never told us that," I said, tears once again springing to my eyes, though happy ones this time. Brie had been only a few years old when Granny had died, but I remembered her well—mostly by smell. True to her "Granny Smith" moniker, she often smelled like apples and butter and cinnamon; the woman was perpetually baking an apple pie. It warmed my heart that Brie could get to know her this way, through their mutual love of food.

Brie simply shrugged. "I wanted to keep it to myself for a while. I'm afraid someone will want to take it."

"We would never," I said. "You're Baker Brie, remember?"

She giggled at the childhood nickname, when we'd always poke fun at her permanent attachment to her Easy-Bake Oven.

Although, even then, we openly enjoyed reaping the fruits of her labor, just as we do now.

"Anyway," my sister said, at last removing the tinfoil from the plate with a flourish. "I present to you...baklava cheesecake."

"My two favorite words."

Honestly, there was no heartache a bit of home cooking couldn't cure.

At least...that's what Granny always said.

chapter 27
Calvin

I RETURNED TO MICHIGAN the middle of the following week, three days before the Labor Day weekend festivities were set to begin, feeling refreshed with a renewed sense of purpose.

I was going to get my girl back.

Spending a week with my parents had been truly cathartic, though. I hadn't realized how badly I needed answers about my upbringing—about why they'd raised me the way they had—until I'd gotten them. And now, knowing how much they truly loved me and had only been doing what they thought would be best for me in the long run? That made it a lot easier for me to see all the ways in which I'd fucked up with Amara, and all the mistakes I needed to fix.

Truthfully, when it came to her and the company, I'd been doing what I thought was best for all parties. In those early days, I hadn't known Amara the way I did now. I hadn't *cared* to learn more about her beyond what I'd seen from her the night we met and our scattered interactions around the winery after until she'd

332

taken over.

And even when she'd taken over, I'd refused to give her the benefit of the doubt. As Owen had so aptly informed me when he called me the other day to ream my ass out for not telling him *I was going to be a father*, I'd been operating from an outdated playbook. Once she and I had gotten together, I'd started to piece together the picture of the real Amara, the highly intelligent and impressive woman with a business acumen that would rival most men I knew. The funny and sassy woman who was unfailingly loyal to anyone she held dear, most notably her sisters. Even after that shit Delia had pulled with the game of truth or dare at Owen's cabin, Amara hadn't flinched, hadn't hesitated to pass off a partnership opportunity with Owen to her.

The woman who had stolen my heart that very first night and never really given it back—even when I'd been prepared to offer it to another for a lifetime.

The woman who was carrying my child.

The woman I loved more than I ever thought possible, and who I wanted to spend the rest of my life with.

So once again, I found myself sneaking around behind her back, seeking out her sisters to aid me in my latest scheme.

Only this time, instead of forcing Amara out, instead of pushing her away, I wanted—*needed*—her so much closer, and I was willing to do whatever it took to bring her back to my arms.

Exactly like that day nine months ago, when I popped into the kitchens to find Brie, Ezra informed me she was at the bakery, so I hopped in my truck and headed to town.

The sense of déjà vu was strong as I pushed through the door, that same little bell tinkling above my head. The girl working the counter was different now—another twenty-something presumably on summer break from college looking to make some extra cash before she went back—but the place still smelled the same. I inhaled deeply, branding that scent on my memories, knowing it might be the last time Brie Delatou would allow me to darken her shop's doorway.

"Welcome to Brie's!" the girl at the counter said, tone cheerful, a bright smile on her face.

I couldn't help but smile back. "An iced Americano and a cheese danish, please," I said, withdrawing my wallet from my back pocket. "And, if you don't mind, I'd like to speak with—"

"What the fuck are you doing here?" the woman in question asked as she stepped out from the kitchen, her deep brown hair tied back with a colorful, abstract-print scarf, some sort of pink frosting marring her left cheek.

"I need to talk to you."

Brie didn't budge; her face didn't so much as twitch. "You know, the last time you came in here asking that of me, it was because you wanted to force my sister out of her company. Tell me, Cal, how well did that work out for you?"

I cut my eyes to the barista, who watched our exchange unabashedly.

"Please," I pleaded with Brie. "Just sit down and talk to me. Five minutes."

With an epic eye roll that I would've expected from Delia or Ella before I ever saw it on Brie, she untied her apron and disappeared into the back once again while I paid for my order.

"So you're Cal," the girl said as she swiped my card.

"Sure am."

"Makes sense now."

I gave her a smile that I'm sure was more of a grimace but kept my mouth shut. I had no desire to learn what she meant by *that* comment.

Brie appeared a moment later, and I barely withheld a groan as I bit into the danish she handed me. The savory cheese combined with the slightly sweet and flaky dough—it was borderline orgasmic, which was not a word I should be thinking in regards to anyone but Amara.

Still, the littlest Delatou knew her way around a puff pastry.

I fervently prayed this wasn't my last.

Brie dropped onto a chair and the moment I was seated, said, "Speak."

"I'm a fucking idiot."

Brie chuckled, instantly clamping down on the sound I knew she hadn't meant to make. "Tell me something I don't know."

So I did. I laid my entire fucking heart bare for this woman, who looked so much like her sister and yet didn't.

It was the eyes, I realized as I spoke to her, maintaining eye contact the entire time. The moment I'd met her, I had been instantly transfixed by Amara's eyes, hypnotized by those pools of liquid honey. Brie was a beautiful girl—all of the Delatou women were—but her pine green gaze simply didn't cut me the same way as Amara's golden one did. It was almost easier, I thought, to be making this speech to someone who could easily be Amara but wasn't. To be explaining to someone else how badly I'd messed up, how I never should've gone after her in the first place, and how I should've done everything in my power to make sure her tenure as head of the company was a success

335

instead of looking for ways to weaken her leadership.

How I should've trusted her, believed in her.

How I should've done my goddamn research instead of flinging baseless accusations at her for so long.

"Have I mentioned lately that I'm a fucking idiot?" I asked when I finished.

"Once or twice," Brie said. "So why aren't you telling her all of this?"

"She won't text or call me back. I'm sure your dad would have me arrested if he knew I set foot on CD property earlier when I went looking for you, so I'm not anxious to go back and try again. Short of showing up at her house…"

"Definitely don't recommend that," Brie said. "She'd probably beat you over the head with something and throw you in the lake."

I chuckled, but the thought of Amara causing me physical harm, the thought that she might *want* to, cut right to my heart.

"How is she?" I asked softly.

I didn't miss the pity in Brie's eyes as she said, "Okay. Scared."

I ground my teeth together to avoid shouting that she didn't have to be scared, that I'd be there every step of the way. Exploding right now wouldn't do anyone any good. In fact, it would almost certainly have the opposite effect on my bid to win Amara back.

"I love her, Brie."

"I know," she said with a sad smile. "But you need to tell her that."

"That's why I'm here. I need your help."

Waiting for the weekend to end was the purest form of torture, mostly because my entire body ached to be near Amara. Knowing she was so close yet I couldn't touch her, taste her, simply wrap her in my arms and promise her everything would be okay was slowly eating away at my insides.

I was up before the sun on Monday morning—Labor Day—and decided to get up and take Skye for a run, needing to do something to burn off the excess energy burning beneath my skin like an itch I couldn't scratch.

The Labor Day festivities at the winery were getting started early so that many of the sales team managers who would have a significant distance to travel this afternoon could get home for work tomorrow. I knew from Brie that Amara was kicking off the party with a little speech thanking them all for coming, and that's when I'd make my move.

The winery had been closed for the day in deference to Amara's party, and I waited until the last possible second to come out of hiding in the kitchens and take up a spot along the wall.

Amara's parents stood on a small, raised platform that had been erected at one end of the flagstone patio. To my right was a table laden with all the goodies Brie and Ezra had cooked up, sitting perpendicular to a bar where a tall, blond man poured canned cocktails for the partygoers. Each of the sisters was present, milling about and mingling with the crowd. The excitement and buzz in the air was palpable, and a little bubble of pride rose in my chest. Despite my protests and failure to see the point, she'd pulled off this event perfectly.

Even if I had yet to see evidence she was actually here.

The clinking of a utensil against a glass rang out over the crowd, and everyone turned their attention to the stage, where Leon approached the microphone.

"It's weird for me to be standing up here knowing I'm no longer the man in charge. This whole speech making thing was my job for so long, so you'll forgive me if I have difficulty giving it up." The crowd chuckled indulgently, and Leon grinned. "But damn am I proud of the woman who *is* in charge, not only because she's my daughter, but because she's accomplished so much in her first three quarters as head of this company, and I know without a doubt that my grandfather's, father's, and my legacy are in good hands with her.

"This entire weekend was her idea, and I hope you all had a great time experiencing all we have to offer here at CD. I hope you understand now that this has been and always will be a family run operation from top to bottom, and we're proud to have your company representing us in the market. I can't wait to see those Q4 sales reports," Leon said with a wink. "And now, without further ado, let's welcome to the stage my daughter and Delatou, Inc. CEO, Amara Delatou!"

Amara stepped to center stage, and I nearly fell to my knees.

My god, she was stunning. I didn't know if it was simply because I hadn't seen her in a while or if she was already getting that pregnancy glow people were always talking about, but she positively shined up there. Her melon colored top tucked into a tangerine pencil skirt that hit just above her knees offset her olive skin—darker now thanks to the summer months spent in the sun—perfectly.

She was, simply put, the most beautiful woman I'd ever laid eyes on, and I couldn't believe I'd fucked it all up. If I couldn't convince her to take me back, convince her to give us another shot, I'd spend the rest of my life lonely and celibate, kicking myself in the ass for letting her slip through my fingers.

"First and foremost," she said when she stepped up to the mic, "I want to say thank you to my dad, and my entire family, really, for believing in me. I'm sure you're all aware it was never the plan for me to take over, but I can't deny—I'm quite pleased with the way things shook out." The crowd laughed, and Amara smiled as she pressed on. "I started working at Chateau Delatou when I was fourteen, bussing tables in the restaurant for extra money that I spent on candy more often than not."

"Watermelon tutti frutti, right?" I asked, peeling away from the shadowed awning and stepping into the sun. Amara squinted down at me, a thousand emotions warring on her face.

I raised a mental fist of triumph when hatred didn't make an appearance.

This wasn't part of the plan, but I couldn't help myself. There was no way I was standing here another second, watching her without letting her know I was here.

We'd been fairly quiet about our relationship up until now, in deference to our jobs and her parents. My name had never been mentioned in any of the TikTok videos that featured me, despite heavy implications in the comment sections. But now that the proverbial cat was out of the bag, I wanted to hard launch. I wanted this girl to be *mine* in every sense of the word. I wanted her in my bed, in my life, in my fucking soul—forever.

There was no way I was letting her go another moment without knowing I was fighting for her, for *us*.

"Yes," she said quietly. "Watermelon tutti frutti." Bringing her hand to her forehead, she heaved a sigh and started again. "I've worked a lot of jobs around here over the years, but there was never a doubt in my mind that I wanted to be involved. I always knew being here"—she swept her arms out at the vineyards that stretched far into the distance to her right—"spending my days surrounded by these fields and the people I love most was my dream job."

"I love that about you," I said. "How loyal you've always been to this company—and your family. How much work you've done behind the scenes."

Amara huffed a breath but ignored me.

"I would've been happy not to go to college at all when that time came, honestly. I didn't think there was anything I could learn at *some state school* that I couldn't learn simply by working side by side with my father every day."

I bit back a chuckle.

There she is. My girl was still in there. Mad as hell at me, but still there.

"The London School of Business, right?"

The crowd gasped, exchanged impressed glances and murmurs with their neighbors.

"Well, I went to Tennessee first," she said with a smirk. "Daddy wanted me to get out and experience being a regular college girl before I...what was it you said, Dad? Oh, right. Shackled myself to this place for the rest of my life." More laughs, and I smiled, easily able to imagine that conversation between them. Stubborn Amara, wanting to get to work immediately, and equally stubborn Leon telling her no. Sending her away couldn't have been easy for any of them, but I'd admit—it had all worked out perfectly.

"So I went to UT," Amara continued. "Joined a sorority, though those sisters could never replace my real ones."

"Became president of your chapter too, didn't you?"

Yet another thing I'd managed to learn in my extensive deep dive into her social media, though I wished she'd felt safe enough with me to share these things herself. In hindsight, I hadn't always made it easy for her to be vulnerable, and I could see why she hadn't told me. In her mind, telling me something like that only opened her up for further ridicule. And honestly, the guy I'd been four months ago certainly would've fit the information neatly into the party princess picture I'd already painted of her.

"I did, Calvin. Thank you for pointing that out." *Calvin*. God, my name on her lips again was a balm to my soul. "And then, as Calvin so graciously pointed out, I moved to London, where I attended the London School of Business during the week and spent my weekends..." She trailed off, tapping her finger to her chin as though she couldn't quite articulate what she wanted to say next. "Help me out here, Calvin. What did I do on the weekends?"

She was baiting me, and I'd happily engage if it kept her talking to me. "You traipsed around Europe partying."

She offered the group—ever single member of which swiveled their heads as we volleyed back and forth—a self-deprecating little smile and shrug. "That *partying* paid off, though, because it increased our international distribution by three hundred percent in the first year."

A staggering number, one I still hadn't quite believed even after running the figures five times to confirm they were accurate.

My woman was damn good at her job.

"I'm sorry I ever doubted you," I said, taking a step closer to the stage where she stood. "I love you, Princess, and I'll spend forever proving it to you."

Amara held up a hand, halting my progress, and she covered the mic with her hand to whisper to me. Though the party was so quiet, I doubted anyone missed her words. "I love you too, but this is not the time for this conversation."

I gave her a mock salute even as my grin nearly broke my face. Hope and joy and an effervescence that was pure *Amara* bloomed in my chest. I remained where I stood, watching her finish her speech.

Someone pinched my elbow, and I whirled to find Brie standing behind me, arms crossed petulantly.

"What happened to the plan?" she hissed.

I winced. "I'm sorry," I said. "I saw an opening and I took it. But how's the cake look?"

In a smooth move, she grabbed the towel draped over her shoulder and whipped it at me, the sting on my arm making me hiss in pain as I rubbed the spot.

"The cake looks amazing, you jackass," she said, then stormed away, muttering about how men would be the death of her.

At last, Amara wrapped up her talk to thunderous applause.

I had a feeling the Q4 numbers for the winery would be through the roof.

Not that I was surprised.

I meant what I'd said earlier—I *was* sorry I'd ever doubted her. There was nothing to doubt. There wasn't a person—man or woman—more suited for this job than she was.

The truth was, losing my job was a gut-punch. But losing Amara was a knife to my heart, and honestly, I didn't deserve to work for her. She needed people around her she could trust, people who would believe in her one hundred percent, who wouldn't pull shady shit behind her back and attempt to shove her out of her own company.

I'd never do that *now*, of course. But if she'd have me, Amara and I were about to enter into a new relationship—one full of love and navigating the wild and crazy world of parenting. I didn't want a business relationship to put any strain on the family and life I wanted to build with her.

Now I just had to convince her of that.

I'D BEEN TRYING MY damnedest to enjoy the day's festivities. This was, after all, entirely my idea. I could at least *pretend* to be excited to be there. But honestly, the heat was making me dizzy, my skirt was too tight, and my shoes were pinching my pinky toes.

Oh, and I had a hole in my heart about the size and shape of Calvin Ryder.

So when he appeared during my speech, his words preceding him into the middle of the crowd, I thought he'd been a mirage. He couldn't possibly be that insane. To show up here knowing full well my dad wanted to kill him and my whole family hated him?

My heart stopped dead in my chest at the sight of his perfect face. Those thick eyebrows, that strong nose, full lips, sharp jaw. His hair was disheveled, more red than brown under the bright light of the sun. God, he was gorgeous.

And it began beating again when he spoke, like a defibrillator bringing me back to life, jerking me back to sense.

How had it only been two weeks since I'd last seen him, yet I felt like I'd gone years without his deep timbre filling my ears?

"Watermelon tutti frutti, right?"

Not only was he here, but *he remembered.* He had to know what that would mean to me.

"Uhh, princess…" Cal said from behind me, his tone concerned. "What is this?"

I turned to face him, finding him holding a bag of candy—a bag of watermelon tutti frutti to be exact.

"They're candy," I said. "What does it look like?"

"I get that they're candy," Cal said. "I can read. I'm just wondering why there's a giant bag hiding out in your nightstand."

"I wasn't hiding it," I said with an eye roll. "They're my favorite. I've got bags of them stashed all over the house…and my office."

"Do you know *how bad this shit is for your teeth? And you're telling me you have* bags, *as in multiple, hidden around here and the office?"*

"When did you suddenly become my father, worried about my oral health?"

"Since I discovered my girlfriend is a child trapped in an adult's body!"

"It's not that big of a deal," I said with a laugh. "It's just candy."

"There's gotta be a story here, Mar. You don't just wake up one day suddenly addicted to fucking watermelon tutti frutti."

I smiled as the memory came to me.

Oh, there was a story alright.

My sisters and I fought over everything *growing up. Toys, what we deemed the best slice of cake, which one of us Mom and Dad loved most, clothes, boys as we got older, and, inexplicably, candy flavors. One Fourth of July, Chloe and I had gotten into a legitimate shoving match on the side of Main Street over the last of the tutti frutti a passing float had thrown that nearly ended with me being run over by a firetruck. The incident had snapped my father at last.*

"We weren't even allowed to go down to the park for the daytime festivities that year, he was so pissed off," I chuckled, and Cal nodded solemnly; he was more terrified of my dad than ever, and we hadn't even officially announced our relationship. "So he sat us down, dug into our candy bags, and withdrew five flavors of tutti frutti. One by one, he sat them in front of us and told us from now on, that was our flavor. We were stuck with it for life, whether we wanted it or not. 'If you're going to act like children, I'll treat you as such,'" I said, mimicking my dad's deep voice.

"How old were you?"

I grimaced, not wanting to say. Cal hauled me onto his lap and dug his fingers into my ribs, tickling me until I relented through fits of laughter.

"Chloe and I were sixteen and fifteen."

"Amara," he said sternly.

"What?" I protested, leaping from his lap. "I really fucking love tutti frutti!"

Cal rose to his feet and stalked toward me, snaking his arms around my waist and tugging me close.

"Well, the good news, Princess"—he pressed a kiss to my nose—"is that I don't eat candy, so you'll never have to fight me for the last tutti frutti."

"Lucky me."

"Yes," I said quietly, answering him at last, my voice steady despite the maelstrom of emotion swirling in my chest. "Watermelon tutti frutti." I brought my hand to my face, suddenly feeling faint with Cal's eyes on me. At last, I heaved a sigh, letting it out in a *whoosh* that reverberated through the speakers, and began again. "I've worked a lot of jobs around here over the years, but there was never a doubt in my mind that I wanted to be involved. I always knew being here"—I gestured to the vineyards to my right—"spending my days surrounded by these fields and the people I love most was my dream job."

I loved this place. I'd grown up traipsing through the vineyards with my sisters, playing hide and seek among the vines, always coming home sticky and stained. Yet our parents never scolded us, never got mad at us for turning the vineyards—which were, in essence, our family's livelihood—into our personal playground. They simply let us run amok through the rolling hills. It may have been a bit unorthodox as far as upbringings were concerned, but I wouldn't have had it any other way. I knew from a very young age that there was nowhere I'd rather be than here on the peninsula, surrounded by the fruits of generations of my family's labors.

"I love that about you," Cal said, stalking slowly through the crowd. "How loyal you've always been to this company—and your family. How much work you've done behind the scenes."

I huffed a breath but ignored him. I couldn't risk indulging him and getting derailed again—and I couldn't afford to stop and savor his words.

"I would've been happy not to go to college at all when that time came, honestly. I didn't think there was anything I could learn at *some state school* that I couldn't learn simply by working side by side with my father every day."

Yeah, that was a dig at him, and his answering chuckle told me he knew it. Told me he was remembering that day in the cellar the same as I was, when he'd lobbed that insult at me. Something told me he knew now how far off the mark he'd been that day, and he confirmed it with his next words.

"The London School of Business, right?"

Noises of shock rose from the crowd, and what could I do but grin? An MBA from the London School of Business was a daunting undertaking and one of my proudest accomplishments.

"Well, I went to Tennessee first," I said, shooting Cal a smirk. "Daddy wanted me to get out and experience being a regular college girl before I...what was it you said, Dad? Oh, right. Shackled myself to this place for the rest of my life."

My father grinned, nodding, and the crowd broke into laughter again. That conversation was as fresh in my mind as if it had happened yesterday. Me begging to forgo college so I could stay home and work. Him pushing me out the door.

The man was more stubborn than me—which explained where my sisters and I got it from, though none more so than yours truly.

"So I went to UT," I continued. "Joined a sorority, though those sisters could never replace my real ones."

"Became president of your chapter too, didn't you?"

How the fuck did he know *that*?

"I did, Calvin. Thank you for pointing that out." *Calvin*. God, when had I last called him *Calvin*? It felt weird, too formal, the syllables tasting wrong as they came out. But I plowed ahead. "And then, as Calvin so graciously pointed out, I moved to London, where I attended the London School of Business during the week and spent my weekends..." I trailed off, tapping my finger to my chin in fake contemplation, zeroing in on Cal again. "Help me out here, Calvin. What did I do on the weekends?"

I was clearly baiting him, and he rose to the challenge without missing a beat. "You traipsed around Europe partying." The accompanying smirk told me he knew that wasn't all I'd been up to.

Seemed someone had finally done their research.

I offered the group a modest little smile and shrug. "That *partying* paid off, though, because it increased our international distribution by three hundred percent in the first year."

A staggering number, one the company had never seen before or since.

I grinned widely at Cal, narrowly holding myself back from telling him *I told you so.*

His own smile shifted from delight at our verbal back and forth to something softer, something secretive.

Something for just me.

"I'm sorry I ever doubted you," Cal said, taking a step closer to me and the stage. "I love you, Princess, and I'll spend forever proving it to you."

I love you I love you I love you.

The words were a balm to my soul.

What else could I do but say them back?

With a hand covering the mic, I whispered, "I love you too, but this is not the time for this conversation."

His responding grin could've powered the entire state. With a mock salute, he moved to the side of the stage, where I'd come down once I wrapped up my speech.

Which I did so quickly now that Cal wasn't standing in front of me, distracting me with his apology and his smile.

Though, by the time I finished, I was beginning to have second thoughts. He'd hurt me deeply, and I couldn't just...forgive that, could I?

I mean, I'd *fired him*. Undoing that wasn't going to be easy. But I was a weak woman, and god, I missed him.

The man from nine months ago who'd gone behind my back and tried to push me out from my own company wasn't the same man standing before me now. He wasn't the man who'd shown me more pleasure than I'd ever known, but also made me feel safe and treasured and *wanted*.

And it was clear Cal had done his homework in our time apart. Now, he saw me at last. There were no more secrets between us. Nothing holding me back from giving myself to him completely.

On shaky legs, I moved to the edge of the platform amid applause, but everything in me steadied when I found Cal waiting for me. His hands were shoved deep in his pockets, a wide, sheepish grin on his face.

I practically threw myself at him. I was tired of pretending every cell in my body wasn't begging to be in his arms again.

He caught me, an *oof* leaving him as I crashed into his chest.

"How about we go somewhere and talk?" he said quietly into my ear. I could only nod against him, barely holding back the tears I'd been fighting since he appeared in the middle of my speech.

I let him lead me inside the winery and along the familiar halls until we reached my office.

The place where it had all begun.

Seemed fitting that we have this conversation here.

Refusing to let go of him for even a second, the moment Cal sat down, I climbed onto his lap.

"You're too long for this," he said, though he cuddled me closer, one arm around my back, the other pulling my legs across his lap.

"You love me."

"I do," he agreed.

"What was it you said before?" I asked. "The rest is just bureaucratic bullshit?"

"Mar…" he said with a sigh.

"Before you launch into what I'm sure is a well thought out and carefully rehearsed speech, I need you to know I've already forgiven you."

"Doesn't mean I don't need to apologize."

I nodded. "Get on with it, then."

"Bossy, aren't we?"

"Well…I *am* the boss."

"Just…stop talking and let me say this."

So I did. I sat there, curled on his lap, as he poured his heart on *my* lap.

"I went to visit my parents," he began.

"I know. Owen told me."

"You talked to Owen about me?"

"I was worried about you."

"I'm so fucking sorry, Princess," he said, burying his nose in my hair. "I'm sorry I ever doubted you. I'm sorry for ever making you feel less than. I'm sorry I made you fire me. But most of all, I'm sorry I ever hurt you."

"I'll admit," I said slowly, "that I could've taken any opportunity over the last nine months to clue you in on my experience. I just...there was that thrill I told you about. The one I got from the look of surprise and awe on your face every time I did something that impressed you. I thought if you knew about the international distribution that you'd stop looking at me like that, and I wanted your praise so desperately that I wasn't willing to give it up. Not even in favor of the truth that would make things between us so much easier at work. I'm not proud of it, but I'd gotten so used to you underestimating me that I was afraid what would happen if you no longer had a reason to.

"And I'm sorry I fired you," I added. "I may have...been a bit hormonal. I wasn't exactly thinking straight, and I've made a whole mess of things."

"I love you, Mar. There's nothing you could do to change that," he said with a vehemence that surprised me, capturing my face in his hands. "I stopped underestimating you a long time ago, right around the time you told me to get on my knees and crawl."

I choked on a laugh. "I think that was the night I got pregnant."

"Really?" His eyes widened, and tentatively, he settled a hand on my belly.

I nodded. "I'm about ten weeks, so if I do the math...yeah, I'm pretty sure it was then."

"I don't even understand," he said. "You were on the pill.

This...shouldn't have happened."

"The pill isn't foolproof." I laid my hand over his. "Are you mad?"

"*Mad*?" he asked, incredulous. "Absolutely not. This baby is a gift. So we're starting our family a little sooner than we would've planned. I'm not mad, Mar. I'm fucking ecstatic to be doing this with you." He paused and looked up from our hands, his bright green eyes shining. "Assuming you'll have me."

"I don't know," I said thoughtfully. "Will you still love me when I'm nine months pregnant and crabby and cursing you for doing this to me?"

Cal moved forward and pressed a slow, soft kiss to my mouth. Against my lips, he said, "Princess, I'm going to love you forever."

epilogue

Calvin

I WIPED THE SWEAT off Amara's brow for what felt like the thousandth time in the last two hours.

And I'd do it a thousand more.

"You're doing amazing, Princess," I whispered. "You're a fucking rockstar, and I'm so damn proud of you. Just a few more, okay?"

I glanced down at the doctor, who gave me a small headshake.

"Cal," Amara hissed, squeezing my hand so tight that my bones ground together uncomfortably. "What's the hold up?"

"Doc?"

"The baby is stubborn," the doctor said with a little laugh.

"Like its mother," I said.

Amara gathered enough strength to glare at me. "Like its stupid ass father who got me pregnant in the first place."

I watched the doctor check his watch then heave a sigh. "We're approaching three hours of you pushing, which is the danger zone for babies—and you. So we can do one of two things: let you keep going until we hit that three hour mark and if the baby hasn't come by then, we do a cesarean. Or…"

"Whatever the second option is," Amara said.

The doctor smiled indulgently. "Or, on your next contraction, I can give you an episiotomy."

"Episi—what?" I asked.

"He's going to create an incision that'll make it easier for the baby to come."

"Is that…safe?"

"Safe enough that I perform them more often than not," the doctor said. "I'm confident the baby will be here within a few pushes if we go that route."

"Do it," Amara said, dropping her head back onto the pillows and taking a deep breath.

"Can you feel anything down there?" I asked.

"No, thank fuck," she said. "It's more like…I can feel the pressure of him taking that scalpel to me right now, but there's no pain. The only pain is in my head and my neck and shoulders."

"I'll give you a nice long massage once the baby is here," I promised, raising her hand to my mouth and pressing a kiss to the back. "I love you."

She gave me an exhausted smile. "I love you too."

"Alright," the doctor said, passing the scalpel off and refocusing his attention between Amara's legs. "When I tell you to, bear down and push, okay?"

Amara only nodded, and I helped her sit up a bit to make it easier on her. A nurse stood at each side of the doctor, holding Amara's feet, giving her something steadier—and less impersonal—than the stirrups to throw her weight against.

The doctor studied the readout from the monitor attached to Amara's belly, and when it approached her next contraction, he said, "Now!"

Amara's face screwed up as she gave her next push everything she had, and a loud groan tore free from her throat.

"The head's out!" the doctor said. "One more, Amara. One more and you can meet your baby."

Our baby.

Finally.

Amara bore down again, and I watched as our baby slid free, directly into the doctor's waiting hands. One of the nurses handed him some surgical scissors, which he held out to me.

"Wanna cut the umbilical, Dad?"

I blinked slowly, coming back to myself quickly as our baby let out a healthy cry, and I sprang into action. The moment the cord was severed, the nurses ushered the baby away for measurements and clean up, and I turned to Amara. Tears ran down her cheeks, and I surprised myself when I choked up right alongside her.

In a flash, a nurse was bringing the baby back.

"Congratulations," she said. "You have a beautiful baby girl."

The nurse set the impossibly small bundle on Amara's chest, and I leaned over them both, brushing a corner of the blanket out of her face so I could take a good look at my daughter for the first time.

My daughter.

I had a daughter.

This impossibly strong woman and these teeny, tiny baby were mine.

My girls.

My whole world.

"Fuck," I said quietly as tears poured down my cheeks. "She's perfect."

"She's the most beautiful baby I've ever seen," Amara agreed.

"There's no rush on any of this," one of the nurses said, approaching Amara's bed from the other side, "but we will need to get the birth certificate filled out. Do you guys have a name picked out?"

Despite my happy tears, I couldn't hold back the chuckle that escaped me. In true Amara and Calvin fashion, we'd argued endlessly about names for the last several months. Anything I liked, she hated, and anything she loved, I wasn't a fan of.

Finally, last week, she'd been reading a book, looked up, and spoke a name.

I'd agreed instantly, and looking at her now, I couldn't imagine a more perfect fit for my baby girl.

I didn't know what we would've done if we had a boy.

"Cora," Amara said quietly. "Cora Mae Ryder."

I blinked in surprise. "Ryder?"

Amara turned and gave me a watery smile. "As long as you promise it'll be my last name one day too."

I grinned broadly enough to strain my face muscles, and then I bent and planted a tear-soaked kiss on Amara's mouth.

"Whatever you want, Princess."

"This is all I want," she said quietly, returning her attention to our daughter and drawing mine there too. "You, me, and Cora."

"Me too, baby. Me too."

We had twelve hours with just the three of us before the Delatou family descended. I'd called my parents last night to tell them they had a granddaughter, and they were excited, of course, but it was nothing compared to the sheer joy Leon and Lena Delatou brought with them to the hospital.

They'd just gone through this six weeks ago with Chloe, who had also given birth to a baby girl they named Aleah, but I doubted the shine of being grandparents would ever wear off for them both. As far as in-laws went, or whatever the I-promise-to-make-an-honest-woman-out-of-your-daughter-one-day equivalent was, I couldn't have asked for better. Despite the drama when Amara made the announcement that we were expecting, despite the firing and the breakup and the getting back together, Leon and Lena had quickly welcomed me wholly into the fold. I was no longer that expendable employee I'd been for the first five years of my tenure with Delatou, Inc., and for that I was thankful.

Now, though, I was officially part of the family, and they were never getting rid of me.

Especially since I no longer worked for Delatou, Inc.

After our reconciliation, Amara and I had a long and difficult talk about how she wasn't giving me my job back. At the time, it had been a gut punch, but when she explained her reasoning, I could admit it made sense. We'd have enough on our plates with baby Cora now, too much to add any potential work disagreements to the mix.

Thankfully, Owen had been ready and waiting to offer me a job as his financial manager and advisor, a position I settled into quickly and happily. Working with my best friend was much easier than working with Amara had ever been—mostly because I didn't want to fuck him, and he didn't fight me at every turn. Now that the distillery was open, we were moving onto our next project. The work was fresh and exciting, and I got to be home every night for dinner with my girl.

Now my *girls*.

True to form, Lena went straight for Cora, who was resting peacefully in my arms. She didn't even ask before taking her from me. Anyone else, that would've pissed me off, but I knew Lena was just too excited for formalities.

Leon, meanwhile, made a beeline for his daughter, who was looking much better today after a shower and that massage I'd promised, which I'd given her while Cora slept for a few hours last night.

He murmured something to her, pressed a kiss to her forehead, then moved to his wife's side to take in his new granddaughter.

The sisters filtered in one by one not long after, and soon the room was filled with coos and crying—and that was mostly from the sisters. Cora, for her part, was completely content being passed between the arms of her grandparents and aunties, who she already had wrapped around her teeny tiny fingers.

I couldn't wait to get both of them home, to settle Cora into her nursery and start the rest of our lives. Amara and I had moved in together by the time the first snow fell, and in the intervening five months between early November and now, we'd quickly settled into a rhythm that worked perfectly for us. I was anxious and excited to add Cora to the mix.

Once everything was out in the open between us, things were just...easy.

It was easy to love someone who had seen every part of you—good and bad—and loved you through all of it.

That was us. Perfect because of our flaws.

Win or lose, it would always be us together. Side by side, fingers laced, shoulders squared against whatever the world wanted to throw at us.

I wouldn't have it any other way.

extended epilogue
Amara

"MAR?"

Cal's soft voice filtered down the hall, greeting me through the open door. I moved toward it, peeking my head out. "In here," I whispered.

He rubbed his tired eyes as he approached, then followed me inside.

"What're you doing?" he asked quietly.

I moved deeper into the room, coming to a stop and staring down at the most perfect thing I'd ever seen in my life.

My daughter.

"She's one," I whispered back, not bothering to hide the emotion choking me up. "Our baby is one." I turned to him then, my vision going blurry with unshed tears. "How is that possible?"

"Time is a thief, Princess," he said quietly, sliding his arm around my waist and pulling me into his side, joining me in watching our daughter sleep.

As she'd grown, she'd developed my olive skin and her dad's

deep red hair, plus the most perfect hazel eyes, a mix of my gold and Cal's green, making her the most beautiful baby in the world.

Today was her first birthday, and I couldn't believe we'd already had her for twelve months. The days before she came into our lives are a dull gray blur, and everything after was as vivid as a full color, 4K, seventy-inch TV screen.

I certainly had never planned on being a mother out of wedlock, but Cora was the best thing to ever happen to me, and I wouldn't trade her for anything.

Cal was the cherry on top. He has been my rock through everything from morning sickness that lasted well into my second trimester, gestational diabetes, and being on bed rest for the final four weeks until Cora was born. I'd never planned on him, either, but I couldn't have asked for a better partner.

Some days, I couldn't even believe I could say that, couldn't quite wrap my brain around the fact that Calvin Ryder was *mine*. I'd fully expected to hate the man forever, but that summer had changed both of us in ways I was still learning.

"Come on," Cal said, curling his fingers around my hip and pulling me toward the door. "Let's get you back to bed."

"But—" I tried to protest, but Cal placed his index finger over my lips, effectively shushing me. And when we stepped into our bedroom, and his mouth replaced his finger, and I let him make love to me until my limbs were deliciously wrung out and I fell easily into a dreamless sleep, straight until my alarm blared at eight on the dot.

And by alarm, I meant Cora, chattering away in that barely intelligible baby way of hers to the lone stuffy we let her sleep with—a downy soft bumblebee that Chloe had given me the day she was born. Her sweet voice filtering through the monitor in the morning was my favorite way to wake up.

"I got her," Cal said, pressing a kiss to my bare shoulder before throwing the covers off and rising.

I knew he'd bring Cora in before we got up and faced the day, so I rolled over and scrounged around on the floor, coming up with Cal's haphazardly discarded tee and throwing it over my head just as he entered the room, our baby in his arms.

And let me tell you something—if I thought my man was attractive before, it was nothing compared to seeing him hold our daughter. My ovaries exploded every time I saw the two of them together. He looked at her like she was the center of his universe, and Cora looked at her dad as though he hung the moon.

We were very lucky girls.

"Mama!" Cora shouted, and I grinned. That had been her first word, and I'd never tire of hearing it—just like I'd never tire of reminding Cal of that fact. We might be deeply in love and in a committed relationship, but we were still *us*. We still endlessly needled each other and pushed each other's buttons.

The upside now was that he made it up to me with his beautiful mouth and perfect cock at the end of the day.

Have I mentioned I'm a lucky girl?

"Happy birthday, peaches!" I said when Cal handed her off to me, peppering her plump cheeks and chubby little neck with kisses.

"Birtday!"

"Yes, honey," Cal said, sliding into bed next to me and gathering both of his girls into his arms. "It's your birthday! We're going to have a big party later to celebrate *you*." He punctuated his final word with a little *boop* of her nose, and Cora's giggle filled the room.

"Speaking of," I said, craning my neck to look up at Cal. "I guarantee my mom will be calling any second, wondering why we're not already at the Villa getting set up."

"The party doesn't start for another five hours!"

I raised an eyebrow. "You remember my mother, right? Tall, cloud of dark brown hair, obsessed with her grandchildren?"

"Doesn't ring a bell," Cal said, and I poked him in the side.

As if on cue, my phone rang, the creepy Siri voice informing me it was none other than my mother calling.

With a groan, I handed Cora off to her dad and rolled toward the nightstand, swiping my phone up right before it went to voicemail.

"Mom," I said by way of greeting.

"Where are you?" she asked, and I shot Cal a *you see?* look.

"We just woke up," I said.

"Well get your ass in gear, Mar. I'm not setting this up all by myself."

"There are five hours until the party, Mom," I said with an eye roll. "How about you let me have my baby to myself for a few hours before you steal her from me for the rest of the day?"

I could practically see my mother's pout as she said, "I just love that little girl so much."

I sighed, softening. "I know you do, and she loves her Gigi. We'll be up there at eleven and not a minute sooner."

"Fine," Mom said, then hung up.

"Told you," I said to Cal, who only nodded then turned his attention to our daughter.

"What do you say, peaches?" he asked her. "Want breakfast?"

"Pacakes!" she shouted, clapping excitedly.

"Yes, pancakes!"

With that, Cal rose and took her from the room. I could hear them chattering as they moved down the hall toward the kitchen.

Once Cal was safely out of earshot, I made a phone call.

"Is it ready?" I said when Delia answered.

"They finished late last night," she said excitedly. "He's going to lose his mind."

"He better," I said. "It cost me a fortune and was headache after headache to complete on time, especially given its winter."

"He'll love it, Mar," my sister reminded me.

"I hope so."

Keeping this secret from him for the past six months had been the most difficult thing I'd ever done. I just hoped he appreciated it for what it was—a gift. Not just for him, but for our little family.

Delia rambled on about the absolute shit show last night had been, working overtime to finish everything up, but I barely heard her. I was caught up picturing Cal's face when I showed him tonight.

"Is everything set for tonight too?" I asked.

"Yep," she said. "The guys are coming over as soon as you leave for the Villa."

"Okay, great. Thank you so much for running point on this when I couldn't be there. I appreciate you more than you know." From down the hall, Cal yelled something to me, and to my sister

I said, "Shit, gotta go. I'll see you later."

"Love you!" she yelled as I hung up.

Finally, I dragged my ass out of bed and went to have breakfast with my family.

Cora's first birthday party had been a hit. My entire family, all of my mom friends, and all of their kids had gathered at the Villa to celebrate my baby turning one. We laughed and played, gorged ourselves on good food, and showered Cora with endless gifts and love.

It was nearing five p.m., and Cora, who hadn't napped today, was nearly passed out in Cal's arms as my family and I loaded all of her gifts into Cal's truck. When we were done, we bid our farewells to my parents and sisters, then strapped Cora into her car seat and set off for home.

"There's a stop we need to make first," I said to Cal. "Take a left up here."

Cal raised a brow and shot me a sidelong glance, but did as I asked.

The sun was approaching golden hour, limning the sky and trees and everything else in our path. There were days like today when everything was so perfect I was simply thankful to be alive. Grateful that I was put on this earth to experience these moments. To watch my younger sister shove my daughter's cake in her face, Cora's squeals of laughter making everyone else in the room chuckle along with her. To see my parents dote on her. To see how easily my family welcomed Cal into the fold despite our rocky beginning.

To see the sun sink toward the horizon with the love of my life next to me and our baby in the backseat.

Once Cal made the left turn, I directed him to drive down the poorly-paved two lane road for a few miles until an unmarked dirt path branched off to the right, in the direction of the water.

"Turn here!" I shouted, always forgetting how quickly the drive came up.

"Are you sure?" Cal asked skeptically.

"Yes, I'm sure," I said with an eye roll.

"If you get me arrested for trespassing, I'm going to—"

"You'll what, exactly? Spank me?"

"Maybe."

"I'd let you if you asked nicely. It's not like you haven't before."

We might be parents now, but the sex was as hot as ever. I was grateful for that too.

Cal boomed out a laugh, and my own mouth curved into a satisfied smirk.

Before Cal could say anything else, we reached the tree line and drove into the middle of a sizable plat of lakefront land. Straight ahead, the flat expanse gently sloped toward the beach and the waters of West Traverse Bay beyond.

And smack dab in the middle was a large, two-story home.

Our home.

The exterior was white-washed with black frames popping against the bright paint. There were windows everywhere, enough that I knew the entire interior would be bathed in natural light while the sun was up. To the left was a garage attached to the main house by a mudroom that had a small half bath with shower and a dog washing station for Skye.

The whole thing gave off modern beach cottage vibes, exactly as I'd intended.

"What is this?" Cal asked, shifting in his seat to look at me.

"Come on," I said, getting out of the truck and heading to the back to carefully take Cora out of her car seat. I didn't want to wake her, but I wanted the three of us to cross that threshold together.

With my daughter in one arm, I met Cal at the hood of the truck and extended my hand to him. Wordlessly, though I didn't miss the confusion pinching his brows together, he laced his fingers through mine.

I led him up the steps of the wide wrap around porch, pausing in front of the heavy walnut door, pulling my hand free of his, and digging the key Delia had slipped me earlier from my pocket.

"Want to do the honors?" I asked, holding it out to him.

"Mar..."

"Just open it."

Cal once again did as I asked, slowly inserting the key into the lock and twisting, shooting me a surprised glance when it clicked free. With a gentle shove, it swung open, and Cal gasped.

I decided then and there it was my favorite sound.

Who said only men could make grand gestures?

Before he crossed inside, Skye greeted us at the door, tail wagging excitedly, welcoming us to our new digs.

Cal turned to me again, settling his hands on my upper arms, and said in a quiet voice, "Tell me what the fuck is going on."

"This is our house," I said simply.

"How?"

"I had it built."

"When?"

"Caaaaaaaaaal," I said with an eye roll, dragging out his name in the way I knew reminded him of the spoiled party girl he'd thought I was for so long. "Can we save the twenty questions for later? Preferably after we're inside? It's freezing out here and, in case you didn't notice, I'm holding your sleeping daughter."

"Fine," he said with an exasperated sigh, then took my hand again and towed me over the threshold.

I had painstakingly selected every detail of this house, from the wide oak plank floors to the white-washed beadboard cabinets and black hardware in the kitchen, the pale cream walls, the three oversized sofas in the living room, the sprawling office with workstations for both me and Cal, and the playroom in the back corner.

And that was just the first level.

Upstairs were four bedrooms, including the master with an en suite, two that shared an adorable Jack and Jill, and a guest room with its own bathroom next door.

Cal spun in a slow circle, taking it all in. There was, admittedly, a lot to see. Lucky for us, we had a lifetime here. He had all the time in the world to poke around, to learn the layout, to teach our daughter to ride a bike on the front lawn. To hose her—and Skye—down in the mudroom when they came in sandy from the beach. To fill this house with endless memories that would make it a home.

There were boxes everywhere, and I was silently impressed by the moving company and how quickly they worked. The instructions had been simple: pack up our entire house while we were at Cora's party and move everything here. I'd packed us bags of toiletries and jammies earlier, and if the moving company did their jobs, our bed and Cora's crib would both be setup. We weren't spending another night anywhere but here, in our forever home.

"I still don't understand," he said at last, turning to look at me. "This is...ours?"

I nodded. "When I was eighteen, my dad signed the legal title to this forty acre section of land we're standing on over to me. For the last twelve years, it sat vacant. I could never figure out what I wanted to do with it."

After spending nearly five years in Europe, I discovered how much I loved traveling, and though I came home for the express purpose of taking over management of Delatou, Inc., I just hadn't been ready to put down those kinds of roots. It seemed silly to me to spend all that money building a house I would live in alone. I couldn't bear it.

And then Cal came along and everything changed.

"I didn't even know I was ready for a family until you gave me one," I said, giving him a watery smile. "I never pictured this life for myself, never imagined I'd get this lucky. But I want to spend the rest of our lives right here in this house. I want to decorate these walls with family portraits and Cora's art projects. I want our babies to grow up here, and for this to be a place where they feel safe and loved and happy."

"I love you."

"I love you."

"Marry me."

Now it was my turn to blink in shock.

"*What?*"

"Marry me," he said again, digging into his pocket as he stepped away from me, then dropping to a knee right there in the entryway of our new home.

"Cal..."

"Just...let me say this." He took a deep breath, and the tears I'd only just dammed up fell down my cheeks once again. "The night we met, if you would've told me we'd end up here, I would've called you crazy. But you have continued to surprise me at every turn, have continued to be the strongest, most intelligent, infuriatingly sexy woman I have ever laid eyes on. I wake up every morning praying that when I open my eyes, our life together hasn't been a dream. You coming into my life was the best thing that ever happened to me, and I love you more every day."

He sniffed, his eyes lined with silver. "And then you had to go and make me a dad, and watching you bring our daughter into the world and be the best mother imaginable to her has simply reinforced that I don't deserve you, and I'll never understand what I did right to end up here. But"—he opened the velvet box clutched in his hand, flashing the stunning square-cut solitaire on a simple gold band—"I promise I'm going to spend forever loving you and Cora the way you deserve to be loved and cherished. So please, Mar. Take my name. Take everything I have. Marry me."

"Yes," I said before he'd even fully finished speaking, and he choked on a laugh as he shakily slid the ring on my finger, then scooped me and our daughter into his arms and twirled us around. Cora squawked, clearly pissed off that her dad was interrupting her beauty rest.

Once he returned us to our feet, I fused my mouth to his. "As soon as possible," I said against his lips. "I want your last name before I start showing too much."

Cal pulled away and swept his gaze across my face, his entire heart and love for me and our daughter—and now our unborn child—shining brightly in his eyes.

"When are you due?" he asked quietly.

"Late October or early November. I haven't gone to the doctor yet. I actually just found out yesterday."

"You've been sitting on this for twenty-four hours?"

"I wanted to tell you today. One more gift in a day full of them."

Cal grinned at me. "Fuck, I love you."

"I love you more," I said, rising up to press a kiss to the tip of his nose. "I was thinking of having a beach wedding in May. Right out there." I pointed to *our* beach. "How does that sound?"

Cal wrapped his arms tightly around me and our daughter and said, "It's a date, Princess."

acknowledgements

As always, I wouldn't be here without the constant love and support of my family. Every time one of them asks me how writing is going, or how book sales are, it gives me the motivation to keep going. It's a simple thing to have people believe in you, and I'm so grateful for their unwavering faith in this dream of mine.

To Grammy and Grumpy, who I miss more and more every day. I know you never got to be here to see me achieve this life-long dream of mine, but I know you're always watching and guiding me through every up and down.

I say this every time I write another book, but I could write a fucking novel about what you mean to me, Mer, and how blessed I've been by your friendship. We had this conversation recently where I said, "You know I've just reached the stage where I'm gearing up for these characters and this story to fully exist outside of me and it makes me anxious lol." Your response was, "I do know this. And you also know that I'll be here to tell you to chiiiiill and give it the time and attention to detail it deserves." I know this isn't what you bargained for when we bonded over Joey B two (TWO!!!!!) years ago, but I'll never take having you in my corner for granted. Thank you for always having my back, for shooting me straight, and for pulling me back to earth when I'm acting crazy. Thank you for the 20 minute FaceTime calls when I tell you I'm on the ledge, for being the first person I want to share any and all exciting news with, and for reading all 3847829948882949 iterations of this book. I could not do life without you.

To Hannah. Your feedback on this story was invaluable, and as someone who has been with me from the very beginning, the fact that you loved these two—something so different from anything I've done before—in all their messiness and drama...I'll never be able to thank you enough.

To Sam. There isn't a single thing I could say that I haven't already. Let's just keep making covers together forever, yeah? I love you and appreciate your friendship so much.

To all of my author friends. Having a community of people like you around me makes me really damn lucky to be in this space. Thank you for the hype, the help, the excitement to read my words. I appreciate you all so much.

To my street team. We almost didn't make it! But I'm glad y'all have stuck it out with me and that we keep getting to shout about these books together. I couldn't do this without the support of readers and friends like you!

To Meg Jones, the creator of the "dicktionary," for letting me incllude one in the back of this book, and to Hailey Dickert for the "spread your" pages wording. Appreciate you both so much!

And lastly, to my readers. The buzz around this book has exceeded my wildest dreams, and whatever happens with it and my career going forward, I couldn't keep doing it without your support. Every page read, every post, every reel, DM, and recommendation to a friend—it all makes a difference, and it's the difference between me not doing this and me being one step closer to my dream of making writing my full-time gig. There aren't words for how grateful I am for each one of you, whether you've read one page of one of my books, or all five of them cover to cover. THANK YOU.

about the author

Amanda Chaperon realized her passion for books, and for writing, at a young age. Growing up, she was rarely found without a book in her hands, a hobby she carried into adulthood. After joining bookstagram in 2020, she felt the pull to try her hand at novel writing. She writes what she loves to read: messy, relatable characters, lots of steam, and always a happily ever after.

She currently lives in Michigan's Upper Peninsula with Gryffin, her Golden Retriever. She loves all things romance, fantasy, young adult, and thrillers that keep her up at night. You can follow her on Instagram, Threads, and TikTok at @achaperonwrites.

Dicktionary

My dear sweet reader, please use this guide to avoid (or seek out) the spicy scenes, which can be found in the following chapters:

Chapter 11
Chapter 13
Chapter 16
Chapter 18
Chapter 20
Chapter 22

Spread those pages, my friend.